D1294027

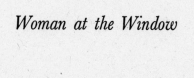

Woman at the Window

Also by Nelia Gardner White

DAUGHTER OF TIME
BROOK WILLOW
NO TRUMPET BEFORE HIM
THE PINK HOUSE

THE BAKERVILLE LIBRARY

Woman at the Window

A NOVEL BY
Nelia Gardner White

New York THE VIKING PRESS *1951*

October 20, 1951 — Gift

W

COPYRIGHT 1951 BY NELIA GARDNER WHITE

PUBLISHED BY THE VIKING PRESS IN SEPTEMBER 1951

PUBLISHED ON THE SAME DAY IN THE DOMINION OF CANADA
BY THE MACMILLAN COMPANY OF CANADA LIMITED

This book appeared serially
in *The Ladies' Home Journal*

acc. no. 2667

PRINTED IN THE UNITED STATES OF AMERICA
BY AMERICAN BOOK–KNICKERBOCKER PRESS, INC., NEW YORK

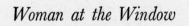

Woman at the Window

*E*LIZABETH BURKE, new job in the bookstore securely hers for Monday next, sat on the hassock in her cluttered room and celebrated future affluence by eating oyster stew. It was no special job but in the six years since college it was the first job she had secured on her own, with no help from her sister Anna or a friend of a friend of Anna's. Lollie Parsons, the fat little teacher of subnormal children, sat on the daybed, scooping up stew in companionable silence. Lollie lived across the hall, shared Elizabeth's bathroom, but bothered her very little. They shared jokes, surprising good fortunes, but rarely bad fortune. Lollie's gift was for laughter and when she laughed her cheeks went red and her eyes disappeared in side rays of wrinkles. Wise without sourness, that was Lollie, and Elizabeth Burke treasured her friendship and never presumed upon it. All over the walls were tacked drawings by a former art student who had had the room. The student had gone off, not paying her rent, and perhaps thought she had left treasures in lieu of her bill. Elizabeth had never taken the pictures down and found pleasure in looking at them, especially at the one of the ballet dancer with muscles like a prize fighter's.

Elizabeth scraped the bottom of the bowl and said, "There, the seven lean kine have eaten up the seven fat kine."

"Something wrong in that analogy," Lollie said. "Wait—I'll think it out."

At that moment the telephone rang. Lollie, with a small, bouncing movement, deposited her bowl on the floor. She was round as a dumpling and was given to bouncing. Elizabeth scrambled to her feet, ran over to the phone, which stood on the plain table that served as a desk and depository for library books, mail answered and unanswered, a dozen other small items. "Hello!" she said in her brisk, sensible, slightly husky voice. Then, when there was an answer, she dropped to the chair by the table, sprawled out a little, her shaggy brown hair that looked as if it had been cut by herself with blunt kindergarten scissors bobbing forward against the phone. Lollie Parsons saw her face as she said, "Oh, *hello*—is anything wrong?" and then looked away. But she was not deaf and the one-sided conversation came to her with a strange ominousness, the gaps filled in by something not understood, and yet dramatic. "No, no, I couldn't. . . . It's not that. It wouldn't work. . . . Why? Why would she? She never has before. . . . Look, I'm not trying to be mean. I'm just being practical. I drive her mad and always have. . . . I'll just say no and let that be the end of it. No need to run up a long-distance bill in arguments. . . . Aren't you hitting below the belt? Yes, I could, but not for long. Could she? . . . Well, we all have our moments of weakness. . . ." Then Lollie heard something that was like a sigh of surrender and Elizabeth said, "Wait a minute. I'll come. Friday—there's a train gets in around six, isn't there? I'll come then. But don't forget I protested. . . . Tell Johnny hello for me. . . . See you Friday. Good-by, Adrian."

The phone being returned to its place was a slow sound, like the sigh of surrender. Then Elizabeth sat there by the table for as long as a minute. There was something tragic about her face.

"What's up?" Lollie said.

"She's never going to walk again—my sister."

"The one who had the accident? Good heavens!"

"The only one I've got," Elizabeth said.

She came slowly, picked up the bowls, carried them behind the screen in the corner where her small electric grill stood. When she came back she stood still in the middle of the floor, looked around her. "Did I sound heartless?" she asked.

"Stubborn," Lollie said.

"He made me sound loveless," Elizabeth said. "I know how I sounded."

"Don't you like your sister?" Lollie asked, jumping plumb into the middle.

"Like her? Like Anna? I'd die for her. . . . But she wants me to take care of her. Adrian says she wants me to look after her. It isn't the new job—I suppose it isn't such a hot job, when it comes right down to it. It isn't the job. It won't work, that's all. He says I might lay aside my personal idiosyncrasies for the moment. . . . I *did* sound loveless."

"You sounded stubborn," Lollie repeated. "That's all—stubborn."

"We're so different. We're a different breed, Lollie. I rub her the wrong way and always have. She's out of another world—Anna. Oh, Lollie, I can't *do* it!"

"I gather you're going to," Lollie said dryly.

"How could I say no? It was so heartless to say no. He was so mad he almost hung up on me. But I know what I do to Anna; what she does to me, for that matter. She tries to make me over—I get bristles all over me. . . . It sounded as if I didn't love her, but I do. Oh, Lollie, if I could just make someone understand!"

"I can understand quite a lot," Lollie said in the same dry tone.

"It's just—it's just that it's taken me a long time, Lollie, to get to be myself. I'm slow at it. Anna's special and I'm run-of-the-mill—I know that. I knew it when she was nine and I was six. But accepting it is something different. I was just getting so I did. . . . But, you see, it's always been that I've wanted her, she's never wanted me, never needed me. Of course I have to go. It was wicked not to say I would right off. Adrian'll hate me. I'm all she's got. Since mother died there hasn't been any family but us. . . . I couldn't imagine it, that she won't walk again. Graner—he did the operation—he was so hopeful. I can't *believe* it. . . . Look, Lollie, I'm talking too much. I know I am. But the bottom seems to have dropped out of things." Her voice was flat, as if this were something that could not be understood by anyone.

"You were right the first time," Lollie said. "Don't go."

"How can I not? She has asked for me."

"Relatives shouldn't look after each other. You're right," Lollie said.

"I am right—but of course I must go. But look, Lollie, I want to keep this room. I want to hang onto it a while. Could I borrow two weeks' rent from you? They're going to pay me something, I don't know what, but the truth is that if I settle up things here, get my ticket and all, I won't have much left."

"I'll take care of the room till you let me know otherwise," Lollie said. "Anything I can do about packing?"

"I won't take much," Elizabeth said. "I haven't much to take."

Lollie was silent for some time, her comical round little figure taking on a curious dignity. Then she said, "I would make it for a definite time—two weeks—a month."

Elizabeth gave her a quick, grateful smile but did not answer, and presently Lollie went back to her own room.

In the morning she rapped at the door and said, "Leaving my car out front, Elizabeth. You use it to catch up on things today—I'll take the bus."

"Thanks. I will, if you don't mind, Lollie."

She stood in the bookshop and told Mr. Danvers that she couldn't after all take the job. Illness in the family called her away. He was surprised, for she had been so happy to get the job. "I don't suppose it will be open when I get back, but I'll come and see," she said. She walked out of there, feeling she had cut some cord to safety. It wasn't much of a job, that was true, but it was her job.

She paid her bill at the cleaner's, took her library books back, bought a present for Johnny, and finally one she couldn't afford for Anna. She went home, picked up the newspapers spread beneath the clothesline stretched across the living room, took down her blouses, took down the line itself. She sprinkled the blouses in the bathroom, rolled them up for ironing. She packed all she could. She limited herself, standing some minutes before her shelves of books, putting a hand now on *The Journal of My Other Self*, now on *Novel on Yellow Paper*, taking the hand away, leaving all here as hostage to return.

A numb, cold November day, that was. In the morning it was raining. Elizabeth rose at seven, put coffee on, went to Lollie's door, called softly, "Come have coffee with me!" Lollie had to leave the house at eighty-twenty for her school. She came very soon, in the blue suit that was her school uniform and which made her more dumpling-like than ever, though neat.

"The car was a godsend yesterday," Elizabeth said.

"Look, Elizabeth," Lollie said, "I'm worried about this. You're all tied up in knots. Can't they get a nurse?"

"Adrian says not—they have one, but she's no good. I'm all right. . . . I'm just so ashamed that I didn't say yes at once. I don't know how to face Adrian after acting like that."

"It isn't only that." Then Lollie laughed and said, "Sorry—I'm so used to digging in to see what makes folks tick. Don't want to be the schoolteacher out of school."

"I suppose it boils down to 'I'm jealous of Anna,'" Elizabeth said.

"Never struck me as a jealous gal," Lollie said.

"No, but you never saw me growing up beside Anna," Elizabeth said. "I think there must be something very nasty down there in my subconscious— Wait . . . it's significant I never have any pictures of Anna around, wouldn't you say?"

She got up from the card table she had set up for their breakfast, went to a book, took out some snapshots, and brought them back to Lollie. "That's Anna," she said. Lollie sat there, solid and merry in her blue suit, looking down at the pictures.

"I see," she said at last. "I see."

"You don't see maybe that she's always gay and generous as well as lovely to look at. But, Lollie, she's never needed me, never. And now, when this awful thing has happened, she's asked for me. I've wanted so hellishly much all my life that she'd want me—and now she does and I'm reluctant. I'll be ashamed of that forever—but, you see, Lollie—oh, I can't explain myself. I don't believe there is any explanation that will excuse me."

Lollie's round face was sober. She got up and said, "I've got to go." Then she put her hand on Elizabeth's and said, "Bless you. Make it two weeks, definitely. There's a boy, isn't there?"

"Yes, Johnny. Five years old."

"Don't get to feeling too sorry for him and stay on. Two weeks, remember."

She hesitated as if wanting to say more, but finally with another "Bless you!" went back to her room, picked up her books, bag and car keys, and departed.

Elizabeth took a taxi to the station. She had intended to manage by bus, but it was blowing and raining, so she called a taxi. She looked around her silly little room before she picked up her suitcase—looked at the student drawings on the wall, her rows of books, her desk, so unfamiliarly tidy, the worn carpet on the floor, the daybed with its red cushions. It looked beautiful to her, dear, her own. Then she picked up her suitcase and went out fast, through the rain, and, wet already, fell into the taxi.

It was a dreary ride in the train. Half the time you could not even see beyond the veil of the rain against the windows.

When you could see, there were only sodden fields, dreary farm-houses, some banked against winter, with rutty drives and machinery rusting in the farmyard. She had always said November was her month. She had been born in November and she claimed kinship with it. But her November had clear skies and a hard ground and bare trees clear and stark against the sky, brown leaves skittering in the wind, a promise of snow in the air. This was some no-man's land of the seasons and Elizabeth Burke felt lost in it, unable to see any borders.

We've had Graner's report—she's not going to walk again, Adrian had said in an angry voice. Angry, and yet tired.

I suppose I can't believe it. I suppose I didn't believe it—I couldn't have acted that way if I'd believed it, she thought miserably. She looked so hopeful in the hospital, so exactly the same. Anna couldn't not walk. . . . But she wouldn't have asked for me unless—unless what? Unless she desperately needed someone of her own blood kin beside her. And she, Elizabeth, was all there was left. . . . I thought of myself first, she admitted. I was protecting myself—will I ever be forgiven for that? Will I ever forgive myself?

She kept seeing Anna, Anna in the hospital, flowers all around, looking amused at all the fuss, amused at her, Elizabeth, for rushing down to see her, so absolutely sure that this was just a silly interlude between fun and fun, making even this fun. And other people coming in so that there wasn't even much time to talk. . . . And Anna standing in the rain in the cemetery beside their father's grave. With a look of such sadness, and with the rain falling on her fair hair. Anna laughing with mother, when mother was trying so hard to get a job and worrying about her clothes. Anna coming in after a dance, pulling mother to her feet and whirling her around the room, making her laugh, making her be gay, though mother had been so serious, so earnest, so hard-working. Anna standing on a chair, at Number Seven, holding up the new French curtain stuff and saying, "France—isn't the very word beautiful?"

as if she had known all the world and chosen France for her own. And Anna taking the challis scarf from her head, saying teasingly, "You look as if you'd just landed, darling! Wait!" and then snatching up her old black velvet beret and putting it on Elizabeth's head with a "That's more your type, sis!" And of course, it was. It was. . . . And mother saying, that last day, "Isn't Anna here yet?" . . . And Anna coming toward them through the snow, in her old gray jacket with the red lining, her hands thrust into the pockets, her fair head bare, not seeming even to see them till she was right up to them. "This is my sister Anna," she'd said helplessly to Adrian Suydam.

It wasn't that I wanted him, she insisted to the streaming window. I hardly knew him. I liked him, but I didn't truly want him, not that way. I suppose I just didn't want it to be so easy for her—and yet if I'd been a man, I'd have loved her, just seeing her walk to me out of the snow that way. . . . And I love her too. I've always loved her, loved so terribly much that it's almost finished me. I've wanted her to want me till I've almost died of it. . . . And now she wants me—she says. She won't want me long, and then I'll have to start getting myself whole and free all over again. That's what bothers me so, I suppose.

The mournful sound of the whistle echoed through the train, out into the early night, and the conductor called out, "Lakeville! Lakeville!" She saw Adrian before she came down the steps, lugging her suitcase. He stood under a light, but the rain obscured his face in some way, turning it dim and tired. His raincoat was hunched up around him, making him old. Then he was reaching for her suitcase, saying, "Hello, Liz," moving at once toward the car. Someone said, "Hi," and Adrian said, "Hello, Hux," did not pause. Hux—he was the one who had flooded the hospital room with flowers, the one who had been driving the car when . . . He had looked very tall and gaunt, passing them in the rain and dark, like a ghost. Adrian put the suitcase in the back, opened the front door for her.

In the car they said nothing till they were out of the big graveled place by the station, then Elizabeth said, "It's understood—this is a mistake, Adrian. But here I am."

"If that's your attitude, of course it will be a mistake," he said without friendliness.

"Don't be like that—I'll do what I can. But it won't be for very long."

"That'll be up to you, Liz."

He had always had a calm she liked. He was a man, firm and capable. But he was irritable now. He didn't speak again till they came to Number Seven, till he'd stopped the car.

"Wait a minute, Adrian," she said then. Her heart was pounding unaccountably. "We can't start like this. All I meant was—some people you don't want with you when you're sick. I'm one of those for Anna. It hasn't anything to do with love."

"Hasn't it?" Adrian said coldly.

"No. Does she know?"

"Yes, she knows."

"She was so sure—Dr. Graner was so sure . . ." she said helplessly. "He said it to me—'Your sister's going to be all right'—he said it to me."

"Damn Graner," Adrian said tonelessly.

"But—did something go wrong?"

He did not answer, but put his hand on the door handle.

"Adrian . . ."

"Let's go in," he said. He took her suitcase out and together they went up the hollowed stone steps of the old house. "I'm sorry!" she mumured, but he did not seem to hear her and she didn't even know why she said it. She loved the house, though she had been in it seldom and for brief hours. It was one in a block of brick houses, painted white, built in Revolutionary days. Though it had common walls with other houses, it maintained a separate dignity and importance. Adrian opened the moss-green door, and they were inside the hall. Johnny sat on the bottom step of the stairs in a good blue reefer. His thin, sharp little face was a mask of waiting.

"Oh, Lord, Johnny," Adrian said quickly, "I'm sorry. I know I said you could go to the station, but I got held up at the plant." He spoke crossly and Johnny looked straight at him with eyes that said, You forgot.

"Hel—lo, Johnny!" Elizabeth said.

"Hello," he said, not moving. She gave a little tweak to his ear and walked straight back to the kitchen. "Hi, Bunce," she said. Bunce was fat, not like Lollie, but with a spreading sort of fatness, but she could cook and she was very fast, despite the fatness. She had small black eyes.

"Hello, Miss Burke. You got here all right, I see," Mrs. Bunce said.

"Why not? You'll have to brief me on my duties, Bunce. But you can do that after supper."

"As I said to Mr. Suydam—" Mrs. Bunce began.

"As you said to Mr. Suydam—there's nothing you couldn't do for Anna, there's no need to get that girl here when you could do everything as well as not and no bothering with outsiders. You're right, Bunce, but here I am. We'll make out somehow."

Mrs. Bunce looked at something on the stove and said, "Well, we could have made out all right, Miss Burke. We know her ways. Maybe you can keep the boy out from underfoot."

"Oh," Elizabeth said, "Johnny? Is he underfoot?"

Then, for an instant, she stood there in the bright kitchen, feeling panic, knowing she was putting off the moment of going upstairs, knowing Mrs. Bunce knew it too, knowing Adrian knew it.

"Dinner's 'most ready. You'll be wanting to go up and see her and wash up maybe. Everything's about ready," Mrs. Bunce said.

Elizabeth walked out of the kitchen and toward the stairs.

Johnny still sat there and she said, "Take off that elegant coat, Johnny. I'm here—you can't meet me now. . . . I've got something in my suitcase for you." She went on up the stairs, down the hall to the big front room that looked over the street and had ever been Anna's and Adrian's room.

Oh, Anna, Anna! The Blessed Damozel! The May Queen under the elms at college! Elaine the fair, Elaine the lovable, Elaine the lily maid of Astolat! Rapunzel leaning from the tower! Snow White—Aelfraeda—all the fair ones of the world since time began. Anna. Anna. She sat in a wheel chair by the window, with a little table pulled near her for her supper. Her jacket of amber satin had a mandarin neck and was the color of her eyes, and her hair, like warm sand in color, was pulled up in little curls to the top of her head. Her delicate triangular face was all light and she said, "Oh, *Liz!*"

Elizabeth couldn't speak. She came to her, bent and kissed her, hunted for words, found only "Oh, dear, I meant to comb my hair. You always make me feel as if I'd just come out of the bush!"

Anna gave a small chuckle, gay, amused. "Darling—that's how you always do look!" she said.

"I know. It's *partly* comparative, though." She sat down on a hassock close to Anna's chair, because she couldn't stand up. "I told Adrian this was a damn fool idea," she said too quickly. "And of course it is. But here I am. . . . It's hell not to walk—but being an invalid is becoming to you!"

She talked too fast, talked nonsense, feeling shock, a shock she had not expected to feel, and wondered why she had not expected to feel it.

"I hope so," Anna said. Her voice was just the same, such a gay, expressive voice, with no self-pity in it. "I'd hate to be one of those stringy invalids who smell of medicine. . . . Oh, Liz, I had the most horrible nurse, so full of endearments—the worst of it was, she liked me."

"And you thought I'd be a change?"

"You won't call me dearie, anyway, will you? No, I just wanted someone of my own, that's all."

It was the voice that brought everything back so, all their common past, that unforgettable voice with that teasing, wise, loving laughter always just under the surface.

"Adrian's your own, isn't he? And Johnny. And Mrs. B.?"

"My own blood kin," Anna said. "Oh, they've all been wonderful to me, Liz. Cornelia'd lie down and die for me, I do believe—she's the most tactful mother-in-law in captivity. I can't find any fault with her—isn't that appalling? But they're all worn out—Adrian with trying to be cheerful, Cornelia with running up and down stairs; Johnny, Johnny's been afraid I was going to die. I hope you can make him know I won't—he doesn't even like to come in here. . . . Oh, Liz, I am glad you're here!"

Elizabeth didn't answer. She hugged her knees and her brown face looked gypsy-like and weathered in the lamplight. She was trembling and she hugged the knees tight to stop it.

"Like the room? We'd just had it done over when I had the smashup. I think it's lovely," Anna said.

Elizabeth gave a brief glance around and said, "Looks like Marie Antoinette's boudoir."

"Too fussy, you mean?"

"Oh, no. It's exactly right—for you." A swift vision of the little room across from Lollie's came, went. "Well, Bunce has warned me supper's ready. Do I bring your tray up, or what?"

"Would you? Bunce is really too fat to climb stairs, and Adrian's mother—well, she's thin as a rail, but she's not young, you know."

Elizabeth made for the door. "Be right up," she said gruffly.

She hung her brown coat over the stair rail untidily. Underneath the coat she wore a white blouse, a gray cardigan sweater and a brown-and-gray plaid skirt. Bunce was coming through the kitchen door with the tray and Elizabeth took it from her. Through the very tray passed Bunce's reluctance to let anyone else serve her mistress. Elizabeth said confusedly, "I might as well, Bunce. That's what I'm here for."

But as she went back upstairs she said to herself, I'm shaking like a leaf. Just like a leaf.

She set the tray on the table, wheeled the table closer.

"Cut up your own meat and everything?" she asked.

"Why not? . . . What a frightful skirt!"

Elizabeth looked down at the plaid. "Yes, I guess it is," she admitted. "Gray and brown—very distinguished-looking together, as they said. So they said. Does it matter?"

"Of course it does, darling. But I won't start pecking at you right off. Think you could wear my skirts?"

"Heavens, no! Not unless they have pleats for letting out."

"Somebody ought to. I've one of a heavenly chartreuse wool. Cornelia's clever with the needle—maybe she could fix a couple of them."

"Skip it, Anna. I'll wear my own clothes. Don't try to make me over."

"Thorny Liz! I don't want to make you over. It's just . . ."

"I know. I know. It hurts you to see an ugly skirt like this in the room. But I can't change now, Anna. I can't even try."

Anna laughed, reached out a hand and touched Elizabeth's hand. "All right," she said gently. "Now you've established your independence. Go eat your supper."

Like a child Elizabeth moved obediently toward the door. That was what Anna could do to her, turn her into a child with no will. In the doorway she paused and said, "Would you like to have Adrian eat up here with you?"

Anna's brown eyes sobered. "No, I wouldn't. I wish people wouldn't keep thinking I can't stand it to be alone a minute. I *like* being alone, Liz. And—well, this is a long-term proposition—I don't want to start things, make habits . . ."

"All right," Elizabeth said, and went slowly away, down the stairs. At the stair landing Jonah from an old Biblical print stared at her with martyrlike resignation from the whale's mouth and the small brown vine in the wallpaper crept down the stairs after her. . . . If she had cried . . . if she had clung to her. She had not cried, she had not clung, unless sending for her was crying. But she was just the same, just exactly the same. How *could* she be just the same? No one had that much courage.

"How do you do, Mrs. Suydam?" she said, and put out a hand. Adrian's mother's hand was thin and dry and cool. Her small face had no beauty but great dignity and restraint.

"It's kind of you to come, Elizabeth," Mrs. Suydam said. "To give up your job and all."

"Kind?" Elizabeth said. "It wasn't much of a job—and I hadn't even started on it."

They sat down at the table. In spite of its darkness the dining room had always seemed a pleasant room. There was Chinese furniture, with red and gold tracings, and there were always flowers and candlelight. Where was its charm now?

"Mrs. Bunce!" Adrian said sharply.

Mrs. Bunce came hurrying through the swing door.

"Where are the candles?" Adrian demanded.

"They're right here," Mrs. Bunce said, her flounce saying, Candles are for them as candles do something for!

Adrian lit the candles, pulled out the overhead light. But then shadows took them all over and Johnny's small sharp face looked sharper, more unchildlike than ever.

"Anna looks wonderful, doesn't she?" Elizabeth heard herself saying.

"She always looks wonderful," Mrs. Suydam said quietly.

"Yes—but well, too."

"She tries to—for our sakes."

"Oh, I don't think you could fake it!" Elizabeth said.

"You haven't been here all these months," Adrian said sharply.

"No," Elizabeth said. She put her hands down in her lap, held them tightly together. "I know she's been through a lot. Still, she does look really well now." The shadows deepened and the faces all came to her with unreality, even Adrian's face with eyes turned toward her filled with dislike. "Johnny," she said, hands still tight together in her lap, "I went to a country fair last month and saw the biggest pig in the world. He was so big he couldn't stand up."

"What's a fair?" Johnny asked. His voice was thin, like his face. Where had they got Johnny from? There was none of Adrian in him, Adrian, fair and solid, like a Viking—there was none of Anna's grace or life. She began to talk very fast about country fairs. Horses, cows, chickens, canned things, enormous pumpkins and squashes, crocheted tidies, the ox-pulling contest. Johnny had good eyes, she thought as she talked—intelligent eyes, that said he had opinions, even if he kept them to himself. But suddenly Adrian was saying, "All right, Johnny, eat your supper. We'll save the rest of the fair till some other time. . . . We try to keep table conversation more or less adult." He smiled at Johnny to take the edge off that, but his voice had an edge of its own.

Elizabeth picked up her fork, then said almost rudely, "All right, Adrian. Now you say something adult and interesting." She was ashamed, but the shadows or Johnny's thin face or something compelled her. She was more ashamed when Mrs. Suydam smiled at her without anger and said, "You've made a point there, Elizabeth. To tell you the truth, it was always Anna who made our conversation interesting. But we may learn."

"Sorry," Elizabeth said. Sorrow went over her drowningly. She could not even meet Adrian's eyes. It was so damnably true—it was Anna who made the light, who turned dullness to brilliance, who, even up there alone, away from them, was more exciting than all of them put together. Did she really like eating up there alone or was she just trying, as she said, not to establish patterns they might get tired of? *Oh, Liz! Oh, Liz!* That had been all, all that said anything was any different.

Adrian took his coffee upstairs and Elizabeth said, "Want to help me unpack, Johnny?"

"We've had to give you the little room next to Johnny's," Mrs. Suydam said. "It's comfortable but small. Adrian's been sleeping in the guest room."

"That'll be fine," Elizabeth said.

Johnny sat on the bed and she hung away her few things. She came on the package for Johnny and gave it to him. "You'd better like this!" she said. "I hunted all over town for the filings. . . . They don't have blacksmith shops up our way any more—but when your mummy and I were little there was a blacksmith shop and they used to give us filings." He had opened the package, which had a magnet and a box of iron filings, close to dust. "They're awfully magic, aren't they?" Elizabeth asked. Funny, she thought anxiously, you don't know whether he'll like magic or not.

"I don't know what it's for," said the thin voice.

"You don't? You've never had a magnet? Just take it in your hand and hold it over the box—don't let it touch. Then watch."

The filings jumped up to meet the magnet, made a little tail on either arm and Johnny said, "It jumped!"

"I told you it was magic."

"There isn't really any magic," Johnny said, but his eyes were still wide on his treasure.

"All right. Be scientific if you want to. I call it magic." She lifted a tissue-wrapped object from the suitcase. "It looks small," she said dubiously, "but what there is of it is good. How would you like to take this perfume in to Mummy? Tell her it's a present from Aunt Liz?"

Johnny kept his eyes on the magnet and did not answer.

"Do that for me, Johnny?"

"You can take it," Johnny said.

She didn't insist, but busied herself a few minutes without

talking. Then she said, "I'm going in to Mummy's room now.
Do you want to come along and say good night?"

He didn't answer but began to fold his present up very carefully. Then he slid off the bed and picked up the package. "I
have to put it away," he said. She went next door with him.
He went to the plain chest by his bed, opened it, and put the
package inside. There were, she saw, no toys cluttering the
room. Then without a word he took hold of her hand and went
along with her to his mother's room. His hand was small and
thin and too cold for a child's hand. In the doorway the small
hand gave a sudden pull away from Elizabeth's hand. "Good
night," he said quickly and vanished.

Anna gave a small sigh, then laughed ruefully. "My loving
little son. I suppose sickness is frightening to a child. But I
have tried to make it seem not like sickness. You know, I always imagined I'd have a little girl who was mischievous and
bold—I never imagined a little boy like Johnny. You'd think I
was cruel to him—but I'm not."

"I should hope not," Elizabeth said.

"The trouble is, you never know what he's thinking. It isn't
like a child to keep his thoughts so hidden—is it?"

"All children aren't alike," Elizabeth said. "Do you go to
bed now or sit up awhile?"

"I think bed. . . . Liz, don't tell Adrian, or he'll go into a
panic, but this is really as much of a day as I can take right
now. In time I'll no doubt sit up as late as I ever have—but
right now . . . I don't know whether you can get me into bed
alone or not. Bennett was strong, I must say. She could have
slung me over her shoulder like a bag of wheat and I used to
think maybe she would someday. But there is a little lift from
the chair to the bed and maybe you'll need Adrian to help you.
It would be easier if you didn't, though. . . . Clean nighties are
in the middle drawer. I put it on here—that's simpler."

Elizabeth helped her. She folded the jacket neatly and hung

it over the end of the bed. She got the nightgown on and wheeled the chair over. She brought a bedpan. Then she told Anna to put her arms around her tight and lifted her over onto the bed.

"You're light as a feather," she said, troubled by the lightness.

"That sounded just like Bennett," Anna said. Her voice had thinned a little.

"Well, I'm not very subtle," Elizabeth admitted. "Thistledown, shall we say?"

"Liz—if you're awake around ten or eleven—*would* you bring me some milk? I don't want to upset the household, and I don't want you staying up for it—but if you *are* awake."

Ten o'clock. What an unearthly hour to go to bed! Probably be good for her, though. "I am bone tired," she said, turning out the light. Then she thought of Anna dancing in the dawn, Anna trying the ski jump off Camp Hill, Anna walking down Main Street with the collie they used to have when father had the paper in Katawa. Back then she'd worn her fair hair long. She'd looked like Alice in Wonderland. She still does, Elizabeth said to herself. You turn romantic as—as Rossetti, just looking at her. . . . And there was that man Huxley at the station—he's in love with her. Does Adrian mind, I wonder? And then she heard Adrian walking down the hall to the guest room. He walked slowly, reluctantly. How horrible for Adrian, having to come to terms with a guest room! she thought, then flushed.

She really wanted me, her thoughts raced on. I mustn't mind about the skirts, things like that. She really wanted me. I mustn't get like a stone wall about being changed. God knows, a little changing wouldn't hurt me. I'm not so special, even at best. . . . Still, I'm *me*. I'll never be Anna—I mustn't forget that. I know it's not important to anybody else that I stay *me*— but it's important to me. It's true, what I told Lollie, it's taken me a long time to be anything. . . . Still, it's wicked to be thinking about myself when Anna's like this. I know that, Anna. Oh, *Anna!*

Way back then—she couldn't have been six yet—she saw Anna lift the teapot to pour tea for her mother, a special concession. Anna's face was so grown-up, so exactly like that of a fine lady, pouring tea, and her arm was so graceful lifting the pot. It had stayed in the mind forever, that moment, as something so desirable, so unattainable. "Do you take sugar?" Anna said, and her triangular face with its curly mouth was so gracious and concerned below the long fair hair. Even the ribbon that tied her hair hadn't made her a little girl. . . . When she'd had her turn weeks later, she'd spilled the tea, spilled the sugar, almost dropped the teapot. Such a little thing to remember.

The clock began to strike eleven, softly, clearly. Elizabeth slipped out of bed, put on the plain brown flannel robe, went down the stairs, and got some milk from the refrigerator. Anna hadn't said she wanted it warmed, but Elizabeth remembered Anna sitting on the arm of the old sofa at home after a party, a cup of steaming milk in her hand, so she got a pan, heated the milk, carried it upstairs. She went in quietly, but Anna said at once, "Is that you, Liz?"

"Yes. Refreshments."

A small light was on the bed and Elizabeth brought the milk, set it down on the table by the lamp. "Want to be pulled up a bit?" she asked.

"Just ram a couple of pillows under me. . . . Oh, hot! How heavenly! You're going to spoil me, darling."

"No, I'm not. Haven't you been to sleep yet?"

"Not yet. I always feel so sleepy—and then I don't sleep. But I like to lie awake and think about things. . . . I think the rain's turned to snow—has it?"

Elizabeth went to the window and it was snowing—small sharp flakes.

"Yes, it's snowing," she said.

"Remember how we used to watch the ice in Dobbs' Pond—to see if it was thick enough for skating? Remember the Bartrip boys—like birds or something? I can't think of anything that was ever so exciting as skating on Dobbs' Pond in the moonlight—can you?"

"It was fun," Elizabeth said. Her voice was dull because she didn't want pity in it, but her throat felt thick with pity.

"I never see why people want to go where it's warm in the winter. I even remember a red pleated skirt I used to wear for skating, and a white cap and scarf. . . . Do you ever skate any more?"

"Sometimes. In the park," Elizabeth said.

"You must teach Johnny. I don't know if you can—or whether he'd even like it. Sometimes he seems allergic to fun. . . . I mustn't keep you up all night—the hot milk was wonderful. Made me all nostalgic and young again. It *is* nice you're here, Liz!"

Elizabeth came and took the cup, pulled the pillows out, kissed Anna good night. "Sleep well," she said. Then she hesitated, glanced toward the other narrow bed on the opposite wall. "Maybe you wanted me to sleep in here," she said.

"Oh, no. I have a bell—I *do* like being in a room alone, don't you? You always used to."

"Yes. But you might want something."

"I'll ring if I do."

So Elizabeth carried the cup downstairs, went back to bed. I ought to have sat down and reminisced, she thought. I really should have.

*A*DRIAN SUYDAM came back into the hall and said, "You've got my telephone number, Liz?"

"Yes."

"Don't hesitate to call me at any time."

"I won't. But everything will be all right."

"Dr. McIntry will come in a minute—his number's right over the phone there."

"Adrian, don't worry so. I'll take care of her."

He frowned as if there were more he must say, but he went at last.

"Does he always fuss like that?" Elizabeth asked Mrs. Bunce.

"He's a husband in a thousand," Mrs. Bunce said. "But then, he's got a wife in a million. He's been just out of his mind with worry."

"But he can't go on worrying like that," Elizabeth said. "He'll go to pieces. I mean—it's terrible, but it's the way it *is*, the way it's going to be."

"He's got a heart, Mr. Suydam has," said Mrs. Bunce.

So have I, Bunce. So have I. But you can't live like that. But she didn't say it aloud.

Mrs. Bunce gave her a look of dislike and turned to her

dishes. Elizabeth went slowly upstairs. "Look, Anna," she said
directly, "you don't *like* all this solicitude, do you? Or do you?
You look as lively as a cricket and they all act as if you were
still on the danger list."

Anna's brown eyes crinkled up in delight. "Oh, Liz, I'm
glad you're here! I said you didn't have any sense of humor—
I told Adrian that—but you *do* have—I'd just forgotten the
kind it was. But it's just that I was on the danger list so long.
They've got the habit. It's going to be a bit of a trick to make
life normal and exciting again, but between us, we'll manage
it. . . . You know, Liz, when they first brought me up here,
from the hospital, I looked around and I thought, *These four
walls, just these four walls*—I'll die here. But I won't die.
That's the whole point, I won't die here."

"Anna, I thought Graner was so sure. I don't even know
what happened."

"Graner." Anna said the word in a whisper that sounded like
hate.

"Did—did he fumble the operation? What *happened?*"

"Which operation? There were three. He wanted to do one
more—at least he told me it might be the end of me. Perhaps
a chance in a hundred that it wouldn't. But I'll take a half-life
any day to a chance in a hundred at a whole one. And I'll
make the half-life seem whole, too."

"Oh," Elizabeth said slowly. She heard Adrian's cold, passion-
less voice saying "Damn Graner." She heard his steps going
slowly down the hall to the guest room. Everything seemed
suddenly changed, and yet she did not know quite why. She
said abruptly, "Shall I have a go at that hair-do now? You've
certainly picked a complicated one!"

"It wouldn't hurt you to find a good barber," Anna said.
"Good heavens, someone's at the door already!"

The someone was an old Italian woman, Mrs. Campanini,
with some pizza for Anna.

"Oh, you angel!" Anna said to her. "They try to feed me on

chicken breasts and suchlike tidbits, Mrs. Campanini. I've got
the appetite of an elephant! How's Nick?"

"Nick, he all the time the same," Mrs. Campanini said. "He
say to tell you he fix your shoes for nothing." Then her warm
brown face creased up and she began to cry at the enormity
of what she had said.

But Anna said, "There, there now—I'll hold him to that,
Mrs. Campanini. And don't you dare cry over me! You just
come up with some pizza now and then and tell me all the
news."

And presently they were all laughing and Mrs. Campanini,
her fat fingers surprisingly deft, helped fix Anna's hair. "Soft,
like a baby's!" she kept saying.

That was moving, seeing Anna with Mrs. Campanini, but
they were essentially of different worlds. It was perhaps more
moving to see her with two young women of her own world,
two women who came in at different times but whose calls
overlapped. Jen and Lucy, they were called. It was not so hard,
Elizabeth saw, to be brave before Mrs. Campanini, but to be
brave, to show no sign of self-pity before these two friends,
that took courage of a very high order. Yet Anna showed no
self-pity. They sat there in the bright room and Anna told
them stories of the hospital—not of herself in the hospital, but
stories she had run across in passing through. There was one
of a doctor who had had an affair with the hospital scrub-
woman who worked there nights. Under Anna's telling some
romantic truth came through. "You know, I could understand
it," Anna said. "I truly could. She must have been forty but
she was strong and she had something about her eyes—something that said she knew what life was all about. The staff
was shocked to the bone, but, if I were a man, that's just the
kind of woman I'd go for. Remember how father used to say,
'She was able for life,' Liz? That woman was just that—able
for life . . ."

There was a little pause, as when people have been listening

to a story from a loved book. Then Lucy smiled and said, "Oh,
Anna, you're wonderful! I was coming in to cheer you up—
shame on me! I'm the one who's been cheered up. That little
scene with my darling Judy that I was telling you—well, I'm
going to take her across my knee and give her an old-fashioned
spanking when she gets home from school. Just to show I'm
'able for life'! . . . Come on, Jen. See you later, Anna—but not
much later. We'll make ourselves a nuisance. . . . How about
bridge some afternoon soon?"

"Love it," Anna said.

"Grand Central Station, I calls it," Elizabeth said after they
had gone.

"Aren't they nice?" Anna said.

The mailman said, "How's Anna?" his cross, stubby face
really interested. Letters flowed across the bed and Anna said,
"Oh, listen, Liz—Carol is so *fabulous!*" And people jumped
out of the letters, came real in the room. Such gay people, such
interesting people. Did Anna know only the interesting ones,
or did people become interesting with the touch of Anna's
friendship? "Oh, I feel so warm at mailtime!" Anna said.

Elizabeth had one friend, Bessie, that she wrote to often—
but sometimes, when Bessie was deep in writing—she wrote
children's books—there would be a lapse of months. There
would be an occasional quick scrawl from Anna. Not so much
else.

"Where is Johnny, I wonder?" Elizabeth said suddenly. "Is
he always so quiet as this?"

"Yes, he's always quiet," Anna said. "Always."

He hurts her, Elizabeth thought. He hurts her.

So the morning went and then there was lunch, then a brief
nap, then more people. The last one was the paper boy, who
came up the stairs with muddy shoes and said, "Hi, Mis'
Suydam. Here's your paper!"

At supper Elizabeth asked Mrs. Suydam, "Does Anna always
have so many people dropping in?"

"Anna is greatly loved," Mrs. Suydam said.

So it was no special day. This was the way life was at Number Seven. This was the way Anna was loved.

"Just don't let her get too tired," Adrian said.

"Well, it would tire me to death, but she seems to like it," Elizabeth said.

She took a filmy brown nightgown with a circle of yellow lace at the neck from the drawer. "If you don't mind the ironing—I do love a fresh nightgown every night," Anna said. "Adrian must have looted Bonwit's or something!" Then, after she was in bed, she added, "Do you think you can manage, Liz?"

"Yes, I can manage."

"I know you were watching me like an old mother hen today —but I do love people coming. I do love life so, Liz."

"If you can take it, I can," Elizabeth said. "Shall I let Adrian come up now?"

Anna gave the briefest pause before she said, "Yes, let him come. He has so little of me, poor darling."

Later Elizabeth heard again those slow steps going down the hall to the guest room. I must make him *know* I love Anna, she thought anxiously. He doesn't believe it. That's my punishment for being reluctant. I suppose he'd hate me anyway, being so strong, having my good two legs, even if they're stubby. It's her courage that breaks your heart. How did she get so much courage? Always everything has come to her easily —but it's real courage. Father died so bravely—and mom certainly had courage afterward. She always had it. But Anna's never had to *practice* at it. Never. How did she have the strength to *decide*? What would I have done? I couldn't make a half-life seem whole. No, I couldn't do that. I might bear it, but I couldn't make it seem whole. She makes it amusing and interesting and beautiful—no, I wouldn't have what it takes to do that. I've always thought she was a fair-weather girl. I don't know whether I can even stand it watching her. Those lovely nightgowns. It takes more courage than to walk straight into a possible death, a lot more courage than that.

When she got into bed, she said to herself, You wouldn't know there was a little boy in the house.

A week later she looked from Anna's window out on bare trees, on streaks of dry snow along the curbs and steps, and said with wonder, I'm still here. She was not only there but she seemed to have been there forever and the life at Number Seven was a routine that had been established long, long ago. She had sent the money for the room to Lollie, said only, "I may be here longer than I planned." She had thought that Anna herself would tire of her, be annoyed with her, would send her away, but with the loving, teasing dismissal that was familiar from another existence. But Anna didn't send her away. She teased her still, laughed at her clothes, her dull life, but seemed to want her there. She said more than once, "Oh, Liz, you're such a relief after Bennett! She was coy—if you touched her, she'd begin to ooze out somewhere. I ought to be ashamed—she cried when she left me—but I couldn't bear her in the room." The work wasn't hard. It was even a pleasure to take care of someone so fastidious and lovely as Anna. Yet Elizabeth Burke was often tired and she was glad now to go to bed at ten o'clock. It was, she thought, staring out the window while Anna read her mail, that it was wearing living up to Anna's bravery. Wearing to put on the face that meant life was just the same, to be lived fully, when it wasn't true that life could be lived so. And yet Anna did make it seem possible. Mrs. Suydam had been right when she said Anna was greatly loved. All of Lakeville seemed to come in and out of that room. It was amazing, an incredible feat, that Anna should make this invalid's room so much a center of life and light. Even Adrian, when he came home at night, came straight up here as if the whole day had been working toward the moment. He was often impatient with Johnny, short with Elizabeth, but his gentleness with Anna was a warm and beautiful thing. It didn't matter what he thought of her, Elizabeth admitted, so long as all was well between him and Anna. It didn't matter that Bunce didn't accept her, either, if she was useful. She'd made several attempts with Mrs. Bunce.

"How's your friend, Miss Potts?" she'd asked her. Miss Potts worked by the day for the Realses, Huxley's father and mother, and she and Mrs. Bunce spent time off together and went to the Baptist church together on Sunday.

"Maisie? She stays the same," Mrs. Bunce had said.

Another time Elizabeth said, "It's wonderful for Anna that she has you here, Bunce. People don't make things shine so any more—everything here always looks as if it had just been polished for company."

"H'm!" Bunce said. "Little elbow grease is all. Never been afraid of using elbow grease." She had seemed almost to unbend at that. But then she said, "Here, Miss Burke, I'll do that. I'm a good hand at ironing, if I do say so." She took the iron from Elizabeth's hand and began to iron silk with loving care, her very motion saying that Elizabeth left wrinkles where wrinkles should not be.

Mrs. Suydam was polite to her, but remote. She didn't worry about that too much, because she remembered her as always that way. Mrs. Suydam stayed most of the time in her rooms on the third floor, made herself useful in small ways, but never intruded. Tactful, Anna had said, the most tactful mother-in-law in captivity. Yes, she was that all right. She had the look of the born aristocrat, self-sufficient, proud. But she sewed, she answered business mail, she did many small services without any fuss. She didn't pay too much attention to Johnny, though she had been giving him his bath nights. "Why do you call her Cornelia?" Elizabeth asked Anna once. "Why? Why, that's the secret of my success with her. You shouldn't call a mother-in-law 'Mother.' It violates something." "Oh, I'll remember that if I ever have a mother-in-law," Elizabeth said. "And why don't you have one?" Anna asked gently. "Oh, I don't know." "I'll have to put my mind to that," Anna said. "Never mind, I'll take care of it," Elizabeth told her.

Johnny was something else, always a worry at the heart. He made no trouble, he asked for nothing. But that was part of the worry. Ever since the night she had come and had seen him sitting on the step waiting, he had been there fixed in her mind, a worry. Anna could charm a bird off the bough—why did she not charm Johnny? "He mustn't be forced to come in," Anna said once. "No, I don't want that, Liz. He'll come—in time. He'll get used to me this way." And that sounded right, and yet—and yet . . . She went into his room and read to him awhile. Then she said, "I hear you have an electric train—where is it?"

Johnny pointed to the chest. "In there."

"In there? Why don't we get it out and play with it?"

"I keep it in there," Johnny said.

"It can't run in a chest. We could put the tracks under the bed and have it for a tunnel under there."

"I like it inside," Johnny said.

He would sit on the stairs for an hour at a time. People would pass him, give him a careless "Hi, there, Johnny!" sometimes pat him on the head. Sometimes he would say "Hello," sometimes not. He never played with other children. Yes, he worried one. Just because he was no trouble at all, because he kept all his toys in a box. But I think he likes me, Elizabeth thought. He lets me read to him and tuck him in at night. He allows it.

It was good to be useful. Yet, as Elizabeth watched the chill street, heard scraps of Anna's letters, she was aware that she was a little frightened to realize that she had been here a week and seemed to be wanted still.

That afternoon another habit was established—the tea hour. Dr. McIntry came in. Anna sat with a book in her hands and Dr. McIntry said, "You haven't taken to knitting then, Anna?"

"God forbid!" Anna said. "Are you being professional or just coming calling? Don't you dare run up a foolish bill on Adrian!"

"I like to work it both ways," the doctor said. "It would be pleasant to be paid for coming to visit with you a bit. You're the only woman in town who doesn't bore me. This time I'll just call it friendship. . . . You the sister?"

"Yes, I'm the sister," Elizabeth said.

"Sit down," Anna said. "You too, Liz—don't fuss around, we're neat as a pin."

The doctor was a very long man. He folded himself into the chair near Anna and said, "You're very smart, Anna. You won't lack for male callers—this is a man's chair."

"It's Adrian's. But you can sit there this time. You've been neglecting me."

"You don't need me, alas. . . . Meg wants Johnny for Sunday. All right?"

"If she can take it, I don't mind. But I don't know how she entertains him. I know I talk too much, but Johnny—he's so *silent.* If Meg can wake him up, more power to her."

The doctor gave a quick, straight look at Elizabeth. He had a look that was completely honest, a look that made people think he was kind, though he was not. He had shed illusions long since, had Dr. McIntry, and did not even think he could alleviate men's ills more than a little, but some trick of the long features, that honest look that was in truth unconscious of its audience, made people trust him. "Not much like you," he said of Elizabeth. "Sure you're sisters?"

"Always believed so," Anna said. "She's a nice girl—but stubborn."

"Anna's stubborn too. It just doesn't show on the outside," Elizabeth said. "Shall I make some tea?"

"Don't bother," Anna said. "Though it would be lovely if it could just be wafted up without hands."

Elizabeth jumped up and said, "I'll waft it."

Anna laughed and said, "She isn't happy unless she's doing something. I can't understand such incredible energy. You can't imagine how I love to be lazy!"

When Elizabeth came in with the tea, Anna said, "That was a quick waft! We've been watching the people go by—Mrs. Daggett, you know, the caterpillar one with all the humps. It's a game I play. Mr. Botsworth's like a cod. You're my little Shetland pony, darling. Adrian called you that once and it fits. Isn't she a pony, Doctor? Just the way she plumped the tray down—so pony-like! . . . I love tea—I'd have it every day if Liz would sit down to it with me. . . . I'll pour it, Liz. I always feel like such a lady pouring tea from this nice old silver pot. Isn't it a love? It was Adrian's great-grandmother's—Cornelia gave it to me. Why don't you call her down for a cup of tea, Liz?"

Elizabeth went to the stairs and called Mrs. Suydam, and Mrs. Suydam came, quietly, erectly, as was her wont, greeted the doctor and sat down in a small rosewood chair with a coral-colored seat and carved back. She accepted tea. "I've just been telling the doctor what a wonder you are," Anna said. "The tea-pot—you gave it to me and that was the end of it. It wasn't yours any more—that's wonderful, really wonderful. I can remember an aunt—remember Aunt Susie, Liz? How she used to give mother things all the time but when she would come visiting she would check on every present, to see if it was mended or taken care of? Once an old plate got broken and mother didn't want to confess it—Aunt Susie spent a week hunting, going through boxes in the attic, the barn, everywhere. 'Well, it isn't a plate you could mislay,' she kept saying. 'It's a plate for show—you probably wouldn't ever have used it on the table. Probably that cook you used to have put it away where it wouldn't be broken. Where is she now, Elizabeth? I'll just drop her a line and ask her.' That went on day after day. But the things weren't *ours*—they were still Aunt Susie's. That's why I love this teapot. It's *mine*."

She smiled at Mrs. Suydam and Mrs. Suydam smiled back.

"You're easy to give things to," Mrs. Suydam said. "You take such pleasure in things."

"I do love presents. But I expect I ought to grow up on that score. More tea, Doctor?"

He stretched out his long arm, cup in hand, and Anna poured the tea steadily.

It was peaceful there in the bright room. Everything shone there, the silver tea things, the knobs on the fenders, the old gold clock with cherubs on the mantel, the sapphire ring on Mrs. Suydam's hand, the arms of the deep leather chair where the doctor sat. But the light was brightest on Anna Suydam, sitting there in the wheel chair. She had on a jacket of blue brocade that Mrs. Suydam had made from an old party dress. The blue was grayed down to warmness and the silver thread that ran through it was a companion to the silver of the tea things. But in her face the light concentrated, in that thin triangular face with the golden-brown eyes looking around at them all with such love, such an effect of saying, These are my very best people. This is what I like, sitting here talking with my own people.

"Aunt Susie," Anna went back, with a little sigh. "She was a character. I thought she was really hurt when mother died. But right now I had the thought that maybe she was just angry like about the plate—something of hers had been mislaid and she couldn't find it. . . . Have some more bread and butter, Cornelia. Liz, you were always a bread-and-butter girl for tea—no cakes or little rolled sandwiches. But I like it, don't you? It's the only time of day when plain bread and butter seems like a party. . . . Who's sick, Doctor? Tell us the town news."

Dr. McIntry laughed and said, "Tom Trevors has boils—that interest you? The Jones baby is a bouncer—eleven pounds. They rarely come that big any more. The Reverend Prather is having trouble with his conscience—*not* a case of mine. Bill Vine has offered to rebuild the chapel and Prather is having an ends and means argument with himself. If Bill only meant well

2667

THE BAKERVILLE LIBRARY

and was at base a religious man even if he didn't go to church, Prather might just swallow it, but he's so out-and-out non-religious—a really godless man—and there's no doubt about it, he has his tongue in his cheek when he makes the offer—well, can Prather take it? Can he say that the ways of the Lord move that deviously, that the gift will perhaps put Vine in a state of grace, that money that comes into the church is thereby sanctified and its source doesn't matter? It's a pretty little case of ethics and I'm watching to see how it comes out. Prather hasn't any sense of humor, so he takes it seriously."

Elizabeth hugged her knees and said, "It is serious, isn't it? I—I mean that if morals are just expediency . . ."

"What do you think they are, young woman?" the doctor asked.

"I don't know. But it seems as if that's a *real* moral issue. Couldn't you just as well say that you'd be better off if you had more money and therefore you might as well kill your father, who's willed his fortune to you?"

"That wouldn't be expedient, because you might land in jail or the electric chair."

"All right. We'll leave murder out of it, or anything that would hurt the public good. I'll even say the Ten Commandments are in the interests of expediency, if you want to—that the greatest good for the greatest number is served by them. But all the same there's something in you that balks against selling out to a truth you don't believe in—I mean something that isn't your own personal truth. And only you know what that is. That's where morals begin, for me. And I imagine that's what's troubling your Prather. He just don't believe that it doesn't matter where the money comes from for his chapel. It may be that the chapel would balance acceptance, but it doesn't for Prather. For him, taking the money would be a sin—or that's the way I see sin. Sin's an awfully private matter. Isn't it?"

Anna gave that delighted little laugh of hers and said, "You mustn't start Liz off, Doctor. She's awfully earnest, my Liz."

"I see she is," said Dr. McIntry. "But Prather's sin doesn't happen to be my sin—we have a right to be amused by the dilemmas of other people, don't we? If we hadn't, we couldn't bear living. I think Prather's dilemma is funny. And you might as well too, my dear girl. . . . Well, I have to go. Hate to."

He unfolded from the deep chair, got to his feet. He shook hands all around, giving Elizabeth an amused, half-indulgent smile. Mrs. Suydam drifted away and the doctor himself walked to the door before he turned and said, "Oh, Anna—Huxley Reals. Can't you do something about Huxley?"

"About Huxley?"

"Yes—get the guilt complex under control. He'll be no earthly good if he doesn't stop this."

"I'll try," Anna said. "I'll have Adrian ask him in—I have tried, but I'll have another go at it."

"Do that." Then he really went, but he said to Elizabeth in passing, "Don't worry about Prather's sin!"

Elizabeth went, flushing, to the table, picked up the tray.

"He works so terribly hard," Anna said. "I do like to have it like a party when he comes. I think he really rests here."

Elizabeth moved toward the door with the tray. Her voice came back with a touch of desperation. "All the same, it *isn't* funny!"

Anna laughed aloud. "Oh, Liz!"

Elizabeth met Adrian coming up the stairs. "What's the joke?" he asked.

"Anna'll tell you," she said without graciousness. Anna's laughter greeted him, trailed on in fresh merriment.

When Elizabeth set the tray down Bunce turned from the sink. "Is he gone?" she asked.

"Yes."

"He certainly went for that bread and butter!"

"We all did."

"What are you crying about?"

"I'm not crying," Elizabeth said. "I'm a little mad, that's all."

"There's plenty to shed tears about," Mrs. Bunce said. "She was such a pretty dancer."

"Yes, she was," Elizabeth said. "Johnny's invited out for Sunday—by the doctor's daughter."

"H'mph!" Mrs. Bunce said.

Elizabeth went slowly up the stairs, into Johnny's room. He was curled up on the bed with a book.

"Shall I read to you?" she asked.

"I don't care. If you want to," Johnny said.

He handed her the book he was looking at, came and sat in the big chair with her. He was small and bony against her.

"This is pretty old for you," Elizabeth said.

"It's all right," he said. So she began to read about Robin Hood. She came to a place where it said: "He walked deliberately across the clearing," changed it to "He walked slowly . . ."

"It doesn't say that," Johnny said.

"Why, can you read?" Elizabeth said. "I didn't know that. Who taught you?"

"Nobody. Go on," Johnny said.

When she finished, she said, "Next time you can read to me. Or to Mummy. She'd love to have you read to her."

He didn't answer.

"Did you know you were going to go to the doctor's house on Sunday afternoon?"

For the first time she saw real expression come into the small face. A look of—what was it?—delight—relief? It seemed relief.

She remembered Lollie saying, "Don't get to feeling sorry for him and stay forever!" But it would take forever, she thought, to get to know Johnny. What was it about him that hurt one so, made such a sore spot at the heart? Why wouldn't he go willingly into his mother's room? Anna was always gentle with him, said only, "Good night, Johnny," never forced him to come and kiss her. She didn't coerce him. And yet he was afraid of that room, terribly afraid. Everybody in town ran in and out of that room, found it good—but Johnny, flesh of Anna's flesh,

stayed aloof, moved about the house like a lonely little shadow.
It didn't make sense.

Later Anna said, "Would it be too much trouble, having tea
every day?"

"No—it's fun," Elizabeth said.

"Good! It rounds the day off, I always think."

"Maybe Johnny'd join us sometimes. He seems so awfully
lonely, Anna."

"Yes. But he likes to be, Liz."

"Oh, but does any little boy *like* to be lonely? He hardly
makes a sound."

"I know. It doesn't make sense—but that's the kind of boy
Johnny is. You can't know how I've tried, Liz."

Elizabeth said no more. But she wished she could talk with
Lollie about Johnny. Lollie said once, "You can know the pattern from life to death—but every single one is different, all the
same."

Then it was Sunday, a bright, bitterly cold day, with a blue
sky and white clouds scudding across the blueness. Grasses were
brittle in the early morning and even the sun did not warm the
earth much. The fields outside of town were hard and green,
like iron. In the morning the church bells rang and people
walked along the streets in their Sabbath best. After church
the same people walked home again to the somnolent, heavy
Sunday dinners. Mrs. Bunce was a churchgoing woman—Baptist by creed. She didn't like asking favors of Elizabeth but she
did say, "If you wouldn't mind giving an eye to the roast, Miss
Burke . . . I'll be back plenty of time for the vegetables." She
let her bulky figure out the front door, her Bible prominent in
her gloved hands. At the steps her round face grew troubled
and she turned back. "Miss Burke," she said, "I didn't think to
ask. Maybe you was planning to go to church yourself. Mrs. S.
would mind the roast."

"No, I wasn't going. It's quite all right, Bunce."

"You'd be real welcome at my church, Miss Burke. We've

got a good preacher now. Real bedrock religion, that's what he preaches. Of course the Episcopal church is more stylish, but when it comes to real gospel preaching, you can't do better than Reverend Smith."

"I don't care about the style, but I don't believe I'll go today," Elizabeth said.

"Well, God bless you," Mrs. Bunce mumbled, and departed.

That seemed a little funny to Elizabeth and she shared it with Anna. Anna laughed and said, "In an hour you'll see her coming down the street with her friend Maisie Potts, talking sixteen to the dozen—about us. They think it's romantic that Huxley has this silly attachment and today Maisie will say, 'He's asked for tea—he sent her roses this morning—three dozen—and you know what roses are now!' And Bunce will say, 'It's a wonder *he* lets him come! But he knows he's got nothing to worry about.' I'd love to listen in once, but I know what they say as if I were there. The 'real strong' sermon—Mrs. Reals's sciatica—Juliet's new mink—but I don't mind. Bunce is wonderful, really, and she can talk about me all she likes."

When Bunce returned, a little red in the face when her eyes met Elizabeth's, as if conscious of having parted with Potts on a note of family gossip, Elizabeth had done the vegetables. "There wasn't any call for you to do that, Miss Burke," she said. "I have plenty of time between church and dinner. You've got your job to do and I've got mine. We'd better keep it that way."

"Right you are," Elizabeth said cheerfully. "That's the same sermon I'm always preaching!"

At two the doctor's daughter came for Johnny. Elizabeth went to the door. The tall young woman came into the hall, said, "You must be Anna's sister. I'm Margaret McIntry."

"Hello. Yes, I'm Elizabeth Burke."

And between them flashed something, the something that made them individuals, made them Elizabeth and Margaret instead of Liz and Meg, instead of "Anna's sister" or "the doctor's girl," something of instant recognition and liking. "I'll run up and say hello to Anna. Johnny, get your duds on!"

That was all of their first meeting. Anna said, "Meg's the salt of the earth—but she always makes me think of that old farm horse Uncle Jean used to have."

Elizabeth smiled. Margaret McIntry was like a horse, long-limbed, with a long face. And yet so real, without any veneer. "I liked her," she said.

"Oh, Meg's a grand girl," Anna said carelessly. "I don't know what fun Johnny has there—in the summer he swings under the grape arbor. But now—I don't know. Liz, do stay around when Huxley comes, will you? He's a lamb—but a troublesome one. I think I'll rest now till he gets here."

But it didn't turn out just as planned. After Elizabeth had drawn the curtains, left Anna to rest, she went downstairs and joined Adrian in the living room.

"Margaret McIntry's nice, isn't she?" she asked.

Adrian looked surprised.

"Meg? The best," he said.

He picked up the paper, held it between him and Elizabeth. There seemed no more to say. She reached for a book, pretended to read. She wanted to escape to her room but didn't want him to think he could drive her out by silence.

"Did you teach Johnny to read?" she asked at last.

"I? No. Can he read?"

"Very well."

"He's precocious," Adrian said, returned to his paper, and said no more till he said, "Shouldn't Anna be getting up now?"

So she went upstairs, fixed Anna in the chair again. "Don't pull the curtains back," Anna said. "It'll soon be dark and it's so nice this way."

Elizabeth went down to see that everything was ready for tea, then joined Adrian in the living room. When the doorbell rang she moved to answer but Bunce got there first, saying, in passing, "That'll be Mr. Reals." Elizabeth saw Adrian's face tighten but he called out cordially enough, "Go right up, Hux!"

Once Elizabeth had heard Bunce say of Huxley, "He's such a beautiful boy!" He came into the living room, paying that much deference to his employer, pretending that much that he was in no passionate haste to go up to Anna. "Sharp out," he said briefly. He was not a boy. He was a man, as old as or older than Adrian himself, and this fact abruptly changed everything. Anna had laughed gently about Huxley Reals' devotion, seemed to make it a nuisance, nothing else. It was, Elizabeth had thought, like the devotion of a schoolboy to a teacher or a college student to a professor's wife. It wasn't that way at all.

"Tea's coming up," Adrian said. "But maybe you'd like a drink?"

"No, thanks," Huxley said.

He lit a cigarette and Adrian said, "You know Liz, don't you?"

"No, I'm afraid not. Hello, Liz."

"Hello," Elizabeth said.

She had thought it would be simple to accompany him up the stairs. She saw it would not be simple, saw it would be impossible. He was no child but a man, competent, mature, used to having his own way.

"Anna'll be waiting for you," Adrian said.

Huxley turned and moved toward the door. Elizabeth half rose but Adrian restrained her with "Maybe you'd like a highball, Liz?"

"No, thanks." The moment when it had been remotely possible passed.

"He fancies himself in love with Anna," Adrian said. He spoke as if that fancy didn't mean much but was still an annoyance. He wouldn't, Elizabeth thought, have mentioned it if he'd thought it constituted even a remote threat to his own happiness. But Elizabeth knew fright, felt the moment as important, more important and frightening than she had expected. Everything grew suddenly more complex. Because the man was more adult, she told herself, than she had thought.

She saw what Bunce had meant by "such a beautiful boy," but he was not beautiful, only sensitive and fine drawn. His mouth was not a poet's mouth, but the mouth of a man who knew his own mind and would not be swerved.

Elizabeth tried frantically to find some opening for escape, some excuse to join the two upstairs as Anna had asked. She bent her shaggy head forward over a book, but saw nothing on the page. Then she said something she had not had the slightest notion she was going to say.

"Don't you think I've been here long enough, Adrian?"

"That's entirely up to you," Adrian said.

"Not entirely. If I can be useful—but I don't think I am, not very."

"Anna seems to think you are. You'll have to do what you think best."

She stopped, shocked at herself. But there had swept over her a desperate necessity to get back to her homely little room across from Lollie Parsons.

When she carried the tray upstairs, Huxley sat on the hassock near Anna's chair. A look of reproach, apology, flashed between the sisters.

"This is my sister, Liz," Anna said.

"I know Liz," Huxley said, but not looking at her. "At least, I've met her."

"If he isn't polite, pay no attention," Anna said. "I've been scolding him and he's sulky."

"No, I'm not sulky, Anna," Huxley Reals said, got up, and moved the table nearer for the tray. "But I'm not a child to be scolded, either."

"I left out the roses," Anna said. "I forgot to scold you about them. They are lovely and I won't send them back this time— but the company doesn't pay you enough to cover roses, Hux."

"I paid for them, not the company," Huxley said shortly. "Surely I can do what I like with my own money?"

"Well, Juliet would say it wasn't seemly to send me roses," Anna said.

"I don't answer to Juliet."

"Isn't Adrian coming up, Liz?" Anna asked. Elizabeth went to the stairs and called, "Tea, Adrian!"

When Adrian came in, he said, "Hux, you're always underfoot. You might pick weekdays to come calling—not make love to my wife right under my nose."

"You mean—it doesn't bother you if you don't see me doing it?" Huxley asked.

"No, I didn't mean exactly that," Adrian said.

They spoke lightly, but Elizabeth felt a current of something that was deadly and serious between them all the same.

"Lemon?" she said firmly to Huxley Reals.

"No, straight," he said. "You're a funny-looking girl to be Anna's sister."

"It happens in the best families," Elizabeth said.

Then Anna picked up the conversation, made it gay and easy, and they presently began to laugh, while the roses were sweet and yellow all about them and the fire burned softly in the grate and the tea things sparkled. But suddenly—Elizabeth hardly knew how it came about—there came a sentence about dancing—then about dreaming of dancing—about movement in general. "I'm always moving in my sleep," Anna said. "Now don't start feeling sorry for me—it's just one of those things that happen in the subconscious, I suppose. In the daytime I truly love to be lazy. . . ." Then somehow, somehow—she got them talking about things that moved, of skating and boats and planes, and Elizabeth, almost without volition, found herself telling them about the Cape, about last fall when she had taken Bessie Loren's house on the bluff across from Wellfleet—or been given it, really, because it was past the season for renting.

"It was sunny the day I came," she said, "but the next day the wind began to blow and it never stopped for two weeks.

The place was on the cove so you didn't get real ocean waves, but all day long and all night long the water slapped on the shore and the sea grass bent to the wind and the scrub pines bent too, and the bayberry bushes. And the clouds raced and the gulls flew over and over till I saw them coming, coming in my dreams, gliding and swooping, gliding and swooping. I began to feel as if I were the only solid thing in the world, the only thing that could stay put. The house was solid enough, but there was only sand under it and I couldn't see what stopped it from being picked right up and blown out to sea, or at least bending like the sea grass."

"And didn't you love it?" Anna asked.

"In a way. But I've felt bent ever since," Elizabeth said.

"You were all alone there?" Hux asked.

"All alone," she said, with a small grin.

"Yes," Anna said softly, "that's the kind of thing I like to think about at night. You sounded quite poetic, about the gulls, darling. I didn't know you had it in you."

"Well, I have lots in me that you don't know about," Elizabeth said more briskly.

Adrian was standing by the hearth now. He looked with some anxiety at Anna and said, "Would you like to rest now till dinner, Anna?"

It put the rest of them out. Huxley got up and said he must run along. Anna shook hands with him. "Adrian's such a fuss-budget," she said. "But I suppose I'd better have a bit of a doze before supper."

When Elizabeth came downstairs Huxley Reals was just leaving. He paused in the hall, said, "Good day, Liz. Thanks for the tea."

Then he took the tray from her hands, carried it to the kitchen, returned. He put his hand to the doorknob, then said, "That was a pretty bit of cruelty up there."

"Cruelty?" But she knew what he meant. "I didn't start it."

"You certainly contributed your share."

She put out a hand to the newel post. "I know. I couldn't stop. It was hideous."

She couldn't look up at him, but stood there, looking down at the hall carpet. But she was conscious of his tall, angry figure there by the door. Then the door closed and she was alone. She went to her room, shaken. But *I didn't start it*, she kept saying to herself. Still, she had been conscious that she ought to stop and she had gone on and on and on. She huddled on the bed, thinking of Anna's nights, skating and dancing and walking in the snow, and her own body ached all over. Cruelty? Yes, it had been cruelty. Only—only the Cape had come to her so clearly, it had fitted in. It had been so lonely there, lonely beyond belief. She could see the houses and spire of Wellfleet across the cove, but there had been no way to get to them. She had had no car and had had to hire someone to bring her to Bessie's house, bring groceries and milk. But she had loved the loneliness. She had felt she could never get enough of it. It had been such a relief not to talk, not to have to think of anyone. She had slid down the steep bluff and gathered firewood and there had not been a single person within call. But suppose she had just had to sit inside, hearing the wind, watching the gulls? Suppose that? Suppose she had not been able to slide down the bluff, gather wood? Suppose she had not been able to go outside and be buffeted by the wind, but had only heard it howling about the house at night? What then? Would she have loved it as much? Would watching the silver light run across the top of the sea grass have compensated her for not being able to walk along the sand? Would it have been enough to watch the fishing boats and clam diggers at low tide? Would it? *A pretty bit of cruelty*—tears stung at her lids and she wiped at them swiftly and angrily with her sleeve.

She heard Johnny come in and got up quickly, ran a comb through her short hair. Buck up! she said to herself in the mirror, but her own sober, guilty eyes looked back at her, saying, I shouldn't have talked about the gulls!

For a moment, for only a moment, as she lay on the rug before the living-room fire with Johnny, her heart eased. When Johnny said, "I used to pretend there was a little person in there," in the half-indulgent tone a child uses for pretendings gone past, she felt a sudden happiness, a letting go.

"I see him now," she said. "See his peaked cap against the brick."

"It looks like horns to me," Johnny said.

"No, I think it's a little cap, like brownies wear. He looks friendly."

"He never talks to me if anyone else is here, though," Johnny said.

"No. His kind never would. But I may make friends with him sometimes when you're not here."

"If it gets all ashes, where does he go?" Johnny asked soberly.

Elizabeth gave a laugh, rueful for logic in the young, said, "Don't you think he could hide in that little crack in the bricks back there and wait for the next fire?"

"He'd get very cold."

"No, he doesn't feel the hot and cold the way we do. Otherwise, he couldn't live in the fire."

"Sometimes they burn up people that die," Johnny said. "Their bones and everything."

The moment of ease was gone. The room seemed cold.

"Do they?" she said slowly. "Who said so?"

"Oh, somebody. They put them in a big furnace."

"That's true," Elizabeth said at last. "And it makes a very beautiful light too. It's as if you turned all into light—like him in there."

"Do you think he was dead once?"

"I don't know. He looks very much alive now. See him tip his hat to us!"

But the happiness was gone. And when had he stopped believing in the little man?

After she was in bed she said, I'm so tired. The day seemed

to have stretched out from forever, with too much in it, too many relationships, too many tensions. Bunce and Adrian and Johnny, the gulls, Huxley Reals—Anna, dreaming of dancing. She's strong—but she's got a light in her. Everything gets brighter in that light. Everybody is warmed by it. You're helpless in the light. . . . Oh, I'm thinking nonsense!

She brought milk and sponge cake. Anna lay there, wide awake. Thinking what? Tired, too?

"You're two minutes late. You do spoil me—when two minutes can make a difference," Anna said softly.

"I was dreaming over the milk," Elizabeth said.

"I wasn't scolding you, darling, I was just telling you how I depended on you. I do, you know. I feel as wide awake as an owl. Isn't it funny how long night hours are when day hours go by like the wind? Sit down—you aren't sleepy, are you?"

"Not a bit." She sat down near the bed, curled up in the chair, her feet tucked under the brown robe.

"How did you like Huxley? Isn't he the silly lamb?"

"Seemed more like a sick hawk to me."

Anna gave a small crow of laughter. Then she said more soberly, "Somehow I have to take this load of guilt off him. He isn't guilty, not at all. He's all mixed up because he urged me to go to that party—but I must have wanted to go. He said I couldn't waste the yellow dress—and I simply couldn't. It was a love of a dress, with little daisies with brown hearts embroidered all over it. Sounds young, but it wasn't. All I could think of in the hospital was what a pity it was the yellow dress was spoiled. . . . You never feel that way about clothes, do you, darling? But, do you know, Liz, sometimes I get to thinking: If only he had seen that truck. If only he had swerved the car just a few inches—if only—if only—I know it's stupid and unfair, but my mind gets to running that way in the night sometimes. The truth is, he *wants* to feel guilty!"

"He couldn't," Elizabeth said.

"Read your Freud. He likes me helpless. It's an excuse for

coming to call. If he feels guilty about the accident he doesn't have to feel guilty about coming to call so often."

"It can't be easy for him."

"I know. I mustn't be unfair. And he does entertain me. He has a kind of sweetness under all his complexes. His sister's beautiful. She drops in often, to keep tabs on me, I expect. She hates it that Hux is so devoted. She hasn't been here all week— I wonder why? Oh, aren't people funny, Liz? If you look at them from far off? I can entertain myself forever just thinking about how funny people are."

"I guess I don't look at them from far enough off," Elizabeth said. "Often they all seem sad to me."

"Don't pity people, Liz. That's the crowning insult you can give human beings. It's much kinder to laugh at them—much— I hate people who pity me. Really hate them."

"I won't pity you," Elizabeth said gravely. "I promise you."

There was a kind of solemnity in the moment, with the two sisters there so close together, the one so fair and fragile, the other so dark and so sturdy. The "I promise you" seemed to fall into the room with a great weight of love and meaning, covering so much. It was strange, Elizabeth Burke knew, after all the years when they hadn't seemed bound at all, that now, at this late date, they should be bound so tightly. Blood must mean more than she had ever known it did. She wanted to tell Anna what Johnny had said, wanted to say that she might have to pity others, Adrian and Huxley and Johnny—but she didn't say anything. She got up suddenly, said, "Try to sleep now, darling," and went away.

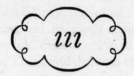

*E*LIZABETH STOOD HOLDING the red dress before her, stared at herself in the mirror. Her brown eyes were angry, but helplessly angry. It's as if I were waiting for something to fight about, she admitted to herself.

Mrs. Suydam had knocked at her door, stood there with the red dress over her arm, saying, "I hope you won't mind, my dear. I like to sew and I've fixed this dress over for you. It was Anna's but it's not been worn much."

Elizabeth said, "But I have clothes enough—of sorts, Mrs. Suydam." That had sounded ungracious and she had added, "But it's kind of you."

"Of course you have clothes—but this is such a pretty dress and it will be something gay for Anna to look at," Mrs. Suydam said.

So she had taken the dress, with difficult words of thanks. She had seemed to hear Anna say, Oh, yes, she is a darling, my little pony, but she *will* wear such dreadful clothes!

It was such a pretty dress, of the softest, brightest red, with gold studs on the belt. It made a gypsy of her in the mirror. Then why had she had the impulse to carry it in to Anna's room and say, I won't wear your clothes! I can't stay here any longer!

It's true, she thought. I do wear dreadful clothes. I haven't a
spark of sense when it comes to colors and the like. I know
what's right for other women—why don't I know what's right
for me? Now, wouldn't I rather have that in the room with me
than my old skirts and sweaters? Of course I would. Anna's
dead right. Then what am I bothered about? It isn't anything
devious—she spoke about it the minute I got here. There's
no point in resisting kindness because you're made into something better by it, is there? Or *is* there?

She hung the dress in the closet but continued to see herself
in it, almost pretty. Why, then, did the thought of wearing it
make her prickle all over? I am not a pleasant character, she
admitted.

Nevertheless, she waited four days before she put the dress
on. In some strange way the wearing of the dress added time to
her stay at Number Seven, was part of the bond that held her
there. Next would be the chartreuse skirt. She put the dress on
at teatime, went in to Johnny, who was sitting on the floor with
a circle of small stones around him like a circle of enchant-
ment. She made a little curtsy and said, "Like my new dress?"

His intelligent eyes lifted, grew secret. "That's my mother's."

"I know. She gave it to me. Isn't it a beautiful color? What's
your favorite color?"

"Gray," he said.

"Oh, no! Gray's so dull! I feel very beautiful in this."

He picked up a stone, held it an instant in his palm as if liking the feel of it, then exchanged it in the circle with another,
lighter stone. He did not answer and she went down on her
knees on the rug beside him. "Of course stone grays are lovely,"
she conceded. "Look at this one, with little specks of gold in it!
Do you think it really is gold?"

"No. There isn't any gold around here," he said.

"I'm going to pretend it really is. A pure nugget of gold. The
white one is my favorite, though. That one by your hand. May
I hold it?"

He held it out to her.

"Isn't it funny how they get warm in your hand? Sometime I wish you could find me one like this for a lucky stone, a white, smooth one. Will you?"

He seemed to consider it, then he said, "You can have that one."

"Truly? Thank you."

She put it into her wide pocket. "Now all good things will come to me," she said. "Well, I have to go now."

He did not protest and she went away, left him sitting soberly in the middle of his circle of stone. No, it was not easy to make headway with Johnny. Still, he had given her the stone. She put her hand into her pocket, let her fingers find the stone, very smooth to the touch, small and perfect.

Anna had a guest. Elizabeth saw the smooth sweep of black hair, the leopard coat, the package in the woman's hands, before Anna said, "Juliet—this is my sister, Liz. This is Huxley's sister, Liz. And she's brought me a present. . . . Doesn't she look nice, my little sister? Excuse me—but she's got one of my dresses on and it gave me a kind of shock seeing someone else in it. But it suits you, darling. It really does suit you. . . . Could I have my present now?"

Juliet put the package into her hands, saying, "I found it at an auction the other day and I thought it would amuse you."

She slid out of her coat, which covered a satin blouse of coral and a moss-green full skirt.

"But what *is* it?" Anna said.

"It's a busybody," Juliet said. "You'll have to get Adrian to fasten it to the window on the outside. They have them in Baltimore, I know—and maybe other places as well. You can watch people coming down the street. Or fix it so you can see who comes to the door. It's just a reflector, really. But I should think they would be fun."

"How enchanting!" Anna said. "How really enchanting! Why, I can know everything that goes on in town! What a heavenly present! I'll have Adrian put it up tonight. What a lamb you are, Juliet!"

Juliet stayed a half hour, telling all the small gossip of town, and there was a good deal of laughter. Finally she went away. "Nice seeing you," she said to Elizabeth. "I didn't even know Anna had a sister till Huxley told me."

"Why, of course you did!" Anna protested. "I've often talked of my sister, Liz!"

"Not to me," Juliet said. "We'll have to see if we can stir up a little fun for you while you're here, Liz."

"Oh, don't bother. I'm content," Elizabeth said. "But thank you."

"We like excuses for parties," Juliet said, and went away.

Anna sighed, said, "It's an awful feeling to be with someone you know doesn't like you. Thank goodness I don't have it often. She never has liked me, from the very beginning, before I even knew Huxley. I don't know just why, because I've never done anything to hurt her. I really haven't. We ought to be the best of friends, but we aren't—even if she does bring me presents. She runs the social life of the younger crowd. I haven't tried to run it, so I don't see why . . . Well, maybe—this sounds vain—but maybe it's because people always seem to have such fun here. She hasn't much imagination and people play bridge at her house, and eat—but they don't laugh much or be gay or talk. But it's not my fault that people always have fun here. It's the house, or something—it lends itself to joy. I really think it does. Funny, that, too, for it's a dark old house in itself. But Mrs. Suydam had such good furniture and all—it only needed curtains and little touches here and there to make it really lovely. I do think it's lovely, don't you, Liz?"

"Yes. It's one of the nicest houses I was ever in."

"I can hardly wait to get this gadget up. It excites me. . . . You *do* look nice in that dress, darling. I didn't mean to speak of it in front of Juliet, but it was such a surprise to me some-how, seeing it again, remembering when I'd worn it. It seems such ages ago—and I was a different person then. But clothes are so strange, aren't they? The same dress on a different person seems a different dress. It's becoming to you, but still, it seems a different dress. It doesn't make you seem like *me*, I mean."

"No, I don't think any dress could do that," Elizabeth said.

It grew dark early, so Adrian didn't put the busybody up till the next morning.

He did put it up then, however, before he went to the plant. It was a bright cold morning, with a deep blue sky and extra-white clouds scudding above the lake. Adrian said at first that he thought he'd better wait till night because there was a man coming at nine that he had to see, but when he saw Anna's face, the slight soberness of disappointment in her brown eyes, he said that, well, it wouldn't take much time. But she'd have to have the window open a bit. He couldn't climb up there with a ladder.

"I'll wait—it's not that important," she said.

Still, he went ahead. With the window far down from the top and the sharp wind sweeping into the room, billowing the curtains and ruffling the bed hangings, stirring the fripperies of the dressing table, Adrian stood on a hard chair with screw driver and hammer and went to work. He called Liz finally to ask her about adjustment, and Elizabeth sat where Anna generally did and directed him.

Adrian turned finally and grinned at Anna, still in bed.

"Snoopy!" he said. "Who ever thought of this one?"

"Juliet. Just you wait—you'll be glad. I'll keep you informed on everything!"

He laughed, came to her and kissed her, and then hurried off to the plant. Anna generally stayed in bed till ten or so, but today she wanted to get up at once. Presently, dressed, combed, she sat in the wheel chair and eyed her new possession. "I wonder who'll be first in it!" she said like a child. "Oh, it's Mr. Prather! How little he is—but how clear! Remember Prather—the sinful one? He *does* look as if his sin weighed on him. How awful, to have a conscience like that! You know, I almost feel like asking him in and comforting him. Would he be surprised! . . . Oh, how wonderful—how exceedingly wonderful and funny —Bill Vine is skulking after him down the street! Bill is, they say, the slot machine king of this section. Oh, it couldn't be funnier! Come look at him, Liz. That's Bill Vine, that fat man. He is a gross creature, isn't he? You could imagine him doing anything."

Elizabeth laughed, caught into Anna's excitement. Then she said, "Let's call Johnny to see it!"

Anna sobered and said, "It's no good forcing him, Liz."

"But something like this—something with a touch of magic . . ." Elizabeth said.

"He's never been one for fairy tales. Funny, isn't it? That he should be such a realist? Or is it? I'm a realist too, I think—underneath. Maybe he does come by it honestly—only I still like to pretend on the outside."

"I think he likes to pretend on the inside and scorns to on the outside," Elizabeth said. "He's awfully smart, Anna. He's got a really good mind."

"Well, why not? . . . There's Mrs. Daggett. You ought to know Mrs. Daggett. She's a character. She's got quite a lot of money but she lives like a pauper. She's had that dress ever since I've been here. Maybe she has one other for Sundays, but that's a century old, too. She writes letters to somebody every single day and trots down to the post office with them. She buys all her groceries herself and carries them home. Not that she buys so many. Some say she starves herself. She's just like a witch. You must someday go into her house—cats all over and nothing ever thrown away. It's a nightmare. Still, I like characters, don't you? There are a lot in this town to watch. I wonder whom she writes to every day? Who's waiting for those letters, I wonder? I've got to find that out—it'll be my mission. . . . I do feel excited, Liz. I'll forgive Juliet a lot for giving me the busybody. When you see people, there's a starting point for speculation—and how I love speculating about people! Don't you? Or do you think it's snoopy?"

"No. I like to, too. People are the most interesting things in the world—to me, anyway."

"I was reading somewhere that curiosity was one of the lower forms of human intelligence, but why? How do you ever find out anything without being curious? Is curiosity any different from interest?"

"Maybe it depends on the use you make of your knowledge," Elizabeth said. "I don't know what it means—I suppose idle curiosity is useless. But curiosity seems infinitely better than indifference to me."

"Doesn't it, though! It always seems to me you can't know too much about people—the more you know, the better you understand them, and yourself. Take Mrs. Daggett—who gets her letters, that she writes with cats crawling all over her? If I knew that, I'd know whether to feel sorry for her or like her better—I'd know what made her tick. Or Mr. Prather—why does he feel it's a sin to take that money from Bill Vine? What kind of boy was he, to have developed such a sense of guilt? Oh, there's no end to it, is there?"

"No, no end," Elizabeth said.

Later, in her own room, Elizabeth thought about that. She had always thought the same, that you couldn't know too much about people, that every facet of human relationships and behavior was interesting. Why, then, had someone said that curiosity was one of the lowest manifestations of intelligence? Maybe the somebody defined curiosity otherwise than she did. Wasn't curiosity just wanting to know? And why shouldn't you want to know? What was the mind for but just that? And even gossip, Elizabeth had always felt, was not entirely harmful. Not if it was something other than just passing malicious rumors. It was eternally interesting, talking about people. You could use it to develop the mind, not stultify it, couldn't you? You could understand the world better, couldn't you, because

of it? It was true that some people didn't, but that wasn't the
fault of the process itself, was it? Still, something about the
statement on curiosity troubled Elizabeth, made her search her
own mind and heart. Wasn't it, though, this very curiosity that
made Anna so able to bear her life, made her have courage to
go on living? Wasn't it interest that let her be gay and at least
outwardly happy in these ugly circumstances? Yes, and yet—
Elizabeth was troubled.

At lunch she told Johnny about the busybody. "You must go
in and see it. Everything in it is so clear and little. You can see
all that goes on in the street."

"Well, that's more like it for a present," Mrs. Bunce said.
"Some life in a thing like that. Flowers are all very well, but
you get to thinking you're in a hospital or something with
flowers around all the time. If you're shut in you want to know
what's going on outside. I call that real clever of Mrs. Olde.
Real clever."

But Johnny, though he listened and seemed interested, said
nothing at all and did not go in to see the busybody.

But, even without Johnny's interest, the little mirror was a
great success. It made Anna laugh so often, and through it
Elizabeth came to see the whole town. It wasn't that Anna had
not been able to see people from her window before, but she
had seen them going past, their backs. Now she saw them coming and that seemed to make all the difference. Allie Jones,
with her newest baby in a battered old buggy. Mr. Quinn, the
president of the bank, with his huge stomach sticking out before him and his Phi Beta Kappa key twinkling in the middle
of it. Charlotte Wayne, coming to meet Huxley when he got
off for lunch ("She tries so hard—it's wicked. But tough on
Hux, poor dear!"). The old woman Anna always called the
Duchess, with her towering hats and white gloves. Children
going and coming from school. The town began to grow, come
real through the busybody—more real than it was from people
coming in and talking. It began to have a pattern of politics

and social affairs, of money affairs and relationships—the little world of Lakeville, with its seven thousand inhabitants. Elizabeth had lived in a city so long now that she had almost forgotten how tight knit were the relationships in a sprawling village. She had forgotten that you could be interested in whether Juliet Olde had her new coat, after a long campaign for it; in whether Mr. Quinn's son-in-law had his name on a door at the bank because Mrs. Quinn had tried so hard, by heart attacks and various sinking spells, to get it there; in whether Allie Jones was actually pregnant again; in whether or not Mrs. Mowrie was considering leaving the church because Mr. Prather was consorting with Bill Vine.

Yes, the busybody was a definite part of their lives, almost a part of the family. It did, as Anna had said, open the way to speculation.

It had another effect also. It was another tie, like the dress. This knowing all the families in town through reflection, as it were, made Elizabeth feel a part of the town. Sometimes she found herself shutting her mind against interest in the passers-by, as if she knew there was danger in the interest. Yet she was ashamed of this. She often thought of her room in town, sent her rent every week. By now someone else would have her place in the bookstore, she knew, and yet she thought of the job as waiting for her. Yet there was never a sign that Anna was not satisfied with her, never a sign that she was not accepted as a permanent part of this household. Yet who would care if she were here permanently? No one. No one at all but herself. But when the Duchess called and in her snobbish manner discussed the state of the world, Elizabeth couldn't help feeling interested in her because she had seen her sweeping so often down the street. And the girl Charlotte who wanted Huxley Reals— when she came into the room, half defiant, half embarrassed, she felt she had known her a long time, and when Charlotte eyed the chrysanthemums that had come from Huxley that very

morning, she felt a sharp understanding of the strange, sad look
in her light-blue eyes.

"I think maybe you're right—I mean that writer was right—
you ought not to know too much about people," she said to
Anna one day.

"What brought that on?" Anna asked.

"Oh, I don't know. It just seemed true suddenly. You go too
far in—where it should be secret."

And one day soon after that she said something about the
busybody she wished she hadn't said. She went up to Mrs.
Suydam's rooms for something that morning. She had been
there rarely and never with more than a message. The rooms up
under the eaves were very nice, with good pieces of furniture
and a kind of immaculateness that was appealing. There were
also some good paintings and on this day Liz paused before
one of them and said, "I do like that!" Mrs. Suydam was surprisingly still, though she was always quick and quiet in her re-
sponses. The picture was of docks with mist folding over them.
At last Mrs. Suydam said, "Yes, I am fond of that one too. My
son painted it."

"Your son?" Elizabeth said in astonishment. "Not *Adrian?*"

"Oh, no. My son Alex, who died."

"I'm sorry," Elizabeth said awkwardly. "I didn't know Adrian
had any brothers."

"He has been dead fifteen years," Mrs. Suydam said distantly
and stiffly.

"He must have had great talent," Elizabeth stumbled on.

"Yes," Mrs. Suydam said.

Later as she combed Anna's soft curls and twisted them over
her fingers, Elizabeth said, "You never told me Adrian had had
a brother."

"Well, it was long ago," Anna said.

"Fifteen years," Elizabeth said. "That's not so terribly long
ago."

"It was long before I knew Adrian. I forget it, I suppose. Adrian never talks of him."

"But he was a really good artist. He must have been very good indeed—I don't see how he could not talk of him."

"Who's talked of him to you?"

"Mrs. Suydam. Oh, not much. I just asked about the paintings up in her rooms and she said her son Alex had done them. I was so startled."

"That's odd, you know. She has never talked to me of him, never. I mentioned him a few times, but she just didn't talk of him. I wonder if there was something queer about him. I thought it was just grief, maybe, I didn't like to pry—but if she's mentioned him to you . . . Adrian told me he was drowned in a boating accident—said there was quite a difference in their ages and he hardly knew him, that was all."

"It seems strange," Elizabeth said. "Too bad you can't turn your busybody on that life."

Anna laughed and said, "Well, maybe I will. Maybe I should. Have you anything special to do this morning? I wondered if you'd mind going down to Mr. Willis's drugstore and asking them if that butttermilk soap has come. I do love that soap and nobody else carries it here."

"Yes, I'll go," Elizabeth said.

She asked Johnny to come with her but Johnny was busy on some project and seemed reluctant to leave. The project was, so far as Elizabeth could see, nothing but arranging some pieces of paper on the rug in a pattern. They followed the somewhat geometric pattern of the carpet itself. So she went by herself. She had been to the stores a few times since she came, but only a few. It seemed good to be out in the air by herself, almost an event. When she came out of the drugstore, someone called to her from a door or two down the street: "Oh, Elizabeth! Miss Burke!" and Margaret McIntry was coming toward her with a basket of groceries. She looked very tall, plain, and hardy in

the autumn light. She wore a scarf over her head and an old
gray raincoat, though it was not raining.

"I was just thinking about you," she said as she caught up
with Elizabeth. "Here the days are going by and we aren't getting acquainted. How about walking home with me right now
for a few minutes? It isn't so far. Come along."

Elizabeth hesitated, but then said, "I don't know why I
couldn't. Mrs. Suydam is with Anna this morning."

So they walked past Number Seven and on to the doctor's
old house, the sturdy Shetland pony and the rangy old farm
horse. Though it wasn't too long since breakfast they sat at the
kitchen table and drank coffee and ate some hard dark bread.
They didn't talk about anything important and yet conversation flowed easily between them. "Like these blue dishes?"
Margaret asked. "Bought them at the auction the other day.
Chipped here and there, but cheerful, aren't they? Paid only a
dollar for a whole set."

"That must be the auction the busybody came from," Elizabeth said.

"Busybody?"

So Elizabeth explained the busybody and Margaret McIntry
laughed and cut two more slices of the black bread. "Sounds
like Juliet," she said.

"Did you ever know Alex Suydam?" Elizabeth asked suddenly. Margaret looked up quickly. Her long face sobered. She
wore an ugly old sweater over a plain blouse, and for an instant
her face seemed to go with the sweater, though ordinarily it had
much vitality.

"Of course. Grew up with him," she said. "Why?"

"I just wondered. They don't talk about him. I never knew
he existed till today. That seemed so strange, somehow."

"He killed himself," Margaret said.

"Oh. How terrible. And he was so talented."

"Yes. Didn't go off half-cocked on abstractions. Modern,

though. Come on in the other room." She led the way into the crowded, happy-looking, cluttered room and made a brief gesture toward the picture above the bookcases. It was of the lake here on a gray November day—cold seemed to come out of the very canvas. The shadowy buildings along the shore were cold too and all was grayed down to bleakness. "He did that when he was eighteen years old," she said. "In fact, did it in this very room. Had some sketches he'd made but this he did right here by the window. I don't know—I just don't know. He was in college and got in some sort of jam and was sent home. But it was more than that. He was destined for the plant and hated the thought. He was here the night before. He liked my father —he liked to come here. My father was out somewhere that night and Alex didn't stay long. He acted strange, tired and dull, though he could be lively if he wanted to. When he left he said. 'Well, it's no use, Meg. Nothing's any use any more,' and the next morning he went out on the lake and didn't come back. They said it was an accident, but he had known boats all his life and could swim like a fish. No, it wasn't an accident. I've never known whether to like Mrs. Suydam or not since. I just don't know. Because she was the ruling spirit in that house and she could have set Alex free to paint if she had wanted to. I was young—fourteen, but I was big as I am now. Too tall and gangly. Alex treated me as if my brain was as big as my body, and I was grateful to him. Well, that's a sad old story. I'll drop it. But that picture is good—I'm proud to have it."

She turned abruptly from the picture and began to talk of other things. She made Elizabeth laugh and finally Elizabeth went away, feeling better than in a long time. There was something wholly likable about the doctor's spinster daughter. She was blunt, entertaining, humorous. There was nothing oblique in her approach to anything. The doctor's house was stuffy and untidy but Elizabeth had the feeling of having breathed great draughts of fresh air.

Mrs. Suydam was still sitting there with Anna when Elizabeth came in. Anna had, Elizabeth saw, changed her jacket to one of yellow. "Hope I didn't hold up anything," Elizabeth said. "I walked along home with Margaret McIntry for a few minutes. I got the soap."

"Anna was a little worried about you," Mrs. Suydam said.

"Fiddlesticks! Anna knows I'm an able-bodied female."

"Well, I didn't think you'd get lost in Lakeville," Anna admitted. "And you certainly ought to be able to walk home with Meg or anyone you like. It's just—well, I expect I'm getting selfish. It's bad for me to be waited on from morning to night. I'm getting to expect it. . . . But if you can get any fun out of Meg, for goodness' sake do it!"

"I do think she's fun," Elizabeth said. "She's so honest, so forthright. I like that."

"Do you? Well, within reason, I do, too. But Meg's close to the line of bluntness for bluntness' sake. She's good, so they say—but remember how mother used to say she'd rather anything would be said of her than 'She's got a good heart'? You want to be reasonably good, but extreme goodness is so *dull*."

"Oh, I don't think she's as good as that!" Elizabeth said. "I certainly don't find her dull. She knows all about birds, for one thing, and I've always intended to know something if I ever got the time."

"Yes, I know she fancies herself as an authority on birds. But that's—"

"Don't say it's frustrated motherhood or something like that," Elizabeth protested. Mrs. Suydam frowned faintly.

Anna gave that soft chuckle of hers. "Thorny darling! No, but it *is* frustration, all the same, isn't it? Maybe I wrong her. But I notice that all these plain, healthy, youngish women get to be an authority on *something*. And the more authority they are the less chance they have to live like ordinary females."

"With a man, you mean? I don't think she acts at all frustrated. I think she really finds birds interesting. I don't think she gives a damn whether she's married or not. She doesn't act

bored or unhappy." She spoke almost angrily, wishing she
wouldn't defend Meg, who needed no defense.

"What's the matter with you, Liz?" Anna asked. "Don't get
mad at me about Meg McIntry. I don't care how much you
like her. She's all right—she just doesn't happen to be my cup
of tea. But, then, I don't suppose you'd like the ones who are—
so we're even there. I think I'll take a little rest before lunch."

So Elizabeth got her into bed, drew the curtains, and went
away, feeling prickly and ashamed. That night she was sitting
in the living room about nine when Adrian came downstairs
and joined her. He lit a pipe and just sat there smoking for
some minutes in silence. Elizabeth had a feeling of unease, as
if she were about to be scolded. But she kept on reading and
did not speak. At last Adrian surprised her by saying, "Are you
contented here, Liz?" He didn't sound like a friend, but more
like an employer being politic with an employee about to be
fired.

"Contented? That's a funny word to use," she answered.

"Why so? Are you?"

"I don't know how to answer you. I've never been a very contented sort of person. I'm all right, though. You know how I
feel about being here, Adrian. I don't see that we need to talk
about it."

"Anna thinks you are getting restless."

"No. Why does she think so? Because I went to Margaret
McIntry's for a half-hour this morning? Did she complain of
that?"

"Of course not. Anna doesn't complain, you know that.
Quite the contrary—she thought perhaps she'd been selfish,
kept you too confined. I told her it was a job and jobs kept
anyone confined."

"I certainly don't overwork," Elizabeth said. "And I don't
want to be entertained. But I met Margaret and walked home
with her. I like her and I knew your mother was with Anna.
If I shouldn't have, I'm sorry."

He frowned. "I'm not complaining, either," he said with that evenness which just escaped complaint. "I was just wondering if you found things too difficult."

"Not at all," she said as evenly as he.

"My mother would be willing to take over a few hours now and then to give you some time off. Anna is very anxious that you have some fun if you can find it. But I don't want her left alone."

"Aren't you making a lot of fuss over a half-hour?" Elizabeth asked. "Anna is never left alone, but the truth is she likes to be alone. She really likes it, Adrian. Before she was hurt she had plenty of time to herself. People need time alone, you know. People don't want to be hovered over every minute. Wouldn't you hate it yourself?"

"I dare say I would. But Anna has always had something going on. She likes people."

"So do I, within reason. But not all the time. . . . Adrian, it would be more to the point if you worried over someone being with Johnny. He's the one who needs companionship. Anna has enough people in her life every day to tire her out. Johnny has no one."

"Good heavens, he has the whole family, doesn't he?"

"I mean children. Why doesn't he ever play with any other children? He's by himself too much."

"There's no reason he can't play with other children. There are neighbors," Adrian said. "Johnny's on the neurotic side, I'm afraid."

"But why? Why is he? You and Anna aren't neurotics, are you? Why is Johnny?"

"Look, Liz, we'll take care of Johnny. He has everything any boy ever had. He's going to be a bookworm—that kind doesn't seem to need friends. Other children don't like him, that's the simple truth, and he doesn't seem to care. But that's our problem. You don't need to worry about it."

"But I do worry about it. He has very strange thoughts for a boy of five. I know you give him everything. He's got a chest full of toys up in his room and he just keeps them in the chest. He won't run his electric train or anything. He's afraid, Adrian. He's desperately afraid. He won't go into Anna's room. He never talks to her. Why?"

He sighed, knocked out his pipe against the andirons, said, "Anna thinks he got worried because he thought she was going to die. She's sick about it but she doesn't want him dragged in. I tried to talk to him—it's hard to talk to Johnny. I suppose it isn't normal for him to keep to himself so much, but I've had a lot on my mind these last months. He's so quiet you almost forget he's in the house."

Elizabeth was abruptly troubled and ashamed. He had sounded suddenly quite human and worried himself. "I'm sorry," she said. "I wasn't trying to add to your worries. But Johnny's such a puzzle. He's got a brilliant mind—but he's so somehow sad. I can't stop thinking about him. You don't mind my giving what spare time I have to him, do you?"

"Lord, no. Only don't force him into Anna's room. She doesn't want that."

He excused himself abruptly then and went upstairs. It was the most prolonged and intimate conversation they had had since Elizabeth's coming. Elizabeth found herself liking him better than she had. He really didn't have too much time to give to Johnny. He had a business and heavy responsibilities. He wanted, naturally, to spend his precious evenings with Anna. Anna made him laugh. There was always gaiety, laughter, about her. And he had had a tough time all summer, still had it, for that matter. It wasn't an easy life for him, not easy at all. He had been angry because she had gone off duty for a little while. But maybe he was right about that, from his point of view. The truth was that Anna really did like to be alone. She liked to watch her new toy, the busybody, have a little time for speculation. But she must have told Adrian about the half-hour.

Not complainingly, though—Adrian had said so. Only wondering if she, Elizabeth, had enough time for fun.

The next day Mrs. Suydam came to her in her bedroom and said, "We've been thinking that you ought to have a full day off every week, and perhaps every other Sunday, to do with as you like. I'll be glad to tend to Anna, with the help of Mrs. Bunce. We've been thoughtless, I'm afraid."

Elizabeth was angry, she didn't quite know why. "Nonsense!" she said. "I have plenty of time, Mrs. Suydam. And I'd rather be here to help Anna in and out of bed. I'm strong as an ox. If I want some special time, I'll ask you. I'm not overworking. But I told Adrian, and I'll say it again—Anna shouldn't be coddled so, watched over every minute. She has a bell and so long as someone is within call, she is all right. You—you get a crowded feeling when someone watches every breath you draw. Let her have some hours of peace when no one is there!"

Mrs. Suydam put her fingers up to the pin at her throat.

"My dear," she said at last, with gentleness and patience, "even though Anna is your sister, I'm afraid you don't know her very well. Anna lives for people. I like time to myself and perhaps you do, too, but Anna does not. She gets very lonely and depressed when no one is there. She has plenty of time alone at night when she can't sleep."

"I know Anna very well. I was brought up with her, I ought to," Elizabeth said stubbornly.

"I doubt if that proves anything," Mrs. Suydam said, still gracious and kind. "Sisters don't always know each other, Elizabeth. She said to me yesterday—she was really worried about you, you know, for all she tried to cover it up afterwards—she said to me, 'You take it for granted that your sister would rather be with you than with anyone else. It just isn't true, is it? I must see that Liz has a chance to have her own friends.' And she is very insistent about it now. It's her idea that you should have a day to yourself. It will work out better so."

"If that's the way she wants it," Elizabeth assented stiffly.

This, then, was the beginning of the end, Elizabeth said to herself. She felt confused, part angry, part relieved. It was just as she had expected—she became part of Anna's life and then, just as her role in it seemed real, she was rejected, made to feel unimportant, unwanted—put in the wrong. She remembered a few weeks long, long ago when she and Anna had walked to school together every day. It had been in the fall of the year and the days had stretched out in a haze of crimson and gold, touched ever with the warmth of Anna's laughter. And then one day a girl called Jessie Leake had called and Anna had run down the stairs and out to Jessie and after that she and Jessie had walked to school together every day and Elizabeth had had to find some other companion. No, she had generally walked alone. And yet, with a word, with a smile, Anna could make you forgive all, make such things not matter at all any more. It's the busybody, she said to herself helplessly, incoherently. But she knew what she meant. She meant that she was now too much *inside* the town, *inside* the family. She had been asked in —she hadn't wanted to be there. Now she was going to be let out and would have to begin all over again walking to school by herself.

So, not wanting it, not knowing how further to prevent having it, she had her days off, every Friday and every other Sunday. She didn't like to think of Mrs. Suydam or even Mrs. Bunce lifting Anna in and out of bed, going up the steep stairs with trays. It made her feel guilty. She had nothing to do with her time, except to spend it with Johnny. That she would have liked, but not at the expense of neglecting Anna, not at the expense of feeling guilty. She did feel guilty and was angry that she felt so. Perhaps she *had* hurt Anna, perhaps it *had* seemed she wanted to escape a bit. But more probably, she told herself defiantly, Anna wanted to escape her for a few hours.

Her first Friday was a strange one, long and strange. In the morning she looked over her clothes, sewed a button on, washed

out a few silk things. Mrs. Bunce had given her her breakfast
in a series of disapproving thumps, making her inclined to say,
This is none of my doing! She went to Johnny's room and
found him lying on the bed with a book. "Look, Johnny," she
said, "this afternoon, let's go exploring around the town, shall
we? You can show me things. I haven't even been down to the
lake yet. You could show me the lake. Will you?"

"All right," Johnny said. "Do you want to read to me?"

So she read to him for an hour, though even that seemed
wrong. A little boy of five ought to be racing through the house
in the morning hours, having a hundred projects of activity.
Still, there was sweetness in having his thin little body curled
up beside her in the chair, his head resting trustingly against
her arm.

Then after his brief nap Elizabeth bundled him up and they
went out exploring. "Where shall we go first? What is the best
thing to see?" she asked him.

"We could look in Mr. Campanini's window, if you want
to," Johnny said.

"Well, where is it?" Elizabeth asked.

They went down to the business center and looked in through
the window at Mr. Campanini mending shoes. He wore a
leather apron and he had huge old-fashioned mustaches. He
looked up and winked at Johnny and then went on tapping.
"Let's go in!" Elizabeth said, but Johnny flushed and said, "No,
I like to look through the window." They stood there till they
were chilled and then moved on down the street. They paused
before a jeweler's window and Johnny pressed his face against
the pane and said, "They used to have a dagger with jewels on
it." He examined everything in the window, the watches and
bracelets and diamonds, but the dagger wasn't there.

"I'd like to see the lake, if you aren't too cold," Elizabeth
said at last.

Johnny led her on to the next little side street and they
walked down its short steep length to the lake. The bluff ended

somewhat abruptly at the corner of the block where the Suydams lived. Here along the narrow shore were only small shacks and a fishing goods store. It looked lonely and deserted down there on this chill December afternoon. There were a few old boats and one good motorboat tied up to the brown posts along the shore, but they looked lonely too. Farther along the shore you could see plainly the long narrow buildings of the Suydam Boat Company.

"That's where my father makes boats," Johnny offered.

"Did you ever go to watch him do it?" Elizabeth asked.

"Once, I did," Johnny said.

"Maybe you could take me there someday and I could watch too."

He did not answer. A wall seemed suddenly erected between them and Elizabeth felt a wave of despair. You simply couldn't get really close to Johnny. They walked along the shore, seeing one small gull riding the wind, meeting one small boy who surely should have been in school but who was kicking an old tin can ahead of him on the uneven macadam of the narrow walk.

They stood still a moment looking out toward the lake, Elizabeth conscious that this was, after all, a somewhat mournful way to spend a holiday. Then as they turned to go on they saw Huxley Reals coming toward them along the shore walk from the plant. He wore a topcoat but his head was bare. He had an elegance out of place there by the lonely waterfront and his long, sensitive face stood out in the grayness, more lonely than the scene itself. And yet, back of the loneliness, you could see purpose, that purpose which drives a man into usefulness despite any personal sorrows, that purpose which inspires respect.

It did not take him long to reach them, but it was long enough. Long enough for Elizabeth Burke to remember again the challis scarf, the knowledge that it "didn't suit her," long enough for her to feel a sharp anger against life, against the truth that there was never any equality in love, that the ways of the heart were devious and illogical. Long enough to remember saying so helplessly to Adrian in the snow, "This is my sister, Anna." *No*, her heart cried out. *No*. She thought foolishly of the checks she kept sending to Lollie for the room.

"Why, hello!" Huxley Reals said. "Hi, there, Johnny. I was just thinking about you."

Almost any little boy would have grinned shyly at that, but Johnny just looked up at him and waited without smiling at all.

"Well, I *was*," Huxley insisted. "Don't look so skeptical. They are opening up the new roller-skating rink tomorrow afternoon and they have some extra fancy skaters here as a send-off. I thought maybe you and I could go watch them for a while. How about it?"

Elizabeth wanted to shake Johnny, he was so cool about it, so reluctant. He certainly showed no sign of excitement. At last he said, holding Elizabeth's hand tight, "If Aunt Liz goes, I will."

Huxley Reals laughed. "Well, Aunt Liz can go too if she likes. Though I thought just us men. . ."

"I'm a boy," Johnny said.

"All right. All right. We'll take Aunt Liz."

"Johnny, I'm afraid I'm going to be busy. I'll be staying with mother tomorrow."

"My father will be there. It's Saturday," Johnny said.

Huxley Reals laughed and said, "I'll fix it up with Anna. You're hooked, Aunt Liz. What are you two doing down here on a day like this?"

"We're exploring," Johnny said gravely.

"You are? Come with me then and I'll show you something, something very special. It's just a step. Once a week or so I have to come down to see what's keeping old Cripps home. Sometimes it's the misery, sometimes the bottle. He'll be harmless, even if it's the bottle. He's our best man at the works but he has weaknesses. . . . Here we are."

Johnny looked up at Elizabeth questioningly. "It's all right," she said, and they went with Huxley Reals up three rickety steps into one of the shacks they had just passed. A small ancient figure sat at a bare table in a clean but bare room. All over the wall were pasted or tacked pictures of ships. The old man squinted up at them out of narrow but bright blue eyes. "Bloodhound," he said. "Snooping around."

"Right you are, Cripps. Why aren't you at the plant? We've got a job on—remember? Let Johnny see what you're doing there. Look, kid—how do you like that?" The old man was making a ship inside a bottle. His thick, callused fingers did not look as if they could possibly manipulate the tiny masts but the ship was almost done.

The old man squinted up at Elizabeth and said, "Who be you?"

"She's Aunt Liz," Johnny offered unexpectedly.

"That's right. I'm Aunt Liz," Elizabeth said, with a grin at Mr. Cripps.

"How do you get the sails in?" Johnny asked.

"Well, boy, you watch. I'll show you."

"And I suppose you'll expect us to pay you for showing him," Huxley Reals said.

"Don't give a hoot in hell whether you do or not," the old man said. "I got my days where I don't feel up to making that trip up there. My legs is bad. Don't jiggle the table, son."

They all watched the delicate operation with anxious eyes. Old Cripps looked exceedingly impatient but he had infinite patience for this small job. Now and then his blue eyes would meet the gaze of the boy with a quick blue squint. "Well, son, that's the way it's done," Cripps said at last, and they all sighed with relief that it was done and done successfully.

Then the old man got up and he was very bent of figure and limped. His body did not seem to go with his tough, lively, weathered face. He went to a plain, unpainted cupboard with a spool for a handle, opened the door and took out a smaller

bottle with a smaller ship inside it. He gave it an oddly regretful, apologetic look, then brought it over and handed it to
Johnny. "You take that home with you, son. I made that for
you," he said.

A look that was childlike, full of wonder, came over Johnny's
sharp little face. He took the bottle into his hands. Then he
said, "You didn't. You didn't even know me."

The old man gave a small cackle. "That's where you're
wrong, boy," he said. "I know you, all right. You're the boss's
boy. I'd've knowed you in Timbuktu, I would. You're the spit
of your uncle Alex, kid. Now you come again—but don't you
bring no bloodhounds with you. Reals, you leave me alone
now. If you want to give my job to somebody else, you sure as
hell can. I'll get by."

"Some of these days I will," Reals said. "I will, Cripps. You
get away with murder. You show up tomorrow."

"See how I feel," Cripps said.

At the door Johnny turned. "Thank you," he said clearly.

"Don't mention it, old salt," Cripps said.

They stood an instant there in the narrow street by the cold
lake before Huxley Reals turned back toward the plant.

"That was exciting," Elizabeth said. "Thanks."

Huxley Reals frowned and said, "Interesting old malingerer.
Might have thought of it before—but a certain—well, lack of
responsiveness. . ." He let his glance drop to Johnny, who stood
holding the bottle with great care.

"I know," Elizabeth said.

"Try to think up some more spots. Like to help out. Well,
Johnny, so long. I'll pick you and Aunt Liz up tomorrow."

So Elizabeth and Johnny walked home. "What a wonderful
treasure," Elizabeth said. "Mummy'll be surprised at that!"

But when they reached the house, Johnny carried his treasure
straight to his room.

"Look, Johnny, put it on top of the bookcase," Elizabeth
said. "It'll get broken in the chest."

"No, it won't."

"But I like to look at it when I come in," Elizabeth said.

He hesitated, then opened the chest and with great care deposited the bottle within. "I'll show it to you sometimes," he said.

At eleven that night, in spite of the fact that it was her day off, Elizabeth got up and fetched the hot milk, went into Anna's room.

"Here's your milk," she said, "and I'll slap you if you say it's my day off. Such silliness I never heard of!"

Anna laughed softly and said, "Oh, Liz, it has been the longest day. Bless you for coming in! They all mean well, you know—and so do I. You *do* need some time to yourself, but I've missed you."

"Good."

"Tell me, what have you done with your day? Did you see Meg?"

"No. I sewed on a button and read to Johnny and went exploring the town with Johnny."

"What a holiday!"

"It was fun, only I didn't need it. It seemed silly. We had one little adventure." For an instant she hesitated, then went steadily on. "We went down by the lake and we met your Huxley Reals and he took us to see an old man named Cripps who was supposed to be working but hadn't showed up for it today—he took a fancy to Johnny and we watched him making a ship in a bottle. Huxley Reals asked Johnny to go with him to the opening of the skating rink tomorrow."

"The lamb!" Anna said. "He does try so hard, poor Huxley! I can't imagine anything he'd less rather do than take Johnny to the skating rink, can you? He's sweet—I'll have to rescue him from that."

"Why? It'll be fun for Johnny and it won't hurt Huxley, will it?"

"Well, Adrian could take him if he wants to go, couldn't he? That's Adrian's job, it seems to me."

Elizabeth didn't say any more about that, not even about Johnny's insistence that she go too. "Did you have fun today?" she asked instead.

"Not too much. I *was* having fun watching people in my busybody—but then Cornelia felt she ought to fuss over me a bit and I couldn't put her out. A lot of people seemed to drift in this afternoon. Dullish ones, except for my Doctor McIntry. He never bores me. . . . I saw something really sweet in the mirror —enchanting. That daughter of Juliet's, Patsy Olde—she was coming down the street and Bunn Middleton was stalking her. She's about thirteen and he's fourteen or fifteen. He caught up with her and they stood talking there on the sidewalk. She would move her foot around in the leaves by the sidewalk and look up at him sidewise and he was all awkwardness mixed with showing off. It was simply lovely. Their books dangling and her full skirt—black and red plaid—swirling when she moved her foot in the leaves. . . . Oh, that age is so entrancing. I'd almost forgotten what it was like. It made me remember the picnics in the old pine grove. Remember? Remember Chuck Simmons? Oh, how wonderful I thought he was! I wore a pink dress, swiss with those little dots, and a pink ribbon in my hair and I was so afraid he wouldn't come and sit with me when we ate but then when he did I couldn't think of a thing to say to him. Painful, wasn't it? But sweet, too."

"Sweet?" Elizabeth said slowly. "Was it? No, I'd rather be me of now than me of then."

"Oh, I too! But if I were a writer, someone like that, I'd be grateful for seeing them that way. To remind me. You do forget so fast. I mean, it was the *essence* of something."

"Yes, I know. I know what you mean."

"Darling, would it be too much bother for you to straighten out my bed a bit? It seems all full of creases. Adrian insisted that he could do it, but you know how men are with a bed!"

Elizabeth fixed her bed and then she said, "Good night!" and went away.

She knew she should have said something about going herself to the rink, but she hadn't been able to. She couldn't and wouldn't go, and that was that. And yet she thought that Johnny ought to go, that it would be good for Huxley Reals himself, maybe. More useful than sending yellow roses, that kind of thing. It was something that he had thought of doing it.

I will not pity him, Elizabeth thought. And it may be Anna is right—he likes having her helpless so he can justify his slavery. Then she retracted that thought, remembering the strength of his face past the loneliness. He was as strong as Adrian, and Adrian was truly strong. He was strong, but he loved Anna. That was the whole story. It can't happen to me like this, she told herself, but she could not deny that it had happened.

The next day at three on the dot Huxley Reals appeared at the door. "Ready, Johnny?" he asked as soon as he came into the hallway and found Johnny curled up in a living-room chair with a book. "Get your things on. Where's Aunt Liz?"

"Upstairs," Johnny said.

"I'll go up and say hello to your mother. You get your things on," he said and went up the stairs. He walked into Anna's room. Adrian was there and Elizabeth. "Hello, Anna," he said. He nodded to Adrian, who grunted a greeting. "I'm taking Liz on a bat," he said then, boldly. "Where's your coat? Johnny won't go to see the skating without his aunt Liz. . . . You'll hold the fort while we're gone, won't you?" he asked Adrian.

"I'll be here, if that's what you mean," Adrian said.

Anna gave a glance toward Elizabeth. "Why, you didn't tell me you wanted to go too, Liz," she said.

"I don't," Elizabeth said uncomfortably. "It was just that Johnny wanted me to. He's shy, you know. But I'm not going. I'm sure he'll go with you, Mr. Reals, without me."

"Well, run along," Adrian said, with some irritability. "I'll be here."

"I'd rather not," Elizabeth said. "It's almost teatime and—"

"I can carry up a tray."

Anna laughed and said, "Adrian, why don't you and Liz take Johnny to the rink and let Huxley entertain me? He'll bring the tea. . . . It's really Johnny's father's job, Huxley, don't you think? Though I know you mean to be kind. Go on, Liz—I'll really be quite all right."

Before she knew it Elizabeth was out in the street with Johnny and Adrian. Adrian was angry and it was an unpleasant walk to the rink. Johnny was silent, with none of that wonder in his eyes that had been there yesterday when he had seen the ship. He was dressed well, in a thick blue coat and cap to match. His knees were bare to the wind, but he looked smart enough.

At the entrance, Adrian did come alive enough to say, "Well, here we are, Johnny." They found places on the sidelines and several expert skaters were doing their stunts. They had hardly got settled when Johnny said he needed to go to the bathroom. Adrian said, "Oh, Lord!" and Elizabeth said, "I'll take him." She threaded her way through the crowd, Johnny's hand in hers. In the ladies' room, Johnny said, "My father can go home if he wants to." His thin voice had a note of desperation. "But he doesn't want to," Elizabeth said, knowing she lied. "He wants to have some fun with you, Johnny." Johnny gave her a look that said he knew she had lied, then he took her hand again and they walked back to their places.

Juliet Olde was sitting where Johnny had been. She and Adrian were laughing. Adrian lifted Johnny to his lap and said, "This is a better spot to see from, kid!" Juliet smiled at Elizabeth and said, "So Anna's letting you walk out with her husband? How come?" "Oh, we have all manner of methods, Juliet," Adrian said. "We work it out." Johnny said in his embarrassingly clear voice, "Mr. Reals is staying with my mother."

Juliet gave a little crow of amusement. "I'll just bet he is!" she said. "Look, those two are good, aren't they?" So they watched the skaters and the awkward moment passed.

After an hour, during which Juliet chatted quite gaily and Adrian answered her in kind, Adrian said, "Well, had enough, Johnny? We'd better jog along, I think. Nice to have seen you, Juliet."

"You mean you couldn't evade me, darling. But I always like to see you, Adrian. Patsy has this passion for skating at the moment and I had a notion I wanted to see the kind of place this was." At that moment a thin, very pretty young girl in a red-and-black plaid skirt skated up to them and called out, "Don't go yet, mom!" Elizabeth remembered the clear picture of her that Anna had given. She was a lovely young thing, with a certain lack of sophistication that seemed odd in Juliet's daughter. Juliet sighed and said, "If they'd only do something halfheartedly for once!"

"Oh, nonsense—did you at that age?" Adrian said. "Come on, Johnny, shove your arm in here!"

They were out in the street again, walking toward home through the early dusk.

"Well, did you enjoy that?" Adrian demanded of Johnny. "I hope so! I used to do that for hours on end. It seems a long time ago and very silly now. But I thought I was having fun at the time."

"You probably did," Elizabeth said.

Johnny hadn't had to answer and that was a good thing, Elizabeth thought. For he hadn't enjoyed it. He hadn't enjoyed it at all. They stepped into the hall and heard laughter from upstairs. But when Huxley had finally gone, Anna said, "I thought you'd never, never come back. I hope you had fun."

"Well, I guess Johnny did," Adrian said. "Though one never knows."

When Elizabeth put Johnny to bed that night, Johnny said

to her suddenly, "You won't ever go away from here, will you?"

Elizabeth paused, sat down on the edge of the bed. "Yes, I probably will someday," she said. "This isn't my home, you know. I'm going to stay awhile, though. I'm going to stay quite a while. Long enough so we can do some exploring and things like that."

"You could have this for your home."

"No, I couldn't, Johnny."

"If my mother died, then you could."

Elizabeth felt a cold shock along her spine.

"*Johnny!*" she said. Then she was ashamed of having heard desire in the small voice. It *couldn't* have been desire. "Look, Johnny, your mother isn't going to die. Did someone say so? She's going to be lame, that's all. But she's all well, except for that. She can't run around and play with you any more and that makes her very sad. So you'll have to come and play with her. You could think up all sorts of games to play in her room. Hide the thimble and things like that. Of course, when she was in the hospital, you couldn't go in, because that's the rules—but now you can. You could read to her sometimes—she'd like that. But she's *not* going to die, darling. You mustn't worry about that any more."

She knew she was talking too fast, filling up the vacuum after the shock. Johnny took his gaze from hers as she talked, seemed hardly to be listening.

When she could see his grave, intelligent eyes, Elizabeth felt a great tenderness for him, but now all she could see was the sharpness of his chin and small nose, the too-clean high forehead. Then he looked straight at her again and said, "But if she *was* dead, then you could stay forever."

"No," she said sharply and baldly, "no, I couldn't. Not even then." She stood up and walked away without a "good night." She went into her room and sat down on the bed and covered her face in a movement of revulsion, though the small face was no longer there to see. She was trembling and could not stop.

"How horrible—how horrible," she whispered. "How—monstrous!"

Presently she went to the bathroom, washed her face, looked in the mirror there to see if the horror was wiped out, started toward Anna's room. She came to Johnny's door, would have passed, but something stayed her, some small sound. She walked in and Johnny was huddled there under his blanket, crying almost soundlessly. She sat down beside him, put a hand on his hair, smoothed it back from his forehead. "There, there," she said. "Good night, darling." He made no movement toward her but she bent and kissed him. She knew there was something else she ought to say, but she could not think what it was. She didn't want to condone what he had said, but she couldn't let him go to sleep crying. He stopped crying and shut his eyes. She waited a moment but he said nothing, so she went out and into Anna's room.

I'm frightened, she said to herself. I've never been so horribly frightened.

Adrian was with Anna and also a young lawyer, Henry Masters, who dropped in occasionally with or without his wife. Elizabeth said she thought, if Anna didn't mind, she'd write some letters. Anna was propped up in bed. She looked beautiful as always but Elizabeth thought her eyes were tired. She wanted to warn Adrian about keeping her up, but she didn't. She went back to her room and took out her writing things. But she didn't write. She sat there, the pen held in her square fingers, and stared toward the door.

I'm frightened, she said again to herself.

MRS. BUNCE AND MISS POTTS sat close up to the big
coal stove in the little sitting room of Miss Potts' cottage. It
was a funny room, clean as soap and water could make it, only
some thirteen feet square and very crowded with incongruous
pieces of furniture. A horsehair sofa stood along one wall. It
had a number of very ugly cushions standing stiffly on it, one
of them of huck toweling with that zigzag stitch that was the
vogue a good many years ago, one of plush with *Atlantic City*
across it in gold letters. This sofa took up a good deal of space
and was plainly never used. There were two well-padded comfortable chairs in which the two women sat close up to the
zinc-edged piece of linoleum under the stove. A coal scuttle
stood beside the stove. In one corner was a whatnot with odd
bits of china and on the wall was something that looked like
fishnet into which an unbelievable number of photographs and
snapshots were stuck. There was also a small table, a good one
that had come from the Realses' attic. It had had a leg broken
but this was mended and polished till the break scarcely showed.
On this was a maidenhair fern in a dish with cupids disporting
around the edge. On the wall just past the stove was a picture
of Jesus blessing little children. The two women rocked com-
fortably but Miss Potts' faded eyes were a little anxious.

77

"I'm certainly glad to set," Mrs. Bunce said with a sigh. "Been on my feet since sunup. She had kind of a bad day. Too many people in, if you ask me. You'd think we was a theater, the way folks goes in and out. Course she's always glad to see folks and she wouldn't hurt anybody's feelings, but the truth is, she gets awful tired. She had a *bridge party* this afternoon— can you imagine!"

"Well, it's nice she's got the strength for it."

"She hasn't, that's what I mean. But she won't give in that she's not as strong as she ever was. I wisht you'd tell that Mrs. Olde to stay home—she pecks at her, in a catty way, if you know what I mean."

"You ought to see her side of it, Leora. Hux is her only brother. He's old enough to be settling down—that's her side of it."

From where she sat Miss Potts could see the clock on the oak sideboard in the dining room and she let her glance slide toward it, while a small frown made a straight vertical line between her nearsighted eyes.

"He's old enough so it's none of her business, the way I look at it," Mrs. Bunce said.

Always when Mrs. Bunce came Miss Potts immediately went to the kitchen, made coffee, and got out a coffee cake or cookies but tonight she just sat and talked and watched the clock surreptitiously.

"Isn't it awful, how high meat is?" she asked. They exhausted the price of meat. They discussed Reverend Smith and some of the doings of the godless Episcopalians. Still Miss Potts did nothing about coffee cake. The little room was unbearably hot but neither mentioned that. They discussed Elizabeth. Something was not quite right, and Mrs. Bunce realized it. At last she said frankly, with her kind laugh that was so much a part of their intimacy, "Well, Maisie, aren't you going to give me a cup of coffee? My tongue's hanging out and I didn't take any at dinner!"

Miss Potts' thin face grew unpleasantly flushed.

"I thought I'd wait a little while," she said. Then with an effort she rushed on. "You see, Leora, Mr. Botsworth's going to drop in for a cup with us. I don't know just how it came about—we got to talking about coffee's going up in the shop and one thing led to another—you know, folks always say I make first-rate coffee and I don't do anything special, just make it the old-fashioned way with an eggshell—but one thing led to another and the first thing you know he was saying he'd come in and have a sample some night and then he said he'd be along to-night. You don't want to get ideas in your head, Leora—it was all sort of in fun. It don't mean anything. But as long as he said that, I thought we might as well wait and have it all together. And maybe it was all a joke and he won't come anyway . . ."

Her voice trailed off. Mrs. Bunce stared at her, shocked. She had been coming to Miss Potts' cottage for years, and of all people in the world Miss Potts was the last to think of as having a suitor. Mrs. Bunce was truly shocked. And bewildered and hurt as well. Not even the accident to Anna Suydam had upset her as had this confused announcement. She had been a widow a good many years and she had never thought of marrying again. She had been, praise the Lord, she often said, contented with her lot. But she had not realized till this moment how much of her contentment lay in the fact that all this time she had had these evenings with Maisie Potts, gossiping, laughing, talking over the state of the world in general and their employers in particular. Not since she had walked out of the room where lay John Bunce, gone in his early prime, had she had such an empty, lost, betrayed feeling.

"Why, Maisie Potts!" she said at last.

"Now don't you go thinking things," Maisie Potts said weakly.

At that moment there was a knock on the door and Maisie, reddening afresh, jumped up and went to answer the knock.

Mr. Botsworth looked, as Anna had so aptly stated, like a cod. But he was a genial man with a hearty voice. "Took you up on it, Miss Potts!" he announced himself. "Where's my coffee? Well, hello, Fatty!" He had called Mrs. Bunce Fatty when she was a little girl and he still did so. "What you doing here?"

"Leora often comes to keep me company," Miss Potts said. "Just sit down, Mr. Botsworth, and I'll go make us some coffee. Just sit down and make yourself comfortable!"

"Whew!" he said, laying off his overcoat. "Mind if I take off my coat too? It's hot as an oven in here."

"Just be comfortable," Miss Potts said again.

So he took off his suit coat and sat in his shirt sleeves by the stove in Miss Potts' chair. "How's your missus coming along?" he asked Mrs. Bunce.

"Fine. Just fine, considering," Mrs. Bunce said.

"Too bad. A dirty shame, that's what it is, a pretty young thing like her. The Lord's ways are certainly past finding out, I say. Couldn't we turn that damper down a bit?"

"Seems just cozy to me," Mrs. Bunce said.

"Guess I'm more used to the cold. Always keep the shop so cold."

Mrs. Bunce had a moment of rejoicing in the heat, hoping it would roast him out. He took out a clean white handkerchief and wiped his forehead.

"This is a good little house," he said finally. "Remember when Matt Spears built it. Made of the lumber from the old Tidings barn—good stuff, though, better'n what you get nowadays. All this unseasoned stuff makes you sick. Used to be you could build you a real fancy big house for ten thousand—now you don't get more'n a shack for that." He put up his fingers to his neat bow tie as if he considered removing that and looked desperately at the damper.

"You've got a good house yourself," Mrs. Bunce reminded him coldly. Looking around on Maisie's house as if he owned it!

"It's all right. Don't have the feeling for it now, though, not since they cut down those two elms. They made nice shade. Well, it's kind of lonesome there anyway, living all stark alone like I do. You eat the darnedest things."

"You could have your daughter Jane and her husband live with you, seems as if. Jane's a real good cook and it isn't as if they had a house of their own. Living over the store like they do, I should think they'd be glad of a house."

"Well, Fatty, you know how that is. Young folks like to be by themselves. That's natural. I don't aim to change my ways—too old for that now. I'll bet it isn't always easy at your place, what with mama always there underfoot. It makes trouble ninety-nine times out of a hundred."

"It don't make trouble at our place," Mrs. Bunce said coldly. "It don't make any trouble at all. Mrs. S. fits in very easy and nice and don't try to run things like some mothers-in-law I know. Anna's good as gold to her—no, we don't have no trouble that way, Ed. And I guess if you wanted to you could make out to be polite yourself."

He chuckled and said, "Mebbe I don't want to. Young folks seem kind of silly to me, and that's a fact. I'd rather mosey along my own way. And I'll bet, underneath, your folks get on each other's nerves sometimes too. It ain't human, not to. . . . Well, about time, Miss Potts, before Fatty and me get in an argument. Is your kitchen as hot as this? If so's it ain't, I'm for having coffee out there."

Usually Miss Potts and Mrs. Bunce sat by the stove with their coffee, but tonight Miss Potts said, "We can sit here in the dining room. So if you'll just come now . . ."

Miss Potts had made an angel food and Mrs. Bunce noted the fact with a sinking heart. She knew quite well that Miss Potts made angel foods only on birthdays and special holidays.

"Well, now, you didn't go and make a cake for me, did you?" Mr. Botsworth said.

"Oh, no," lied Miss Potts, flushing. "Maisie and I always

have a little snack together. Just sit down and I'll pour the coffee. I've got a feeling after all my talk that it's too strong!"

Mr. Botsworth took a sip, scalding hot. "Strong enough to sink a battleship," he agreed. "But it tastes like coffee, I'll say that." He took a large triangle of angel food, began on it at once. "That certainly slides down," he said. "Haven't tasted angel food like that since I lost Angie."

"Nor before," Mrs. Bunce said. "Angie was no cake baker, Ed. She was a nice girl, but she was no cake baker."

Mr. Botsworth gave her a codlike, surprised stare, if cods can be surprised.

"Her things always tasted good," he said stubbornly.

"Of course they did," Miss Potts soothed him. "Because you were happy, I expect."

"Darned if we weren't," Mr. Botsworth said. "You know, sometimes I come in at night and I look over at that old Singer sewing machine, thinking she's going to be settin' there. She was always sewing—Jane was dressed nice, if I do say so. Still is. She's got the same knack Angie did. Guess when there isn't much coming in, women have to learn. Shop goes well enough now, but in those days it was kind of a struggle sometimes."

"It ought to be going well, the prices you charge," Mrs. Bunce said.

"I can't help the prices. It don't mean any more to me because they're high. You know what I paid for a steer the other day?"

"I guess you ain't going in the red, Ed," Mrs. Bunce said. She couldn't seem to eat her cake, though Maisie had never done better and it would melt in your mouth. Sadness deepened in her, because she had always fancied food Miss Potts gave her. She ate her meals in such a hurry at the house—here she had savored them.

"No, but I have to keep humping to pay taxes and all. You can't compete with the chain stores, but I give good value and

the folks that's used to me, they stick by me. . . . I'll have a
mite more of that cake, Miss Potts. It's real tasty."

They talked on but all the time Mrs. Bunce felt emptier
and lonelier. Ed Botsworth acted so at home, as if it wouldn't
be any effort for him at all to move right in. And those silly
red spots on Maisie's cheeks, and the way her hand shook when
she cut the cake, and the foolish way she bridled when Ed
asked for more of that coffee. And the eating in the dining
room, which seemed chilly after the warmth of the sitting
room. Oh, it was all over, all over and done—she could see it
plain. He was ripe for it and Miss Potts was acting like a schoolgirl. The poor fool—she'd find out it wasn't all roses, having a
butcher for a husband.

"Well, I've got to work tomorrow if you folks haven't," she
said suddenly. "Hate to break up the party, but I'll be getting
along now."

Miss Potts looked at her with some distress. Ed Botsworth
said, "I'll walk you home, Fatty!" He gave a hearty laugh at the
thought and Mrs. Bunce said sharply, "You'll do no such
thing. You set right still and gorge yourself on that cake if
you're a mind to. I don't want anyone toting me home! I'm
fifty-six years old and I haven't been bothered for some time
. . ."

She got her coat and hat on, pulled on her cotton gloves.
"Good night, Maisie," she said. "Good night, Ed."

"See you Sunday," Maisie Potts said, her blue eyes anxious,
knowing what was happening but quite unable to stop it.

"You generally do," Mrs. Bunce said, and departed. But
when she was safe in her own back room at Number Seven,
undressed and in her bed, tears came to her eyes.

Well, that's that, she tried to say philosophically, but she
couldn't stop the tears from coming. Her little snug room was
suddenly too snug. It was all she had. She didn't know how
much Miss Potts' cottage had enlarged her world till now that
world had shrunk to this.

In the morning when Johnny wandered into the kitchen she didn't tell him to get out from underfoot, as she was wont to do. She had always maintained stoutly that she was lucky not to have had any children, being as she had to earn her keep after Bunce died. But this morning she couldn't help feeling that she ought to have had children, something of her own to put her mind on.

"Here, now, young fella," she said, "suppose you dry this silverware and I'll get going on my pie."

Johnny carefully dried silver and Mrs. Bunce got out the materials for making pie crust. She let Johnny have a small piece of dough, pour a little molasses on it and put it in the oven. She made a cream filling, beat up egg whites for a meringue. At last it was out on the kitchen table, cooling, and Johnny's little molasses pie as well.

"It smells good," Johnny said.

"Let it cool a spell. Yes, molasses pie smells like something, that's the truth. Land, my legs hurt me. I'm going to set five minutes."

When Elizabeth came down to the kitchen for something, Mrs. Bunce sat just inside the door of her room, which was the old storeroom Mrs. Bunce had cleared out for a bedroom so as not to have to climb stairs at night, and she was rocking back and forth, Johnny in her arms, singing clearly in her uninhibited Baptist voice: "Jesus loves me, this I know, for the Bible tells me so—Little ones to Him belong—We are weak but He is strong. Yes, Jesus loves me. . . ."

Elizabeth, not knowing what impulse had brought about this tenderness, was startled and touched. She said nothing to them but all the way upstairs and later she kept remembering Johnny's head against that broad bosom, the clear voice, the rocking chair. Was it as simple as that, the way to Johnny? *Jesus loves me*—was that the way? Elizabeth remembered one day when she'd been very small, how old she didn't know, she'd been lying in the grass in a farmyard under a mulberry tree. It was the only mulberry tree she remembered ever having seen. The branches came down almost to the ground so that she was inside a little house, a cave. She could see the sky through little chinks, but it was almost dark in there. She had had the sensation that the tree was God, bending wings over her, keeping her utterly safe and secure. She had never been so happy—never before, never since. She hadn't asked herself whether she believed in anything, she had just felt God's wings over her, that was all. Maybe all Johnny's silences meant was that he was hunting for a still place such as that had been. Maybe Johnny *always* was one with God. Then she remembered his eyes when he had said, "But if she *was* dead, then you could stay forever," and she shivered. No, he had been one with Lucifer then. Yet he had looked so young, so relaxed, so content, there against the bosom of Mrs. Bunce. Maybe I'm just not fat enough, she thought foolishly.

In Anna's room Anna looked up with excited brown eyes and said, "Oh, Liz, run down and ask Mrs. Daggett in! She's coming down the street."

"But—how could I?"

"Why not? Bet you two to one I'll find out whom she's writing to! Run—before she gets by!"

Elizabeth ran down the stairs and opened the front door. Mrs. Daggett was humping along with a string bag dangling emptily from her arm.

"Oh, Mrs. Daggett!" Elizabeth said. "My sister wonders if you wouldn't come up and say hello to her!"

The old woman paused. She didn't straighten, because she couldn't, but she peered up at Elizabeth with an odd expression in black eyes pouched and veined of lid.

"She must be bored," she said clearly, in a voice Liz had not expected from her. It was a worldly, even a cultured voice.

Elizabeth laughed uncertainly and said, "No, she's never bored. She just wants to see you."

Mrs. Daggett began to come up the steps. "I must be at the

post office before eleven," she said. She came into the hall,
her black eyes took in the contents of the hall, the wallpaper.
"So Anna fell for this paper, did she?" she asked. "I have some
of the original in my back bedroom." And as she passed the old
prints on the stair well, "Don't these pictures frighten the life
out of Johnny?"

"I don't think he even sees them," Elizabeth said.

"Kind of thing a boy always sees," Mrs. Daggett said.

Anna called out gaily, "Have to go out and drag you in to
see me! Shame on you, Mrs. Daggett!"

Mrs. Daggett put her bag on a chair, came and shook hands,
then sat down, bent forward a little as if about to run off
again. She did indeed look like an old witch, with her queer
figure, her old black clothes, her dark, piercing eyes and
wrinkled face.

"Anna, you didn't want to see me any more than you
wanted to see Bill Vine," Mrs. Daggett said. "You saw me in
that contraption of yours up there and thought you'd surprise
me."

Anna laughed, a young girl's laugh. "True," she said, "but I
did want to see you. I see the same old faces over and over.
I wanted a change."

"Told your sister you were bored."

"I'm not. That's something I never have been. I'm just interested in everybody and I thought, Here comes Mrs. Daggett and I don't really know her at all. Why don't I begin?—
and here you are."

Mrs. Daggett gave a small grunt, then without changing her
position said, "Remember this room well when it was old
Mrs. Suydam's—Adrian's grandmother's. It had brown paper
with gold medallions and brown velvet curtains. She took
enough medicines to stock a drugstore and kept them in a
cupboard over her bed. She had a dose for everything."

"It doesn't look like that now, does it? I don't keep so much
as a pill in sight!"

"Looks elegant. Like you," Mrs. Daggett admitted. "Except for that Dresden vase."

"But that's the love of my life!" Anna protested. "What's wrong with that?"

"Doesn't fit, that's all. I mean, if you want to make a picture of this room. Never tried to make anything fit myself. Being house-proud's not my line."

"But you've got a lovely old house," Anna said.

"It's got everything in it that ever happened to settle there," Mrs. Daggett said. "I never made it. Houses have rights, I've always thought."

"Well, I think so too," Anna said. "I truly do. But their right is to be as beautiful as they have it in them to be."

The black eyes narrowed reflectively. "Is that the way of it?" The voice had, Elizabeth thought, a touch of scorn. "Always seemed to me all the life that's been lived in them ought to show somehow."

"Well, I mean the same thing," Anna said. "I mean—well, this is my life," and she waved a hand about at the lovely room.

"Yes, but where's Grandma Suydam's life? Can't see it. And she'd have dropped dead to see those heathenish prints on the wall out there in the hall."

"But you don't want me to live her life, do you? I've got a right to put my life on top," Anna protested.

"Certainly. Certainly," Mrs. Daggett said.

"Oh, I am glad you came in!" Anna said. "I knew you'd give me something to think about." Then she plunged, with a suddenness that almost made Liz jump. "And it wasn't any sudden urge to see you, Mrs. Daggett. I see you going by every day and wonder if you'll drop in. I think about you a lot—I truly do. I wonder if you're lonely and whom you write to every day, things like that. When you're shut in you speculate on *everything*. Do tell me whom you write to every single day, so I won't have to brood over *that* any more!"

Mrs. Daggett was silent. The room seemed to stop breathing for a moment. Then Mrs. Daggett reached for her bag with an awkward spiderlike motion, got to her feet. "No, I'm not any lonelier than any of God's creatures," she said. "I must run along now. Good day, Anna."

Elizabeth followed her down the stairs and opened the door for her. "Thanks for coming in," she said embarrassedly.

Mrs. Daggett peered up at her from the bottom step. "I like the looks of you," she said. "Come and see me, young woman."

When Elizabeth went into Anna's room again she said, "Two to one, eh?"

"Oh, just wait. I'll know yet!" Anna said. "Isn't she a character?"

It was later that day when Elizabeth stopped to look at the prints with eyes that really saw. There was the one of Jonah with that look of holy martyrdom, one of Elisha being devoured by the bears, one of Samson bringing down the roof of the temple, one of Sodom's destruction, with houses falling in and lightning flashing in an ominous sky, and one of Abraham's son tied up on an altar, with faggots under him for lighting. Elizabeth had glanced at them with laughter before, but now she saw them with eyes a little shocked. They were horrible. If one took them seriously. But Johnny was a realistic little boy and he would know better than to take them seriously. Or would he? If he could find comfort in "Jesus loves me," perhaps he could find horror in these pictures too.

"You know, Mrs. Daggett is right—those are rather monstrous prints out there in the hall," she said to Anna.

"Monstrous? They're really very funny," Anna said.

"To us. Maybe not to Johnny."

"But Johnny's not one for fairy tales, you know that. He probably never sees them."

And there the matter rested. She couldn't bring them to Johnny's attention if he never had noticed them much. She didn't want to make an issue of them. And yet they troubled her. She had seen them as funny too, but she was an adult. Children had different eyes. She watched Johnny once or twice as he climbed the stairs but he never glanced toward the prints. She had to pretend to believe that it was always so.

"We have to think about Christmas," Anna said that night. Something in her voice made Elizabeth feel great compassion for her.

"You do the thinking," she said. "Would you like the tree up here?"

"I suppose it better be. If it wasn't too big—but I do love big pines with long needles—but we could have a slim one in the corner there. We have always been very gay at Christmas, with lots of parties. But we could have open house one day, couldn't we? Only you'll have to do such a lot of shopping, Liz."

"I don't mind. Only there are so many places you can write to nowadays. I'll get catalogues, shall I? And you can shop yourself."

"I seem to remember so many people. I didn't realize how many. It's nice to have friends—I'm lucky that way—but at Christmas . . ."

"Don't worry about it. We'll manage everyone. What about Johnny? What would he like, I wonder?"

"What he'll really like is books, nothing but books. He always gets a lot of toys—but it won't matter to him. Oh, Liz, I don't know what to do about Johnny. I try to think we'll get together and be friends again, but we don't. I don't want to force him, but it's all wrong, darling. He doesn't even kiss me good night."

"Yes, it's all wrong," Elizabeth admitted. "But it will come out right. You've been very patient with him. Maybe you ought not to be quite so patient. You could charm him out of his brooding, it seems to me."

"Oh, I've tried that. No, I just don't know where I'm at with Johnny. Well, good night, darling."

At breakfast, Elizabeth said to Adrian, "We must have a bang-up good Christmas."

"Yes. Yes, of course," he said.

"Anna'd like open house someday. We could do that, couldn't we?"

"I suppose so. Yes, we could. If Bunce'll stand for it."

"Of course she will. We can all help."

He did not answer and presently he got up, brought his coat and hat. He went up to say good-by to Anna, then came slowly down the stairs. He hesitated at the dining-room door, then said, "I don't see how she can be so excited about Christmas. I can't be, I'm afraid."

"I don't know that she is," Elizabeth said. "I think part of it is pretending, Adrian. There are all the presents to think of—it's tiring. But we can pull it off somehow."

He stood there in the doorway, looking tired and somehow defeated.

"I'd like to skip the whole damn thing this year," he said. Then he went away.

CHRISTMAS CANNOT BE SKIPPED, not with the fixed American habit of letting the year work ever toward that day.

"What's the matter with Bunce?" Anna asked. "She doesn't have much Christmas spirit this year."

"I don't know. Something," Elizabeth admitted.

Mrs. Bunce, down in her small, tidy room back of the kitchen, took the last stitches in the afghan she had been making for Miss Potts, pressed it, wrapped it carefully in tissue, and put a card on it for her loved mistress. Her dark eyes snapped as she performed this act, and one would have thought her angry instead of hurt. But she could not bear the thought of Ed Botsworth lying on the horsehair sofa with this afghan over him.

Elizabeth said one morning, "I never thought I'd spend Christmas at Number Seven."

"I didn't think you would either," Adrian said. "Are you getting used to us?"

"Some. Still, I'm surprised I'm here. If you could just say 'Merry Christmas' and let it go at that. Wouldn't that be easier?"

"You get tired of all the hullabaloo too?"

"Sometimes. I love it—but I just want to *feel* it and not do so much about it. I remember that Christmas when father was sick, awfully sick, and we didn't have a tree or anything. Mom said we had to be quiet. I think we had something in our stockings, but that was all. In the afternoon it snowed. Father asked mom to bring us in and she told us to be quiet and go in. He smiled at us and asked mom if she wouldn't like to read the Christmas story according to St. Luke. And mom read it and we went out. . . . It was my best Christmas. The snow came down so softly—big wet flakes—and mom's voice was so solemn and steady—do you know what I mean, Adrian?"

"The storekeepers have seen to it that that kind of Christmas is dead and buried," Adrian said. "You don't give because you want to any more, but because the other fellow does and you're made to feel small if you don't. It's a racket."

"Oh, not all, Adrian, not entirely a racket. It's only . . ."

"I know. But I guess we can live through it, Liz," Adrian said. It was the friendliest thing he had said to her.

Anna saw little Dolly Maule stop by a lamppost and look inside a tiny red pocketbook so anxiously, counting her pennies. She saw Peg Jones rushing along to the store before school closed, with that last-minute horrified look of having forgotten Aunt Dorcas. She saw Meg McIntry walking with her hands empty—at Christmastime.

Young women kept running in to show Anna what they had purchased for this one or that. "Oh, Anna, do you think this sports coat is all right for Ed?" or, "Anna, do you think Joan will like this ski suit?" And Anna would be truly interested. "I really think a tweed with a little blue in it would be better, Joan—Ed's eyes are so blue!" Or, "Well, if she doesn't like it she'll be an ungrateful brat." And when Elizabeth protested that an open house the day after Christmas would be just too much—people would be so tired, Anna said, "No, that's the perfect day. People are so sick of tissue papers and all—they want to get out!" It seemed people did. Everyone was coming.

In the rush of preparation Elizabeth didn't take her day off and Anna let it pass—for this once, this twice. But never after Christmas, she said.

Letters came for Elizabeth from Bessie Loren and Lollie Parsons. Anna always had mail but Elizabeth seldom. "And who's your letter from?" Anna asked. Elizabeth had a strange moment of not wanting to share Bessie with Anna, of not wanting Bessie's charm dissected. Bessie was her own friend. Not that Bessie wasn't interesting in her way, interesting as Anna's friends were interesting, but she had the oddest style— jumping from one thing to another and leaving you to find the connection. There always was a connection, and that was the fun of trying to keep up with Bessie. But as if she had spoken the words Elizabeth could hear Anna say, She sounds like a telegraph machine, doesn't she? . . . Wait—wait a minute! I missed something there! Then Elizabeth was ashamed, for Anna shared her letters, so she read Bessie's letter aloud and even found herself telling Anna the worldly things about Bessie's success as a writer to build her up in Anna's eyes. "Why, you never told me you knew her!" Anna said. "But I hope she doesn't write books in the same way she writes letters!"

Elizabeth didn't read her Lollie's letter. In it Lollie said, "Look here, it's time you came back. They've got a girl in the bookshop, but she's temporary. I seem to get a note of depression even through the lines of your too-brief notes. Mrs. B. has had several chances to rent your room but I tell her to hold her horses—you'll be back. I don't know why she'd care, she's getting paid and there's no work. But seriously: you don't want to be The Spinster Aunt in the House, now, do you? You're old enough to know your own mind, but I seem to worry about you . . ."

I'm worried about myself, Elizabeth admitted, shoving the letter into her pocket. I ought to say to Anna that I will stay till such-and-such a day—even if it's Easter. I ought to make it definite, not let her think that my life doesn't count to me outside of this house. That's what she would do and that is what I ought to do. Then why don't I? Because I can't bear to be thought unloving—I'm not unloving. It's something else that tells me to get out before it is too late. I will be The Spinster Aunt in the House—that's just what I will get to be. I will grow old and die in this house.

Then one day she went downtown to get a record for Bessie, and in the music store Huxley Reals was standing, discussing some record machine with the proprietor. He looked half embarrassed when he saw her and said to the man, "Well, I'll let you know tomorrow." But he waited till she had made her purchase and walked out of the store with her.

Now be your age, Liz, she said to herself. Yet, just walking through the snowy street with him changed her, frightened her. It was in a way like the fright when Johnny had asked her about staying forever. It was connected with it, in a way she hated.

"I never asked you how the skating party went off without me," he said in a friendly voice.

"Well enough. No, not so very well," she contradicted herself. "Adrian didn't really want to go, you know."

"Well, I didn't either," he admitted. "Or at first I didn't. But I'd worked myself up to a desire to get acquainted with Johnny. I've never known him."

"He's hard to know."

"He scares me, to tell the truth. He looks as if he knew more than I do. He liked the ship though, didn't he?"

"Yes, he liked that."

"Meg McIntry was lecturing me—said that taking on Johnny would be more useful than sending roses. D'you think so?"

"Better for whom? If you begrudged doing it, I'm quite sure Johnny would know it."

He laughed and the laugh surprised her. It had real humor in it. "You don't coddle people, do you, Aunt Liz?" he said.

"Why should I?"

"Why should you, indeed? What do you think of a record player for Anna for Christmas? I know they have that big one downstairs—but perhaps a smaller one for her room. She loves music, I know—so I wondered . . ."

Elizabeth thrust her hands into her big pockets, said, "Yes, she loves music, but—must you be such a fool, Mr. Reals?"

She hadn't known she was going to say it, she wanted to take it back, but the words hung there on the air, spoken. He had been talking to her in an easy, friendly way, but now he stopped dead still on the sidewalk, turned, and stared hard at her.

"A fool?" he said. Then, more quietly, "Yes, I must be a fool, if that is what you call it."

"What do you call it? I don't know why Adrian doesn't throw you out of his house, out of his plant. He's not a gentle man—nor an unseeing one. Palely loitering around his wife!"

She was aghast but couldn't stop. To her amazement he laughed, began to walk again by her side.

"What a temper you have!" he said. "I didn't like that 'palely loitering' crack. But to tell the truth, I'm past shock treatment, Aunt Liz. Nothing like that matters at all."

"Don't call me Aunt Liz. And don't think I don't know what Anna does to you. She's terribly exciting as well as beautiful—all the same a record player costs a couple of hundred dollars, doesn't it? That's downright silly."

"But would she like it?"

They had come to Number Seven and paused at the steps. A light snow lay everywhere and the world of Lakeville looked beautiful and peaceful. This, Elizabeth Burke said to herself, she did not deserve. She could give her life to looking after Anna more easily than she could bear this.

She gave him a sudden smile and said, "I think she'd love it."

He grinned at her in a puzzled way, walked away.

When Elizabeth went into Anna's room, Anna said, "Are you stealing my swain?"

"Heavens, no! He's having a struggle trying to decide what to give you for Christmas!"

"And what? What is he going to give me? I ought to suggest a new refrigerator."

"You'll find out. I don't know where we're going to put it, either. Could I give Johnny a dog for Christmas?"

"He's allergic to cat and dog fur," Anna said.

Then Christmas was there. In Anna's room, there was the heart of the house. There was one bad moment when Elizabeth didn't know whether Johnny would even come for the tree, but Bunce came to his door, took his hand and said, "All right now, Johnny—looks as if Santa's been here, all right!" And Johnny went with her to his mother's room. Adrian distributed gifts and Anna was excited and loved everything.

"Oh, it's too much! Aren't friends wonderful! You're all wonderful," she said.

Johnny had plenty of toys, puzzles, and books and a new tricycle, water colors, and all the odds and ends that fall to children's lot these days of too many things. He managed a few reluctant thank you's, prompted by Bunce. Bunce gave her afghan to Anna, and Elizabeth saw that Bunce kept looking at it with sadness and she wondered about it. But all in all, everything went well.

Anna was like a child with presents. She had sense enough not to speak to Johnny much, not to press him for thanks or excitement. Of the record machine she said, "The extravagant darling! But I can't send it back—you don't want me to, do you, Adrian? The records are wonderful—remember the Christmas before we were married? How we listened to dance music on that old machine at home? And danced?" Then she cast a glance toward Johnny and said casually, "That red piece comes next, doesn't it, Johnny?"

The next day was the open house, with all of Lakeville wandering through the house, with laughter high, with singing, sitting around Anna's chair, Anna's own alto coming through clearly and truly. A gay party, a good party. Juliet Olde said to Elizabeth, "I thought we were going to get together for lunch or something." Huxley Reals once caught her eye as music was coming from his gift and gave her a small smile. Then it was all over, the last guest gone, the things carried away from the dining room, the ash trays emptied, the big eggnog bowl carried out.

"Are you awfully tired?" Elizabeth asked, getting Anna into bed.

"Unto death," Anna said, half serious. "But it was fun, wasn't it? I am lucky, Liz—having so many friends."

"Yes, you are. And everyone was so happy."

"Wouldn't it be awful to have a dud of a party? I never have, but one could. Oh, bed does feel good!"

"Maybe you'll sleep and won't want any milk tonight."

"Maybe I will. . . . Oh, come in, darling. It was fun, wasn't it? And now—*sleep!*"

Adrian stood uncertainly by the bed, then bent and kissed her, went out. Downstairs, he said to Elizabeth, "She got too tired."

"Yes, she's tired. But aren't you? You always get tired after a party. But it was worth it."

"Why didn't Meg come? She didn't have to look after Johnny."

"I don't know. She said she didn't like big parties."

"It bothered Anna."

"Why should it? Anna doesn't even like her much, does she?"

"Doesn't like her? There isn't anyone in the world Anna doesn't like. It seemed rude of Meg."

"For goodness' sake—there were a hundred or more people here. And it was a good thing to have Johnny over there. Go to bed, Adrian—you're too tired to stand up."

The next afternoon Dr. McIntry dropped in. "Well, you

haven't lost the knack, Anna," he said. "A good party. I expected to find you in bed."

"Cornelia's the one who's exhausted," Anna said. "Run up and see her before you go. She did work too hard. But it was good, wasn't it? I saw your car coming in my busybody and I willed you to stop. I was just scheming about you. Wondering whom to marry you off to."

"Stop. Stop right there, Anna. I don't want to marry anyone. I'm too old and too set and I get along."

"But suppose Meg married—then how would you get along?"

"Meg? She won't marry. We're both content—so put your mind on something else. I've been through the experience of matrimony."

"Was it so bad as all that?"

Dr. McIntry's face lost its habitual look of kindness. "It was bad enough," he said shortly. "But I got Meg out of it. . . . Aren't you losing weight?"

"No. It's just the day-after-the-party look. I'm fine. I even thought in an idle moment of Liz here for you. She'd make the perfect doctor's wife—steady as a rock—all that."

Elizabeth made a little face at him and he laughed. "No, I won't have you, Liz," he said. "Besides being old enough to be your father, I wouldn't want to be badgered about my sins."

"Would you rather have Mrs. Daggett?"

He gave a snort, took out his pipe. "I'd rather be left alone," he said. "I'm so busy I wouldn't have time to speak to a wife. Meg's got used to shorthand. . . . No, Anna, you can't tempt me—even with Liz."

"She takes getting used to, but she'd grow on you," Anna said, with a little giggle. "Everybody ought to be married."

"Just because you're lucky doesn't make all marriages lucky," he said. "I don't want any part of it, Anna, and that's the truth. I was married once—and it was bitter medicine. I'm wary of marriage and I do very well as I am. If you want a husband, Liz, I'll find you one—among the young fry."

"I don't," Elizabeth said. "It wasn't my idea. I don't even like you very much."

Anna gave a crow of laughter. "My Liz! But he'd grow on you too, darling. He's nice, really, even if he does laugh at Prather's dilemmas!"

After he had gone upstairs to see Mrs. Suydam, Anna said, "But why don't you like him? He's one of my favorite people."

"I don't know. He's got a cold heart."

"Dr. McIntry? But that's not true. You can't believe how nice he's been to me, how gentle and how patient."

"To you, yes. But you're special, Anna. He's a little in love with you."

"Oh, nonsense! But, you know, I hope he is—just a little."

On Thursday afternoon Mrs. Bunce had a telephone call. This rarely happened and she shouted "Hello!" boomingly into the receiver. "It's Maisie," Miss Potts' prim anxious little voice said. "You'll be over tonight, won't you, Leora?" "No, I guess not. Don't want to butt in!" Mrs. Bunce said. "Oh, don't, Leora. You know you wouldn't be butting in." "Well, I'll see," Mrs. Bunce said and hung up.

When Elizabeth went down after supper she found Mrs. Bunce, huge and sad, standing in the middle of the kitchen floor doing nothing at all. "What's the matter?" Elizabeth asked. "Nothing. Not a thing, Miss Burke," Mrs. Bunce said. "I was just wondering whether to go out or not. It's so chill, I guess I'll just stay home."

But at eight o'clock, in her black coat and little black hat with the feather at the wrong angle, Mrs. Bunce was walking down past the stores to Miss Potts' house. When she got there she walked onto the low porch and through the window saw Mr. Botsworth, his coat off, sitting by the stove. She had argued to herself that maybe Mr. Botsworth's call had been for just that once, one of those things which just chance, as Miss Potts had tried to make her believe, but it hadn't been so. She had wanted to tell Miss Potts all about the party, the

Christmas presents, but she wouldn't go in there tonight. Then
the thought of the afghan came, shaming her. She had sent a
little apron down to Maisie, that was all. She began to move
swiftly and softly off the porch, but before she had gone down
the step the door opened and Miss Potts called out, "Why,
Leora—where are you going to?"

"I don't want to intrude," Mrs. Bunce said with dignity.

"You come right in here."

Mr. Botsworth's figure appeared in the doorway behind
Maisie's. "Hello, there, Fatty! Come on in with us old folks!"
he called out genially. So she had to go in, not being able to
refuse with dignity. As she went in, Mr. Botsworth gave her
a little smack on her broad behind. "I've got her to turn the
damper down," he said. "We thought we'd have a little game
of three-handed rummy. Or don't you Baptists allow that?"

"Why, we're not so behind the times as all that," Miss Potts
said. "We don't object to simple little games like rummy.
You've got the wrong idea about the Baptists, Mr. Botsworth.
They aren't as strict as they used to be when we were children.
Gambling, they don't like that, but a game of rummy's all
right."

Mr. Botsworth winked at Mrs. Bunce. "You got cards?" he
asked. "I can recall the day when a pack of cards in the house
was downright consorting with the devil."

Miss Potts got out a pack of cards and they sat at the dining-
room table and played rummy.

"No gambling, eh?" Mr. Botsworth said after a few hands.
"A little stake makes the game exciting, but just as you say,
girls. Just as you say. I wouldn't want to cause your downfall
from grace."

"You can play poker with the men down in Bill Vine's place
if you feel that way, Ed," Mrs. Bunce said.

Mr. Botsworth gave a guffaw and said, "What do you know
about Bill Vine's place, Fatty? No, I like a nice game at home,
but I don't hang around Vine's. I'll tell you, Miss Potts—how

about putting up that extra fruit cake you got out there on the shelf? You told me it was given you by the Realses—it won't be any loss, now, will it? So long as you've got another to go with our coffee. Winner takes the fruit cake home. You wouldn't call that gambling, would you, girls?"

Miss Potts flushed and said, "You can have the fruit cake and welcome, if you want it."

"No, no. Just want the fun of trying to get it."

"I guess there wouldn't be any harm in that, would there, Leora?" Miss Potts asked.

"I don't see as it makes any difference one way or the other," Mrs. Bunce said. She did think it made a little difference, but it wasn't, of course, like playing for money.

Mrs. Bunce liked to play rummy and in spite of herself enjoyed the game. When it was done she found herself in possession of a fine fruit cake. "You take it home, Ed," she said. "I can make my own cakes."

"I'll bet you can," Ed said. "But fair's fair, Fatty. It's yours. I'll have another try when Miss Potts gets another donation."

Mrs. Bunce walked home with the cake under her arm. It bothered her. She wanted to throw it away but it was a good cake and she put it in the cake box. She felt she had done something wrong by the tenets of her religion and had been enticed into it by that foolish old Ed Botsworth, or by the fact that she felt guilty about the afghan and didn't want to add any more to her guilt by way of incivility. And she was angry because she had gone to Maisie's at all after having decided not to.

She sent some cake up for tea next day, and Anna said, "Where did this cake come from, I wonder? Bunce never made it—fruit cake's not her line and it's certainly not store cake. Someone must have sent it in. Don't you love it all black and full of things like this?"

When Elizabeth took the tray down she said, "Anna wondered where the cake came from. It was terribly good."

A dull red went up Bunce's face. "I won it," she said bluntly. "Playing rummy with Maisie and Ed Botsworth."

"Why, Bunce!" Elizabeth said, exploding with laughter.

"I don't see as it's so funny," Bunce said. "When I was seven years old I signed a pledge I wouldn't ever dance nor drink nor gamble. I never broke it till now. You can have fun over a game without getting something for it."

"Yes—but the cake was so good."

"That fool, Maisie Potts—at her age," mumbled Bunce and bustled off as if dismissing Elizabeth.

Elizabeth went back and reported and Anna laughed till tears stood in her eyes.

She managed to have Bunce come up later and she said to her, "Let your conscience be at rest, Bunce. You gave us a wonderful tea party today. Don't tell me Maisie has a suitor?"

"That's what she has. I should think she'd see she was making a fool of herself. She's sixty if she's a day. And a butcher— he's just looking for a cozy home, that's all he's looking for. I always thought Maisie Potts was sensible, but she acts like she never had a beau before. Simpering and baking cakes—not *that* one, 'twas one the Realses gave her Christmas—but don't she see he's just after her house and her cooking?"

Anna glanced toward the afghan, which lay over the foot of the bed. "I wondered about that afghan," she said, but smiled affectionately at Mrs. Bunce. "You told me you were making it for Maisie long ago. But she's got a right to have a little happiness, hasn't she?"

Mrs. Bunce's dark eyes were wet with angry tears.

"I wasn't going to go to all that work to have something for Ed Botsworth to lie under!" she said.

Anna laughed. "Oh, Bunce!" she said helplessly. "I see your point—but why not Ed Botsworth for Pottsy? Why not?"

"Because it don't make sense. It's just the cooking. You ought to see him dig into her cake and swill down her coffee— at ninety-seven cents a pound."

"Well, I wouldn't want to be married to him. He looks like a codfish to me. But Pottsy may see him through other eyes—he may be Adonis to her. Oh, it's lovely, Bunce. I haven't laughed so in months!"

"It don't seem funny to me," Bunce said stubbornly. "Maisie's independent and comfortable. She won't be any more so—she'll be less so married to a butcher."

After Bunce had finally gone, Anna laughed again, laughed and laughed, and Elizabeth with her.

Then Anna said, "You know, Maisie and Bunce have always interested me. If we were in a town where they make light of such relationships, folks would call them on the queer side. But really they're both as sensible as the day is long. They're both Baptists and they have us and the Realses to talk over—and I can just hear them talk! Just the same, it's an awful blow to Bunce to have Maisie getting serious over a man, even if it's Ed Botsworth. I knew something was wrong with her, but I couldn't imagine what it was. There ought to be some way I could insist on the afghan going where it really belongs, but I don't know how now."

"She'll have to work out her own salvation. It's funny—but it's sad too," Elizabeth said.

"Can't you just see her reluctantly cutting that sinful cake! Oh, it's wonderful. I wonder if Hux knows—about Maisie. But, then, I presume she would go right on working. She's been going there by the day for twenty years and more."

Elizabeth sat down on the stool, hugged her knees. Her brown face was suddenly grave. "Look, Anna, while we're on the subject of marrying and giving in marriage—I wish you'd leave the doctor and me alone. I'm serious—I really wish you would. It's embarrassing to me and to him too. I wouldn't have the doctor even if he wanted me, which he certainly doesn't."

Anna's brown eyes twinkled amusedly and she said, "But he might. I was just planting the seed. Men are funny that way. They don't know what they want. I think it would be perfect.

You'd be almost next door and he'd have somebody of his own besides Meg. I was only half teasing you both. It would be perfect."

"But I don't want any seed planted. I just don't want the doctor."

Anna laughed aloud, a traïling laugh like an echo of the laugh over Bunce. "But you might," she insisted. "He's older than you, but he's incredibly nice and intelligent too. He's one of my favorite people."

"He's not one of mine, though. I mean it, Anna. Don't take it as a joke. I mean it. As I said before, I'll pick my own man if I want one."

"I know you, Liz—you'd pick some lame duck you were sorry for. Someone you'd have to support. There's something to be said for the old days when your spouse was chosen for you by the family. They really did have more common sense about it."

"Nobody picked your spouse for you."

"No," Anna admitted more soberly. "No. Well, you've made your protest—but I may still work on it underground. I've set my heart on it. First thing you know, you're going to begin to take it seriously—and so is he. See, I lay all my cards on the table. I warn you, darling."

Elizabeth was silent. At last she said, looking straight at Anna—and that directness was a painful one, "And I warn you, Anna. Leave me alone. If it's any compliment to you, I know you're perfectly capable of marrying me off to the doctor against my will. But it would be a bitter victory, I can assure you. All right, that's all. But I *mean* it."

"Porcupine," Anna said, with amused affection.

Elizabeth did not smile. "Not unless I'm attacked," she said.

"Oh, Liz! But you always did see enemies behind every bush. I can remember you when you were so high and I came out and found you hiding behind the big maple with a little pile of soft mud and a mud cake in your hand. You were, you said,

going to throw it at Buddy Lee, if Buddy threw any at you.
He never had thrown any—never—now, had he? But you were
ready for him! You haven't changed a bit."

Elizabeth got up and said, "Do you want to go to bed now?"

"Yes," Anna said.

But when she was in bed, she reached out and took Elizabeth's hand, held it tightly. "Don't be mad at me, darling.
Maybe I'm just throwing mud cakes at the world too. If I
stopped being interested in everything—where would I be,
Liz? Oh, where would I be?"

Elizabeth gave a troubled laugh, and with her free hand
pushed Anna's fair hair back from her forehead. "You make
it so damned easy to forgive you."

Adrian came in, saying, "Got my girl tucked in?" and Elizabeth went away and left them together.

She went into Johnny's room and found him already in bed.

"I took my bath myself," he said.

"Good boy. And cleaned the bathtub?"

"As far as I could reach," Johnny said.

"Tomorrow we might go exploring again. Want to?"

"Can we go to Meg's?"

"I don't know why not."

"Aunt Liz . . ."

"Yes?"

"Did you ever see God?"

"No. No, I never did." Then she said gently, "But I *felt* Him
once."

"What did He feel like?"

"Like big wings around me."

"Big as eagles'?"

"Bigger than that."

"Bunce said God was everywhere. I never saw Him."

"If He's anywhere He's everywhere. Something in you tells
you when and how to be good—and some people say that's
God."

"Do you?"

Elizabeth was still for a moment. Then she said, "It's a good name. Yes, I'll call it God."

Johnny lay there, eyes wide, just looking at her. And then he said, "Bunce said God wasn't in the doctor's house."

"I thought Bunce said He was everywhere."

"Everywhere but in the doctor's house, she said."

"There too, Johnny. There too," Liz said. "Now good night."

She told Adrian she was going out for a few minutes, put her coat on and stepped out into the dark, cold street. Her cheeks burned and she walked very fast up North Lake toward the parkway.

I'm certainly not very hot as a theologian, she said to herself. But what difference does it make whether you call it God or conscience? Can a child take anything beyond a personal, anthropomorphic God? Maybe no one can. Good and evil are here—that is true enough. I was born to be a Puritan, and yet I'm nothing at all. Anna thinks I'm preoccupied with sin, and maybe I am. I did feel Bunce's sin about the cake. It was a sin to her and she's going to have to expiate it, somehow. It was funny—but it wasn't so funny as we made it. Maybe you have to take a very long view to see the humor in humanity. I've never stood off far enough. She doesn't want me to marry the doctor at all. It's just something to think about and work at, something to laugh about. I shouldn't have taken it seriously. I ought to have laughed too. Only—only I don't like to be pushed around, even to make Anna laugh. I don't . . .

She had come to the statue and stood there near it a moment. The statue was of an airman, a sailor, and a soldier and had been erected after the first World War. The figures were elongated, surprisingly modern for having been done all those years ago. Around the base were names—names—names—boys who had gone away from Lakeville never to return. Elizabeth looked up at the strange El Greco-like figures and felt a sudden rush of tears to her eyes.

Life's so funny—and so short, she said, and her thought seemed to stand out like a written cliché against the night. There isn't time enough to work it out.

Johnny and Anna and her room and—and Huxley Reals. It was too much. She had promised she wouldn't pity Anna, but tonight she had thought her heart would break when Anna spoke about the mud cakes. Still, you couldn't let her marry you off to Dr. McIntry because of that, could you? *Could* you? Not that the doctor wanted her—only, only it happened so often that the things Anna thought of actually came to pass.

When she went in, Adrian was still with Anna. She went to her own room and began a letter to Lollie. She could see Lollie's round wholesome face as she wrote: "I'm concerned with the matter of sin tonight, Lollie. You've always called me 'independent as a hog on ice!' I think I have been. But I wonder if being that independent doesn't preclude love. I mean love in general, not boy and girl stuff. You can get to thinking the preservation of the self is the whole duty of existence. I'm mixed up and I wish you could say 'Tommyrot!' to me and unmix me. You talk about the selfless people—you call them saints. . . . Take the doctor, I've told you about Anna's doctor—he really gives himself to humanity as represented in Lakeville. All his time, all his energy. But is that giving the *self*? He seems like a completely self-centered man to me, in spite of his usefulness. And yet I ought to like just that sort of thing, hadn't I? . . . I get to feeling so wicked, because I remember my *self* in a place where my individuality doesn't matter at all. If you knew how much courage Anna had—and it is real courage, Lollie—you would think me a selfish fool. She's been magnificent—and I resent everything. I resent having clothes given to me. I resent being given a day off when I don't need it. I resent Adrian's never seeing me (don't get any idea from that that I have a romantic feeling for Adrian—never!). I resent making a joke of the whole human race. Oh, I am a fool. I know it—and I keep right on. I want to do my job. I want to

be useful to Anna. And yet I must want to eat my cake and
have it too. I want to keep on being Liz Burke. Not a sturdy
little Shetland pony, not a carrier of trays, not a nursemaid to
Johnny, not a prospective wife for Dr. McIntry. Just Liz
Burke. . . . I was trying to explain God to Johnny tonight. I
can hear you laugh. I don't feel like laughing. I feel desperate.
That's a strong word for my mild life. Maybe I had the delu-
sion that I was God. That I didn't need any everlasting arms
around me but was my own everlasting arms. I expect I have
felt just like that. Bunce is so sure of her right and wrong. I'm
just not sure about anything. . . . I'll enclose a check for the
room for next month. I ought to give it up, but I have to hang
onto it to be sure I exist at all. . . ."

She heard Adrian coming out of Anna's room and she folded
the letter quickly, went in to Anna. Anna was already in bed.

"It's been a long day," Anna said. "Most days go by very
fast."

"Yes, it has, rather," Elizabeth said. "Would you like a
pill to make you sleep?"

"Yes," Anna said. "Yes, I believe I would—don't let me do
it again. But just this once."

Elizabeth brought the pill and water. "I won't wake you at
eleven if you're asleep," she said.

Anna closed her eyes and did not answer. When Elizabeth
was back in her room she looked at the folded letter on the
desk, flushed and tore it into small pieces, let the pieces flutter
into the wastebasket.

At eleven Anna was sound asleep and Elizabeth crept back
to bed. But at two the little bell by her bed woke her and she
went quickly to Anna's room.

"Have I waked you at the crack of dawn?" Anna said. "Nature must be served, that's all."

"It's only two," Elizabeth said.

"Two. What a ghastly hour."

Elizabeth felt hours stretching away to the real dawn. "How about some toast and milk? I'd like some too."

"It would be heavenly."

As she came up the stairs, Adrian came out of his room. He looked young standing there under the hall light in his flannel robe. "Is anything wrong?" he asked anxiously.

"Not a thing," she said. "Anna took a pill last night and she slept till now. I just got her a little snack. Go back to bed, Adrian."

"Nothing I can do?"

"Not a thing."

They had their milk and toast, and Anna said, "I ought to be ashamed to get you out of your warm bed. That's the penalty of being a sister—you can ask things you wouldn't of anybody else in the world, not even your husband. Adrian will worry so—oh, he's terribly sweet—no one could be more patient than Adrian—but he couldn't bear it to have me lie awake at night nor to want an ordinary thing like milk at two in the morning. A sister takes it for granted that you're still a human being, even if you can't run around any more. Oh, Liz, how I do want to keep on being a human being!"

"You needn't worry. You still are. Very much so."

"I can't bear it to have people feel I'm *sick*."

"Well, I don't believe many people do."

"Adrian does. He treats me as if I'd fall to pieces if a breeze hit me. It's wearing."

"It's just that he loves you so much."

"I know. I'm not ungrateful. I'm not—only . . . I was lying here thinking about the busybody. I think about it a lot. About seeing the world going about its ordinary business, unawares. It gives you such a feeling of—I don't know what. Of holding the whole world in the palm of your hand and looking at it. Only that's the way I like life to be around me—people going on doing ordinary things, not changing anything because I can't join in. But to see them doing it—that I do like, if you know what I mean. I'm incoherent—it must be the pill."

"No, you're very coherent," Elizabeth said. "You'll never be anything but. I know what you mean, all right. And yet—and yet when Adrian loves you so—he can't help worrying. I can see that too."

"I know."

"It makes him angry at the whole world."

Anna turned away, as if suddenly sleepy. "In the palm of my hand," she murmured. "Night, Liz."

*I*N THE MORNING Adrian said, "Anna all right?"

"Yes. Or she isn't even awake yet."

"Does she take sleeping pills often?"

"No. It's the first time. There were a lot of people here yesterday and she was tired. Don't fuss over her, Adrian. She hates it."

He frowned. "Look, Liz, don't instruct me on how to treat my wife."

"Sorry. I am sorry, Adrian. Only she does like everything to be ordinary."

He slid into his coat, still frowning. "The hell of it is, things aren't ordinary," he said.

Elizabeth went out to the kitchen where Johnny was drying dishes for Bunce. "Good egg," she said. "Don't forget we've got a date this afternoon."

She wanted to say something comforting to Bunce, but Mrs. Bunce was busying herself over the sink and did not turn.

In the doctor's old brown house Margaret McIntry came into the office and said, "Mrs. Daggett's sick. You'd better drop in there as early as you can make it."

"Daggett? She's always bragged she never took a pill or had a cold. What's the matter with her?"

"I don't know. But she's sick."

"See her?"

"No. Just my extrasensory perception. She didn't go to the post office yesterday."

"For heaven's sake!"

"No, I mean it. You must go," Margaret said.

But when he came in at noon he confessed he hadn't been to see Mrs. Daggett. "Look, Meg, be your age. I don't go call on Daggett just for the fun of it. I wouldn't have any excuse for stopping there." He dropped down at the table, reached for the coffee pot. Meg brought his lunch, sat down with him. "You can drop in on her if you want to," her father said. Then he gave her a look that was quizzical, but friendly, and said, "Say, Meg, I've been wanting to ask you, but never find the opening—are you thinking of marrying anyone?"

Margaret McIntry dropped her fork on her plate with a little clatter. A red spot appeared on either cheekbone but she gave a short laugh, more like a snort, and said, "Marrying anyone? Are you out of your mind?"

"Then you're not? Good. I didn't know who it would be, but I didn't want it on my conscience that I was keeping you here doing my housework—not that you're such a housekeeper, kid."

"I'm as good as you deserve," Margaret said tartly. "No one else would put up with you. What brought that matter to your conscience?"

"I've been prodded toward matrimony myself—with a 'what would you do if Meg married?' sort of nonsense. You needn't go into shock. I'm not convinced. Not likely to be. I didn't think you were yearning after anyone but I decided I'd better make sure." He grinned at her as if the matter were settled for all time and helped himself to sausage.

"And who put that bright idea into your head? Never mind, don't tell me. It was Anna Suydam. And whom has she picked out for you? Has she told her all your distressing habits—how careless you are and how ugly?"

He laughed, throwing back his long head. "Her sister, Liz," he confessed. "Thank God the young woman's got brains enough not to take it seriously."

"And did she pick out someone for me too?" Margaret asked sharply, so sharply that her father stopped laughing.

"Oh, you know Anna, how she likes to play with ideas," he said. "It'll stay in the idea stage, never fear. The girl's young enough to be my daughter—besides being plain as an old shoe."

"Plain? Elizabeth Burke? She's not plain at all. It's just that she gives out a different sort of light," Margaret said. "If you married, which you won't, being completely heartless, it won't be anyone like Elizabeth Burke. You wouldn't be that lucky. Nor does Anna have any notion you would." Then she grinned at him forgivingly and said, "Not completely heartless to me. You let me have my own life—I'm grateful for that. But even that—isn't even that because you don't want to be responsible for me?"

"You're making me out a very unpleasant character."

"Well, you are. But I like you all right. At least, I'm used to you. You wouldn't marry Helen of Troy, let alone Elizabeth Burke. Though you needn't consider me if you want to. And never use my welfare as an excuse for doing something you want to do anyway."

"Meg, such penetration of male vanity isn't becoming. But you don't have much of a life when it comes right down to it. You probably ought to marry, though what in time I'd do without you I don't know. But the truth is you're a born spinster."

She sat quite still and stared at him. He looked up after the silence became noticeable and said, "What's the matter? Shouldn't I have said that?"

"No," she said. "You shouldn't have said that. It's quite in character, though. I don't know why people are always saying to me, 'The doctor's so *kind.*' You needn't worry. I am not going to marry. But I am not a born spinster—and you'd better get into the office."

He got up, his face more embarrassed than it often was.

"That's not a good note to leave you on," he said, trying for laughter.

"It's good enough. Quite good enough. Go on."

"Look, Meg—"

"Go on!"

She cleared the dishes away, washed them, then got her coat. But before she had reached the door the bell rang and there were Elizabeth and Johnny on the porch.

"Oh, you were going somewhere!" Elizabeth said.

"Come in. I'll put it off a bit. I was worried about Mrs. Daggett. She didn't go by with her letter and I wondered if she was sick. But come in."

"We could wait for you," Elizabeth said. "Or I'll tell you—Mrs. Daggett asked me to come see her. Suppose I run in for a few minutes and leave Johnny here with you? How would that be? I needn't stay long."

"Sound idea," Margaret said.

"Could I do the birds?" Johnny asked.

"Sure could," Margaret said. She went to the corner and took out a big rolled chart, spread it on the floor with a book on each corner, got a box from an overflowing desk and handed it to him. In the box were little cutouts of birds and on the chart were colored pictures of the Land Birds of America. "He matches 'em," Margaret said. "Well, hurry back, Elizabeth."

Mrs. Daggett did have a good house, plain of line but big and dignified, as if worn and in need of paint. Elizabeth Burke rang the bell and there was no answer. She rapped on the door then. Still no answer. She stood there hesitating, when a woman passing called out good-naturedly, "She uses the side door!" So Elizabeth went around to the side door and rapped again. At once she heard that deep, surprisingly cultured voice call out, "Come in. Whoever you are, come in!"

Elizabeth stepped into a room that might once have been a
library. At least there were many shelves crammed with books.
But there was a couch too and a sewing machine and piles of
magazines and hundreds of other things. It was a room where
lives certainly overlapped, where one life had not crowded out
another but only attached itself to another. On the couch lay
Mrs. Daggett in her black dress, with her witchlike face drawn
and white.

"Oh. You," Mrs. Daggett boomed out. "Good. I've sprained
my ankle or broken it maybe. Thought nobody was ever going to
stop in. Yelled at the milkman but he's deaf as a post. Want to
get hold of McIntry for me? The phone's in the kitchen."

Elizabeth found her way to the kitchen, called the doctor.
He said he'd come as soon as he could. Might be half an hour.
He gave some orders about compresses, then said, "No, wait—
I'd better stop in and have a look first. Darn Meg and her crys-
tal ball anyway!"

Elizabeth went back and said, "He says I'd better not do anything till he gets here. Is it very painful?"

"Well, I've stood it for twenty-four hours. I guess I can stand
it for another. But I could swallow a cup of tea if it wouldn't
be a bother. But first would you put some milk out for the
cats?"

Elizabeth fed the cats, found tea, made toast, and brought it
in. The kitchen, she saw, was not too well supplied with food
and she remembered Anna's saying that the neighbors said the
old woman starved herself through stinginess.

"That's not much. Wouldn't you like an egg or something?"
Elizabeth asked her.

"That'll do for a start, my dear. But it's just in the nick of
time. I was hollow clear to my toes. Food's something I never
think of—but I've been thinking of it all day. Sit down. How's
your sister, spying on us all in that contraption of hers?"

Elizabeth said slowly, "She hasn't so much else to do, Mrs.
Daggett. She doesn't spy. She's just interested in everybody."

Mrs. Daggett said, "H'mph! Feel the breath of life in me again. That hit the spot." Then she gave Elizabeth a penetrating look, as if weighing her trustworthiness. "Look, girl," she said then, "will you do something for me? I'm a crooked old stick, I know, but I've always been sure on my feet. Never thought I'd do a fool thing like this, just climbing on a chair. Over on that desk you'll see two envelopes and there's stamps in a little bowl there somewhere. If you'll just bring me those two envelopes, I'll be grateful." Her sharp black eyes never left Elizabeth's face. Elizabeth walked over to the desk and there the two envelopes were. She couldn't help seeing the face of them, though she willed herself not to look. One stood out because it was addressed to a number in black angular figures and letters. Elizabeth got the stamps, brought all over to Mrs. Daggett. The old woman put one envelope inside the other, affixed the stamps. Then she said quietly, "I suppose you saw that address?"

Elizabeth said slowly, "Yes, Mrs. Daggett."

"I think you're a young woman who can keep quiet on things that are none of her business."

"I hope so."

"I hope so too. Will you bring me some paper and writing things over near by where I can get my hands on them? I think I'm going to be laid up a bit."

When Elizabeth had finally found paper and pen, Mrs. Daggett said, "Sit down. I don't think I make mistakes about folks very often. I've lived a long time and I keep my eyes open. . . . That's my grandson and he's in prison. He's been there four years, but he'll be out soon now and I want him to come to me. I don't want everybody in this town knowing where he's been. He's all right and he's going to have a chance if I can manage it. You're new in this town and you don't know what they can do to a boy. But I think I have it fixed so he'll get his chance. . . . You see, girl, I didn't do right by my boy. He married a bad woman, a very bad woman, and I quarreled with him. I

did just the wrong things and probably pushed him right into
it. We never were friends afterward. But there's this boy and I
think he's all right. He's had that woman for a mother and he
got into trouble. He took a car and had an accident and killed
a man. It sobered him up and he wrote to me. I've been trying
to make up for what I did to my boy, but of course you never
can make up. I want that boy here and I want him to get a decent start. I write to him every day and I don't want him to
miss my letters. I send them to Sarah Horne—she's an old
friend. That woman in the post office, she's as easy to get in-
formation out of as an open faucet—if you'll mail a letter for
me every day till I get on my feet again, I'll be grateful."

Elizabeth hesitated. She didn't know how she was going to
manage that. But she said, "Yes, of course I will. Thank you
for telling me."

"Know I'm taking a chance, with that sister of yours who
can't rest till she knows everything, but I made up my mind
about you the other day. . . . Is that McIntry?"

McIntry came in with his bag, grunted out a surprised
"What are you doing here?" and went at once to Mrs. Daggett. "Well, let's see what you've been doing to yourself. Left
an officeful . . . That's a nice one! How'd you do it?"

"Fell off a chair."

"We'd better get you over to the hospital. Don't think it's
broken but we'd better have an X ray."

"It's not broken. You ask Jennie Leavitt to come over here
and wait on me. I'm not going to any hospital."

"You are if I say so."

"I'll stay right here. You can tell if it's broken—what'd you
go to school for?"

"I don't think it is but I don't like to take chances, Mrs.
Daggett."

In the end he got Jennie Leavitt, fixed Mrs. Daggett up as
best he could, let her have her own way. He took Elizabeth
back to the house.

"Meg told me to stop there this morning," he said. "She hadn't
seen the old girl go by and she was worried about her. But I
didn't stop. Ought to have listened. I'm sure it's just a sprain
but she ought to have gone to the hospital . . . Only house in
town that's more cluttered than mine."

"I like clutter," Elizabeth said.

"You do? Theoretically I don't. But I live in it. Always
thinking when I get around to it I'll make me a house like the
Suydam house—a house that makes sense. Got more room—
just don't make anything of it. Never seem to have time and
Meg's not one to hanker after antiques and the like."

"You've got a good house," Elizabeth said. "It looks so
lived in."

They had reached the doctor's house now and Elizabeth
went in and collected Johnny. "No, I can't stay to supper.
They'll be expecting me," she said. "Sorry I was so long."

"They wouldn't care," Johnny said hopefully.

They wouldn't, except for Bunce, Elizabeth thought, but she
put his things on and said maybe another time they could stay.
They walked home in the winter dusk and Johnny was quite
talkative and happy. She left him at the house and walked on
down to the post office with Mrs. Daggett's letter. How she was
going to get that letter and mail it every day without telling
Anna what her errand was, she didn't know. But somehow she
must do it.

At the supper table Dr. McIntry let out a sudden guffaw.
"Sensible girl—good as a nurse. I might do worse!" he said.
"And she likes clutter."

His daughter's long face grew grim and angry. "I told you
she was too good for you. As well as being a thousand years too
young. Let her alone."

He laughed again. "Just a thought," he said.

"Well, think again. Anna ought to be ashamed of herself."

He stopped laughing. "Why so? She wants some kind of life
for her sister—what's there in that to be ashamed of? I thought

you said I didn't need to consider you in the matter—but you're acting as if I should."

"You don't need to consider me. But consider yourself— whether you want to be led to the altar by Anna Suydam. At least, do your own choosing."

"What's got into you today, Meg? Don't be so crabby. I'm not marrying anybody, but I don't want to be told I'm a fool if I mention it. You *do* sound like a spinster, and no mistake. Swallow that, my girl!"

It was the next day that Peggy Jones told Anna about the kindergarten Corinne Lemon was going to open. "I'm sending Susan," Peggy said, "and I wondered about Johnny. Not that Susie needs getting used to other children—but it would be a break for me. I'm tired of the house being bedlam every morning. It's going to be more like a nursery school, I fancy— though she trained for kindergarten work and she'll have all the equipment. She'll give 'em lunch and a nap in the afternoon. They'll have to be taken there, though—I mean, she won't do any collecting. It'll be near for Susie, but quite a walk for Johnny. Thirty a month, she'll charge. But I'd take in washings to pay for it, really I would, Anna."

Anna laughed and said, "My maternal Peggy!"

"Oh, I'm maternal enough. Or I was till I experienced Susie. Normal gregariousness I can take. The boys have their gang too—but Susie's gang encompasses all Lakeville. Will thinks it's crazy, in a town like this, to pay thirty a month for nursery school for Susie—but he just has her Sunday mornings when she's reasonably calm for Sunday school. . . . Well, I think Corinne's going to drop in on you, so I thought I'd brief you on the thing."

After Peggy had gone, Anna said, "I wonder if I ought to consider it. Adrian's had so much expense."

"I think it would be money well spent," Elizabeth said. "Good heavens, I'll take a cut to pay for it. Or let it be a present from me. I don't have anything to spend my money on and hate to be getting any, only Adrian wouldn't have it any other way. Just don't mention it to Adrian and I'll take care of it."

"Nobody could want Johnny out from underfoot," Anna said soberly. "He's never underfoot. It's going on four months now that I've been home—I don't know what to do that I haven't done, Liz. I swore I wouldn't make him come to me, but there's a limit to what you can bear. Even Christmas morning—I did think maybe with the tree here on Christmas—but he could hardly wait to get out. Look, out there now, those two little boys playing in the snow. Look at them laugh—and see their red cheeks. They aren't any bigger than Johnny—but Johnny never laughs and he's as pale as tallow. Yes, it might be a good idea to have him go. And I'll even let you pay for it for now, darling. I'll give you an IOU for it though, if you like. There's no reason Adrian can't pay for it, only right now, with all the hospital bills and everything . . ."

"I'd like to," Elizabeth said. "And without any IOU."

Elizabeth told Anna about Mrs. Daggett and Anna's eyes brightened. "Oh, dear—that may slow me up on my detective work! But I'm making headway. It isn't to her son, because he's dead. And her son's wife Daggett wouldn't wipe her feet on. Quote, that is. The vampire type she was, I hear, and years older than the son, which would make her getting on by now if still alive. Maybe Daggett writes to her, but it doesn't seem logical, does it? Unless she's making up for the quarrel with her son. That's an idea.... Bunce always has soup going, I suppose you'd better take her some."

So that day was taken care of by the soup. But Anna wouldn't send her with soup every day. Anna said to her before she went on her errand, "You might feel around a bit—make her aware that friends ought to have someone to notify in case of accident!"

"No, I don't think I could do that," Elizabeth told her.

"Oh, *I* could," Anna said. Then added, "I know—just offer to mail her letters for her!"

At Mrs. Daggett's, Elizabeth sat down by the couch. Jennie Leavitt was working noisily in the kitchen, whistling as she worked.

"You don't hear folks whistle much any more," Mrs. Daggett said. "Used to be, when men started off for work mornings, they often whistled. Old Jim Pease, he was a master whistler. 'Annie Laurie' was his favorite."

Old days came real to Elizabeth Burke, sitting there by Mrs. Daggett, days when men walked past this house, whistling "Annie Laurie." Days of long mustaches and dirt roads and singing societies and Browning clubs.

"I would have liked living then," she said. "It was simpler, wasn't it? Or do we just imagine so?"

"It wasn't simpler—it was just more hopeful," Mrs. Daggett said. "Things hadn't flattened out so. Easy to say human nature's always the same. Don't know as it's true, though. We talk too much about everything and don't feel much any more. Or do I just imagine that because I'm getting old and my feelings are getting atrophied? Seems as if people are smarter about their heads now but not so smart about their hearts. Religion's gone sour for a lot, but it's not the same thing—psychology and God the Father. Maybe it'll work out in a few hundred years."

"Maybe. I wonder. Mrs. Daggett—about the letters—Anna asked me to ask you if I could mail them."

Mrs. Daggett's black eyes sought Elizabeth's face. "Warning me, eh? Show them to her if you like. I've known Sarah Horne for fifty years. I knew I liked you, girl. You're responsible. It's not so common."

That night Elizabeth said steadily to Anna, "There's no secret really. They're just to an old friend of hers called Sarah Horne, out west somewhere. I told her I'd mail them till she was on her feet again."

"Letters every single day to an old friend?" Anna said doubtfully. "Every single day? What a friendship!"

Elizabeth took Johnny to kindergarten his first day. She took

him firmly by the hand first and led him into his mother's
room. "Well, we're off!" she said.

"So you're really going to school, Johnny!" Anna said. "How
exciting—but we'll miss you, darling. You must tell us everything that happens."

"Good-by," Johnny said.

"How about a kiss, kid?" Elizabeth said. Anna looked at her
with something close to anger but Johnny walked toward her
stiffly and Elizabeth saw Anna bend and put a light kiss on the
top of his smooth hair. "Be a good boy and learn a lot," Anna
said.

When Elizabeth saw his sharp face against the blue of
Corinne Lemon's dress, saw his passivity beside the excitement
and giggles of the other children, she suddenly regretted bringing him, and when she finally walked away from him she felt
guilty. And yet, why not? But she had thought it would be a
relief to have him out of the house, to be free for a few hours
a day from the strain of waiting for him to come into his
mother's room. She was ashamed to have felt that. And yet,
wouldn't it really be good for him? Wouldn't it be a relief for
him too? As far as smartness went, he could hold his own with
any of them. But what did smartness avail you if you were a
misfit? All education nowadays seemed to be bent toward making you one of many, not toward strengthening individuality.
You had to fit in or you were maladjusted. Was that all there
was to life—fitting in? Was she old-fashioned because it still
seemed important to her to make the self strong enough to
force the world to fit to you? Was she hanging onto something
completely outmoded? . . . There was Anna, completely ad-
justed to the world about her, and greatly loved because of it.
There was herself—not loved much by anyone because she so
jealously guarded the self. The truth is, I don't want to be loved
by the whole world, she said to herself, walking quickly home
through the snow. I *want* to keep a little apart from everyone
and I want everyone to keep a little apart from me. I don't

know as I even want Johnny to be just like every other little boy—I only want to know what's hurt him so. He's the kind that's going to be hurt all his life. But he's not a fool and will manage his own hurts. Only he's so young. Sometimes it hurts me when I see Anna being worshiped so by everyone—just jealousy. And yet I don't want to *be* Anna. And maybe that's pure arrogance. Oh, dear, I wish I could talk to Lollie.

"Did he cry?" Anna asked.

"Oh, no. Susan was climbing over tables and looking quite capable of creating bedlam for Miss Lemon. But Johnny just stood there politely waiting for someone to put him somewhere."

Anna sighed. "I hope it was right. I do hope it'll work out."

For all Johnny was so unobtrusive, the house seemed different with him gone. Bunce said at lunchtime, "I suppose that boy'll pick over his food, same as at home. You ought to have told the teacher he likes his milk first."

"He'll have to get used to it the way it is for the rest," Elizabeth said.

"Easy said, Miss Burke. Easy said. He don't get used to things like some boys."

"True. But let's try not to worry. They have to begin sometime. . . . He can read, that'll be a help, maybe."

Bunce gave a grunt. "He set right there by that table and the oatmeal box was sitting there and he said 'That's an O, Bunce,' and I said 'Sure enough—O for Oatmeal.' And he set there and looked at it a spell and he said, 'It's *shaped* like oatmeal, Bunce.' And I shoved his mug up, the one with his name on, and I said, 'And that's shaped like *Johnny!*' And after that there was no stopping him and he got all the things off my shelves and looked at the words. I never could get that *oz.* straight in his head, because it wasn't shaped right. I learned my ABCs when I was a girl—I never learned by the shape of words. Miss Burke, sounded crazy like, but it wasn't any time before he could read right off the cornstarch box."

"But that's wonderful, Bunce. No one seemed to have taught him and I didn't see where he'd learned."

"Well, I didn't *teach* him—he just sort of figured it out by shapes like I told you. And I don't know as it's so good for a boy his age to have his head filled up with reading and things like that. It ain't childlike."

"No. But all children aren't the same. At least, his head *is* filled with something!"

There were friends in that afternoon and Mrs. Suydam came down and said she would go for Johnny. "Oh, *would* you, Cornelia?" Anna said. "We're right in the middle of a rubber." Eliabeth put her cards down and said, "I think he'll be expecting me, Anna." "Oh, sit still, Liz. Cornelia'll like the walk." But Johnny never seemed very close to his grandmother and Elizabeth couldn't put her mind to the game. Johnny would want a friend waiting. It may have been a terribly long day to him. But when he came in a half-hour later, Elizabeth heard him going through the hall, with an "Oh, *Bunce!*" Anna gave a sorry little grin around and said, "He'd rather tell Bunce about his first day than me! But of course she has the cooky jar on her side!" When Cornelia came in, Elizabeth looked up anxiously and Anna said, "Well, he seems to have survived." Mrs. Suydam said, "Yes. I think it will work out very well."

At the supper table Adrian said, "Well, well—our big schoolboy! How did it go, kid?"

"All right," Johnny said. Then he lifted those large, knowing eyes and said, "Miss Lemon let me read a story to the whole class."

"She did? What do you know about that!" Adrian said. "I thought reading came in the first grade. Didn't you have any games?"

"Kind of. In a circle."

When Liz tucked him in bed, he said, "I read a story to the whole class."

"Yes, you told us. That was fun."

"They all listened to me."

Elizabeth frowned a little, then said, "Of course. You always listen when somebody reads."

"Miss Lemon skips. That's silly, a lady skipping."

"No, I don't think so. I think it might be fun. She does it to show the rest how. I don't think it's silly. Did you skip?"

"No. It's silly. I read a story to the whole class."

Elizabeth laughed, bent and kissed him. "So you did. So you did. Vanity, vanity, all is vanity."

When she went in to Anna, she said, "He's terribly proud of having read to the whole class. Does that mean a lust for power, I wonder? By the way, Bunce taught him to read. Off the oatmeal box—graduating to the cornstarch box."

Anna laughed. Then she said, "He doesn't seem the actor or the politician type, would you say?"

"No, I wouldn't. But you never know. Or maybe he's just compensating himself for having no power at home."

"No power?" Anna said, almost sharply. "I don't know what you mean by that, Liz. He's got all the power there is. He can certainly make everyone uncomfortable. No one's ever tried to hold him down."

Elizabeth remembered Adrian shutting off the account of the fair on her first night, but she didn't say anything.

"Aren't the anemones sweet?" Anna asked. "For all he's a nuisance, Huxley does have taste about flowers. I'd miss them if he suddenly turned cold to me."

Elizabeth turned and began to tidy unnecessarily, then she said, "Doesn't Adrian ever mind?"

"Heavens, no! Hux doesn't let anything interfere with business—he's a good designer and Adrian wouldn't want to lose him. He wishes he wouldn't bother me, that's all—he knows quite well I don't take him seriously."

"I don't blame him—Huxley, I mean—but it seems a waste," Elizabeth said.

"A waste? Yes, I suppose it is—but it would be a waste if

Charlotte married him, too. Or Meg. Juliet wants him to marry Meg. But you might put it down to the credit side that he's being saved from an unfortunate marriage." Her voice teased Elizabeth.

"I think it might be awfully good for him to be married to Meg," Elizabeth said. "She's not beautiful—but she'd make a wife one could depend on."

"Oh, *Liz*," Anna protested.

"I like her. I like her very much," Elizabeth protested.

"But for *Huxley*? No, Huxley deserves someone pretty special to look at, and sensitive to boot," Anna said. "And anyway, he's never given a romantic thought to Meg. Maybe to Charlotte, I don't know. She's the cuddly kind—sweet and all that, but too cuddly, wouldn't you say?"

"I'd prefer Margaret," Elizabeth said.

"Why do you call her Margaret? No one does."

"I like it. It suits her. It's her name, isn't it?"

Mrs. Suydam came into the room, and Anna said, "Where have you been all day? I've missed you! Look, Cornelia, do you remember a Sarah Horne who used to live here?"

"Of course," Mrs. Suydam said. "Her husband was the doctor here before Dr. McIntry. She moved to California."

"What was she like?"

"Like? Why, she was just Sarah Horne. They were much liked, she and the doctor."

"Were she and Mrs. Daggett great friends?"

"I don't know. They knew each other, of course. Mrs. Daggett was a good-looking woman in those days—though you might doubt it to see her now. Sarah never forgets us here in Lakeville. She sends me a card every Christmas."

"Does she really?"

"Why do you wonder about her?"

"Oh—Daggett sends her a letter every single day. Doesn't that seem odd?"

"It does, rather."

"Every single day. That intrigues me. Such a friendship— how long has she been gone?"

"A good many years now."

The next day Anna asked Bunce, "Do you remember Sarah Horne, the doctor's wife, Mrs. Bunce?"

"I should say so! The doctor saw Bunce through that operation he had and she used to come with him more'n once—she was kind, Sarah Horne was."

"Were she and Mrs. Daggett good friends?"

"Not that I ever knew of. Mrs. Daggett was kind of high and mighty in those days and Sarah Horne was friends to everybody. They wasn't anything alike."

That day when Elizabeth went to Mrs. Daggett's and got the letter, she walked slowly to the post office, having the feeling that Anna could see her going, see through the frail outer covering of the letter in her hand, knowing a kind of fear. She met the doctor in the post office and he laughed when he saw her, or rather let his face crease into a grin. "Hello, Liz," he said. "Shall we set the day now?"

She dropped the letter in the slot, feeling it still not safe, then said, "If you don't look out, you'll find it happening."

"I've been giving it thought," he said. "It doesn't seem quite so impossible as at first reading."

"That's what I mean," Elizabeth said. She was aware of the postmistress's sharp eyes looking out at them between the wickets of the little window and she said quickly, "But I'm not in the market."

She gave him a not too friendly smile, walked past him and out of the post office. She almost bumped into Juliet Olde, and Juliet said, "Oh, how nice to see you! Look, couldn't you come home with me for lunch?"

"No, I couldn't. Sorry," Elizabeth said.

"Well, when could you?"

"Friday," Elizabeth said. "I could come Friday."

"Good! I'll expect you!" Juliet smiled at her more intimately than their brief acquaintance warranted, and went on.

When Elizabeth told Anna, Anna said, "Good old Juliet. She'll try to persuade you to persuade me to leave her precious brother alone. Do go and give me a full report!"

Elizabeth saw at once what Anna had meant about Juliet Olde's house. It was correct, even elegant, but it did not look like a house in which people had fun. The table was handsome, with fine appliquéd linen mats and a centerpiece of freesia, and good silver—but you did not feel you could sit at it and laugh and gossip and be gay. You could sit up straight and eat what was put before you and that would be the end of it. And yet, she thought confusedly, Anna's house was elegant too. It must be the personality of Anna herself, nothing else, that gave the house its charm. Juliet Olde was as beautiful as Anna, as smartly dressed, but she had no warmth, she could not give out that note of the romantic, of amused laughter. But over the coffee, the coffee in the good Royal Dalton cups, Juliet lost for a moment her air of good breeding and control and said with sudden gravity and sincerity, "I asked you here because I wanted to talk with you, Miss Burke. Or could I call you Liz?"

"Of course," Elizabeth said.

"I want to talk about my brother," Juliet said. It was plain that it was painful for her to be frank and that only a real concern would have driven her to it. "You must know how he feels about your sister."

Elizabeth felt the room swim away from her but she said, "Yes, I know."

"Perhaps you'll say it's none of your business. But I happen to love my brother, Liz. I love him very much. He's the best of our family. And he's letting himself be nothing—nothing but her slave. It's wicked."

Elizabeth moved a spoon on the mat, put her hands in her lap, said, "If you want me to use my influence with my sister,

Juliet, you might as well stop. I don't have that kind of influence."

Some earnest hope in the fine dark eyes faded and Juliet Olde said, "Sorry. I've been so anxious about Hux. And it's all wrong—wrong for him and for Adrian—and for her. Why doesn't Adrian do something?"

Elizabeth said slowly, "Because he knows that it doesn't matter—not to him."

"Then that makes Hux the more a fool," Juliet said.

I am called on for something and I can do nothing, Elizabeth thought. "Does it? I don't know," she said. "I just don't know. Does really loving someone ever make you a fool?"

"The hell of it is," Juliet said, and Elizabeth knew she did not speak that way often, having too great a respect for her own dignity, "that I can see how impossible it is not to love her. She's got everything."

"Has she?" Elizabeth asked. "Everything? It doesn't seem so to me. She just makes it seem that way to others."

"Yes," Juliet said, humbled, "that was a mean thing to say. Wasn't it? Well, that's that. I don't know why I thought of this, anyway."

"I know why," Elizabeth said. "But I can't help you."

They went into the living room and talked for a little about books and such things, things removed from what was in their hearts, and presently Elizabeth said she must go. When she shook hands, firmly, as always, Juliet's hand seemed to cling to hers, though Juliet was not the clinging kind. They said no more of Huxley but there was, in spite of themselves, a bond between them.

Elizabeth found she didn't want to go back to the house, didn't want to report to Anna. It's my day off, she said defiantly to the air. She couldn't get Johnny for a walk because Johnny was still in school. She might go to meet him though it was a little early as yet. She might go to see Margaret McIntry, but she didn't feel in the mood for more of the doctor,

should he be at home. Still, he would probably be busy with
the office calls. She walked toward the old brown house and
found herself sitting with Margaret. It was queer about people—she liked Juliet Olde better than she'd thought to but she
could not be easy with her as with the doctor's homely daughter. She and Margaret didn't even have to talk to feel at ease.
It was snowing outside, gentle big flakes coming almost singly
past the window. Inside it was warm and bright and the snow
outside emphasized the warmth inside, gave them a snug,
happy feeling that flowed into their talk. And they found themselves talking of pity.

"Anna says it's a capital sin to pity people," Elizabeth said.
"And I think in a way she's right. I know I don't want to be
pitied and yet—and yet I pity myself sometimes—and I'm always feeling sorry for people. I can't bear it, thinking how people suffer, over little and big things."

"But you have to give them credit for enough strength to
bear their own sorrows, don't you?" Margaret said.

"Yes, you do. You truly do. But Anna doesn't even pity herself. That takes a lot of courage."

"It does indeed." There had come an odd note to the voice
of the long-legged, long-faced young woman in the old brown
chair across from Elizabeth.

"I worship courage, I think. Maybe because I have so little
of it," Elizabeth admitted.

"Courage takes such curious forms," Margaret said, almost as
if she weren't thinking of her companion at all. "Physical
courage—spiritual courage—they aren't the same thing at all."

Then there fell a little silence between them, while Elizabeth
thought that it had taken courage on Juliet's part to tackle her
on the matter of her own sister.

Then the doctor's daughter gave a brief, sardonic spurt of
laughter and said, "I hear Anna's started trying matchmak-
ing!"

Elizabeth laughed too, laughed more heartily than she had

expected to, and the whole silly business of the doctor became nothing.

"Have no fears," she said. "It won't come off."

"I should hope not, though I'd turn him over to someone willingly enough. But not to you. I warn you, though, he's begun to take it seriously."

Elizabeth sobered and said, "The funny part is, it could happen. I mean, Anna could make it happen. No matter whether we wanted it or not. That's what I mean about courage—I don't have much courage when it comes to Anna."

"You'd better, on this. It wouldn't work."

"I know that—but, you see, I was always the little sister— I've always done what Anna wanted me to do. Always."

"You look as if you had some spunk of your own," Margaret McIntry said. "Use it." Then her face took on a look of age, so that Elizabeth knew how she would look as a very old woman. "I lack courage, too," she said. "You see, I was engaged to Adrian once."

Elizabeth looked up with astonishment. "To Adrian?"

"Yes, to Adrian. My mother died—it didn't seem the time. There was my father to look after. Then he met Anna. But if I'd had the courage, I would have married him and let my father struggle as best he could. He would have managed. He didn't, I must admit, even know I was engaged, but I doubt if it would have mattered had he known. He is an interesting but not unselfish man—I love him, but I know him. I've never mentioned this before and I won't again. But Anna and Adrian and Johnny are not people to whom I am indifferent and it is better that I don't see them too much or even talk of them too much. He was ashamed to tell me about Anna, but he did tell me. Adrian has always had courage, and you need not pity him."

"Adrian," Elizabeth said in a whisper. "How strange. I said to Anna what a good wife you would make—for Huxley—for somebody—but I never dreamed . . . Does she know?"

"I don't know."

"Don't other people know?"

"I doubt it. We went around together—but it had just happened when mother died. No, I don't think so."

Elizabeth stood up. "I must meet Johnny," she said. Then, confused, troubled, "That's why you love Johnny so."

"Partly," Margaret said. "Let's not speak of it again. I don't know why I told you—it came to me that I must."

"I feel sad," Elizabeth said childishly.

"You needn't. It's all right."

Elizabeth walked in the snow and the sadness wouldn't go away. The wrong people, always the wrong people loving each other. So many people being hurt by love. So many, many people. And I'm tied more, she said, meaning the town felt ever closer to her, meaning that through knowledge she was bound to these people, meaning the little room across from Lollie was growing dimmer, more unattainable, meaning that she was losing the vision of herself getting away from Lakeville, being just Elizabeth Burke again, going to a daily job that might be dull but was still of her own getting, maybe spending a week or two a year with Bessie, talking over things with Lollie, making her own niche in the world, even small. But as the snow brushed her face she felt Margaret McIntry as important to her, like Bessie, felt it would be wrong to leave her alone in Lakeville. It was that damnable inclination toward pity in her. She felt responsible too soon. Juliet and Margaret McIntry in one day— it was too much. It had been a real shock, knowing of Adrian and Margaret. When she'd said Margaret was nice there had been an odd but earnest note in Adrian's voice as he said, "The best," and he had been troubled because she hadn't come to the house for the party. Yet she knew he loved Anna wholly. But there was a bond there with Meg all the same.

She saw Mrs. Suydam and Johnny coming toward her and knew she had stayed too long with Margaret. Johnny walked sedately, not clinging to his grandmother's hand. "Hello!" Elizabeth called out. "I'm late!" She turned and walked with them, on the other side of Johnny. "Anything really interesting happen in school today?" she asked.

"We cut out snowflakes," Johnny said.

"Well, *that's* interesting. I wish you'd cut some for me."

"Betty brought her dog and it can do tricks," Johnny said.

"And you didn't even sneeze? Look, look at that big flake on your sleeve! You can see the six sides, even!"

As they neared the house Johnny ran ahead of them and Elizabeth said to Mrs. Suydam, "I think school's awfully good for him, don't you?"

"Yes. Yes, I do. Miss Lemon says he has the highest IQ in the class, if that means anything any more. I don't suppose it does—you have to use your intelligence and there doesn't seem any assurance that you will."

"Oh, I think Johnny will use his. Give him time." Then, her mood of the day or some loneliness in the older woman made her say, "Mr. Cripps—he's the old man from the plant who makes ships . . ."

"I know Mr. Cripps," Mrs. Suydam said.

"Of course. He said Johnny was the spit of his uncle Alex. Is he?"

"Of Alex? How strange. Perhaps he is—I had never seen it."

"There must be something, because Mr. Cripps had never seen Johnny before and when he told Johnny he'd made a ship for him and Johnny said he couldn't have because he didn't know him—the old man said of course he knew him, he'd know him anywhere, because he was 'the spit of his uncle Alex.' I hope he'll be as talented. Margaret McIntry showed me a picture she had of his and you never forget it."

"Johnny!" Mrs. Suydam called out with an urgency Elizabeth had never heard in the controlled voice. Johnny turned on the top step. Mrs. Suydam looked up at him with a look of hunger and questioning, then said, "Nothing, dear. Change your clothes when you go in."

As they came in, Bunce was lumbering up the stairs with tea.

Elizabeth wanted to take the tray from her but somehow refrained, knowing Bunce probably waited for this one day when she had Anna to wait on. There were voices above and laughter.

But this is my day off, my day off, Elizabeth thought. "I know where Bunce has some tissue paper," she said to Johnny. "Come on out in the kitchen and cut me some snowflakes."

When Bunce came down she gave a clucking sound of disapproval and said, "Can't you find some other spot to make a mess? I've got to get the dinner going!"

At eleven Anna said softly, "You've been away years!"

"I know. It's silly," Elizabeth said. "You *would* make me have a day off."

"Well, you need it—I'm sure you must. All the same—tell me, what did Juliet have to say?"

Elizabeth hesitated, then said, "What you expected she would. But I wasn't any help to her. Love's something you can't meddle with." Then she grinned and said, "And you remember that when you're planning my life, darling."

Anna laughed. Then she said, "In a way, I like it, having Hux devoted. I suppose I'm vain. It's a nice civilized game that doesn't mean a thing."

"Not to you, maybe. It might to him."

"Well, he's unattached. It doesn't hurt anyone. If it bothered Adrian I'd send him packing—but Adrian doesn't mind."

"Are you sure?"

"Yes, quite sure," Anna said, and her voice was, indeed, sure.

$\mathcal{A}$DRIAN SAID AT BREAKFAST, "The lake's safe for skating at last. Johnny, maybe Aunt Liz could take you down to try your new skates."

"I'm afraid I didn't bring my skates," Elizabeth said.

"Anna has some around somewhere. Bunce will know. I'm not going to the plant this morning so I'll stay with Anna if you want to go. . . . Mrs. Bunce, do you know where Anna's skates are?"

"They're hanging in the closet," Mrs. Bunce said. There was an instant when hate came out in waves from Mrs. Bunce and from Adrian too, for anyone who should dare to use Anna's skates, but Elizabeth said, "How about it, Johnny? Shall we try it?"

"All right," Johnny said.

The day was cold and dry and still, a perfect day for skating. Johnny carried his double-runner skates over his shoulder in comical adult imitation of Elizabeth. There were other children on the lake and quite a few high school youngsters. Someone had swept snow off for quite a distance and the ice looked thick and smooth. Johnny sat on an old box and Elizabeth fastened on the new skates.

"Hello, there. Want any help?"

"No," Johnny said.

I do. I need help, Elizabeth thought. I don't want to see you or think about you. She looked up with a grin and said, "That was final, wasn't it? What's the matter with the boat business today? Is there a holiday?"

"Matter of fact, there is. We just finished off an order and Adrian decided to close down till Monday. Come on, Johnny. Skate with me while Aunt Liz gets her skates on."

Johnny's face set in obstinate lines, but Elizabeth said, "All right, Johnny. I'll be ready in a minute."

He was good with Johnny, taking falling down as part of the fun, praising Johnny, when praise was due, acting as if he were enjoying himself. Elizabeth's skates were on and she stood up, moved toward them, with that joyous feeling she always had on the ice. *Remember the Bartrip boys?* The words came in Anna's lovely voice, touched with nostalgia. I feel guilty—I won't let skating be spoiled, Elizabeth said to herself, knowing that it was spoiled a little already, that she would never again feel quite so much like a bird, free and able for all things again, that in spite of any resolve pity would slow her feet, slow her heart.

"All right. I'll take over," she said, took Johnny's hands. Huxley Reals skated away and his red pullover sweater made a spot of color, vanishing up the lake.

It didn't take Johnny long to learn to stand alone and presently they were moving together, Johnny's small hands firmly in Elizabeth's, and they laughed together and were almost gay.

"I can do it! I can do it!" Johnny said once.

"Of course you can do it," Elizabeth told him.

"But of course I haven't got just one thing on my skates like you have—I guess that would be harder," he admitted.

"Well, you always start on two—next year you might manage one," she told him.

Then they saw Corinne Lemon skating toward them and to

Elizabeth's surprise Johnny called out to her, "Look, Miss Lemon! I can skate!" Miss Lemon stopped and said, "Well, I should say you could! That's wonderful, Johnny!" She gave Elizabeth a look of—what was it?—respect, then said, "How about having a try with me, Johnny?" He went willingly with Corinne Lemon and Elizabeth was left standing alone there in the bright day.

"All right, Elizabeth—let's go!" Huxley Reals said.

He took her hands and they were off.

"I remembered not to say 'Aunt Liz' that time," he said.

"It doesn't matter," she said. "It's just—well, you like to be yourself, not just an aunt, sometimes."

"Naturally. I feel guilty. Do you?"

"Yes."

"You skate awfully well."

"I've skated all my life. I mustn't leave Johnny alone."

"He's having a wonderful time with Corinne. The only time I feel I could take the world by the tail and swing it is when I'm skating."

"Don't talk," she said.

He stopped talking and they swept up the lake, clear to the plant, then turned and came back to Johnny without a word. She said, "Well, Johnny, we'd better get home for lunch."

So they took their skates off and went home. Johnny even waved a good-by to Corinne Lemon, put his skates over his shoulder proudly.

"That was fun," Elizabeth said. "You did awfully well for the very first time."

"I could probably do it on skates like yours," Johnny said.

"Probably. Or probably you'd land on your head, you little boaster you!"

"Well, I think I could. I can balance the best of anybody in the world."

"Indeed!"

"Well, I can."

Adrian asked him at lunch, "How did you make out, son?"

"He thinks he's Sonja Henie already," Elizabeth said. "Don't ask him."

"I skated with Miss Lemon," Johnny said. "I didn't fall down, either."

"Good for you!"

"Aunt Liz skated with Mr. Reals and I skated with Miss Lemon."

"Oh," Adrian said.

When Elizabeth put Anna to bed for her nap, Anna said, "Did you have fun skating?"

"Yes. Johnny quite took to it."

"I thought of you all morning."

Elizabeth looked down at her ugly plaid skirt. She had looked so plain this morning in this old skirt and her gray jacket and brown scarf.

"Your swain was there," she said. "In a red sweater."

"Was he?"

She closed her eyes and Elizabeth went away. She felt sore all over, but she had promised—she had *promised* not to pity Anna. Only, how could you not? Never was anyone in the world so graceful as Anna, skating. The old red pleated skirt and the white cap—but should you stop moving? Should shame at having two good legs be so great as that?

The next morning after Mrs. Suydam had gone off to church, Elizabeth heard someone moving about downstairs. Adrian was with Anna, so it wasn't Adrian. She went down and found Bunce frosting a cake in the kitchen.

"Why, Bunce, why aren't you at church?" she asked.

Mrs. Bunce did not look up as she said, "I just thought I wouldn't go today."

"But you always go! Don't you feel well?"

"I feel all right," Bunce said.

She carried the cake to the shelf, put the big aluminum cake cover over it. There was unhappiness in the way she moved.

But she said no more and Elizabeth had to leave it at that. When she went upstairs she said to Anna, "Mrs. Bunce didn't go to church. I wonder what's the matter."

Anna said, "I wonder! Bunce is the main pillar of the Baptist church—she never misses. It's Potts. She's had a quarrel with Potts, over the cod!"

Then she told Adrian all about the romance between Potts and Ed Botsworth. About the sin of the fruit cake. They couldn't help laughing.

"I should think she'd feel proud that Miss Potts had that much appeal," Adrian said. "She doesn't seem the jealous type."

Anna sobered and said, "But Potts is all she's got, Adrian, except us. She's her friend."

"Couldn't she still be her friend, married to Ed?"

"It wouldn't be the same," Anna said.

Right after dinner, before Anna had gone to bed for her small nap, Huxley Reals appeared. When Elizabeth went to get the tray he sat in the leather chair that was Adrian's special chair, but he hadn't taken off his overcoat. Anna was telling him about Bunce and Potts.

"Pottsy? It's incredible!" he said. "She's as dry as a chip, not an ounce of romance in her."

"But it's true. They're courting!" Anna said.

Then Huxley stirred, stood up. "But I haven't come acalling," he said. "I'll do that around teatime, if I may. I came to borrow Johnny and your sister for an hour or so. For skating."

Elizabeth said quickly, "Sorry. Not me. But Johnny'd love it."

"No, I want you too," Huxley said. "You don't mind, do you, Anna? Not with Adrian home?"

"Of course not," Anna said. "It's a heavenly day for skating."

"Thanks, but I'd rather not," Elizabeth said after a brief pause.

"Nonsense! You love skating," Anna said. "Run along! Only, darling, do put on something more fetching than that plaid skirt. Hux is a fastidious young man."

"Wear anything you like," Huxley said. "Only hurry up. The sun doesn't last long these days."

She stubbornly put on the plaid skirt, because it was short and full, put on the old gray jacket, the brown scarf, got Johnny ready. This, she knew, she should not do. She didn't know why she had been allowed to do it, any more than she had been allowed to go with Hux to the roller-skating affair. But she was forced to go. When she tied Johnny's blue scarf about his throat, she found her hands were unsteady. Even Adrian, coming out into the hall, sensed that this was an odd occasion, that it needed explanation.

But he said only, "So long. Have a good time!" and went up to Anna.

In the street, Huxley Reals said, "I managed that pretty well, didn't I?"

"Amazingly well," Elizabeth said dryly.

"I thought so. It's part of a course of treatments."

"It would have been more—more efficacious had you taken Meg or—Charlotte Wayne."

"Well, one has to start somewhere," he said. "You were close at hand. The idea wasn't to make her mind, however."

"What was it, then?"

"That *is* an ugly rig you've got on. What's the matter with the red number?"

"If you take me skating, you take me as I am," Elizabeth said.

They had come to the street going down to the lake and could see the ice thronged with skaters. All the town seemed out.

"I see Miss Lemon!" Johnny said excitedly.

"Good!" Huxley said.

Huxley left his overcoat on a bench. They got their skates on, took turns skating with Johnny. At last Huxley said, "I wonder if Miss Lemon wouldn't like to take over for a few minutes. Oh, Corinne!"

He managed that amazingly well too and they went swinging up the ice toward the plant.

"Don't say, 'Don't talk!' now," he said. "Because I'm going to talk. I'm going to tell you what the idea is."

"You needn't."

"But I'm going to. Because you're responsible."

"I'm not responsible for anything to do with you," Elizabeth said. "I don't want to be."

"But you can't help yourself. And it wasn't your calling me a fool, either, if that's what you're thinking of. Maybe I am a fool, you know, but that wasn't it. I was used to that. Juliet and Meg have used that word before and it doesn't have any effect."

"Please—skip it," Elizabeth said. "I'd rather not know any of your emotional problems. I'd rather just skate."

"I don't care whether you want to know or not. I'm telling you. It was that 'And don't call me *Aunt Liz*' business. It stuck."

"I don't know what you mean."

"I think you do. I just don't want to lose my own identity—and I was close to it."

She said helplessly, "I don't know whether it's important. I used to think so but I don't know any more. Maybe it's all there is to it—we're made to give ourselves away. I just don't know any more."

"Hey! You're not helping me! I don't believe that, anyway. Or I never have. You can give away till there's nothing left to give."

"Can you? That's what I don't know. Maybe giving creates too. I don't know."

"No. That's not the way it is," he said, almost angrily. "Look here, don't start mixing me all up again. I'm not against giving —only against giving the entire self. When you said, 'Don't call me Aunt Liz,' I had the feeling that I knew something important suddenly. Not only about you, but about myself as well. You weren't just a *thing*—you were Elizabeth Burke, with something past the taking care of Johnny and Anna and all that. And I was Huxley Reals, who designs boats and writes an occasional scientific article on engines—not a doormat. I mean, I had something that was dying, something I don't want to have die. I would die for Anna, if need be. . . ."

"Physically, you mean?"

"All right, Maybe you've got something there. Maybe I didn't mean that. Maybe one kind of death's no different from another. Take this skating—when I put on skates yesterday for the first time, it seemed like a betrayal. A wicked, cruel betrayal. But I said, 'I've got to do this—if I'm to stay Huxley Reals, I've got to do this.'"

"Let's go back," Elizabeth said.

They skated halfway in silence, then Elizabeth said, "I do understand. I understand all too well. But I don't know the answers. I'm mixed up too. . . . You see, Anna is worth loving, even loving hopelessly, I should think. I love her too. It isn't only that she's beautiful—she—she's Anna."

"Yes, she's Anna."

"I keep paying rent for my room in town—so I do understand. Yet there seem times when I think that loving someone is all that matters—that it's only a silly kind of pride that makes you want to keep part of yourself away. What good does it do? What do you do with the self you save? I didn't do anything special with mine—just lived in a poor little room and went to a dull job day after day. Life wasn't half as exciting as here. It isn't that I don't think about it—I just don't know the answers."

"I see," he said quietly. "Well, Johnny, I see you don't even need help any more. That's not bad, you know, not bad at all! You're learning faster than I did."

He gave Elizabeth an odd smile that said Johnny was one of the ones who liked to be on his own, too, apart, self-sufficient. Then, after Johnny had exhibited his prowess for a few minutes more, they took off their skates and went home.

"Next Christmas, I hope I get some skates with just one run-
ner," Johnny said.

"What's your rush, kid?" Huxley said. "It's very pleasant to
have two, I should think. Very pleasant indeed."

"I think I could do it with one," Johnny said.

Huxley laughed and Johnny's serious eyes came up to meet
his questioningly. But Huxley Reals did not explain his
laughter.

Strangely, there was no one in and Adrian was reading to
Anna. Anna wasn't up, but was bolstered up in bed. She looked
tired, Elizabeth saw at once. Adrian put the book down and
said, "Let's have a drink downstairs, Hux—Anna's a bit tired
today and wants to skip tea."

So they went downstairs and had coffee and cake. And to
Elizabeth's amazement Johnny came and sat on the arm of
Huxley's chair and even ate some cake with them. Adrian and
Huxley talked of some plant business and Adrian was friendly
enough, but still Elizabeth was glad when Huxley went.

"I'm worried about Anna," Adrian said. "She hasn't been
doing anything extra, has she?"

"No. She had some of the girls in playing bridge yesterday—
today there's been nothing."

"She didn't want to get up after her nap. That's not like her.
I'll have the doctor look in tomorrow."

"Adrian?"

He looked around half impatiently.

"Adrian, I think it tired her to think of us skating. She used
to love it so. Be honest—tell me if you think it's cruel that we
do things like that. It seems cruel—yet, life does have to move
along. You can't stop everything moving."

He sat down, leaned forward with his head in his hands. He
was a good-looking man, fair and full of force, but his body
looked inexpressibly weary. "Oh, I don't know, Liz," he said
at last, looking up. "She especially wanted you to go. But that
may have been it. I don't always know what's the right, the

kind thing to do. We've just got this big government order—
it's going to mean a lot of overtime work at first. Even that
seems wrong—that I have to give time to the government, I
mean. But as you say, life does have to move along. I have to
earn a living."

"Of course."

"Only, you see, I know she feels it that I have such little
scraps of time to be with her. I ought to give more time to
Johnny. I can't."

"I think Johnny's going to be all right. School is doing him
good—making him positively cocky. Yes, he'll be all right,
Adrian. I know I worried you about him before—but I was
worried. He was so terribly remote and introspective. But he's
changing. A month ago he wouldn't have joined us for the cake
as he did today. It's only—well, Adrian, you must just tell me
if you think I'm doing anything that isn't kind. I don't always
know. She never, never says I've hurt her, but often I feel I
have."

"If she knew we were talking about her—that would hurt
her," he said.

"Yes, you're right."

She got up and went to her room. Yes, Adrian was right—
that was the kind of thing Anna would hate bitterly. Wouldn't
she hate it herself? Having two relatives or friends talking her
over for her own good? Of course she would.

Later she curled up in the chair by Anna's bed and said,
"You look so beautiful in that brown nightgown, darling. But
I don't think it's the nightgown at all, it's the way you enhance
everything you wear."

"Why, what a compliment, Lizzie!" Anna said.

"You enhance a house, too. I was thinking about that at
Juliet's on Friday. She's got a very nice house, as good as yours
really—and yet something's missing—it's you, I decided. You
put a charm on things."

Anna's eyes crinkled up in amusement. "Why, Liz, you're embarrassing me—this isn't like you!"

"I know. I'm always grudging about compliments. I don't know whether I'm afraid they'll be taken for flattery or what. When people say—and they are always saying it—'You're wonderful, Anna!' I always cringe a little. But you are wonderful, and that's the truth."

Anna looked at her almost gravely and said, "No, I'm not wonderful. But I happen to love life terribly much, Liz. Really love it. Even half a life."

"That's what I mean—you make it seem whole. That's the wonderful thing. Could you spare a piece of that toast? I'm hungry!"

So they laughed, and the moment of earnestness passed. But after Elizabeth had gone back to her room, she flushed suddenly, as if she had been seen in a silly act. *Had* that been flattery? *Had* she only been trying to make up for the fact that she had skated on the lake with Huxley Reals and loved doing it? *Had* she been apologizing for having discussed Anna with Adrian? She had thought she felt the necessity of some special kindness, some honest word of love—but was she deluding herself?

The doctor did come in next day. "This is professional," he said. "So none of your gossip, girl. Let's get you into bed and give you a look-over."

"I'm fine," Anna said. "I really am. Yesterday I was low in my mind for some reason—you'll allow me a low day now and then, won't you?"

"Into bed with you," the doctor said.

He gave her a thorough checking. She didn't say much, only once when his long hand ran down her leg in a strictly professional manner she said, "I hate my legs getting thin. I was proud of my pretty legs."

"Liz massage them?"

"Yes. But they're getting very thin."

"You're all right," the doctor said, but his eyes were troubled. "You're fine, you are. Adrian's a fuss-budget. Want to get up again?"

"I'll get up later. Sit down—are you in a rush?"

"I'm always in a rush. Thought when that young Lowe got here things would ease up a little. They don't."

But he put his bag by the door and sat down near the bed.

"Given any thoughts to matrimony?" Anna asked with teasing affection.

"Well, I'll tell you, Anna—I quizzed Meg as to her intentions but it seems she hasn't any, so I haven't any excuses."

"Then maybe I'll have to work on Meg."

He gave a little snort and said, "Meg's not one you can work on, my girl. At least, I've never been able to. No, you let us alone. We get on all right."

"It's intriguing," Anna said. "I'll bet I could work it—if you gave me time. Liz, don't look so black."

"I feel black," Elizabeth said. "I feel black as a thundercloud. But you're safe from me, Doctor. Completely safe."

The doctor gave her a quick grin and said, "You do grow on me, Liz. You do, for a fact. It's a pity you're so young."

"You don't grow on me," Elizabeth said. "Not a bit."

She was standing by the window and she said, "Betty and Jen are coming. They'll want some bridge. Would you like to cut in, Doctor?"

"Good heavens, no! Or I wouldn't mind, but I've got a dozen calls to make. Take care of my girl here. Don't let her think she's got the strength of Samson! She might find the temple falling down on her!" He patted Anna's thin hand on the cover, went away.

"Quick—help me up," Anna said. "I hate being found in bed."

So when the girls came up the stairs, Anna sat as usual in the wheel chair by the window. "Oh, Betty, you've got your hair a new way! How elegant!" she said as soon as the girls came in. "Nothing so gives you a new start on life as a new hair-do! . . . How's your doddering mama-in-law, Jen? Sit down —tell me all!"

Laughing, the girls sat down, told her all. Then they played a little bridge, had tea, went reluctantly away. But as soon as they'd gone, she said, "The doctor thinks I'm not so good, doesn't he?"

"He didn't say so."

"No, but that's what he thought. You get so you read a little extra solicitude. . . . My legs are getting thin, Liz. So long as they *looked* just the same, it was easy to pretend. It gets harder."

"Still, you will," Elizabeth said.

"Yes, I suppose I will. I have to. But don't leave me, darling. I couldn't manage without you."

"I haven't left you," Elizabeth said. "Have I? Don't be silly."

But she felt a sharp, wild sensation, as of beating wings against bars.

The next day Mrs. Daggett went past, using a stick and hobbling along, but making her own way to the post office. Anna saw her and said, "Well, your errand days are over, Liz. Such a funny old witch she is—I worry away at her mystery all the time."

"Oh, let her go, Anna. It's her business," Elizabeth said.

"I know. But I feel as if I have to know."

When Johnny came home from school that day—Mrs. Suydam was going for him every day now, and once Elizabeth had seen him clinging to her hand as they came down the street and she felt inordinately pleased about it—when he came today he rushed up the stairs with more noise than usual and called out, "Aunt Liz!"

"I'm in here," Elizabeth said and did not go to him. He came to the door and said, "I made the best clay thing of all and Miss Lemon showed it to the mothers!"

Elizabeth felt her heart pounding but she said only, "Johnny, you're getting as proud as a peacock. What did you make?"

"I made a cat. It looked just like a cat," he said.

There was something so triumphant about his voice, something abnormally triumphant. Why didn't Anna speak, give him some word of praise or even of censure for boasting? But Anna said nothing, just sat there, looking remote and still.

"Well, good for you! Bring it home and show it to us. . . . There's some cinnamon toast left—want a piece?"

He took two steps into the room, held out a hand for the toast. It was like luring a bird closer with crumbs. But then Mrs. Suydam called from down the hall, "Did you take your things off, Johnny?" and the spell was broken and he was off. They heard him scrambling up the stairs to his grandmother's rooms.

"School's really doing a lot for him," Elizabeth said, but her throat felt dry from the drama of the brief event. "He's getting bold—and he needs to be bold, even if he overdoes it for a bit."

"Life's going to be so hard for him," Anna said slowly. "So terribly hard. He never hits the happy medium."

"Well, it may be exciting for him."

"Is he bragging like that much?"

"Some. He reads to the class, and that's a big honor—or he can stand up alone on his skates, and he's pretty cocky about that—but still, it's better than not doing anything, Anna. I'd rather have that than silence."

"I suppose so. I don't like it, though. But I don't seem to have much influence over him any more."

"He'll be all right, Anna. He's waking up."

"Liz, I think I'll ask Adrian to come up and have dinner with me tonight. He'd bring his own tray."

"Fine! I'll tell him."

When she told Adrian, his face lighted up as if someone had given him a present. How terribly much he loves her! Elizabeth thought.

VIII

WHEN, THE NEXT SUNDAY, Bunce again did not go to church, Elizabeth said to her, "Bunce, what's wrong? Have you lost your religion?"

"I hope not. Maybe I have," Mrs. Bunce said.

Elizabeth sat on the high kitchen stool, though it was plain that Mrs. Bunce would have liked her to leave.

"I hope not too," she said. "One day I came down you were singing 'Jesus Loves Me' to Johnny. It sounded so beautiful. I mean, as if you meant it so. It isn't because this is my Sunday off?"

"No," Mrs. Bunce said. "I just don't feel for going."

"You mean—it's none of my business," Elizabeth said, curling an apple peeling into a letter.

Mrs. Bunce fitted the top onto an apple pie and did not answer.

But later, up in Anna's room, Elizabeth came upon Bunce, standing wiping tears from her small black eyes, a monumental figure of grief. She did not interrupt, but later Anna told her. "Poor Bunce. She *has* quarreled with Pottsy. It's a tragedy for her. I hope I talked some sense into her. I tried to incite her into planning a slap-bang wedding for Pottsy. . . . But it hurts to have friends fail you."

Elizabeth said, "How do you know? You've never had one fail you, have you, darling? You're right, I expect, though. Her whole way of life is at stake."

"I'll see they make up, somehow. I couldn't have a mournful Bunce around permanently."

In the afternoon Elizabeth took Johnny skating. Huxley Reals wasn't there, however, and when they came back they heard him talking upstairs with Anna and Adrian. Elizabeth stayed downstairs reading to Johnny till he went. As he was sliding into his overcoat in the hall he turned and saw them sitting by the hearth in the yellow chair.

"Hi!" he said.

"Why didn't you come skating with us?" Johnny asked.

"Why?" He came into the room. He looked very tall standing there by the door. "Well, I backslid, that's why. Was it good?"

"Very good," Elizabeth said.

"Let's make a date for next Saturday, shall we? Saturday afternoon? If the ice holds?"

"No. Sorry," Elizabeth said. "Johnny could."

"All right," he said. "Johnny, then. But we like you along."

"Thank you," she said stiffly.

"What are you reading?"

"*Alice in Wonderland.*"

"Oh? Never thought that was a child's book. Never was for me."

"Depends on the child," Elizabeth said.

"Very adult sort of humor. Well, I'll see you Saturday, Johnny."

As the door opened, Johnny said, "Off with his head!"

Elizabeth laughed and said, "Not Mr. Reals, Johnny. His head's on too tight."

In the middle of that week Anna had a caller, a Mrs. Tye, who was a great gossip. After she had gone, Anna looked excited and said, "Know what I've discovered? Mrs. Daggett has a grandson! That boy of hers who died—who was such a no-good man and married that awful woman—well, they had a boy. Mrs. Tye knows it for a fact. Maybe Sarah Horne knows him and keeps tabs on him for Daggett. For Daggett swore never to have anything to do with her son as long as she lived —and Daggett is a woman of her word! Do you suppose it *could be?*"

"How do I know, Anna?" But her voice seemed to her to carry a load of knowledge.

"It's something. I'll work on it. I just don't believe that Daggett writes to Sarah Horne about Lakeville news every single day of her life. It doesn't make sense. I'm going to watch for Daggett and have her in one of these days. I know the son moved west."

"Oh, let her alone!" Elizabeth said. "What does it matter?"

"It matters to me. I can't have things dangling like that. Does it seem snoopy, Liz? It's like a book, really. Only better than a book, because you're one of the characters."

"But that's the difference between books and living—you're allowed to know everything about characters in books, but you're not allowed to know everything about people."

"I am," Anna said. "I allow myself."

There was a sleet storm on Saturday and that would, Elizabeth saw, spoil the skating. But about eleven Anna, watching her busybody, saw Mrs. Daggett coming slowly down the street, using her stick still.

"Call her in, Liz!" Anna said.

Elizabeth was cutting off some faded flowers. She hesitated, then said, "No, not now, Anna."

Anna looked around at her, astonished. "Yes, right now— run!" she said. "I really do want to see her."

"Then don't quiz her," Elizabeth said.

"Silly! I like the old caterpillar!"

Elizabeth went slowly down the stairs. She hoped Mrs. Daggett had gone by and couldn't hear her if she called, but Mrs.

Daggett was just by the steps as she opened the door. "Anna says you ought to stop in and see her," she said.

Mrs. Daggett peered up at her. "Well, I could on my way back," she said.

"The stairs are pretty steep," Elizabeth said. "Maybe you ought not to be climbing them."

"I can manage," Mrs. Daggett said, and went on.

She couldn't stop it, felt the morning moving toward disaster, toward pain.

Mrs. Daggett sat in the straight rosewood chair and Anna said, "I ought not to have made you climb the stairs, with your bad foot. But I do love to visit with you, Mrs. Daggett. You give me things to think of. Last time it was about houses—I haven't forgotten anything you said. What shall we talk about today? Let's talk about old days in Lakeville, before I came here. Tell me about Prather. Was he from Lakeville?"

"Born and raised here," Mrs. Daggett said. "And a wild one, to boot. Never thought he'd make a minister—but he did. Good one, too, I'd say."

"It was nip and tuck there about the money for the chapel," Anna said. "I didn't know whether he'd hold out or not. But I hear he did—and I suppose there'll be a thousand bazaars and bridge teas and the like to raise the money. In a way, it's silly—and yet it's interesting, seeing how minds work, isn't it?"

"Went away to study music—stayed away ten or twelve years and came back here to St. Paul's an ordained clergyman."

"How exciting! I never knew that. What do you suppose happened?"

"I wouldn't know, Anna. Last person in the world to have a 'call,' I would have thought."

"That I will have to know more about," Anna said. "He always seemed stiff and very much the clergyman to me—and here he's got a past and everything."

"A past?" Mrs. Daggett said. "I wouldn't say that, any more

than any of us have pasts. I dare say you can be a good man and
a musician at the same time."

"But you said he was wild when he was a boy."

"Not wilder than many others," Mrs. Daggett said. "Don't
make stories where no stories are, Anna."

Anna spoke then very gently, "I know, I can't help it. I do
love people. But you had what they called a 'wild boy' too,
didn't you? And he turned out all right too. What's his boy
like? Is he wild too? He does have a boy, doesn't he? Someone
said so, it seems to me."

Elizabeth was standing. She hadn't been able to sit down
since Mrs. Daggett came. Now she wished she were sitting, for
her knees felt weak and she was cold all over. Then Mrs. Daggett turned and looked up at her. Her dark eyes were sharp,
yet filled with pain and reproach. Elizabeth tried to let her eyes
deny guilt, deny gossip, but she felt they denied nothing. Mrs.
Daggett acted then as if she hadn't heard Anna. She gathered
her gloves and stick and said, "Well, I'll have to get along,
Anna." She moved toward the door and Elizabeth moved to
accompany her. Mrs. Daggett said coldly, "You needn't come
down. I can find my way, thank you."

Anna's brown eyes sparkled as Elizabeth turned at the closing
of the front door. "I was right!" she said. "I was right!"

Elizabeth walked out and into her own room, sat down at
the small desk and dropped her head upon her arms, let scalding tears flow against her arm. Never, never would Mrs. Daggett
trust her again—maybe she would never trust anyone. Maybe
she would not now have her boy come here when he was re-
leased. And yet—and yet, wasn't she to blame too? Hadn't she
talked over everybody in the town with Anna, felt excited at
all the stories that unfolded through the mirror? But she
couldn't seem to stop crying. She couldn't even go to Mrs.
Daggett and tell the truth. Mrs. Daggett wouldn't believe it—
how could she?

Presently she went to the bathroom and washed her eyes, powdered her face to hide the tears, but her eyes still looked red and strained and when she went to Anna, Anna said at once, "What's the matter, Liz?"

"Nothing."

"But something is. You've been crying."

"It's nothing," Elizabeth insisted.

Anna said no more then, but later that afternoon she said, "Look, Liz, you're happy here, aren't you?"

"Happy? Happy as it's my nature to be," Elizabeth tried to say lightly.

"I'm worried about you. You were crying this morning—are you bored staying with me, darling? I suppose it does get to be a tedious chore."

"No, I'm not bored. And you're never tedious. You said you ought to be allowed a low day now and then. Can't I have one too?"

"Liz, you haven't a beau back in town, have you?"

Elizabeth laughed and said, "None that counts. You needn't worry about me. I'm all right. I was crying for my own sins— and I told you long ago that my sins were private affairs."

"You could tell them to me, couldn't you? I'm the best confessor in the world. I really think I am—I don't know why it is, but I seem to be a repository for all the troubles in Lakeville."

"Well, you won't be a repository of mine. I've never believed that open confession was good for the soul."

Anna leaned her fair head back against the chair. She looked so fragile, so beautiful, and for an instant Elizabeth wanted to kneel beside her, put her head against her and rid her heart of all its problems. There was something in her that drew confidences, made you feel she would understand everything.

"And you are happy?" Anna asked suddenly. "You don't want to leave me?"

"Of course not," Elizabeth said.

"I've got so used to you, Liz. But I don't want to be selfish.

I've even got used to that dreadful haircut of yours. You seem to *belong* here and—now I'll confess—in the beginning I was afraid you wouldn't. You used to have such bristles—but maybe I like bristles better than I used to or something—anyway, it seems as if you'd always been here and it was right."

"That's good," Elizabeth said.

Anna reached out and touched her hand, so gently, so lovingly.

"My little sister," she said.

That night Elizabeth wrote to Lollie and said that this was the last check she would be sending. Mrs. B. could rent her room any time she liked. There were some books there—would Lollie store them for her till she could get to town and take care of them? But after she had written the letter, she wept again. She was not one for crying, never had been. She had learned early that tears got you nowhere and eased nothing. Still, the tears would come. "This seems to be my place," she wrote to Lollie.

But after the letter was gone, she felt changed, a different person, committed to this life, with no ties elsewhere. The tie to her room in town had been a feeble one at best, but it had been real. It had given her a kind of strength, and now she felt lost and weak. Nothing had changed except that the frail tie to another life had been cut; yet she knew she had changed, had given up something.

In the morning she said to herself, Well, this is it. This is all there is.

Yet she knew it was much. There was Anna, there was Johnny. There were all these people whose lives she had touched. Meg and Juliet and Mr. Cripps and Mrs. Daggett—the girls who came in and out, played bridge with her, talked over their problems before her. There was Huxley Reals. And in that other life, what? Nothing really but independence. And was she not independent here? Wasn't she doing a job, for money? And did you have to have isolation to be independent?

Still, the sense of newness, of strangeness persisted. Life was not the same thing it had been before she had written that letter to Lollie. She thought suddenly of what it must have been like to Adrian when he knew there was no longer any hope that Anna would walk. It must have been like this, something you had to accept, get used to. No wonder he was irritable and sometimes rude. He had had to accept this, come to terms with a fact that was ugly and heartbreaking. No, I'm not the only one, she admitted, and found herself going down to breakfast with Adrian, found herself talking with him more gently than she had yet done.

And when Mrs. Campanini, with her great liquid eyes and soft voice, came up the stairs later, Elizabeth looked at her with new eyes. Up to now most of the people who came to this room were like people on a boat. You saw them very clearly for a moment, knew a kind of intimacy, yet knew that the intimacy would not last, that they were only characters in a play, not part of living at all. But, if she were to have life in her at all, now they were and must be a part of it. So she found herself saying to Mrs. Campanini, "How Johnny loves to watch Mr. Campanini working at the shoes! Whenever we go to town he makes me stop in front of the window."

"Yes, yes, the poor little lamb!" Mrs. Campanini said. "Poor little lonely lamb!"

"He's not so lonely now. He goes to school," Elizabeth said.

"Our Lord makes some to be lonely," Mrs. Campanini said. Then she gave her gift of pizza to Anna and said, "My Nick, he make a surprise for you! I bring it, maybe Saturday."

"Bless Nick—and bless you too," Anna said. "You are too good to me."

There was something about the little scene that stayed in Elizabeth's mind, would stay there no doubt till she was old. Except for the doctor's daughter, she had not really put out a hand to anyone in this town before. She had stayed in her place of transient nurse, talked with them all, but as an outsider. To

Mrs. Campanini she had tried for an instant to speak as to a friend, one with whom she would speak again. She hadn't said much, true, perhaps no more than at another time, but her self had gone with the words, admitting Mrs. Campanini into her world.

Yes, all that day everything seemed new, as if done for the first time, done under new management, so to speak. Even Mrs. Bunce—when it came churchtime she went downstairs and said, "Bunce, it's none of my business—but do go to church. Go and pray for us all."

"You could go and pray for yourself," Bunce said.

"I know. I've lost the knack of prayer—and that's the truth, Bunce. Life's awfully short, at best, Bunce. It *hurts* me to think of you and Potts quarreling."

"It hasn't anything to do with you," Mrs. Bunce said.

"Only it has," Elizabeth said slowly. "You—you're so special here, Bunce. I can't bear to think of you unhappy."

"Well, I don't plan to go," Mrs. Bunce said. "I don't think it's the place for me, thinking unChristian thoughts right under the pulpit, like I do."

Elizabeth stood leaning against the sink. Now she flopped the bangs off her forehead and looked at Bunce and said, "All right, Bunce. Still, pray for me. When you're making pie or anything—pray for me."

Bunce was thrown off balance by the words. Elizabeth had always had an easy way with her, but had kept her distance. Now her brusque voice had had a real appeal. She, who never entered the door of a church, had sounded as if she meant it when she asked for Bunce's intervention before the throne of God.

"Is something wrong, Miss Burke?" she asked awkwardly.

"No. Or only inside things, Bunce—like worrying about you and Potts—like not knowing how to show you love people, things like that."

The black eyes darted a puzzled look at her. Then Mrs.

Bunce walked into her bedroom without a word and in two minutes was back in her black dress, pulling her coat over it. "If you'd baste the chicken about quarter to," she said.

At noon she came walking down the street from the Baptist church beside Maisie Potts, and Anna said, "Oh, the duck! She listened to me, she really did!"

That afternoon Huxley Reals came. He nearly always dropped in for an hour on Sundays. More often than not Adrian left him alone with Anna, as if mocking Huxley by his very generosity. Sometimes others were there but that never embarrassed Huxley. Today Jen Smith was there when he came and he said to her, "Oh, Jen, you can come calling weekdays—run along and let me visit with my girl!"

"Shameless!" Jen said, making up a little face.

"Sit still, Jen—don't let him drive you away," Anna said.

But Jen got up, pulled on her camel's-hair coat, shoved hands into green angora mittens. "I have to go. I left the children to Martin and he can only take so much. 'By, darling—so long, Liz."

"So long," Elizabeth said. "But first—did you make those mittens?"

"Yes."

"Will you show me how?"

"Of course. Miss Hitchens carries wool—the best. Just get some and some needles—any time."

After she had gone, Anna said, "Good heavens, Liz—knitting? I never expected knitting of you!"

"Nor I of myself," Elizabeth said. "I just thought of it this minute. But why not?"

Yes, every contact was new and strange on that day. Even the meeting with Huxley. She had said to herself, This will end. I will go away and after a while, after a long time, it will fade out, become unimportant. But if this is my home—if I live here forever, and see him every few days—how will it be then? He sat there in Adrian's chair where Adrian himself had so little time to sit. He had on a tweed coat and brown slacks and his brown hair was a little ruffled. A collegiate costume, Elizabeth tried to say scornfully, but he did not look like a college boy. That was what hurt so, that he looked so much a man and behaved so like a boy.

"If you don't need anything, I think I'll go get Johnny while Mr. Reals is here," she said aloud.

"It's early yet," Anna said.

"A little, but he wasn't planning to stay for supper today."

But as she was going out the door, Adrian said, "Where are you off to?"

"I was going to get Johnny. He's at the doctor's."

"I'll come along," Adrian said briefly.

She was startled, but she waited and they walked down the steps and up the street together.

"Wanted to get a breath of air," he said. "And I see Hux every day and can get along without him on Sundays."

"Yes, he's omnipresent," Elizabeth said, laughing a little.

"I'd fire him—only it would be for the wrong reason and everyone in town would laugh and say I was jealous of him. Which I'm not. But I get tired of having him around."

"I know. He takes up time—and there's so little time to spare."

"Anna can't bear hurting people—but sometimes I wouldn't mind telling Hux where to get off at."

"Then why don't you?"

"One of those things. He'd think he'd got under my skin. Be bad at the plant."

"Well, he does get under your skin."

"Yes, but not the way he hopes he does. . . . Meg needn't think she has to have Johnny every Sunday."

"She likes to have him."

They came to the doctor's old house, and Adrian went in without ringing. As if he were used to that house and opened the door without thought. Sadness swept over Elizabeth at the gesture and all its implications. Then he was embarrassed at having walked in and said, "I might have rung."

Margaret was sitting at the table with Johnny and they were working on a big jigsaw puzzle. "We're used to having people walk in," she said. "How are you, Adrian?"

"I'm fine. Ready to come home, Johnny?"

"We've just got a corner to do," Johnny said.

Adrian reached over and put a piece in place, then dropped down beside Johnny and began to hunt for more pieces. Elizabeth stood there watching them, saw Margaret McIntry's hand slow down on the pieces. But finally it was done and Johnny said, "You're quite good at it, Daddy."

"Get your coat, kid. It's almost suppertime." Then he gave an odd look about the room, and Elizabeth felt she knew exactly his sensations. It was just the same, the very same cluttered, homely room as when he had come here years ago. Nothing in it had changed, not even Margaret.

"I could give you some coffee. We don't hold with tea," Margaret said.

"No, thanks. We have to get back. Don't tell me you still drink your eight cups of coffee a day!"

"Yes. All right, Johnny—I'll leave the puzzle up, shall I? Come again. How is Anna, Adrian?"

"She's fine. Well, I don't know whether she is or not. She won't say and I thought the doctor was a little disturbed about her the other day. She has a beau calling today."

"I saw him go by," Margaret said. She wore a tan blouse and a dark-brown skirt and, with her brown face, seemed all of a piece. Then she looked straight at Elizabeth and Elizabeth knew that her eyes had betrayed her. She smiled and said, "He's a nice beau, anyway. I've always liked Hux."

"He's all right. Just off his beam at the moment," Adrian said.

"You can't blame him for that, can you?"

Adrian smiled at her with a sudden warmth. "Meg, you're

an angel," he said. "Come on, Johnny. You've dawdled with those overshoes long enough."

And they were out in the street again, going home, Johnny between them.

"Have fun?" Adrian asked Johnny.

"Kind of," Johnny said.

"If you'd come out with an unqualified 'You bet!' once, I'd drop over," Adrian said. But his voice was kind enough and he held Johnny's hand in his all the way home.

Johnny went out to the kitchen and Adrian and Elizabeth went up to Anna's room. The tea things were there and Anna said, "Where have you been so long? The tea's cold."

"Doesn't matter. I'll have some cold," Adrian said, holding his cup out. "We've been calling on Meg. Doing a jigsaw puzzle with her, if you must know."

"How wildly exciting!" Anna said.

"It was fun—kind of," Adrian said. "Hux, that's my chair—how about letting me have it for half an hour? Doing jigsaws is wearing."

Huxley Reals looked at him in surprise but Adrian had risen and come toward him as if waiting for compliance and Huxley did get up, standing half a head taller than Adrian, but complying. "You only boss me weekdays," he said, "but you can have your chair."

"If you're going to be underfoot all day Sunday too, I'll boss you then as well," Adrian said. "Why don't you get yourself a girl you can keep, Hux?"

"Adrian, what are you trying to do?" Anna said. "Scare away the source supply of my roses?"

"I'm trying to pick a quarrel with Hux," Adrian said.

"You're almost succeeding," Hux said. "Have you got any girls to offer—as nice as the one I can't keep?"

Adrian's fair face reddened and he said, "Take Liz here. Take anyone. But for goodness' sake, don't take *all* my Sundays—as well as my chair!"

Anna laughed and said, "Have some cold toast, darling, and calm down. What *has* got into you? I'm ashamed of you both."

Adrian took the cold toast, looked at it with some distaste, but began to eat it and to drink his tea.

Huxley said, "I'd better be going, Anna. I do believe I'd better be going. Keep your shirt on, Adrian. I'll be seeing you tomorrow, unless you want me to resign as of now. So long, Elizabeth."

There was a silence in the room after he had left, then Adrian laughed. "I've been wanting to be mean to Hux for quite a while," he said. "I feel better."

"You certainly were mean," Anna said. "You don't really mind Huxley's coming here—you know you don't. Why all that, then?"

"I don't know. No, I don't mind in one sense. In another, I do. I don't like to see anyone making a fool of himself—Hux has too much on the ball for that kind of nonsense. And for a minute there, I did see red—not on account of you, Anna, but because I wanted my own chair."

They all began to laugh, laughed helplessly.

But afterward Anna said, "I'll miss him, all the same. And he won't come again."

"Of course he will. He can't afford to let Adrian make him angry. Too much is at stake," Elizabeth said.

"I'm second to the chair," Anna said ruefully.

"No—he's sure of you. The chair's all he's got to be mad about and he knows that. It was funny, though."

But it wasn't altogether funny. It was frightening too. It was out of character for Adrian, who was always controlled, before Anna at least. Maybe the extra work at the plant had put him on edge. Had she had a share in it, asking him why he didn't tell Huxley where to get off at? He'd been reasonable enough then, or seemed to be. Oh, life was so muddled! Margaret McIntry's hand slowing on the puzzle pieces . . . *Take Liz here. Take anyone. . . .* And where was pride—gone into hiding? That she could love a man who was chained so to another man's wife?

At night Anna said, "I ought not to confess it, but I was even a little excited to have Adrian blow off steam today."

"I know what you mean," Elizabeth said dryly. "It's always exciting to have men fight over you."

"No, not that. Though maybe it is. But Adrian doesn't do things like that—it made *him* seem different."

"Yes."

The next day when Johnny came home from school he came straight up to Anna's room, the first time he had ever done it since Elizabeth came. He walked right over to Anna's chair and held out his small clay cat that he had made in school and of which he had been so proud on Friday. "It's for you," he said.

Anna took it, but slowly, almost reluctantly. She set it down on the table before her and said, "That's very good."

It was good, for a five-year-old. It was a real cat.

"It's for you," he said again.

"Thank you," Anna said. But there was no love in the voice that knew every cadence of love. "Thank you very much, Johnny."

"You're welcome," Johnny said, too politely. Then, "Well, I'd better put on my old overalls," and he backed out of the room.

"You know, that is very good indeed," Elizabeth said. "And, you see, he thinks of you more than you realize."

"Yes, he must," Anna said, but her voice was still cold.

"It may be that he does take after his uncle Alex, who was such a good artist."

Anna did not answer. A half-hour later, when she was reading, she suddenly put her book down on the table, pushing it against the cat so that it tumbled off to the floor.

"Oh, dear! How dreadful!" Elizabeth cried and ran to pick up the cat. Its perky ears were squashed flat and its tail was off.

She began with fumbling fingers to try to squeeze it back into shape. "There, it's almost right," she said relievedly. "It would have been horrible to have something happen to Johnny's present!"

"Horrible indeed," Anna said, but her voice did not sound like Anna's voice. And then Anna said, "I think I'll have supper in bed tonight. It's been a dull day, but I seem to be terribly tired."

*S*O ELIZABETH'S NEW LIFE began, and it did seem like a new life, altogether different from the "few weeks of helping out" she had envisaged. She got red wool from Miss Hitchens and when Jen came in she began to get instructions on knitting mittens. It wasn't much, but it seemed important, a thing of her own, different from anything Anna did, and something that made her touch Jen more closely.

Adrian apologized for his outburst on Sunday and said he didn't know what had hit him all of a sudden.

On Friday Elizabeth suddenly made up her mind to go to see Mrs. Daggett, try to tell her Anna's knowledge had not come through her. She put on the red dress, made herself as pretty as she knew how, went up to Mrs. Daggett's house, went around to the side door and knocked. Mrs. Daggett's voice came clearly. "Come in!" But when Elizabeth stepped inside, her heart pounding uncomfortably, Mrs. Daggett looked at her from a chair by the kitchen stove and Elizabeth knew she could never say anything. Mrs. Daggett was done with her, convinced of betrayal in her.

"Mrs. Daggett, I wanted to tell you—" she began.

"You need tell me nothing," Mrs. Daggett said. "There is nothing to tell."

"But there is. I didn't—"

"Please go, Miss Burke."

There was such finality in her voice that Elizabeth turned to the door obediently. Then she whirled around. "You've got to listen to me, Mrs. Daggett. I didn't tell Anna. I didn't."

But those old dark eyes looked at her unmoved. It would not have surprised Elizabeth to have been bewitched to stone in that moment, or to have felt a knife through her heart. It was hate or perhaps only contempt in those eyes. She went out of the house and homeward.

In her room she tried to write a letter to Mrs. Daggett, but everything she said seemed wrong. She had to accuse Anna to free herself. And no matter what she said, she was sure Mrs. Daggett simply would not believe her. She thought of going to Anna with the whole story, but that would be a betrayal too. Only Anna would know how to fix it up. And Anna was the one who ought to fix it up. No, she couldn't tell Anna. If there were only someone she could tell. Lollie, she might, if Lollie were here. But to put it all down in a letter—that seemed a betrayal too.

She put the letter away. She would try again, she said, but she didn't think that letter would do. Some friend of Anna's was there—it sounded like Juliet's voice—and she was reading poetry to Anna. Then she heard Anna's voice. "Oh, let me read you a favorite of mine!" And Anna's voice, that memorable, expressive voice, began to read "Andrea del Sarto." Elizabeth sat quite still, moved deeply. Anna's voice made Juliet's a childish, untrained one. It pulled tears to Elizabeth's eyes and said that Anna might have been a great actress.

When it was done, there was a little silence and then Anna said, "I suppose I'm old-fashioned. But I like what Browning does to me."

Juliet said, "He'd have liked to hear you read it."

Elizabeth got up, put on her things again, and went to see

Meg McIntry. But Meg was not alone. Huxley Reals sat by the window, smoking a pipe, looking very much at home. Elizabeth tried fast to think of some brief errand, but Margaret said, "Oh, come in!" And Huxley grinned at her and said, "Yes, do come in, Aunt Liz."

So there she was with them, saying, "You do have banker's hours, don't you?"

"More or less."

"Your sister's at the house."

"Indeed! Up to no good, you may be sure. Juliet's apt to think I'm still at the spitball stage. What are you doing off duty?"

"It's my day off. I have to work hard to use it up, but it's my day off. And they weren't talking about you—they were reading poetry—Browning, if you want to know exactly."

"Juliet—Browning? I don't believe you."

"Anna was doing Browning. It was nice too. If it hadn't been my day off I'd have liked to stay and listen in."

Huxley said, "Read something to Meg and me. I feel like being soothed."

He thinks I won't. He thinks I wouldn't dare, after hearing Anna, Elizabeth thought. Then aloud, "I'm not the soothing kind of reader, but I don't mind."

It would be easier than just sitting here where she could watch him, listen to his teasing voice.

She walked over to the bookshelves, reached out almost at random, and took down *The Waste Land*. She didn't even like Eliot much, but she took the book down as if she had been meaning to read that particular poem, sat down in the window seat, and began at once to read. Why this? Why this? kept going through her mind even as she read. *Mein Irisch Kind, Wo weilest du?* She sat there with her hair hanging over her forehead, bent to the book, and outside the snow fell and the room was warm and cluttered and full of friendliness, and the moment began to be beautiful, painfully beautiful. When she came to the mountain part she almost forgot Huxley Reals and Margaret McIntry. *But there is no water.*

She finished at last, sat there, the book still open in her hands, looked out at the snow.

"I remember Alex reading that," Margaret said. "Sitting where you are. It didn't mean a thing to me but he read it very well. It was new then and the young went for it. But it was difficult, no one understood it very well. How strange it seems that now we understand it very well indeed."

Huxley Reals said nothing, just sat there, his head back against the shabby old chair.

"I know," Elizabeth said. "Is it just that we're older—or that the world knows more about waste lands now?"

"Maybe both."

Elizabeth had wanted somehow to tell Margaret about Mrs. Daggett, even if not the exact, full story, but of course she couldn't now. She put the book on the sill, said, "I have to run along now."

"Don't go," Margaret said. The spell of the poem lay still over the room, making words very quiet and important.

But Elizabeth got up, reached for her coat. Huxley slowly rose. Margaret just stood and let them go.

It was getting dusky outside and with the snow falling the world was beautiful, still.

"You're quite a girl, you know, Elizabeth," Huxley said suddenly.

"What called that forth?" But her voice wouldn't come out with lightness.

"Oh, I don't know. Or I do know, but I'm not very articulate. But you always seem to make me take stock—it's a gift, I expect. Why were you so unhappy when you came in?"

She didn't deny her unhappiness. She said, "A private matter."

"When you said, '*But there is no water,*' I shivered. Actually. You seemed to have been there."

"I have been there."

"But let's not talk, eh? All right."

They walked in silence and Elizabeth knew this late afternoon would be in her heart forever, with the snow about them closing them in, the quietness between them, the waste land of their lives too close for speech.

Then there they were at the familiar stone steps, with the green door above them.

"Would you like to come up and say hello to Anna?" she asked.

"No, thanks," he said. "Not tonight, Elizabeth."

He murmured, "Good night," and was gone.

At eleven she sat curled up in the chair by Anna's bed. "You know what," she said, "you ought to have a poetry-reading afternoon. I was listening in on 'Andrea del Sarto.' You're good, sis, really good. You almost made me weep. Why don't you do it?"

"It might be fun, at that. Only I'm selfish about poetry—I can't bear it to have people read it who don't understand it. I found myself almost snatching the book away from Juliet to-day—there wasn't any spark there—yet Juliet's smart enough. But people all like to read and they wouldn't want me to monopolize the thing."

"But they would, once they heard you. Let's really do it. I'll ask the girls, shall I? Bridge is fun, but you don't want to do that every day."

"If you'll fix it, darling."

"You ought to write poetry yourself—or something. You know a lot about people. You could do a novel."

"I've even thought of it," Anna said. "But no, Liz, I don't think I could. It takes a lot of patience. Sitting alone and just working. I don't think I could take it. And I'm a perfectionist about my books. I couldn't bear it if what I turned out wasn't really good. And why should it be? I've had no experience."

"You write awfully good letters."

"That's not the same thing."

Elizabeth looked up and saw the little cat on the very edge of the table. She reached over and moved it to safety. "Your cat almost fell off again," she said. "I'll put it on the mantel where it'll be safe." When she turned from the mantel, Anna's eyes were on the cat. Her expression was strange, but she said only, "Do you know what I heard today? That there was some question about Alex's drowning—that some thought he did it on purpose. I thought I knew Cornelia awfully well, that she trusted me—but she never told me that."

"Maybe she doesn't even know it."

"I think she does. I think that's why she's always so quiet about him. I wondered, but she has always been very open about everything with me—that seems to hurt a little."

"But if it's true, it's something she wouldn't want to talk about. Would you?"

"It depends. Not to everybody, maybe. But we're friends, or I thought we were."

"Anna . . ."

"H'm?"

"I don't think it follows—I mean, because you're friends doesn't mean you tell every single thing, not your greatest sorrow, not things like that."

"It's funny, your saying that, Liz. For if I'm any good at all, it's for that reason—people do tell their deepest sorrows to me. That seems to be the kind of friend I am to people. The secrets I've been trusted with! Sometimes it even shocks me—and yet it makes me feel warm and loved too. Even the Duchess—she told me about having a miscarriage and being frightened of motherhood and refusing to have any more children and how it drove her husband to take up with Sadie Corey. *The Duchess!* . . . And Betty's got a brother in a mental hospital and every time she gets the least bit moody she's scared out of her wits and thinks something's happening to her mind—though she's as sane as a rock. Things like that—I know a thousand of them. It's a good thing I don't have any desire to write a book!"

"But don't tell them to me, those things," Elizabeth said, troubled.

"Oh, I know you're safe, Liz. I don't gossip about them."

"How do you know I'm safe?"

"You just are, darling. And you'd better go to bed or Adrian'll come worrying!"

It was several days later that one morning Elizabeth met Mrs. Suydam coming out of Anna's room, with tears running down her face, which was always so controlled. She walked blindly past Elizabeth and toward the stairs to her own rooms.

Elizabeth went slowly into Anna's room. Anna was just sitting there, looking out the window.

"What's the matter with Mrs. Suydam?" Elizabeth asked bluntly.

"Poor darling—she's been telling me about Alex. It made her cry. I wish she'd told me before. You ought to share things like that, Liz, no matter what you say. Only, in some ways, I wish I hadn't let her. Because I see she loved Alex better than Adrian and I'll probably not be able to forget that. Only I suppose she can't help thinking of him more, because of what happened to him. She's been wonderfully generous to Adrian, to me too. She gave us this house, outright. She didn't even want to live here with us, but finally she agreed, if she could have the third floor and not be asked to join us except for meals. She really has her own life apart from us, and that takes some doing, but of course we feel responsible for her in a way."

"She'll hate having talked to you about it—she's so proud," Elizabeth said.

"She feels responsible—about Alex, because she tried to persuade him to stay in the plant and only paint part time. But of course he knew that being an artist was a full-time job. But Cornelia knew that Mr. Suydam was a sick man—she knew how much of himself he had put into the plant and she loved him. Adrian was too young to take over. . . . Well, he gave in and the next morning he was drowned."

"I wish you wouldn't tell me. I don't want to know," Elizabeth said.

"Of course you want to know, darling. It's sad, isn't it? And all these years she's been so strong and so proud and she's had this broken heart, this load of guilt to carry. It's awful—I felt so sorry for her I almost cried too. But it will be better for her to have got it said once. You'll see it will be better."

"I don't think it will be better, not if you carry it in your mind that she loved Alex best."

"Oh, I didn't mean that seriously."

"It won't be better anyway. Because now it'll be harder for her to be proud and stiff. She depends on that."

"But she oughtn't to—not with me."

Elizabeth said no more. It was later in the morning that she said suddenly, "Anna, I was wondering—wouldn't it be possible for you to use crutches?"

There was no answer. She turned and Anna's face was colorless, her eyes hurt. "No," she said at last. "No, Liz. I don't know whether I could or not. But I won't. I won't *look* like a cripple, and that's the end of it."

That night Elizabeth said, "Mrs. Suydam came down and got a tray tonight. She didn't eat with us."

"Poor Cornelia. Well, all the same, it will be better, Liz. She'll have a low day and then she'll feel better."

And the next day Mrs. Suydam did appear and was her usual, remote, polite self. But she looked older to Elizabeth, broken somewhere, not to be mended. After Adrian had taken his coffee upstairs and Johnny had left the table, Elizabeth said, "Did you see the cat Johnny made? I thought it was remarkably good, didn't you?"

"Yes, it was good."

"Wouldn't it be wonderful if he could be talented the way his uncle Alex was?"

Mrs. Suydam didn't answer at once. Then she said, "I'm not sure, Liz. I'm not at all sure it would be wonderful. Artists live a painful life, or so it seems to me."

"Yes, they do. But they have something to show for the pain. Which is more than you can say for some of us."

"Perhaps you're right. Johnny is very young yet. One doesn't know what will come."

"I know, but he does have the temperament—and that cat was something special, for five."

"Perhaps Miss Lemon helped him."

"Maybe, but I doubt it. Johnny isn't amenable to being helped. . . . Every time I go to Margaret McIntry's, I sit and look at that picture of the lake and think how wonderful it is. It doesn't seem possible that you could give the illusion of the *soul* of a lake that way. But he did. And I get to feeling so sad that he died young. And yet—and yet—how many have as much to show for a long life? Not many, Mrs. Suydam."

Mrs. Suydam was silent and Elizabeth thought, I'm doing the same thing Anna did. Exactly the same thing. Stirring up emotions she wants to hide. Only, they've been stirred up now, and it seems as if to be frank and open is the only way.

"I have a great many sketches—I suppose Johnny is too young to be interested in them yet," Mrs. Suydam said.

"I don't think so. Every time you come to reproductions of famous paintings in his encyclopedia, he looks and looks, though you can't understand what he sees in some of them. Show them to him, Mrs. Suydam. I think he will be interested."

Then Mrs. Suydam excused herself and went upstairs, but in the doorway she paused and turned, gave Elizabeth a smile such as she had not had from her before. But all she said was "Good night, Liz."

Maybe Anna was right, Elizabeth admitted. And about Bunce too, for Bunce was singing about the kitchen this week and Thursday night she went to Maisie as if they had not quarreled. Yes, Anna might be right. The purging of the heart might be very good. And perhaps she, Elizabeth, wanted to purge her own but had no one she trusted fully as a confessor. Maybe pride was only the lack of a proper confessor. But there was Mrs. Daggett. That was wrong, terribly wrong. Mrs. Daggett had not wanted her pride broken, her secret aired. But even Mrs. Daggett had told her, Elizabeth, her secret. She was the one Mrs. Daggett had chosen for her confession. So it might be that even there, the purging had been necessary and it had only been a disaster because Mrs. Daggett thought she had betrayed her confidence. Only—only wasn't it true that after such confidence the bond was a difficult one? Wasn't there always a breach in one's pride? Weren't you always more vulnerable? Mrs. Daggett had trusted her because she cared more about disappointing her grandson than betraying her own secret—she had had to trust someone and she had thought Elizabeth Burke trustworthy. Suppose Margaret McIntry felt the need of purging her heart to Anna? Suppose Anna drew her secret out of her as she so well knew how—what then? Or perhaps she knew it already. No, or she would somehow have said so. But that would only make for trouble, for sadness, for disaster. Yet Margaret had told her, Elizabeth. Because she liked her, though, because she wanted her to understand her position in regard to the Suydams, not because she wanted pity or wanted to confess. She had not wept.

I don't understand life very well, Elizabeth admitted to herself.

But when she saw Johnny go up the stairs to his grandmother, then she thought, Anna is right. She has made something good happen. And when Johnny asked her for some paper to draw on, she knew more fully that something good had come from confession.

She asked some four or five girls to come for poetry on Wednesday afternoon. Jen said, "Wonderful! I might fall asleep, though—I haven't raised my mind above the six-year level in so long!" Charlotte said, "I can't think of anything I'd like better. No one seems to read poetry any more—the times aren't right for poetry, are they? Or do you just stop after college?" And Betty said, "If someone else will read, I'd love it. Just to do nothing, to be read to, is my idea of heaven. I used to think when I first got married that we'd have long evenings of reading aloud—but do we? No. Ed goes through the *New York Times* from beginning to end and I sew awhile or else Ed says, 'Well, we might as well call up somebody for bridge!' . . . Wednesday? I'll be here!" Elizabeth said, "Shall we ask Juliet?" "Oh, yes, might as well. Then that's enough."

So they came, all of them, bringing sewing or knitting, four well-groomed young women, women with good minds and humor and charm. "That I should ever come to a 'cultural afternoon' in Lakeville!" Jen said. "What shall we read? . . . Oh, Anna, why don't you read and let us knit?"

"I'll start if you like," Anna said, "but we'll take turns. Do you like *Tristram*—Robinson's, I mean? It's terribly romantic, but it casts a mood. Let's start it and see if you like it."

And white birds flew over and the gray-eyed Isolde came alive in the room, or not in this room but in her castle on the coast of Cornwall. Needles slowed on bright wool and the faces of the young women changed, became more gentle, younger, caught into a spell with the moving voice of Anna.

"Surely it's someone's else turn," Anna said at last, putting the book down.

"Oh, no!" Charlotte said. "Go on, Anna. Unless you're tired, do go on. It wouldn't be the same if someone else read it. Don't stop."

So all that gray afternoon Anna read. It was time for tea but no one wanted to stop for tea. "We can drink tea any time," Betty said. Then she came to the last words, and they

were still there on the Cornish coast, with the white birds fly-
ing over and the heart aching for love that was so great, so
disastrous.

There fell a little silence. The room was dark except for the
light by Anna's chair. Anna's face stood out in the light and
her hands on the book, thin and graceful, were part of the
story, part of the great love. And Anna, had her eyes been gray
instead of that soft and luminous brown, might have been, indeed had been these past hours, Isolde of the gray eyes herself.

Jen took her handkerchief out of her knitting bag and
rubbed at her eyes. "To think that I'd cry over poetry at my
age!" she said. They gave a small laugh of relief to have the
spell broken.

"Good heavens, my family will be starving!" Betty said. "Do
you see what time it is?"

"I'm sorry—I hate to stop before the end," Anna said.

"Sorry! We wouldn't have let you stop. But you must be
dead tired. It was wonderful. I can hardly wait for next Wednesday! Liz, bless you for thinking of this."

They went away, and Elizabeth said, "That was really fun,
wasn't it? They all loved it."

"I think they really did. I don't know why I love that
poem—it is so *awfully* romantic—I think it's for the lines about
the white birds. They always make me want to cry. I think I'll
get to bed, Liz. That was a long session."

"Next time we will take turns," Liz said. "Nobody will want
to, but for your sake we'll have to. Or we'll have tea to give
you time to rest. But it was a perfect afternoon, really perfect.
They all thought so."

The next day Jen dropped in to pick up her knitting bag,
which she'd left behind, and said, "It's a wonder I didn't leave
my head! I was completely gone from this mundane world of
ours. When you said 'poetry,' I wasn't sure, Liz. But I haven't
felt like that since I saw Eva Le Gallienne in *The Good Hope*,

when I was a little girl and Uncle John took me to New York on a spree."

Juliet wrote Anna a little note and said, "It was so good, the reading this afternoon, Anna. You can have Hux—you can have anything you want! . . ."

Anna laughed a little and said, "Imagine that from Juliet! It must have been good!"

So, with the poetry, with the mittens, with stopping in to see Mrs. Campanini to get Anna's present, which was a pair of the softest bedroom slippers ever made, with going up the third-floor stairs and sitting on the floor to look at Alex Suydam's sketches, with these and other things Elizabeth acknowledged she was bound to Lakeville, to this life and not any other. She acknowledged it too by the hurt about Mrs. Daggett, by her worrying over Johnny's bragging, by her consciousness of Meg's love for Adrian and her own for a man who would never in a thousand years love her.

The next week they read again and she started off by reading "Scarlet Geraniums and Mignonette," and then asking Charlotte to read something by Frost. But then someone said, "Oh, Anna, you read!" And Anna read Aiken's "White Nocturne," and part of "The Land." It was not quite the sustained emotion of the first afternoon, but it was good, and the women were happy and moved, sitting there in the lovely room.

On Friday of that week Bunce called Liz to the phone. "For me?" Elizabeth said in surprise.

She went down the stairs and lifted the receiver, conscious that Mrs. Bunce was looking at her with some curiosity. It must be Margaret McIntry, she thought, or someone with a message for Anna. It was Huxley Reals, and at the sound of his voice she gripped the receiver and turned her face away from Bunce.

"Elizabeth? . . . Huxley Reals. Look, will you do something for me?"

"What is it?"

"It's your day off, isn't it?"

"Yes."

"Then about four-thirty, walk down the lake road, will you? I want to tell you something."

"No, I don't think so. Couldn't you come here?"

To her surprise he chuckled. "Now, Aunt Liz! I'm not in favor at the moment. Come, will you? This is something you ought to know."

"I'll see," she said, and hung up.

She said she wouldn't go. He just wanted a wailing post and she wouldn't be it. But she went, a few minutes late, walked down to the lake road and saw him coming at once. He is not, she told herself helplessly, the kind of man I should love. I should love someone steady and quiet, with no grace that shows on the outside. That man in the bookstore—that is the kind of man for me. It hurts to love a man like Huxley Reals, for he is from another world and it's not my world and never can be.

"Hello, Elizabeth," he said. He took her arm and turned her about and they walked a few steps in silence.

"What did you want?" she asked at last.

"I don't exactly know. But I've come on something I can't cope with. I don't know as you can—but it doesn't seem funny to me."

"Well, what is it?"

"It's Pottsy."

"Miss *Potts*?"

"Yes. I call her Pottsy. She more or less brought me up and I'm fond of her. When Anna told me about her and Ed Botsworth, it seemed funny and yet sad. Potts has never had an admirer in all these years, not that I know of. When I thought it over, it seemed very nice. Well, last night I met Ed going home from his shop for supper and I said to him, 'Ed, I hear you're courting my Pottsy. You treat her well or you'll account

to me!' Something like that I said to him. . . . Elizabeth, he
isn't courting Pottsy at all—it's Bunce. Said he'd been trying
to get her ever since his wife died. Seems he liked her 'way
back when they went to school together. Finally found out she
spent her Thursday evenings with Pottsy and he got himself invited there so he could see her. Said he hadn't made much
headway, but that's the way it was. He was embarrassed as hell,
but forthright enough too—and concerned if he'd given Pottsy
the wrong idea. . . . That's the story. What does one do?
I've even teased Pottsy about him and she blushed and sim-
·pered like a girl."

"How awful. Bunce hasn't an idea."

"I thought not. It's been on my mind all day. Could you tell
Bunce?"

"I don't think so. It's taken her weeks to make up her mind
to stick to Miss Potts, no matter what. It's been a sin to her,
quarreling with Miss Potts—a real sin, I mean. But she's con-
quered it and she went to Miss Potts' house last night as usual.
No, I don't think I could tell Bunce that, any more than you
could tell Pottsy that."

He was silent. They had come to Mr. Cripps' shack and
Huxley paused, stood looking toward the lake. "I wish we could
have some more skating but the sleet's made the ice no good,"
he said. Then, "No, I don't know how you could tell her—
maybe something like 'Why, Bunce, you sly thing! All the
time it's been you Ed's courting!' Something like that. Could
you? Probably not. It would be easier to tell her than Pottsy.
Because she's the gainer."

"She won't look at it that way."

"You know her better than I do."

"But why did you tell me?" Elizabeth asked when he didn't
move, just stood there looking out into the grayness.

"Why you? Why, it's the kind of thing you take seriously,
don't you? I have to have some help on it and you were the

only one I knew who wouldn't laugh at it. I can't help remembering how pleased Pottsy was to be teased about Ed. It's going to be a bitter blow to her."

"Yes. But it'll come sometime. I can't stop it, nor can you."

"I suppose not. Will you try to break it to Bunce?"

"I'll try. But I don't know whether I can. Or whether I should. Affairs of the heart ought to be let alone. . . . I know I called you a fool, but I'm sorry. I shouldn't have. I'm afraid to interfere, and that's the truth."

"Well, I've told you. I feel better, anyway. It's one of those things the town would roar with laughter at—but Pottsy has been good to me and I hate the thought of people laughing at her. She's knitted me socks and sweaters forever and she always had cookies for me when I was a boy—and took my part when I got into trouble, as I often did. Then she's the only person in town, I think, who could have worked for my mother all these years in peace. Mother's wonderful, but she's got a tongue like an adder sometimes and some folks are afraid of it, most folks, I dare say. She's the salt of the earth, but you have to know her to believe it. Pottsy believes it and mother can say anything to her and Pottsy just lets it slide off without taking offense. Does her job year in year out with never a complaint. I wish somehow Pottsy's pride wasn't going to take such a beating."

"But it's something between Bunce and Miss Potts. Only they can make it right. They love each other—it's a matter of whether their love can survive this."

"Yes, I understand that. Maybe we'll just have to wait and let it happen. At least, Ed understands there's been a mistake. He ought to have seen it would be in the beginning. . . . All right, we'll just wait. But I felt as if someone should know, someone who knows them."

They began to walk on.

"Juliet tells me Lakeville has taken to poetry. That's something!" he said.

"Yes, it's something," she said. They came to the corner of

Main Street, and Elizabeth said, "Don't walk home with me. . . . Thanks for telling me."

"Nonsense. Why shouldn't I walk home with you?" he said. He kept by her side till they reached the house. "You're a comfort anyway," he said then. "I don't just know why—you certainly don't help a fellow much—but you're a comfort."

He swung off into the dusk and she went slowly into the house. Bunce was singing as she prepared dinner.

X

"*A*ND WHAT HAVE YOU DONE all day?" asked Anna.

"Nothing. Really nothing much. I wrote some letters and took a walk."

"And where did you walk to?"

"Down by the lake. It was very cold."

How easy, how fatally easy it was to tell things to Anna! How simple it seemed, here in the soft light, to tell Anna all about Bunce and Pottsy, even all about her own love. How almost necessary, as if the telling were something owed to Anna for being forced to lie here and depend upon vicarious experience. Still, she sat there, the dark and shaggy one, and did not tell her sister anything at all.

"How the wind blows!" Anna said. "Remember the night dad's office at Katawa burned down? It was a night like this."

"Yes, of course I remember."

"Sometimes I think that broke his heart—he did love his newspaper, didn't he?"

"I don't think his heart was broken."

"I hope not. He died so awfully young, though. And mom was only forty-six. Are we a short-lived family, I wonder? It seems so."

"Grandpa lived to eighty-two. Don't get morbid, sis."

"Can you remember faces after people are dead? I try and try for dad's face sometimes and I can't see the color of his eyes. Isn't that queer?"

"They were brown, like yours—only sometimes they looked green. Mother's were gray, like sea water—I've just thought: Johnny's eyes are like mother's. Only they don't laugh as hers sometimes did."

"Yes, I think you're right. I always see mom in that brown suit she used to wear to the office. What she thought the well-dressed businesswoman ought to wear! She made out pretty damned well, didn't she, considering she didn't have an ounce of business sense?"

"Yes, she made out damned well," Elizabeth said. "I hope we do as well. . . . Remember how she used to tie on an apron, always bring the ends of the strings around in front, and say, 'I'd like some toasted cheese sandwiches—wouldn't you girls like some too?' Probably she just thought we wanted them. She never cared much what she ate—or whether she ate."

"I remember something she said to me once. I was dying for love of that Lucky Browne—I acted like a fool, I know, but when you're young you often do. But one night mom said, 'Anna, if life is all over for you without that puppy, Lucky Browne, why do you have to wear Aunt Lucia's housecoat to die in?' I had to laugh, and I've been laughing ever since, seems to me. Aunt Lucia's presents were either checks or something wildly unsuitable to our station in life, weren't they? That green velvet housecoat! I can see it plain as day, down to the little bands of leopard across the pockets—I can feel the luscious, swooning feeling it gave me to walk about in it. Mom knew my heart wasn't broken if I could still feel so elegant in that housecoat—and of course she was right. Yes, mom was smart."

"She was very smart."

"Once in a while you make me think of her, the way you move or something."

"Do I? I'm not like her much, though. I think I'm like dad. But I suppose we're combinations. I'd better get to bed if you're going to get any sleep tonight."

"I'd rather talk about old days than sleep any time, wouldn't you? *That* I get from dad! He would sit up till all hours talking about anything under the sun. I remember that. Mom wanted her eight hours, no matter what. . . . I wish the wind would stop blowing. It tires you out. Sleep in here tonight, will you? For some reason, I don't want to lie here alone listening to the wind. I think there are sheets on that bed and everything."

Elizabeth lay across the room from Anna, the light out. Strange, being here. No, natural enough, but frightening. As if the world was getting smaller, as if she soon would not even have the room next to Johnny's, but would be held in this room forever and ever. The wind now led around and down the chimneys and presently there was a sharp sound against the panes as of another sleet storm starting.

"Liz . . . ?"

"H'm?"

"I do remember dad's face. The way his eyes squinted up and sent out little green sparks. I remember."

"You ought to. He thought you were Helen of Troy or Joan of Arc or—no, all the Graces and the heroines made into one. He adored you."

"He did, didn't he? Bless him."

Elizabeth thought, He never adored me like that. He liked me. He depended on me. But his face never lighted up when I came into the room. The way I see him is with Anna sitting on the arm of his chair with her hair falling in that soft storybook way, and his arm around her, and his eyes so gentle, so kind. Yet, he did like me. A lot, in his way. Yes, he liked me.

"Liz . . . ?"

"H'm?"

"Oh, nothing. But we had fun, didn't we? Considering the way things were, we had an awful lot of fun."

"Yes."

The wind and sleet seemed to try to bring down the old house, though the house stood firm as it had all these two hundred years. I haven't played that game in a long time, Elizabeth thought. It was her game to bring sleep. You thought of somebody whose name began with A, brought the face clear before your mind; then someone with a B name, and so on. Nearly always it worked and you didn't even have to think of a Z. A was for Alonzo Rapp. Good heavens, how had she come to think of him, that rabbity little boy from the third grade, with his flax-white hair and his teeth that stuck out and his sly little eyes? B—well, Bill Burke, would be all right, only not fair maybe, because they had just been talking about him. His long face, long pointed nose, and his green-brown eyes that sent out sparks, as Anna said. His hair that was shaggy, like hers, and never stayed anywhere. And the way he smiled at mom when he was so sick there at the last. Stop. Don't think about him. . . . C—Charlotte Wayne, with that eager, frustrated look in her blue eyes. D for Daggett, witch eyes, witch nose, witch black, but not a witch voice. Oh, *Mrs. Daggett, Mrs. Daggett!* E for Eleazar Pratt, the trig professor in college. He fell in love with Anna and sent her books that she never read and managed to walk across the campus with her sometimes. His face did not come clear, only his slouching walk and shabby suits and a certain anxiety in his kind face. F for mom, Fanny Burke. Sitting by dad's bed, her hand on his, her cheerful little face turned to stone. Liz could not see it cheerful and twinkling, though she knew it had often been so. She saw it stone. G for Grahame, that boy who went to Tahiti. A face that hated civilization, that face she often thought of because it was such a product of civilization, so fair, so fined down, so intelligent, so poetic. Had he been caught into the war? What had happened to him? Had he found peace? H—

No, she thought. *No*, I will not think of him.

Now the game was done. The sleet beat against the panes,

against her heart. Here she was, in this room, in Anna's room. She had no room of her own in all the world. She was in this room. Anna would never let her go again. But I do not have to stay here, she said. I do not have to. I can get up this minute and go back to my own room. . . . He makes me think of Grahame—only he has come to terms with civilization, with machines, towns, all that. He manages life in a worldly way. He manages everything but his heart, and his heart has betrayed him and that shows in his eyes. Not in his mouth, which is firm and sure. In his eyes. I must not be comforted that he came to me about Bunce. That is because I am sensible. And that is why Anna wanted me. She knew I was sensible. He likes me—dad liked me too. But it was Anna who sat on the arm of his chair with her fair hair falling against his face. It still has dark streaks in it like a child's hair. You could not help loving someone with a face like Anna's, with that curly mouth, those eyes which laugh and yet know everything, that hair with the childish dark streaks. I almost told her about Bunce. I almost did. She pulls things out of you because she understands everything. *You certainly don't help a fellow much—but you're a comfort.* I must tell Anna I saw him. She will know it somehow, so I must tell her. . . . *I wish the wind would stop blowing.*

In the morning when she woke and found herself in Anna's room, saw the lovely curtains and the soft rug and the little gallery of portraits of friends over the desk, she at first thought she was ill and in a strange place. Then she remembered, got out of bed softly, and went to the bathroom. Anna was still sleeping, looking like a child, a beautiful, frail child.

Elizabeth went downstairs for breakfast. The oatmeal was cooking and the coffee making little pops in the percolator.

"You're late!" Bunce said.

"Yes, I overslept. It was such a storm last night I couldn't get to sleep."

"Mr. Suydam's gone already."

"Is it *that* late? Where's Johnny?"

"There was something going on at school. Mrs. Suydam took him."

Elizabeth thought, Now, this minute, I must tell her, prepare her. But no words came. Instead she said, "Johnny's turning into a real boy. It's wonderful, isn't it?"

"And about time," Bunce said. "It's a good thing Mrs. S. is taking an interest in him. A boy needs a grandma, and I haven't got the time to be a grandma and cook too."

"Yes, a boy needs a grandma. . . . Bunce, I don't see why you've never married again. You ought to have a home of your own instead of just waiting on us all."

Bunce gave a little snort. "I was married once. I don't know as I'd want to go through it again—not that Bunce wasn't a good man. He was."

But Elizabeth couldn't go any further. She took Anna's breakfast and went up the stairs with it.

"Wasn't it a night!" Anna said. "I had such horrible dreams."

At ten, while Anna was reading her mail, Juliet dropped in. Anna had seen her coming in the busybody and said, "There's Juliet—I hope she doesn't stop here. She looks awfully elegant for shopping, though, so she might." She did. She had been to a party the night before and she seemed to have come to tell Anna all about it. "We do miss you so at parties, Anna. They never seem the same any more," she said. Then she smiled at Liz and said, "What were you doing wandering by the lake yesterday with my brother, Liz?"

It came too suddenly. She was not prepared. She turned, but she knew she had not turned quickly enough to hide panic in her eyes and she did not know whether her voice was casual enough or not. "Oh, I was out walking and ran into him," she said. "He walked me home. But don't get romantic notions about me and your brother, Juliet."

Juliet laughed and said, "I can try, can't I?"

But Anna said never a word. Elizabeth did not know what to do with herself, with her hands. She picked up her knitting and

sat down on the stool beside Anna, where she could keep her
face away from her sister. But she never knitted in the mornings. It was out of routine and Anna would recognize that too
quickly.

"I'm new at this," she said to Juliet. "One mitten's going to
be bigger than the other, but they look beautiful to me."

"Lovely color," Juliet said.

"They're to match the red dress Anna gave me."

Anna still had not spoken, but now, with a small laugh, she
drew a letter from her morning's mail toward her and said,
"Listen to this from Marybelle—she's a girl I knew in college
who's married to an Englishman—she's always so funny. . . .
This is private, I know—but you'll never know her and she's
always like a story character, over there in England. . . . 'If I
come home suddenly, don't be surprised. Remember how we
used to sit around and read Edna Millay and those people? "It's
not love's going" etc., "but that it went in little ways"—you
wouldn't mind half so much a tragedy or a great passion but
you do mind your husband kissing the maid or hearing the bar-
maid at the King and Crown, Lulu, her name is, saying,
"Toodle-oo, Henry!" Still, so far, I can laugh and I'm awfully
used to Henry. You'd be amazed at how British I've got, reserved as all getout, all that. But all the same—oh, Anna, I wish
we could sit in the old green chairs and talk it all out.' . . .
That's pathetic, isn't it, but funny too. I don't suppose she'll
ever leave him."

"No, she probably never will," Juliet said. "It's the old story
of—how much should you compromise for peace' sake. And
maybe it doesn't really matter if he does kiss the maid."

"But if he betrays her in little things, eventually he will in
something bigger. But as she says, it's the little betrayals that
hurt—you're ashamed to quarrel over little things. But they kill
love, all the same."

"Maybe love ought to be big enough to cover a lot of little
things like that," Elizabeth said, with a certain desperation.

"Ought to be isn't is," Anna said. "I don't believe there's a woman alive who doesn't die some at betrayals like that."

"Yes, I expect we're all oversensitive—but I know what Liz means too. We are apt not to see the wood for the trees," Juliet said.

"The wood's made up of trees," Anna said. "Aren't we getting serious! What did Jen wear to the party? Did she get the black number?"

Then Mrs. Suydam came back with Johnny and presently Juliet went away. But Anna said nothing at all about Elizabeth's meeting Huxley Reals by the lake. When Elizabeth got lunch ready for Anna, she dropped a cup. It broke into many pieces.

Bunce stared at her in astonishment. "That's one of the best cups," she said.

"I know. I'm terribly sorry," Elizabeth said. "Can I replace it?"

"They're Mrs. S.'s English china—I don't expect you can get 'em here."

Elizabeth got another cup and felt that it too would slip from her hand. But she got the lunch safely upstairs at last. If only now she could bring the matter up herself, lightly, but she could not. If only she had last night said, at once, 'I met your Huxley by the lake and he walked home with me.' But she had not and now it was too late. It was not that she had walked with him, she knew, but that she had not told Anna. Only, at the time she couldn't seem to find words that would cover the meeting, without telling why the meeting had happened. But it should have been easy, and if her heart had not been involved it would have been easy.

"You forgot the salt," Anna said. "But never mind."

She went back down and got the salt.

Adrian came in at three and hadn't had lunch yet. He was working very hard these days on the government order. "Could I have a sandwich and some coffee?" he asked. "That'll be plenty."

Bunce brought him a big sandwich, made coffee. Then Adrian went up to Anna, carrying his small lunch with him.

"You look done in, darling," Anna said.

"No, I'm fine. Just hungry," Adrian said.

"Is that all they gave you? Liz, there was some pie left from last night, I know. Why don't you get Adrian a piece?"

When she came back, Anna was saying, "But I do hate the feeling of a quarrel in the air, Adrian. I do hate it. It makes everything wrong."

"There's no quarrel," Adrian said. "I told you, I apologized."

"But he feels it is a quarrel, I'm sure. Go call him up and ask him over, that's a dear."

Elizabeth said, "But Adrian's so tired, Anna. He doesn't want company," knew the words a mistake. You shouldn't protect your sister's husband.

"He said he was fine. And Hux isn't company. He's one of the fixtures of the house. I won't let him stay long—but just to get past this unpleasantness, so I can breathe again. He's a fool, if you like, darling, but I hate quarrels."

For an instant Elizabeth thought Adrian was going to refuse, but he got up and went down to the telephone.

Elizabeth said, "They say the lake is smooth after that rain this morning—would it be all right if I took Johnny skating?"

"Oh, I don't think you'd better," Anna said. "He was at that school doings this morning—and I heard him sneezing too. No, he'd better not skate today. Perhaps tomorrow."

"Then, if you're going to have company, I think I'll go write to Lollie."

"Oh, stay here, Liz. Help me talk to Hux—Adrian's such a silly. But I do hate having squabbles hanging over."

Elizabeth felt herself getting cold, her skin curiously tight all over. She was not smart enough to escape. She was going to have to meet Huxley, going to have to let Anna see the meeting, watch her face.

Then something odd happened. Adrian came back up the

stairs, but did not sit down. "He'll be over," he said. "But if you don't mind, Anna, I think I'll duck out."

"Oh, Adrian, don't be like that!"

"Like what? Look, Anna, I don't mind your coddling Hux if you want to. But he's a big boy now and I'm not going to coddle him too. You take care of his precious feelings for him—I want to get a little fresh air, anyway."

"Darling—you don't really *mind?*" Anna said. "If you were anyone else, I'd say you were jealous of poor Hux—but not you, Adrian!"

"No, I'm not jealous of poor Hux. Still, I'm going to take a walk."

And he went. That Anna was genuinely astonished Elizabeth did not doubt. Adrian had never spoken like that to Anna in all these weeks. He was always gentle with her, no matter how tired he was, always pathetically anxious to be with her, to anticipate her desires. But he had been very firm and he had gone.

"Why, how could he?" Anna said. "Now I'll have to soothe him! But he simply couldn't mind about Hux."

"He likes you to himself sometimes," Elizabeth said dully.

Then Huxley Reals was there, in the room, sitting in Adrian's chair as if he hadn't been ordered out of it, saying, "Hello, Aunt Liz!"

"Hello," Elizabeth said.

"Where's Adrian?"

"Taking a walk," Anna said, with a small chuckle. "You've been deserting us, Hux."

"No. Not so. We've got a big job at the plant and I've been busy. Besides, I thought I was getting in Adrian's hair and I'd better make myself scarce. I like my job!"

"Oh, Adrian likes to have you come. I don't know what got into him the other day—just his chair, I guess. He likes his chair to be his chair. Yet he's not exactly senile yet."

"No, I wouldn't say so," Huxley said. "But he was really sore—I've known Adrian longer than you have—and he's never been sore at me before. I was sorrier about that than I expected to be. We've always made a pretty good team."

"Just forget it—I'm sure he has. Now tell us all the news."

"There isn't much. I've been working, as I said. My social life is dwindling to the merest trickle. . . . Ah, I'll bet you've missed my posies! But you told me not to waste my money."

Anna laughed and said, "I *have* missed them—but Adrian's filled in the gaps pretty well. But tell me even the trickles!"

"Well, I looked in at Betty's party last night—didn't stay long. It was very dull, though Betty was trying hard. I bought myself a new book on engines but I'm sure that would bore you. I had dinner with the doctor and Meg and got into a great argument about marriage with the doctor . . . Why that Mona Lisa smile?"

"Nothing. I'm working on the doctor. And Juliet must be working on you! Meg is the salt of the earth—but I don't know, Hux. For you? I don't know. But that's none of my business, is it?"

"You don't marry the salt of the earth, more's the pity," Huxley said. "Meg detests me—or, rather, she knows me too well. I don't think she does detest me. But I haven't any notion of marrying Meg, so you don't need to consider whether it would be good for me or not."

"Oh, I like to sit here and spin webs," Anna said. "It's exciting. And what else have you done? You walked home with Liz here one night—I know that. Wasn't that a trickle?"

"With Liz? Oh, yes, I did meet you over town, didn't I, Liz? Shame on you for revealing our rendezvous!"

"Oh, she didn't," Anna said, laughing. "She didn't, Hux. She kept it secret as the tomb. You were *seen*!"

"Well, that's the way it goes in Lakeville," Hux said. "We'll have to be more careful next time, Liz."

Elizabeth managed to laugh, and the moment passed but left its mark on her heart. "I'll get the tea," she said, knew it was escape and looked like escape. She could not help it.

Then he was gone and she sat at the dinner table with the rest and could not eat. Adrian did not seem hungry either and it was a dull, uncomfortable meal. Adrian spent the evening with Anna. When it was bedtime, Elizabeth said, "You don't want me to sleep in here again tonight, do you?"

"Oh, no," Anna said. No more than that. Nor did she talk much when Elizabeth brought the milk. Just, "I'm awfully sleepy tonight."

*N*OTHING SEEMED to happen for a week. Nothing out of the ordinary, though the ordinary at Number Seven contained more excitement than most people's special days. Anna seemed just the same. It was only that guilt made Elizabeth feel she was being punished. It was not Anna. Anna even gave her an old orange velvet dress that Elizabeth knew she had planned to have Mrs. Suydam make into a jacket. Not orange exactly, the dress, but of that tawny shade of bronze chrysanthemums. "I don't know where I'd wear it," Elizabeth said, "but it's beautiful." "Oh, it's to enchant the doctor in!" Anna said. Elizabeth gave a little snort and Mrs. Suydam shortened the dress a little, put a few more fine pin tucks in the shoulders. . . . On Thursday Bunce went to Miss Potts' house and she had not been warned. But it didn't matter so much that week, though Elizabeth did not know this, for Ed Botsworth hadn't been there. His not coming had made some differences in the conversation of the two friends, but that was all. Huxley Reals sent a pot of daffodils and dropped in himself one night for a quarter of an hour. Elizabeth did escape that time, and afterward Anna said, "You aren't afraid of Hux, are you, darling?" "Afraid of him? No, but he comes to see you," Elizabeth said sturdily.

When Sunday came around again, Margaret McIntry called up and asked Elizabeth to supper. Anna said: "Oh, you can wear the velvet dress!"

It was, Elizabeth admitted, guilt that made her submit, put on the dress when she wanted not to. She didn't want to be told what to wear. She went to the doctor's house in the dress and Margaret said, "Why, you look beautiful!"

"Anybody could look beautiful in Anna's clothes," Elizabeth said. "She told me to enchant the doctor in this. I must say I hope he'll be out making calls or something."

"Well, he's out now, but I expect he'll be back for supper. If you weren't so dressed up, I'd ask you to come out in the kitchen while I make the salad."

Elizabeth laughed and went to the kitchen with Margaret, perched on a high stool.

"What's been happening?" Margaret asked, her hands busy over the salad bowl.

"Happening? Not much. Or not that shows on the outside," Elizabeth said.

"It's a good thing the inside doesn't show," Margaret said.

Elizabeth looked up at the long, plain face and thought, She has great dignity—great courage. How I like her! Aloud she said, "A very good thing."

"Elizabeth . . ."

"H'm?"

Margaret put her knife down, stood there, not doing anything for an instant, then said seriously, "In a moment of weakness I told you how things were with me. I want to ask something of you—don't let Adrian come here again."

"Again?"

"You didn't know he'd been here? Well, that's good. Or maybe not. He was here last Sunday and again Friday night. Why is he so tired, Elizabeth?"

"He has this extra work at the plant . . . but it isn't only that. He—he's been through so much this year."

"I know. But he has always been enormously strong. He came in like a man walking in his sleep and sat down in the other room and said, 'Don't talk, Meg, I just want to rest a minute.' And he didn't talk. He just sat there and rested. But, you see . . ."

"I see. No one could take that."

Margaret picked up the knife, went on with her task, then said, "Friday he came in, not knocking or anything, and said, 'Play to me, Meg.' I used to play the old songs for singing— I'm no musician. So I went to the piano and played and pretty soon he got up and went out without saying a word. But he must not come. I'm human, I can't have it."

"I don't know how I can stop it. Adrian is not one you can order around."

"It is too easy to comfort Adrian. I know how," Margaret said. "But why does he need comfort?"

"He doesn't have so much of Anna any more."

Margaret's forehead had a straight up-and-down line in it as she said, "But Anna could make him believe he had—if she wanted to. That's the kind of thing Anna can do better than anyone else in the world. He worships Anna."

"Yes, he does. I know what you mean. It's what I wonder about Johnny. Why doesn't she charm Johnny? Because she could, you know. And Johnny doesn't even go into her room if he can help it. But I think she does manage to make everything right with Adrian most of the time. He was angry at having Huxley underfoot last Sunday."

"But he's never minded Hux, not really minded him. He knows that's all a game, so far as Anna is concerned at least."

"Yes, he knows that."

Margaret gave a sorry laugh and said, "I'm just protecting myself, that's all."

Elizabeth understood her so well that she said nothing at all. She could see Adrian sitting in the old brown chair, his fair head resting against the cushions, exhausted, wanting a mo-

ment's peace and finding it, and Margaret seeing him finding it
and being tempted, tempted to comfort him for all his weariness, all his unhappiness, tempted to take what of him she could
have, even yet. Margaret had no charm, knew she had none,
but she had strength and she had love, and she knew that too
and knew she could give it to Adrian Suydam if she wanted to.

In that moment Elizabeth could have told Margaret everything about herself, about Bunce, about Daggett, about Huxley. But she did not. She just sat there on the stool and
watched Margaret and felt that they knew all about each other
without telling. Then the doctor came in and gave Elizabeth a
grin from the doorway. "My intended!" he said. "You look very
nice too."

They sat at the table and talked and laughed and the doctor
was amusing and caustic and worked up a discussion on politics
in which they all joined heatedly. It was fun, in its way. Or it
was till Elizabeth said, "But you sound as if politics was all expediency. It doesn't have to be, does it?"

"Yes, it has to be. It's the nature of politics. And don't go
idealistic on me, Liz—you're looking very pretty tonight and
you mustn't be too earnest."

"Now and then—now and then you hear a voice, in the po-
litical world, I mean—that rings out, that has something in it
beyond expediency," she insisted. "Once in a great while
you do."

"You can't name ten times in the history of the world," he
said.

She hesitated. "I could if my mind worked faster," she said.

"Name one."

"Stop pushing her around," Margaret said. "Have some more
coffee?"

When it came time to go home the doctor said, "Oh, well, I
suppose I have to see you home, Liz."

"Nothing of the kind," Elizabeth said. "In fact, I'd rather
walk alone, if you don't mind."

"How can I court you here under Meg's eye?"

"I'm not in the courting mood. No, I mean it—I'd rather go alone."

But the doctor came out with her and walked down the street by her side.

"No fooling, you're a nice girl, Liz," the doctor said suddenly. "You do take a pretty moralistic tone sometimes, but you're a nice girl. I could do worse."

"Don't be silly, Dr. McIntry!"

"Of course you are pretty young." His voice teased her, mocked her a little, made her uncomfortable.

"That wouldn't matter if I were interested," Elizabeth said. "But I just don't happen to be. Nor are you, so stop it, please. It's the kind of joke that doesn't amuse me."

"I'm not joking," the doctor said more seriously. "I'm not joking, Liz."

Incredibly, she heard the words. They were honest, faintly ashamed of honesty.

"Well, you'd better be," she said confusedly. "Because I don't like you very much, Dr. McIntry. I'm not joking about that either." They had come to the house already. "Good night," she said hurriedly and left him.

Had she known it, she could have said nothing more calculated to stiffen the doctor's desire. Everybody liked Dr. McIntry.

On Tuesday night when she brought Anna's milk, Anna was wide awake and wanted to talk. "Oh, darling," she said, "I feel so excited! The doctor says he's courting you! Liz, you must take him—I really mean it. It would be perfect. I knew he'd take it seriously once he'd thought about it a bit!"

"That's nonsense, and you know it," Elizabeth said. "I don't want the doctor, and he doesn't want me either. You're trying to spin webs again—don't do it, Anna. Not around us, anyway."

"But why not? I do think it would be lovely. You could be married here—I'd see that you had a very special wedding."

"Please, Anna. I just don't want the doctor. And it isn't because he's too old for me. He's just not someone I could ever care about."

"I don't see why not. He's very lovable. Homely in a nice way. At least it seems nice on him—it's unfortunate it isn't so nice on Meg. I'm not fooling, Liz. I'd love it. Not having you leave me, but then you wouldn't be far away. I want you to be really bound to Lakeville—because I'm selfish, I suppose."

"I don't need the doctor to bind me," Elizabeth said. "I like Lakeville all right."

"But there isn't anybody else, is there?" Anna demanded. "*Is* there, darling?"

"If there were, I wouldn't tell you," Elizabeth said.

"Wouldn't *tell* me! Oh, Liz! Then there *is!*"

The room was in shadow, except for the little circle of light from the bedside lamp. Elizabeth was grateful for the shadows, but had the feeling that Anna could see right through them, that she was terribly exposed, completely unprotected. Suppose right now she should tell Anna the truth, the whole truth? She felt tempted to do so. Suppose she told Anna that Adrian was going to see Margaret because he couldn't rest any more in his own house, because he was missing something that only Anna had the power to give him? Suppose she told her that even if she loved Dr. McIntry, there was something so proud and stubborn in her that she couldn't allow him to be given to her by Anna? The silence grew and was dark and frightening, even though the tightness on herself seemed to be growing also.

"Liz—" Anna's voice was warm like love, like silk. "Liz, you do love somebody else. I *am* selfish—I've never known it or even suspected it. Tell me, darling. Doesn't he love you too?"

"Anna . . . look, Anna, I know I'm your little sister. I know that. But I'm a grown woman now. And so are you. I don't ask you about the state of your heart, do I? And you wouldn't tell me, if I did. So why should I tell you?"

"But you know the state of my heart, Liz. You know I'm married and that I like being married to Adrian. I surely show that, don't I? Aren't you my friend too, as well as my little sister? Don't be secretive—I have all I can take of that from Johnny."

"I'm not secretive. It's just—it's just that I can't talk about some things. I can't, Anna, so don't tease me to."

"Earnest Liz!" But her voice was loving. "All right—only, you see, I'll know somehow, kid. I can turn the busybody on anybody's heart—I really can, you know."

"Yes, I know."

"When you have to take your living vicariously, it takes so little for excitement," Anna said slowly. "I won't quiz you any more, darling, but I'll wonder all the same. I'm wondering right now what kind of man you'd love—some lame duck, as I prophesied once before, I'll wager. And I'm wondering why he doesn't love you—you said he didn't, by silence, Liz, you really did. If you'd let me work on it, I'd soon see he loved you! I can work magic that way—look at the doctor! I said he'd take you seriously, and he has, hasn't he?"

Elizabeth's heart turned over with pity, but she got to her feet somehow, picked up the little tray.

"I think I'll go to bed," she said. "Or somewhere where you can't read my open face. Don't lose any sleep wondering, sis!"

A small trail of soft laughter followed her out the door.

But the next day, though Anna's eyes upon her were sometimes quizzical, there was no more talk of Elizabeth's secret love. That didn't mean, Elizabeth knew, that it was forgotten—only put away till a more convenient time.

It was Wednesday, toward noon, that Anna said, "There's a car in front of the house. I wonder who that little dumpling is? Nobody I know."

Elizabeth went to the window and felt a wave of sudden relief and happiness.

"Why, it's Lollie!" she said, ran out and down the stairs, where Mrs. Bunce was already opening the door. She threw her arms about Lollie, though they were not two who went in for physical endearments. "Oh, Lollie! *Lollie!*" she cried.

"Well, well," Lollie said.

"But why aren't you in school?"

"Had a little virus shindig, took three weeks off. In the pink now, though. Just hope the school board doesn't find out I'm off jaunting. Such a nice day I made up my mind to come see you. How are you?"

"Fine. Just fine. Oh, it's *wonderful* to see you, Lollie. Come up and meet my sister. You never wrote you'd been sick."

"Not important. What an elegant house. You're sitting in the lap of luxury, my girl."

"Yes, I am."

They went up the stairs together, into Anna's room.

"This is my friend Lollie Parsons, Anna—Lollie, Anna."

"Hello," Lollie said. "So this is the fabulous Anna? Glad to know you in the flesh!"

Anna smiled, and when Anna smiled winningly it was something one never forgot. "You're the teacher, aren't you?" Anna said. "How nice of you to come! Liz, you must take the day off. I make a slave out of her, Lollie—but I'll give a dispensation. Tell Cornelia, Liz—and then go on a bat with your friend. . . . Oh, but this is the poetry afternoon! Come back for that, can't you? It's fun, Lollie, and we'd like to have you here."

Elizabeth was trembling, she didn't know why. Yet all was going well. Had she been afraid Anna would make fun of the roly-poly little Lollie Parsons? Been afraid that she would not remember who Lollie was, would say, as Juliet had said, "But I never knew you had a friend Lollie"? No, she was being hospitable and kind. All was well.

"Would you mind?" she said. "We'll go to the inn and have lunch and then come back for the poetry."

"Run along," Anna said. "I'll be fine!"

So Elizabeth called Mrs. Suydam and she and Lollie went out and down the street to the old inn. Elizabeth had never been in it, but it had always looked pleasant. They found a table in a corner, sat across from each other, and smiled with sudden warmth.

"Lollie, how beautiful you look to me!" Elizabeth said. "I was never so glad to see anybody in my life."

Lollie said soberly, "You're too glad. What's the matter with you, Elizabeth?"

"Nothing. It's just that you're real."

Lollie's round face went rounder yet with her grin. "You know, I'm an authority on the psychopathic," she said. "I see what you mean about your sister. Good heavens, what charm! A word I distrust, but she's got it."

"She has indeed!"

"The Blessed Damozel . . . but, look here, what *is* the matter with you? I've been worried. Between the lines I seem to read something pretty devastating. I thought I warned you not to stay here."

"Yes. You didn't need to warn me. I warned myself. But here I am, Lollie. And here I'll be till kingdom come, so far as I can see."

"Nonsense! If you weren't here, they'd get somebody else, wouldn't they?"

"I suppose so."

"Then let them."

"It isn't so easy as that. But tell me about you—and who's got my room—about your children—everything."

"Nothing changes with me, Elizabeth. But I'm not one for change—I don't mind. I like my life all right. . . . No, skip me. Tell me what's the matter. That's what I came for."

The round, sensible face across the table had a light on it. Elizabeth laughed and said, "Funny, but nothing seems wrong, now I can see you. I can cope with anything now."

Lollie said, "I'm not snoopy by nature. Now, am I? Still, I want to know. I want to know what you haven't been able to cope with. Is it Johnny? Is it that blasted independence of yours? Not that I'm not for independence. You know I am. But what in particular binds you here? Just your sister's charm?"

"I don't know," Elizabeth said. "Maybe it's just pity. I've always loved her so terribly much. And she is so courageous, you feel there is nothing you couldn't or shouldn't do."

"But she does make a slave of you?"

"No, of course not. She is easy to take care of. No, I don't work too hard. It's just my mind that won't come straight, that goes around in circles and makes me desperate."

"Desperate. That's a word that rings true. But it's a strong one. Why desperate?"

"There's Daggett," Elizabeth said helplessly. And then she was telling her about Mrs. Daggett, about the hopelessness of making Mrs. Daggett believe in her. Just a funny old witch of a woman, but important in some queer way. And Margaret McIntry, who had been engaged to Adrian—and was afraid to let him come to her house. And Juliet and Bunce and Johnny and the doctor—all of it came out. But in a shamed, not too coherent way.

Lollie just sat there, letting her lunch get cold, and listened, nodding now and then in a serious way. "I see," she said at last. "I see."

"Do you?"

"Yes . . . and this Huxley, I see that too. You love him, don't you? I hope he's worth it."

"He's worth it, but he'll never see me. He saw Anna first."

Lollie picked up her hard roll, took a bite with her strong white teeth, then said, "I was picturing your sister as a kind of Circe. I see it's more complicated than that. You've got to liking the town and the people. And you're in love, which is a fatal condition. I was going to beg you to come back. But I won't. For I can see you wouldn't come. I was going right back after lunch but I think I'll come to this poetry reading."

"Lollie, I don't know what to do."

"Well, I'm not going to advise you. You see the spot you're in. If you see, that's all anybody can ask."

"There's such an awful gulf between seeing and doing."

"True," Lollie said, with wrinkles at the corners of her eyes. "But you'll work it out."

On the way back to the house, Elizabeth gave a rueful laugh. "Anna's always telling me confession is good for the soul—and I'm always contradicting her," she said. "But I guess she's right. I feel a lot better."

Lollie was silent an instant, then she said, "Well, there's a limit on how alone you can be."

"But I'm not alone . . . I mean . . ."

"I know what you mean," Lollie said briskly. "And I don't take it back."

When they reached Anna's room the girls were all there. Elizabeth introduced Lollie all around, then Anna said, "Find a place to sit, Lollie—and why don't we have a new voice for this afternoon? Lollie, why don't you read to us for a while?"

Anger shivered through Elizabeth, then laughter like a giant's laughter. For Lollie could read poetry, not with that romantic note in her voice, but with the greatest meaning and power. It was the poetry in her that made her such a teacher, such a friend, even if no one looking at her would dream it was there. Anna was not being kind, but Anna was going to see a miracle happen, see that genius could be enclosed in a roly-poly nice little body, see magic made. She could see the politeness in the girls' eyes, the faint disappointment, and the laughter in her rose above the anger till she seemed made of laughter.

But Lollie said, "Thank you, but I think I must be getting back. I came to see Elizabeth and now I've seen her. . . . Nice to have seen all of you." And with a pleasant smile she was nodding, going out of the room and down the stairs, with Elizabeth behind her. She went out to her small car and Elizabeth stood there on the sidewalk, silent, cheated of triumph.

"Why didn't you read?" she demanded, with more of meaning in the question than seemed possible.

Lollie said, and her eyes twinkled understanding, "It didn't seem important. . . . None of them was Margaret?"

Elizabeth shook her head.

"I'd have liked to see her. . . . Now, now—you're all right."

"Yes, I'm all right. Bless you for coming."

"Good-by, Elizabeth."

"Good-by, Lollie."

Lollie slid under the wheel, started the car at once, slid away from the curb, giving Elizabeth only one backward look. There were tears in her dark small eyes, but her smile was clear and loving.

Elizabeth went slowly back up the stairs, sat on the floor near Anna's chair. But for once the voices did not get through to her. They came from far away. There was no disappointment in her now, no chagrin at losing what might have been such a triumph. But over and over Lollie's voice went through her head: *It didn't seem important.*

RS. BUNCE, with a coffee cake in the curve of her arm, started out for Maisie Potts' house. The coffee cake was no gift from the Suydams, but had been made with ingredients bought separately by Mrs. Bunce. She had a conscience about such things. Though she did not know it, the gift was an acknowledgment that some small extra must be thrown into the evening if Mr. Botsworth was not there; something must fill the gaps that couldn't be talked about by the friends.

It was a very dark night, but through the business section the world was bright and busy. Then she came to the little tobacconist's shop at the end of the stores, stepped into darkness again. A few steps beyond the tobacco store someone suddenly materialized out of the darkness, as if having waited behind a bush for this moment, fell into step by her side. It was Ed Botsworth.

"Hello, Fatty."

"Ed! Where on earth did you pop from? You almost made me drop this coffee cake."

"Coffee cake, h'm?"

"Yes, and not made for you, either."

"I'll carry it," Ed said.

"No, never mind. You can't sling coffee cake around like a side of beef."

He laughed, too heartily.

They came nearer and nearer Pottsy's house. Ed acted embarrassed, as if he had something on his mind he couldn't get out. Suddenly he stopped dead still on the sidewalk under the big elm by the Peters house and said, "Fatty, I've got to talk to you. Wait a minute."

"To me? What about?" Bunce said.

"Us," Ed said succinctly.

"Us?" Bunce echoed blankly.

"Us. I've come awful close to making a fool of myself without knowing it. I thought everybody in town knew I was making a bid for you, Fatty. Why, I liked you 'way back in grade school. I didn't know any way to get to you but by seeing you at Pottsy's house. I thought you'd see through that quick enough. . . . Somebody's been joking me about courting Pottsy. Good Lord! We're getting on, Fatty—there ain't time to play around like we were kids. I think we could make a go of it. What do you say, Fatty?"

Bunce stood there in the dark, big, shaken. She could see Ed's face, but dimly, remembered Anna Suydam's saying he looked like a cod.

"Are you out of your mind, Ed?" she said at last.

"No, I ain't. I been thinking of this ever since—well, from 'way back."

"Well, you stop thinking about it, quick. I never heard such nonsense."

"What's nonsense about it? You're all alone and so am I. I've got a house and I make enough to support us all right. When Hux says to me he heard I was courting their Pottsy—well, I was that shocked I didn't have any answer hardly. If I've give her that notion—well, anyway, Fatty, it was you I was courting. I've been dumb, I guess."

"Dumb isn't the word for it," Bunce said. "I never had any

idea . . . Come on, now, Maisie'll be waiting. We can't stand here all night."

She began walking on, but he didn't move for an instant. Then he caught up with her and said, "Look here, Fatty . . ."

"Did you ever stop to think, Ed, that a woman my build might not like to be called Fatty?"

"Gosh, no. I've called you that for forty years, I guess."

"Well, stop it."

Then Maisie Potts, in her best gray dress, with the garnet pin at her throat, opened the door to them and they went in. "Why, Leora, what's the matter?" Maisie said. "You look like you were sick!"

"I'm fine," Bunce said. "Here's a bit of coffee cake I made to go with coffee tonight."

"You ought not to have bothered," Miss Potts said. "Ed, now don't go monkeying with that damper. It's just comfortable here." Her tone was almost that of a wife, not quite.

"You'll dry out," Ed said. "It ain't healthy, living in an oven."

Bunce sat down, quite close to the stove. She felt like jelly and couldn't look her friend in the eye. But she saw that Maisie's cheeks were pink, that she had her best cloth on the dining-room table, that she had a new fern to take the place of the one that had begun to go straggly this winter. "Dear God, help me!" she prayed, and prayer with Bunce was very real.

At eleven o'clock Bunce was in her own small room back of the Suydam kitchen. She sat down in the rocker, her coat and hat still on, sat there for half an hour, no strength in her to move. Dear God, help me. Dear God, what shall I do? was all that went through her mind in all that half hour. Then she got up, undressed, crept into bed, her body old and tired. This was like the moment when she had realized the limitations of this room, after believing Maisie lost to her, only worse. Worse. She didn't quite know why it was worse. She had always believed herself sincere when she said she was through with marrying and giving in marriage. But in spite of herself she thought of Ed Botsworth's little house, that she knew Ed had kept spick and span ever since Angie died. It grew big in her thoughts, spacious and full of a queer beauty beside this tiny space where was all her life. Ed, Ed Botsworth, that she had accused of going to Maisie's to get a cook and a home.

If it hadn't been for Maisie, Bunce knew in those long dark hours of sleeplessness, she might have considered taking Ed Botsworth.

In the morning Johnny was downstairs first, as he often was, and when he went out to the kitchen there was no Bunce bustling about. For some reason he felt frightened and lost and he went to Bunce's door and said, "Bunce! Bunce! Bunce!" pounding on the door anxiously.

Bunce said, "Yes, yes," but it was several minutes before she opened her door and came out, trying on her apron as she came.

"It's awful late," Johnny said.

"So 'tis. I overslept," Bunce said. "You set the silver around while I get the coffee on."

"Your eyes look very little," Johnny said. "Do you ever cry, Bunce?"

"Well, not often," Bunce said. "Don't chatter, boy. Get the table set."

Adrian came down and found things not quite ready. "Bunce's eyes look awfully little today," Johnny told him.

Adrian walked on into the kitchen and said, "Out late last night, Bunce?"

"I'm real sorry, Mr. Suydam. I overslept," Bunce explained again. "Just sit right down. I'll have everything on in a jiffy."

"Feel all right?" Adrian persisted.

"Surely. I always feel fine," Bunce said.

When Elizabeth came down, Johnny began again. "Aunt Liz, Bunce's eyes—"

"Hush. Eat your cereal," Adrian said.

Elizabeth went on to the kitchen, picked up the tray that Bunce had ready on the shelf, then she gave a glance toward Bunce, who stood half turned away from her, buttering the toast. Bunce, with a face always as red and fresh as an apple, looked haggard. This is it, Elizabeth thought. She knows. But she took the tray without a word and went upstairs. She returned, ate her own breakfast.

Mrs. Suydam came down, took her place; then, after she had eaten her meager breakfast, got Johnny ready for school and set out with him.

Adrian, at the door, said, "Liz!"

Elizabeth went into the hall and Adrian raised a brow toward the kitchen.

"Something's eating Bunce," he said in a low voice. "Find out what's the matter."

But there was no time then. There was Anna to fix up for the morning. No, it's my day off, Elizabeth thought. But somehow she wanted to spare Bunce Anna's too discerning eyes for an hour or two. So she said, "I know it's my day off, but let me fix your hair anyway and tidy up a bit. I haven't got a damned thing to do and Bunce is busy. Besides, I had part of Wednesday off."

"Oh, that was free," Anna said. "But fix my hair if you want to."

So she did Anna's hair and made the bed and tidied everything. She waited till the mail came. There were some new books from New York and they looked those over. Anna read her mail. But it was one of those blank mornings when no one came in and nothing much happened. Mrs. Suydam stopped in for a few minutes after she came back from school, but she didn't have much to say. She was quiet these days, and Elizabeth fancied that some of her arrogance had gone out of her. Her shoulders, which had always been so straight, seemed to have a slight droop and her clothes, which had always been so modish on her straight small figure, had a dowdy look, as if bought for someone else. Still, she spoke quietly as always, did not evade any of her small duties.

"Cornelia needs a new suit," Anna said, after she had gone. "That one really begins to look seedy."

Then Bunce came lumbering up the stairs.

"I'm kind of slow this morning," she said. "Aren't you going out today, Miss Burke?"

"Oh, please don't 'Miss Burke' me!" Elizabeth said. "Why don't you call me Liz?"

"I don't like to be too familiar," Bunce said. "What would you fancy for lunch, Mrs. Suydam?"

"I'd fancy whatever I got—from you. What's the matter, Bunce?"

"Matter? Nothing, Mrs. Suydam. I don't know what got into me this morning. I never heard the alarm and I was late with the mister's breakfast. It gives me the jitters to get behind in my schedule."

"You look as if you'd had a night out. Don't tell me you have such riotous goings-on at Maisie Potts'!"

"Not without you call having a cup of coffee riotous," Mrs. Bunce said. "You can run along now, Miss Burke. I'll look after things here."

"Bunce, you wouldn't want to bother with one of those mushroom omelets, would you? It would be wonderful."

"That's no bother," Bunce said.

Elizabeth lingered a moment after Bunce went out. "It is a bother," Anna said, "but she's got something on her mind—it'll be good for her to fuss."

Elizabeth went slowly down the stairs. Anna would have it out of Bunce before lunch was over. If only she could stop her some way. Anna would think it funny and romantic, and maybe it was funny and romantic. But it was something more than that. But if she intruded, wouldn't that be just as bad? What would be the difference? The only difference was that she, Elizabeth, knew how much that "something more" meant. Or did Anna know too? She might. She did see what motivated people—she was awfully quick at seeing that.

She walked into the kitchen and Bunce was getting out the things for the omelet, though it was too soon. She plunged in, ashamed, half frightened, but plunging all the same.

"Bunce," she said, "I know what the trouble is. You know about Ed Botsworth, don't you?"

Bunce turned and stared at her out of those small, swollen eyes.

"I knew it two weeks ago," Elizabeth went on. "I tried to tell you, but I couldn't. Huxley Reals told me—that day he called me up. That was what he wanted to tell me. He was worried about you and Miss Potts. He thought you ought to know. But I couldn't seem to tell you."

"You ought to have," Bunce said.

"Yes, I know. I couldn't. It didn't seem my business. It isn't my business now, either."

"That's right," Bunce said.

"It's so awful," Elizabeth went on quickly. "For you and her, I mean. I don't see how it can be made right, no matter how it turns out. I just don't see. I know it's not my business, but I've been thinking about it for all this time and worrying about it. I don't see how it can come out right."

Mrs. Bunce gave a deep sigh, said, "I don't know which way to turn, and that's the truth. I've asked the Lord to show me the way clear, but it all looks dark to me still, Miss Burke, and that's a fact. . . . Well, this ain't getting my omelet made."

Elizabeth felt dismissed and turned to go.

"I don't know if I'm coming or going," Bunce said.

"And that's the first business of man—to know that. . . . I read that somewhere," Elizabeth half apologized. "Will you take lunch up or shall I?"

"I'll take it up," Mrs. Bunce said.

But it was all in vain, all in vain, that little moment in the kitchen, for that afternoon Elizabeth, ready for skating all by

herself, paused in Anna's room. Jen and a woman called Evelyn
Wood were there, and Anna was telling them, with much
laughter, the problem of Bunce. Elizabeth felt darkness growing in her, making her face dark, her mouth ugly and straight.
"Don't talk to me about betrayals!" she said hotly. "That's
mean. That's damnably mean, Anna!"

Anna went on laughing and her brown eyes met Elizabeth's
with no embarrassment, only amusement. "Oh, Liz," she said.
"She'll never know and you have to be able to tell your friends
funny bits of psychology that pop up!"

"How do you know she won't know? And it isn't funny to
Bunce."

She saw the surprised eyes of Jen and Evelyn Wood upon
her but she couldn't stop.

Then Anna sobered and said, "I'm sorry. I am, girls. Bunce
is my great help in time of trouble—I couldn't live without her.
I wasn't trying to be cruel—I couldn't be cruel to Bunce. But
it was funny and somehow you get to thinking about such
things as outside of people, just problems in themselves. But
Liz is right—and don't you dare to spread it around!"

That was a handsome apology and Elizabeth had to let it go
at that. But as she swept alone up and down the lake she said
to herself that Jen and Evelyn couldn't possibly keep a bit of
gossip like that to themselves. It would be known all over town
in a day or two and laughed about. Still, what could she do?
If Bunce had been foolish enough to tell her troubles, what
could be done about it? And maybe it was right to laugh.
Maybe that would clear the whole thing up quicker than anything else. Here she went again, pitying people, not giving
them credit for having the strength to carry their loads, for
having the strength to laugh at themselves. Why, she didn't
even know Maisie Potts except to speak to, and here she was
all torn up inside thinking of that prim, old-maidish little figure scurrying around her little house thinking Ed Botsworth
was courting her. And aching like Billy-o because Bunce had

to choose between a man and a friend. Or was she so concerned because Huxley Reals had been troubled and his troubles were her own? Was that it? Huxley loved Maisie Potts. She had loved him since he was a little boy. He felt he must protect her. But maybe that was wrong—maybe you didn't have a right to protect anybody. Maybe you had to believe in their ability to protect themselves and that was all.

"I don't know either, Bunce," she said aloud. "I don't know if I'm coming or going."

But presently movement itself and the sharp fresh air calmed her and she began to feel almost free, sweeping all alone up and down the smooth ice. That, she thought, was the blessed reality of Lollie—she left you free to decide things for yourself, she granted you your adulthood. But to be an adult wasn't so easy. It was a load to bear. She wished she could say, like Bunce, Oh, Lord, make my way clear! Then she didn't think at all, but moved swiftly, mindlessly, like a bird, up and down the lake. Yes, she thought once of the gulls that swept over Bessie's lonely house on the Cape all day long, all day long, but that was all.

That night Anna brought up the matter of Bunce, saying gently, "I was stupid this afternoon, darling. It was such a wonderful story—but I was stupid to tell it."

Elizabeth said calmly, "Oh, never mind. Bunce will work it out."

"Liz. . . ."

"H'm?"

"My legs are getting so thin. I feel as if I'm vanishing."

"Well, you're not."

"Look, would you mind taking that little cat away? I don't want to look at it any more. Every time I look at it I think of how I'm failing with Johnny."

Elizabeth went over to the mantel and took the little cat down, held it in her hands. "But Johnny will be disappointed if you don't have it up," she said. "And Johnny's all right now. He's doing all right in school and he seems much happier."

"But not with me," Anna said. "Not with me."

"He gave you this. It's a beginning."

"I've really failed with him. I can't bear to fail, Liz. Please take it away."

Elizabeth took the little cat into her own room, stood it on the bureau. The next day Johnny saw it there.

"I didn't give that to you," he said, scowling at it.

"I know you didn't. Mummy said I could have it to look at for a little while. We're so proud of you for having done it—I wanted a share in it."

That was the best she could do and it wasn't good enough. Johnny walked out of the room and, to her amazement, went straight to Anna's room. She heard him say, "You gave away my cat!" She waited, her heart racing, for Anna to say: "Oh, darling—I just wanted you to love me, I don't care about the cat!" something warm and loving, something that would send him to her arms. But Anna did not answer for a moment and then she said, "Make me something else. I've given the cat to Aunt Liz." Her voice was not warm at all. It was almost indifferent. "I'll make you another cat," Johnny said, with an odd fierceness in his voice. "No, I'd rather have a rabbit," Anna said. Johnny came running back. His sharp little face was all screwed up in anger. "I'll make her another cat!" he said. "I will!" "All right," Elizabeth said, but the whole scene had a strangeness, had something she could not understand. And Johnny's face was not a child's face, was ugly with hate. No child ought to look like that. Was it disappointment that Anna had given his present away? Was that all it was? That was enough, but it didn't seem quite that.

On Sunday Johnny went to Margaret's. It was almost a habit now, these Sunday hours he spent in the doctor's house. In a way, Elizabeth felt it was wrong for him to go there every Sun-

day. It was the only full day his father had at home, the only
time he had to get to know his father. And yet it was the only
full day for Anna too, and Anna needed that day. And Johnny
was happy at Margaret's, that was surely something. If he
couldn't be happy here, it was better that he be happy somewhere else. She thought once of asking Adrian about the cat,
but she thought better of the impulse. Adrian had made it
clear that he didn't like interference, and why should he? Anna
was his wife and Johnny was his son. She was an outsider. And
yet she knew there was something there that ought to be understood.

So Johnny went to Margaret's. The doctor called for him and
took him in his car. The doctor said to Elizabeth, with his long
face wrinkled into a grin, "Hello, my prickly pear!"

"Hello," Elizabeth said feebly.

"Why, I believe you blushed!" Dr. McIntry said. "I didn't
know girls did that any more. You must be softening toward
me!"

"Nothing of the kind," Elizabeth said.

"You come get Johnny at five. I'll get in a lick then."

He went up to speak to Anna. When he came down his face
was more grave. "She's worrying about her legs wasting away,"
he said. "They will, though. We can't help that. You've got a
wonderful sister, Liz."

"Yes, I have."

But she didn't go to get Johnny. Huxley Reals came and also
a man and a woman. The couple left soon but Huxley stayed
on and Adrian said he would get Johnny.

"Oh, let Liz go," Anna said carelessly.

"I'd like to," Liz said.

But Adrian went. Huxley was not so full of light talk as
usual. He sat quiet and let Anna do most of the talking. Finally
she said, "You're dull today, Hux. Got something on your
mind?"

"I am dull," he said. "I've been working on this article. I've

done so little writing lately that it's hard going. My first youth-
ful enthusiasm for the written word seems to have dried up.
I've been thinking perhaps I ought to make a change. I'm going
stale."

"Leave Adrian?" Anna said protestingly.

"Yes. Get out of town and make a fresh start."

"Oh, no. Lakeville couldn't get on without you, Hux. You're
our brightest young man about town!"

"Well, being a bright young man about town can't last forever, Anna. I'm just not so young as I was ten years ago. Then
your Adrian isn't so sure I'm useful to him any more. You don't
want to stay where you aren't useful. I never planned to stay
in Lakeville anyway."

"You are in a mood! But forget it—we'd miss you too much.
And where would I get posies from?"

"You said Adrian filled in the gaps, didn't you? You can't
have it both ways, Anna."

"You're just being difficult, but I'm not going to coddle you.
Adrian says I coddle you—but you're too adult for that. Only
it's true—Lakeville would be a different place with you gone
from it. . . . Look, Hux—I need your help on something. Liz,
you go away because you'll think I'm just gossiping again.
You're concerned in this, Hux, because Maisie brought you
up. . . ."

Huxley Reals turned and looked at Elizabeth. But there was
no reproach in his eyes, just a small smile.

"I know all about it," he said. "Liz knows I do. But I'm not
the one to help you. And I don't think anyone can."

Anna's brown eyes rose to Elizabeth's face.

"You didn't tell me you'd consulted Hux on it," she said.

"I consulted her, rather," Huxley said easily. "I don't believe
Liz asks for help much. I didn't get much help, I know. Let's
skip it, Anna. There's nothing we can do."

"But I think I can. I thought maybe you could think up
some excuse to have Miss Potts come to see me. Send some-

thing over—something like that. I could tell her so it wouldn't be more than a prick."

Huxley shook his head.

"No. No, I won't send her over," he said. "Leave it alone. They'll have to work it out themselves."

"That's silly. If you can help you ought to. Well, I'll manage without you. . . . If you're going away, I'll have to, won't I? Oh, dear, I hate changes—I'd hate to have you gone, even if you are tiresome sometimes. You mustn't go, Hux. I know I'm selfish, but I don't want my friends to go away."

Hux got up. He picked a dry leaf off a plant, looked toward Liz almost as if asking for help. But she could give him no help.

"Well, I probably will be here when I'm an old man with a beard and a cane," he said. "I'm old enough to know that fresh pastures aren't always greener. Indeed, I feel as old as Methuselah today."

"And you don't know whether you're coming or going," Elizabeth was surprised to hear herself say. She managed to laugh and said, "That's a quote—it just went through my head."

"No, I know," he said. "I'm coming."

But he contradicted himself by going, almost without saying good-by.

"He was low, poor Hux," Anna said. "What's got into him?"

"You, I expect. He can't see where he's getting anything out of it."

"But what can he expect to get? He's my friend, that's all he's ever been."

"He doesn't seem to find that sufficient," Elizabeth said.

"He won't go away, though. He hasn't that kind of courage," Anna said. "Why, Meg's walking Adrian home! Probably telling him how to bring up Johnny. Only they don't seem to be talking even. She *does* look like Uncle Jean's horse! I must tell Adrian they looked quite like one of those silent married pairs who haven't anything left to say to each other."

"Adrian doesn't like that kind of joke."

"Silly! Adrian likes any kind of joke. I will say for Adrian, he can laugh at himself better than most."

Meg didn't come in. When Adrian came upstairs and Johnny had vanished into his own little room, Anna greeted him with a laugh. "Oh, Adrian, I saw you coming in the busybody! I hardly knew it was you. You and Meg looked so exactly like a *New Yorker* cartoon—the married pair who have no more to say!"

Adrian did not laugh. He sat down in his chair, looked out the window, saying only, "Oh, did we?"

Anna leaned her head back against the chair, said, "Isn't it almost suppertime? Adrian, do eat up here with me tonight! Hux is tiresome and I'd just like to have a really restful hour with you."

He smiled at her, but said nothing, and Elizabeth went off to see about the supper. Elizabeth thought, She shouldn't have said that. Oh, she shouldn't have said it. It put the thought in his head. She thinks he couldn't possibly change; she's so sure he loves her forever and ever. But maybe he might change. No, he wouldn't. He's very loyal and he does love her. . . . But that frightened me. It shouldn't have been said.

XIII

$\mathcal{D}$R. MCINTRY CAME IN late one night and dropped his bag in the office, came into the dining room from the office, and found Margaret making old-fashioned valentines with tissue paper and red hearts and cupids and the like, on the dining-room table.

"Jumping Jupiter!" the doctor said.

Margaret went calmly on with her task, held up a filmy number and said, "That's the way they used to look, isn't it?"

"I can't remember that far back."

"I just wanted to see if I could do it—so I could help Johnny make some."

"That one. Do you think he thinks in Valentine terms? I don't. He's a pretty cold proposition, for a kid."

"Cold? No, he's not."

"Never knew a boy I couldn't get along with—except Johnny. He gives me the creeps."

"Maybe you give him the creeps too."

He went to the kitchen, began to forage in the refrigerator, came back with a sandwich of bread and ham.

"Meg, do you want to be serious a minute, or are you too engrossed in that throwback to childhood?"

"I'm serious. But I'll finish this and be serious at the same time. What is it? Elizabeth?"

"Yes. It was a joke at first, but, you know, I think I'll ask her. I know she's young—and you have told me she is too good for me. But I have my points. I think maybe it would work."

"No doubt you could make it work if you had the chance. But she won't marry you."

"Want to lay a small bet on it?"

"No. It's a sure thing. She won't. She's in love with some-body else."

"Who said so?"

"No one. But she is. I'm used to the signs. No, she won't have you, so forget it."

"She amuses me. She's such a spunky little piece. She wouldn't ever get to be a whiner, Meg."

Margaret McIntry looked up with sudden compassion. She had grown up with a whiner for a mother.

"No, she never would," she said. "But all the same, it's no good. You'll save yourself embarrassment if you don't ask her."

"You're a pessimist, Meg. I'll risk the embarrassment, I think. You wouldn't mind her here?"

"No."

"Didn't think so. . . . It's no life, that of a doctor's wife, I know. No life at all. But life's short, Meg. No use wasting all the spare moments if you can find anything good to put in them."

"You've always seemed to fill them. . . . It isn't that I'd care," Meg said, "but she won't have you. Put your mind on some-body else. That widow who has the two boys, up in the Putney house. She'd take you in a minute."

"No, I don't want just anybody, Meg. I'm more particular than that."

"You're fifty-five years old."

"I've still got all my teeth," he said, got up and went up to his room.

At the same time Elizabeth sat beside Anna's bed. "There's

something that's been on my mind," Anna said. "About Bunce. Why didn't you tell me you knew? Why did you talk it over with Hux? It bothers me."

The shaggy-haired sister burrowed her head deeper into the chair, turned her face away. "Well," she said at last, "you know what happened when you did know. You told all the town."

"All the town? Jen and Evelyn aren't all the town, and they're both very discreet. But I love Mrs. Bunce."

"I know. But do you think Bunce would have liked hearing you all laughing at her trouble?"

"Bunce didn't hear us. I can love people and laugh at them too, Liz. But it isn't that. It's why Hux told you, not me. That bothers me. He's always brought all his problems to me."

"That I don't know," Elizabeth said. "All I know is, he did. Probably he hoped I might do something about it, but I didn't. He felt out of favor here at the moment."

"Was that it? He didn't really take Adrian's storm seriously, I hope. I don't know what got into Adrian that day. It was dreadful. . . . But you might have told me, Liz. Why didn't you?"

"Oh, I don't know," Elizabeth said helplessly. "I don't know. It just seemed something better not hashed over. I didn't see what anyone could do about it."

"But somehow—oh, I don't know how to say it, Liz—but when *secrets* grow up around you, it gives you such a shut-in feeling. It makes this room like a prison. I swore I'd never let it get that way. But if the people around you keep things away from you—then that makes you a prisoner, if you know what I mean."

"Yes," Elizabeth said slowly. "Yes, I know what you mean, Anna. I'm sorry. I'm not very secretive—I do tell you almost everything I know, and some things I don't. I just don't know why I kept that secret. It just seemed to be Bunce's business, nothing we ought to mix into. But of course I might as well have, because Bunce told you anyway."

"I hope you weren't silly enough to think I'd mind your creeping out to meet Hux!" Anna said, with a small chuckle.

"Of course not. Don't be silly. And I didn't creep out, anyway."

Had she said that boldly enough? Too boldly? Anna's head turned on the pillow and the brown eyes searched Elizabeth's face.

"Why, *Liz!*" Anna said, so gently, so lovingly, so knowingly.

"What do you mean by that?" Elizabeth said.

"Liz," Anna said again, in that wondering, loving tone. Then, very softly, "I'm sorry, sis. I'm terribly sorry. I never dreamed it was Hux."

"Hux? I hope you know what you're talking about," Elizabeth said.

"Yes, I know, darling. I don't know why I didn't know before. All this stubbornness about the doctor—but it never entered my head you'd be so foolish as to fall for Hux."

Lollie had said she'd work things out, but what would Lollie do with this drowning feeling, this helplessness, this horror? What would Lollie do with this? Was a lie called for? Was a lie ever called for? Was truth called for? Was she cruel not to share this with Anna?

"Anna, you're out of your mind," she said, and her voice sounded quite normal and sensible to herself. "I hope I wouldn't be such a fool as to fall for someone who worshiped you. No, I protect myself from such misfortunes. I never said I'd fallen for anybody. You made that up out of whole cloth. And I was stubborn about the doctor because I don't happen to like him much—and because I don't like to have my life manipulated—not even by you, darling. You know I like to decide things for myself, but you thought it would be fun to decide that for me. It isn't fun for me, though, Anna. It really isn't any fun. I'm a plain Jane, I know, but I'm proud as Lucifer. As you say, it's probably compensation for my lacks—but it's there, all the same. You *ought* to have been a fiction writer!

It would be awfully dramatic, wouldn't it, to have me have this hopeless yen for Huxley Reals? But I'm smarter than that, darling."

"Are you, baby?" Anna said. "You protest an awful lot!"

Yes, her voice had gone on and on, could not stop. She knew that even while she talked.

"Wouldn't you, in my shoes?" Elizabeth said. "Suppose I said to you that I was going to have to tell Adrian—that you really had, say, a great passion for the doctor, or even for Huxley, that I knew it was true, because one day Huxley was sitting there by your chair with his head against your hands and you were looking down at him too tenderly for friendship—as I did, darling, as I did. Suppose I made up that tale for Adrian? Wouldn't you protest? I'm sure you would."

"Ah, but you see, Adrian trusts me," Anna said softly. "He knows I love him. Even if he did make a scene. He truly trusts me. I don't think that's parallel, Liz. Do you? Well, we'll forget it tonight. Only I do feel hurt, somehow—that you didn't tell me."

"Didn't tell you what? See, there you go again. There's nothing to tell. Nothing. I can't make up a love life, even to entertain you."

Anna laughed, reached out her hand and put it over Elizabeth's.

"Sleep tight, my thorny one," she said.

In her bed Elizabeth Burke lay wide awake. Anna had not believed her. What did words matter, when you knew someone so well that all those words had meant absolutely nothing? Anna knew. And what now? What would Anna do with her secret? Would she present it to the girls? To Huxley? To Adrian? I will have to go away from here, she said to herself. But how? What reason could she give? Was it not the same as a confession if she went away? But at least she would not have to meet Anna's quizzing, loving eyes in some other place. Lay aside her personal idiosyncrasies? Was this just an idiosyncrasy?

No, it was all her life. It was the core of her. It might change. It might wear away, as people were always saying such things did. But when? And how? A fading of this feeling was not something to be desired. How could one desire that love should go, even such a love as this? That was the same as wishing life itself should go. Suppose she had told Anna, had begged for Anna's mercy? Would that have been better? Then she remembered the love in Anna's hand over her own, remembered the words about being a prisoner, and she began to cry, silently but deeply, against her pillow. How terrible, how unbearable, to be an Anna, to be an Anna and now a prisoner. To have secrets kept from you by those who protested love for you. *I don't know, oh, I don't know whether I am coming or going.*

She was afraid to begin the next day, but she did begin it. It was to be a day remembered forever, but it began like any other day. There was the moment of entering Anna's room, meeting Anna's eyes as if last night had never been, but she managed that. There was the moment of leaving Anna alone with Betty in midmorning, straining her ears for laughter, hearing none but distrusting her own ears. There was the moment of going into the kitchen and seeing Bunce's face in the little mirror over the sink, a face old and white. There was the moment of coming on Johnny sitting on the top step of the stairs, a small, silent figure who only moved over against the wall when she passed. There was the moment of Adrian's coming home, going up to Anna—the waiting again for laughter. A long day. A quiet day. A bitter day. A shamed day. But Anna said nothing. She looked at her once or twice with that look of amusement, that speculative, teasing look that was so enchanting and yet today so unendurable, but she said nothing.

The day wore itself away. It was toward suppertime that she said suddenly to herself, I will go and see Daggett tonight. I didn't do it right before. But I can't get hold of myself till she knows I didn't betray her. I can't ever get anything else right while that's hanging over. She had an odd sensation as of having been told to do this by Lollie. Yes, if she was going to make anything of her life at all, she had to straighten that out. And she had to do it without putting any blame on Anna. With this decision, she was abruptly calmer. "First things first," her mother used to say. But she would not have said Mrs. Daggett was first in her mind had she been forced to name first place there. Nevertheless, she felt calmer, as if she had begun to put her life in order.

Nor did she beat about the bush when it came time for going. She hid nothing. Huxley Reals came in, but Adrian did not go out and Elizabeth said, "Adrian, you'll be here all evening, won't you? I'm going down to call on Mrs. Daggett, if you are."

"Go ahead," Adrian said.

Anna said, "Daggett? Whatever for?"

"I want to see her," Elizabeth said.

She went out, down the stairs, out the front door and into the street. There had been a thaw and the streets were full of slush. It was freezing again now and the ruts were beginning to form. It was hard walking. But Elizabeth went steadily along, came to Mrs. Daggett's big old house, went around to the side door. She felt firm, able to make herself clear. The back part of the house was all lighted up. She knocked on the door but no one answered. She knocked again. She heard steps, but knew they were not the steps of Mrs. Daggett. The door opened and Dr. McIntry stood there in the doorway. He stared at her as if she were the last person he had expected to see.

"What's the matter? Is she sick?" Elizabeth said blankly.

He pulled her in, closed the door. "Stroke," he said briefly. "She won't last the night."

"But I've got to talk to her," Elizabeth said.

"She's done talking," Dr. McIntry said.

"Can I see her?"

"See her? Why? Miss Leavitt is with her. She's no sight, Liz. And she won't know you."

"I must see her," Elizabeth insisted.

She followed him into the bedroom and there lay Mrs. Daggett, her eyes half open, her mouth slack, a little moisture dribbling from one corner, and an odd, twisted look to one side of her face.

Elizabeth walked to the side of the bed. "Mrs. Daggett," she said. "Mrs. Daggett."

But the eyes did not change. There was no recognition in the eyes, no movement of the eyes. Elizabeth walked out of the room and the doctor followed her.

"Are you sure she won't get better?"

"No, of course not. It's her first stroke and often people do survive more than one. But this is a bad one. I don't think she's going to come out of it. But I'm not God, Liz."

"I've got to talk to her," Elizabeth said.

"Got to? What about? Well, you can see it's impossible."

"If she gets to—to be herself again, will you call me?"

"Yes, but I doubt she will. Not tonight anyway. She's pretty old, Liz, and maybe it will be better if she doesn't come to herself. Her future wouldn't be very bright. She hasn't got anyone to look after her—she's been alone a long time now."

"But you will call me?"

"I said so, didn't I?"

He was puzzled, but she walked out of the house and on up the street. She paid no attention to the slushy walks, but plodded on as if she had a destination. Then she found herself crying, the tears hot, then cold against her face. She tried to wipe them away with her sleeve. She came to the end of the town, stood there looking off into the dim countryside, with the snow, now ugly and brown over the fields. At last she turned and went home. Her feet were unbearably heavy and it seemed miles she walked, slipping on frozen places, getting her feet wet as she plunged suddenly through ice in a puddle.

Then the block of familiar houses was ahead of her and she came to Number Seven. She hadn't thought at all in all that long walk, only felt this burden that weighed down her heart,

weighed down her body so intolerably. The door opened and
Huxley Reals, head bare, overcoat open, came out and started
down the steps. She put a hand to the railing, waited for him
to pass. But he stood there in the light from the street lamp
and stared at her. "What's the matter, Liz?"

She could feel the rush of tears again, could not stop them.
"I can't stand it," she said.

"Can't stand what? What is it?"

Then he came on down the steps, took her arm. "Come
along with me," he said. "What is the matter? You're shaking."

"I know. Mrs. Daggett is dying."

"Mrs. Daggett? I didn't know she was sick."

"She's had a stroke. She's dying."

He was walking her firmly up the street. It was all a dream.
"But, look here," he said at last, "why the tears? Was Mrs.
Daggett anything special to you? She is a very old woman. I
don't understand. Stop your crying, Liz."

"I'm sorry. I can't seem to stop. I must go home."

"Looking like that? Here, you come in with me a minute and
I'll give you a drink. There's no one home—come along."

"No."

"No? Don't be silly. If ever anyone needed something, you
do. You aren't worrying about your reputation, are you? It's as
dark as pitch out and none of the tabbies will see you—besides
. . . oh, just come on and stop your nonsense!"

Everyone knew he had an apartment of his own. They went
in by the side door and Elizabeth was pushed into a deep chair
in a room that was filled with books. "Coffee or brandy?" he
asked.

"Coffee," she said.

"All right. Sit still."

She couldn't have moved had she wanted to. The weight at
her heart would have held her there, helpless. When he came
back he handed her coffee, said not a word while she drank it.
"Thank you," she said. "I'm all right now."

"You look a degree more normal anyway. Now tell me why you were going into hysterics because old Mrs. Daggett is dying. I'll miss her myself—she's one of the familiar landmarks. But still I don't understand why you are so emotional about it. It doesn't make sense. You generally make sense."

"She thought I betrayed her," she said. "I had a secret of hers—she thought I told it to Anna. I didn't—she thought I did. . . . To have her die and not know. It seemed to me I couldn't bear it. I went there tonight and I was going to make her listen to me. She is dying. She is dying. She can't see or hear or—or even think."

"Hold it," Huxley Reals said shortly, commandingly.

She stopped short. His voice was not the teasing, self-mocking voice he used for Anna. It was a voice he might use in business. It took obedience for granted. She obeyed. Then she got up. The books whirled around her an instant, then she felt steady. "Thank you for the coffee. I will go now," she said.

He did not stop her; instead, he walked with her to the door, out with her into the night. He didn't even talk on the way back to the house. When they came to the steps again, she said, "I'm sorry I went hysterical. It was only—it was a shock to know that I wasn't ever going to get a chance to tell her. It seemed so cruel."

"Yes, it's cruel," he said. "But we have to accept some cruelties in life, I expect."

"I suppose so. Only this one—it will be with me forever. Good night."

"Liz—Elizabeth. . . ."

She paused on the second step.

"Do you want to tell me the secret?"

"No."

"All right. It seemed so important, I thought you might."

Strange conversation. Strange voices in the night air.

"No. But you are kind," she said, wished the words back, for it seemed to her that they were weighted with love.

"Not especially," he said. "Good night, Elizabeth."

Now she was in the house, going quietly up the stairs. The light was dim in Anna's room. Adrian must have put her to bed. She went to her own room, undressed, then went to the bathroom, scrubbed her face hard, put powder on to hide the traces of tears. She stepped to the door of Anna's room, but Anna lay there with her eyes closed and did not speak. Gratefully, she went back to her own bed, waited for eleven. She did not sleep. The telephone might ring. Suppose it rang in the middle of the night? Suppose she got up and left the house without telling anyone—would that make a commotion? When at last she went in to Anna, Anna was wide awake.

"Sorry I wasn't here to get you to bed," Elizabeth said.

"Daggett must have been very entertaining," Anna said.

"Daggett is very ill. She's had a stroke," Elizabeth said.

"Good heavens! Did you know that before?"

"No."

"Poor old Daggett! How terrible! You know, I've been really fond of Daggett. She's always given me something to think about. She's a wise old girl, even if she does look like a ragbag."

"Yes."

"Was Dr. McIntry there?"

"Yes. He doesn't think she will recover. Look, Anna, if the phone rings in the night, it'll be for me. I asked the doctor to call me if—if I could be any help."

"Isn't anyone with her?"

"Miss Leavitt was there. But I thought maybe—maybe I could help."

A faint smile came to Anna's eyes and Elizabeth knew Anna was thinking that perhaps her sister was thinking of the doctor, of helping him, and that she, Anna, was finding some amusement and comfort in the thought. But she did not spoil the thought for her.

"It would make a change in Lakeville if Daggett should go,"

Anna said. "You wouldn't think so, maybe, but it would. A character like Daggett adds a lot to a town."

Elizabeth was silent. Anna went on presently, "I do hate the thought of dying. You die a little yourself, just thinking about it. Yet we all come to it, don't we? The thing itself isn't so important—but the nothingness of it is frightening. It's frightening to think that life goes on without us."

"It goes on, but it changes," Elizabeth said.

"Or does it? Do we just imagine we're important? Sometimes I get to thinking Adrian would die if I did, that he couldn't bear life. But I suppose he could. And Mrs. Bunce—I get to thinking she couldn't manage life without me to look after. But she would, of course. And Cornelia—I know she keeps apart, but I really believe she keeps alive through me. It seems such a responsibility is laid on you to keep alive. But maybe you're just deceiving yourself because you want so much to live."

"No, I think they all would die in part," Elizabeth said slowly. "You do mean a terrible lot to them all. To me too, darling."

"Do I, Liz? Sometimes I feel I'm just a duty to you."

"A duty?" Elizabeth said. "I hate that word. It implies lovelessness. I've always wanted to do something for you. All my life. But you've never had any need of me. Perhaps I'm as bad as your Huxley, wanting you to be ill so I can be of use to you."

She forced herself to say the name but it came out steadily enough when she came to it. Anna's smile at her was like a flash of light, warm light.

"Funny Liz! Have you really always felt like that? One would never have known it."

"You've always had so much, perhaps you didn't know it," Elizabeth said. "But you must have. How could you not have? I was disgusting, I worshiped so hard."

"How strange. You always seem so barbed-wirish—I've always thought you wanted to be left alone, only that."

"Silly. You didn't. If I'm barbed-wirish, that's just my defense mechanism working."

"Defense against what?" Anna asked.

"Against—oh, I don't know, Anna. Against loving too much, maybe. Against being plain. Against everything. Everything that hurts."

Even as she talked, Elizabeth Burke knew that she was giving up a part of her defense, but giving up one fortress to protect another. Stepping back to the last bulwark, but giving up hostages all along the way.

"I *have* been silly," Anna said gently. "I thought your prickles were because you hated having to do your duty. Your keeping secrets from me and all that. I'm not very smart, am I?"

"You're all too smart. And you'd better go to sleep now before I get any more sloppy. And don't notice if the phone rings —it'll just be about Daggett."

"But why you? Why should you go to help poor Daggett die?" Anna asked.

"I just happened to be there," Elizabeth said. "Good night, darling."

She lay awake, ashamed. Could it possibly be true that Anna had never known how she worshiped her? *Could* it? *Had* she been so proud it had never shown? But it could not be, for Anna saw everything. Anna would have known her love, known it in her very bones. It had been there forever, and if it had had some envy in it, Anna would have known that too. But suppose she had not? Suppose her pride seemed real, her resistance to change something like enmity, her hoarding of secrets something like hate? Only, didn't love admit the necessity of a secret place in others, even in the most loved ones? *Didn't* it?

One o'clock, two—three. The telephone did not ring. At last she fell asleep and when she woke it was bright daylight. She jumped out of bed, ran to the bathroom, dressed quickly, went in to get Anna ready for breakfast.

"Did you hear from Daggett?" Anna asked.

"No."

She went downstairs and got the tray ready. Just as she started through the hall with it, the telephone rang. She put the tray down on a chair, hurried to answer. It was Margaret. "Elizabeth?" Meg said.

"Yes."

"Dad asked me to phone you. Mrs. Daggett died a few minutes ago."

"Oh."

"She never regained consciousness."

"Oh. Thanks." She hung up, sickness flowing over her.

"What is it?" Bunce asked.

"Mrs. Daggett died."

"Mrs. Daggett?" Bunce's eyes asked what deep concern it was of Elizabeth's.

"Bunce, would you mind taking Anna's tray up?"

Bunce took the tray, but she was plainly puzzled as to why this should upset the stranger in the house, in the town. Elizabeth sat down at the kitchen table, put her head down on her arms. Now she would never have a chance. Never. Never. It had seemed that some miracle would happen, but none had happened. Mrs. Daggett was dead and would never again creep crookedly down the street with her letter. And out there in the West was a boy who would never get those letters any more, would never have a home to come to. And it might be that this worry had brought on the stroke. That she would never know, but it might be, it might be.

Johnny came down the stairs, into the kitchen. "What's the matter?" he asked.

She stood up abruptly. "Nothing, Johnny. Oatmeal? I'll get it for you. Your orange juice is on the table."

She dished up the oatmeal, brought it in to Johnny.

"You eat with me," Johnny said.

She sat down and tried to eat. Bunce came back and found

them together, frowned a little, still puzzled. Then Adrian and his mother were down and Elizabeth escaped. She went in to Anna and said, "She's gone. Mrs. Daggett."

"Bunce told me. I feel sad."

"I too."

But she did the ordinary morning tasks, spoke no more of Mrs. Daggett. Only she felt something had changed in her. Something had, perhaps, really died. Some belief that ultimately justice would be done, wrongs be made right. This wrong was never going to be made right. All the rest of her life she was going to have to remember that this hurt had been unhealed. It made an emptiness in her but the emptiness seemed to be filling up with stone.

Everyone who came in that day talked of Daggett, but Elizabeth Burke was silent when the name was spoken. Anna spoke of the old woman with great affection. "You know, I believe I really loved her," she said to Jen. "She was so odd, but you liked that oddness—you liked her being different. And she knew a lot about life—I always felt as if I learned something from her. I'll truly miss her."

Jen said, "Oh, Anna, you always manage to make me feel ashamed of myself for not seeing more, not feeling more. I've seen Mrs. Daggett about all my life but she was like a tree, like the monument in the parkway. Now you make me feel I've missed a lot, not knowing her."

But Elizabeth Burke said never a word.

XIV

HE BELL at St. Paul's was tolling. The sound came
solemnly through the storm, for the worst blizzard of the year
was raging through the streets of Lakeville. You could not see
beyond the panes. Nevertheless, the dead must be buried and
this was the day of burial. The bell ran on forever and the
heavy, not too musical, sound made a monotony of warning or
remembrance.

"I wish the bell would stop," Anna said.

Mrs. Bunce and Mrs. Suydam, each dressed in somber black,
had braved the storm and gone to the church. But Elizabeth
had said, "No, I won't go." She thought, though, that all the
rest of her life would be a service to Mrs. Daggett's memory.
It made no difference whether she sat reverently in St. Paul's
and heard the organ and the grave voice of the Reverend Mr.
Prather or stood in a storm-swept cemetery and listened to the
final "Dust to dust," or whether she stayed here in this bright
and beautiful room out of the storm. The storm was within, and
the grief and the regret.

"Remember how she sat here and talked about all the lives
in a house overlapping?" Anna said quietly.

"Yes. I remember," Elizabeth said.

"And how she told us about Prather, going to be a musician, and deflected somehow?"

"Yes, I remember."

"But mostly I seem to remember her humped over, going along the street down there toward the post office. There was a kind of stubbornness, a kind of *faithfulness* about it that you don't forget. It made Cornelia sad too, though I don't believe they were ever intimate. Probably it makes her feel old. It makes me think of her as old, old and precious. Though I never have before. But she's seventy-four. That's not young. But I've never thought of her as changing. She's seemed set and changeless. Till lately. Lately—well, she doesn't seem to care about her clothes like she used to. And now and then she forgets something. She's always had a phenomenal memory. I wonder if you ever know you're old, Liz."

"I don't know. Probably not. I'm twenty-eight years old and I still have a feeling I'm just beginning."

"I wish the bell would stop. . . . It has, I think. Yes, that is the end of that. . . . That's the secret of everything, Liz—to always feel you're just beginning. But sometimes I get the awful feeling that I can't any more, that I'm fooling myself, that everything's ended."

"But, Anna, you're the one who seems to have an inexhaustible supply of life. I don't know how you do it, but you do. That is what makes people come so much, love you so much. You give them life."

"You comfort me," Anna said. "But all the same, sometimes I feel as if I have no more life to give. That's stupid. It's the bells that make me so solemn. I intend to live forever!"

"I wish we hadn't let Johnny go to school."

"Adrian's going to bring him home. He'll go right from the funeral to school. I hope Adrian won't get chilled. It's not the day one would pick to be a pallbearer. I don't know why they asked him—except that he's one of the leading business lights of Lakeville. He's always felt so responsible for Lakeville—as if he'd founded it and had to keep it going."

"Well, that's good. Good to know someone who does feel responsible."

"I suppose so. But it makes him work so hard. And the town would go on if he weren't here."

"Not so well, maybe."

"If he has to fire someone, he's actually sick. But you wouldn't know it. He does it if he has to."

"Yes, he's very strong," Elizabeth said. "I think you could depend on him till doomsday. You're terribly lucky to have Adrian, Anna."

"Yes. Yes, I am," Anna said.

Mrs. Bunce and Mrs. Suydam came home at last but Adrian did not come for some time after.

"I wish Johnny would get here," Elizabeth said.

Then they came. Adrian came upstairs and into Anna's room.

"We were beginning to worry about you," Anna said. "Was it awful?"

"No. But bitterly cold. Johnny insisted on picking up his valentines he'd made at Meg's. That kept me."

"I hope they weren't soaked, the valentines."

"No. Meg put them in a box."

Elizabeth said, "I hope he doesn't keep them there and forget to send them. He has such a passion for hoarding things in boxes."

"Did many come?" Anna asked.

"Yes, a good many, considering the day. The church was almost full. After all, she had lived here a long, long time. A funeral like that makes you know it's the end of an era, or something. Bunce thinks a Baptist funeral is better, with a eulogy and a good long sermon about what is in store for Christian or heathen—but the service at St. Paul's suits me. The eulogy consists of all those people sitting there, having struggled through the blizzard."

Anna looked surprised, as if Adrian was talking out of character. But all she said was "Yes, you're right. Aren't you frozen? Liz, how about making us some coffee instead of tea today? Wouldn't you like that, Adrian?"

"I could take some more," he said. "I had one cup at Meg's."

Anna laughed gently. "What with valentines and coffee—Meg does a lot of coddling of my family," she said.

Elizabeth went out, down the stairs. Bunce had already put coffee on, feeling the need of it herself. Elizabeth delivered the coffee, then left Anna's room, wandered back to the kitchen. "I'll have some coffee down here," she said, helped herself to some, sat down at the kitchen table.

"And what will happen to Daggett's house, with all those lives in it?" she asked suddenly.

"She's no kith nor kin," Bunce said. "Likely it will go for taxes."

"It's a pity the phoenix tale is a myth," Elizabeth said. "If only a new Daggett could arise from the ashes."

Bunce stared at her without comprehension, poured herself coffee.

"Bunce . . ."

Bunce looked up at her, waiting.

"Has the Lord shown you your way clear?"

A trace of the old clear red came to Bunce's round cheeks.

"It don't set well with me, Miss Burke, to have you take the name of our Savior in vain," she said.

"I wasn't, Bunce. I wasn't."

"The ways of the Lord are past finding out," Bunce said. "Pitfalls are digged for us."

"Pitfalls indeed," Elizabeth agreed. "But are the ways of the Lord past finding out? That's what I want to know. Don't you ever get a sign you are in the right road? I'm not being impudent, Bunce. I really want to know."

Bunce sighed. "I've got no sign yet. But maybe He don't show his intent to the sinful."

"You're not sinful, Bunce. I think if He could give a sign, He'd give one to you. I'm looking for a sign too. Somehow, all day I've been feeling this funeral is it. And yet I can't read it. Not yet."

Bunce looked at her with some suspicion, not quite trusting her, and Elizabeth longed to say, I'm your friend, Bunce. We're together, lost souls together, and we're friends, but she did not.

Bunce said, "Well, a funeral does make you stop and think."

"Let's call Johnny down and give him some cambric tea," Elizabeth said, and did get up quickly, call Johnny.

He sat at the kitchen table with a cooky and weak tea. He looked pinched and pale, though lately he had looked much better, and Elizabeth had days when she did not worry about him at all.

"Do bodies go soggy in the ground?" he asked suddenly.

"They put them in boxes, child," Bunce said. "Good stout boxes."

"I put my caterpillar in a pasteboard box. But I guess pasteboard would get soggy, wouldn't it?" Johnny said.

"A caterpillar don't feel much," Bunce said sensibly.

"Did you ever get lost in a blizzard?" Johnny asked.

"Well, once when I was nine or so, I had a hard time getting home from school, the wind and snow were that bad. I thought I was lost but I wasn't more'n a few yards from my own house when I thought that. My ma opened the door and come out after me and I was all right. But I had a minute there when I was scared and thought I was a million miles off and that I'd never get home. You wasn't out in this blizzard today, was you?"

"I went a little way. I couldn't see any houses or anything."

"Why, whatever did Miss Lemon let you do that for? She ain't got any sense if she let young'uns out into this!"

"She didn't let me. She told me to wait, only I thought I'd go home."

"But your daddy found you," Elizabeth said gently. "You see, like Bunce says, you're generally very close to home and there's someone to open the door for you."

"Could your ma walk?" Johnny asked Bunce.

"Yes, lamb, she could. She was always running around like a chicken with its head cut off. Couldn't stop running, seemed as if. She had a lot to do, ma did, and I guess she thought she had to run."

Johnny finished his tea, and then Bunce said, "You want to come and set in my room for a spell with me, Johnny? I'm kind of tired out and want to set a little bit before I get supper going."

Elizabeth left them together, seeing Johnny sitting on the broad lap, his head against the broad bosom. The sight stayed with her for a long time, as it had that other time she had seen Bunce singing "Jesus Loves Me" to Johnny. Was this the sign? This transmutation of personal pain into pity and love? Did Bunce have the only answer there was? *Had* the Lord shown her her way clear, after all? Was this *it*?

The sign came the next day for Elizabeth Burke. It was one so unexpected, so strange, that at first she did not even recognize it.

About ten o'clock the telephone rang and Mrs. Bunce called Elizabeth. She had so few calls and she couldn't help remembering the one from Huxley Reals. But this time it was not Huxley Reals.

"This is Mr. Masters, Miss Burke," the voice said. "I wonder if you could come down to my office this morning? Say in half an hour?"

"Mr. Masters?" Elizabeth said. "I'm afraid I don't know where your office is. And what was it you wanted to see me about?"

"I'll inform you when you come. I'm upstairs, next to the bank. Masters and Winch. Shall I expect you?"

"All right," Elizabeth said.

She went back up to Anna and said, "Funny thing. Mr. Masters wants me to come down to his office."

"Henry Masters? What on earth does he want?"

"I haven't the faintest idea."

"Have you committed a crime?"

"Not that I know of. I'll call Cornelia down."

"Never mind. I'll just sit here by the window and think about things. Run along. I'm consumed with curiosity!"

Elizabeth climbed up dingy stairs and sat in a stiff heavy old brown chair across from Henry Masters, whom she had seen sometimes with his wife calling on Anna but had never known much. He was a thin dry man with a small mole on his cheek that seemed to have a life of its own.

"Miss Burke, I have here the will of Mrs. Will Daggett. It is very brief. I will read it to you: 'I, Amanda Daggett, being of sound mind, do bequeath all my possessions, real and personal, to Elizabeth Burke of Number Seven North Lake Street, Lakeville. . . .'" Signed by Mrs. Daggett, Jennie Leavitt, Lena Jones, Mary Stone."

Elizabeth stared at him. "That's impossible," she said at last.

"It seems to be in order, Miss Burke. It surprised me too, I may say, but there it is. There is a letter to you, marked 'Personal'—here it is."

"It's some mistake," Elizabeth said. "I—I hardly knew her."

"Well, there it is. I'm only the lawyer. She gave me this herself, sealed. I didn't know what was in it."

"When? When did she give it to you?" Elizabeth asked.

"Some weeks ago. It was when she was laid up with that bad foot. Jennie Leavitt called me over there one day."

"I see. It's a mistake." She stood up. "I'll have to think about this, Mr. Masters. I will see you again. I hardly know what to do."

"There isn't much you can do, except take it," Henry Masters said. "The house isn't such a bad old place and with a little fixing might bring in quite a sum. I don't know what she has in the bank. Not too much, probably. She hadn't any kin that I know of—you happen to be in luck, Miss Burke, and I congratulate you."

"In luck?" Elizabeth said, and Henry Masters remembered the strange look in her plain face for a long time. She walked out of his office, down the stairs, home, up to her room.

"What is it?" Anna called, hearing her feet on the stairs.

"Wait," Elizabeth said. She sat down, coat still on, on her bed, read the letter marked "Personal."

"My dear Miss Burke: My common sense tells me that it is completely unwise to entrust anyone in the world with money not meant for him. However, as I lie here helpless, I have come to the conclusion that I must trust someone. My friend Sarah Horne is an old woman, like me, and she has angina and might go at any moment. Up to this time she has been the only human being in whom I have complete confidence. Since her hold on life is so precarious, I deem it necessary to make other arrangements to safeguard my small property for my grandson. It may be I shall live till I am ninety, as many of my ancestors did, and then I will take care of this matter otherwise, but as I lie here I feel unsure of living so long and I want things left in order in case I am taken. There is no legal way in which you will be liable to turn this property over intact to my grandson, and yet I trust you to do so. If I left it to him direct, his place of residence would be known and that, I must confess, I hesitate to have made public. He may not wish to come to this town if I am no longer here, though that has been the plan for some months now. He will be free next November, if all goes well. You can say you have discovered his whereabouts among my papers, anything you like. I enclose the address and that of my friend Sarah Horne. There is something in the neighborhood of eight thousand dollars in the bank. Would a thousand of this be fair to pay you for your trouble? There is also a box of jewelry in my desk in my bedroom. It is not worth much, but some of it is worth wearing. Please accept that. I have put myself entirely in your hands. I trust you. Sincerely, Amanda Daggett."

Elizabeth Burke sat looking at the letter a long time. Her body was numb, her mind too. This could not be. It simply could not be. There must be another will, not yet discovered. She would never have let this stand as her last will and testament. It had been written during that little space when Mrs. Daggett had been compelled to trust her—but now? No, there was another will, of course. But if there was not? She stood up, ignored Anna's call, went down to the telephone, called Henry Masters. "Mr. Masters, I do feel there has been a mistake," she said. "I think there must have been a later will than this. Will you look for it?"

"Why, yes, if you say so, but you'd better just consider yourself lucky," he said.

Then she went to Anna. "Whatever is it?" Anna asked.

"It's too strange to tell you," Elizabeth said. "It seems Mrs. Daggett has left all she has to me. I just told Mr. Masters it must be a mistake, that there must be a later will. So I won't accept it till he searches." Then she thought suddenly that perhaps Mr. Masters might find other things there in the house that Mrs. Daggett would not want anyone to see.

"To you?" Anna said in amazement.

"That's what the will said—to Elizabeth Burke of Number Seven North Lake Street. It doesn't make sense, does it?"

"Why, you hardly knew her!"

"No. Only we did seem friends when I was going to see her when she was ill. I did errands for her—I think she liked me. Only *that* much? It's incredible."

"The heiress!" Anna said. "Was there much money?"

"I don't think so. A little."

"You could get a good price for the house if it was fixed up a little. I never heard of anything so exciting!"

"It's all a mistake," Elizabeth said. "Wait a bit—they will find another will, you'll see."

"You look as white as a ghost. You'd better take what the gods provide and be grateful! She must have taken a fancy to you!"

"The truth is, I don't want it," Elizabeth said. "It's frightening to have something left you like that. Something that shouldn't belong to you."

"Why, it's wonderful! It's like a fairy story! And why shouldn't it belong to you? You as well as another? She was all alone, she could do as she liked with her things. Why didn't I make her like me that much? I'm jealous!"

"Look, Anna, don't tell anybody till they've looked for another will. Please don't. It would be awful to tell it and then find it was all a mistake."

But that night Adrian said, "What's this Anna tells me, Liz?" He seemed, she thought, to look at her as if he saw her, not as if she were just the spinster who looked after his wife.

"I told Anna not to talk about it," she said.

"Well, she just talked to me. That's quite a break, Liz. A surprise, I must say, though."

"A surprise to me too."

"Glad for you, Liz. You deserve it."

Yes, she thought, she deserved it. Deserved this guilt, this responsibility, this awfulness. She deserved it all.

"But I still think they will find another will," she said. "So wait, Adrian. Don't be glad for me yet."

Though they searched the cluttered old house as carefully as possible, they found no other will. They found a snapshot of a young man who was not recognized, but was commented on, because it was in a silver frame, but that was all. When they told Elizabeth, she said, almost coldly, "Very well, I will accept it. You will know what must be done about taxes and such things, Mr. Masters."

Now she had to accept the questions, the wonder, the congratulations. Now she had to be a person looked at. To accept all this in modesty, in silence, not to show her sorrow, her shame, her regret. For to have shown them would have meant some eye would see the source, that her secret should be nibbled away, become defiled. She went to that house, sat in it one day for an hour, saw the pictures on the walls, the clutter of books and dishes and afghans and lives overlapping, till she felt she was sitting in the history of Lakeville itself. Jennie Leavitt was there, working away at cleaning the house, at the request of Elizabeth herself. "Change nothing, Mrs. Leavitt," she said helplessly. "Clean it all, but change nothing."

"There's an awful lot could be thrown out and no loss," Mrs. Leavitt said.

"I suppose so, and yet I don't know yet what is worthless." Nor did she. It seemed as she sat there that it was all a whole and must not be discarded by so much as a paper, a cracked dish. She took only one thing from the house, the box of jewelry in Mrs. Daggett's desk. It was not much, not valuable, and yet as Elizabeth looked at the old brooches, the bracelets and pins, they were like pieces of the many lives that still seemed to exist in the old house. There was one bracelet of enamel and old gold, with small seed pearls for embellishment, and this bracelet Elizabeth put on. It was old-fashioned and yet had a charm, breathed something of love from another day. She had never worn jewelry, never loved things much, but she loved the bracelet. She said to Jennie Leavitt, "Why don't you and your brother move in here and keep the place going for a few months. They tell me that you just have rooms somewhere since your house burned. You might as well be here."

"You can rent the house easy as rolling off a log," Jeannie Leavitt said. "Why don't you rent it, Miss Burke?"

"No, I don't want to. Not yet. I'll tell you—could you pay for the oil to heat it? I'd let that be the rent, that and keeping the place clean. Would you want to do that—say till next fall? I might have other plans then."

"You must be crazy," Anna said. "Why, Jennie and her brother will shuck around in there like peas in a pod. It's a big house. Even with all the clutter, you could get a good rent. And why don't you clear it out?"

"I don't want to," Elizabeth said. "Not yet. Besides, the estate won't be settled for some time. Mr. Masters said there was no reason I shouldn't do what I liked, but still I'll wait till it is all settled."

She didn't want the house closed, life cut off in it. That seemed wrong to her, and that was why she insisted on the Leavitts' staying there. The house must have warmth and life in it. It must not go dead, have the continuity broken.

She wrote a letter to Anthony Daggett. She told him of Mrs. Daggett's death, of the will. As she wrote she took on phrases that seemed to have come from the old woman herself. "You may not deem it expedient to come to Lakeville to live," she said, in words not her own. Or: "I am only a trustee till this misfortune shall have passed you by." She smiled at the formality of the words but did not change them. And once, out walking on a Friday afternoon, she picked up a stick and felt suddenly that she was old, was old Mrs. Daggett herself, hobbling along to the post office. She wrote to Sarah Horne at the same time as she wrote this other letter, told her the facts, said everything would continue as it had, asked her further cooperation.

Then she watched the mails for a reply. There was a strangeness in these days. It was sometimes bitter to her to feel the added respect in people's glances and tones. There was no difference in her and sometimes she felt a sharp scorn for those who liked her better because she had been the recipient of property. Again, she was ashamed of the scorn, only sad that she had not had enough within to draw people to her without property.

One day Johnny said, "Are you going to live in Mrs. Daggett's house?"

"No, darling."

"It belongs to you, doesn't it?"

"So they say. But I am not going to live in it."

"I could live there with you—then you wouldn't be lonely."

"That would be lovely, but I'm just not going to live there. Don't you want to address your valentines? I'll help you."

He spent much thought on the valentines. Bunce, Meg, Miss Lemon, Susie, his father. Then he hesitated. "How do you spell Liz?" he asked. She told him. "And which one for Mummy?" she asked him. "How about this one—it's very beautiful."

"That's the one for you—only now you know," he said disappointedly.

"It doesn't matter if you know. Valentines say 'I love you'— it's nice to know that. Which one shall we write 'Mummy' on?"

"I don't care," he said.

"Then this one," she said firmly, and wrote the word across the envelope.

On Valentine's Day Bunce sat at the kitchen table, her valentine propped before her, when Elizabeth came down.

"You got the prize one," Elizabeth said. "His very best."

"Poor lamb," Bunce said. "Poor little lamb!"

Anna's was put on her tray and she said only, "I see your fine hand in the address. You didn't need to make him."

Adrian, Elizabeth saw, put his envelope into his breast pocket before he went off to the plant. She felt a sudden tenderness for him, a sharp pity. It had meant something to him—but what? You did not know what Adrian felt about Johnny, about anything. But the valentine had touched him.

That night Bunce, in her little room, with the valentine propped against her Bible, wrote a letter: "Dear Ed: I have been upset but I begin to see my way clear. Much as I appreciate the honor you've done me, I can't do it. I'm needed here and besides I don't think it was meant I should marry again. I've been tempted, Ed, but it just isn't right. The right thing is for you to marry Maisie and I know you'd be real happy with her. We aren't young, like you said, and there's no sense in behaving like we are. I'd like it real well for you to marry Maisie.

She's true gold and you wouldn't be sorry. I've made up my mind so don't try to change it. It wouldn't do any good. Yours in the faith . . ." Then she paused. She had been going to write *Leora Bunce*, but she looked up at the valentine and then wrote *Fatty*. There were tears in her small black eyes. That name was her only concession to sentiment. She did not turn back. It was the end of her brief dream, and she accepted it as the end. She didn't even know she had had a sign, but suddenly she had written the letter. Perhaps the sign was the valentine, which had love in it, which called for her love—this poor little lamb who was so solemn, so in need of comfort and joy.

From time to time Anna had said some gentle word to her of Ed, apologizing for having called him a cod, saying that she didn't know how she'd get on without her, things like that. But Bunce had taken that all without comment. But now Anna said to her on a Thursday, "Are you going to Maisie's tonight?"

Bunce said, "I thought I would, if you aren't needing me here."

"Oh, no. . . . Mrs. Bunce, have you told Ed you'd marry him yet?"

"I ain't going to marry Ed, Mrs. Suydam."

"Nonsense! Of course you are!"

"No, Mrs. Suydam, I'm not." And she went out of the room, with a flurry of stiff gingham.

"I'll have to do something about that," Anna said. "I can't let her waste herself on us. She thinks we can't get on without her. But of course we can if we have to—though it would be a wrench."

"Maybe she doesn't want him," Elizabeth said.

"Of course she wants him! It stuck out all over her! Why, I wouldn't know, except that he's a man."

Elizabeth went down to the kitchen. "Bunce—you did get a sign?" she asked timidly.

Bunce looked up from her potato peeling and said, "I don't know as I did. But I've made up my mind, Miss Burke."

"Yes, I know."

She went over to Bunce, bent and kissed the round red cheek. "Bless you, Bunce," she said. For she knew that Bunce had chosen this loneliness in preference to betraying her friend. The "All's fair in love and war" was a falsehood. Bunce knew that it was not fair that she take Ed Botsworth when Maisie thought he wanted her. Only suppose he didn't take Maisie? But he would. Bunce knew he would, in time. That Maisie would comfort him, that his dream would fade, that he would take second best and grow to like it. Yes, that was what would happen. For Ed needed a home and companionship and Maisie would give it to him—he was past the age where he could be true to a dream. But what had been the sign? How had she made up her mind? Bunce herself could not have told her, for the workings of the heart are devious, do not always take place aboveground in the light. She only knew that it had come to her, plain, that she couldn't do this to Maisie, her friend.

Anna said, "I'm going to have Maisie come over here. I am, Liz. There's no point in Bunce being thwarted in this, no point in her not having Ed if she wants him."

"No," Elizabeth said, "you aren't, Anna. It's Bunce's business."

Anna looked at her, surprised, but did not argue, only smiled slightly as if she would do as she thought best. Then Elizabeth surprised her further. "If you do any such thing, Anna, I must leave here."

"Whatever do you mean?"

"What I say."

"You're getting awfully bossy, now you've got a fortune!" Anna said teasingly, but Elizabeth did not laugh. Then Anna went on, as if there were some connection, "What's happened to Hux, I wonder? He's deserted me."

"Oh, I don't think so," Elizabeth said.

She had not seen Huxley since that night before Mrs. Daggett died. Not once.

"Liz . . ." Anna's voice was very gentle.

"H'm?"

"I'd give him to you if I could. You do give so much to me, darling. But Hux isn't the kind to allow himself to be given away."

"I didn't ask for him, did I?"

She remembered again the challis scarf and Anna's beret, plopped on her head so carelessly because it "suited her" better. Just so would Anna give her the doctor, because he suited her—but she would not give her Hux, who did not suit her. No, that Anna would never do. And what kind of person was she who would be willing to take a castoff from her sister, anyway? Her clothes she had taken, the bits of friendship left over from her relationships with the people in Lakeville, a piece of her home —these she had accepted, for expediency's sake. But what kind would she be if, even had she the chance—and she never would have the chance—she should take a discarded lover? She would be nothing, half a person, without pride or common sense.

"I wish you'd get yourself some new clothes," Anna said later. "Henry says there's no reason you can't use some of your money."

"I thought I was very elegant these days," Elizabeth said. "I'm not going to touch the money, not yet. But I could afford a new suit if I'm a disgrace to you."

"No, I want you to go on a real buying binge—really lose your head over clothes."

The next morning Elizabeth went down to the one good clothes shop in town, the one where the smart young married women shopped, and asked to see suits. But when she saw the suits displayed, confusion overtook her and she knew she did not have the clothes sense necessary to pick out a suit that would please Anna. She tried on one but it was plainly not for her, the skirt too tight, the lines of the jacket making her dumpy and plain. She had been so determined when she went downtown, but now she said slowly, "I'm not in the mood to decide. I don't like this, but I don't know just what I do want. I'll come in again." She saw the raised brow of the salesclerk, but she walked out of the shop and stood there before the door in the thin sunlight ashamed of not knowing what she wanted, what would make her acceptable and smart. Spring would come on, everyone would be having new clothes to greet the spring.

Huxley Reals came out of the bank. She saw him as one would see a stranger. Tall, dark-haired, thin, with that look of breeding and grooming that was his hallmark. Firm, not the kind of man who would be a slave forever. She did not move, just stood there in front of the shop and saw him come down the bank steps. Then he turned and saw her, came at once toward her.

"Hello. What are you doing out this morning?" he asked.

"I was trying to buy a suit," she said. "I haven't got enough brains to pick it out and I ran away."

He gave her a sudden grin and put his hand on her arm. "I'll help you pick one out," he said. "I'm good at it. Juliet always takes me along when she buys clothes." He put out a hand to the door, opened it and pushed her in. "Hello, Grace," he said to the salesgirl who had raised her brows at Elizabeth. "We've come to buy a suit. What have you got? None of those slinky things that Juliet wears, now. Something that you can walk in without tripping."

Grace was laughing and affable now. "We've got some tweeds," she said.

"Well, let's see 'em," Huxley said. "There, that one—that check, that's it. Put it on, Elizabeth."

She stood in the dressing room with the suit on. It was of fine brown and cream check and it made her look what she was, a girl who loved the outdoors, walking, common sense, freedom. "It's a little long," Grace said. "Wait, I'll pin it up so you can see—" and she did pin it up loosely.

"I like it," Elizabeth said.

"Isn't Mr. Reals wonderful?" Grace said.

"He's got good taste anyway," Elizabeth said. She walked out into the shop and Huxley grinned at her and said, "Good! That's the one. Buy it."

It was more than she had meant to pay, but she bought it, left it to be shortened, and walked out of the shop with Huxley Reals.

"Thanks," she said. "That was the fastest shopping I ever did. I don't know what happens to me when I get clothes. I'm not so indecisive about other things."

"No one knows everything," Huxley said. "I have an eye for clothes but on some things I'm as blind as a bat. I'm not going back till after lunch, so why don't we have a sandwich in Tony's place?"

"Why not?" Elizabeth said.

They sat in a booth and had a sandwich and coffee and Huxley Reals said, "I haven't congratulated you on your inheritance. That gave Lakeville something to talk about!"

"I know."

"You don't act pleased. Aren't you?"

"Not much."

"I've been pleased for you. It meant she had forgiven you whatever it was you thought she held against you, anyway, didn't it?"

"No. No, it didn't. She—she made that will when she still trusted me."

"Oh. But she could have changed it, couldn't she?"

"That's what I don't know. That's what I'll never know."

They finished their coffee in silence, then Huxley paid the bill, and they walked out. "I have to get back to the job," he said. "Look, Elizabeth, I think she could have changed it if she'd wanted to. I think she trusted you always—because you are a person to be trusted. I trust you."

"You might not, in like circumstances," Elizabeth said.

"Yes, in like circumstances. In fact, there has been a like circumstance, hasn't there? I seem to remember one. I didn't think you'd betrayed me about Pottsy, did I? I knew better. Anna has this fantastic ability to get at the root of a matter by magic—I know that, Liz. I know it very well indeed. But I trust you and I feel sure Mrs. Daggett did too, once she'd thought the thing over. I wouldn't brood about it if I were you."

"I can't help it. It's like a stone inside."

"But you're lucky, if you only knew it, that it is like a stone. You're lucky that you can feel it that much. When you get your new suit, I'll take you out, shall I?"

Elizabeth hesitated, then said, "I'll see. I always seem to run into you when I'm in trouble, don't I? But I'm not always troubled."

"I know. I've seen you skating. Well, be seeing you, Liz," he said and swung back down Main Street.

Elizabeth did not hide this meeting. She went at once to Anna and said, "Well, I've got a new suit. And you'd better like it, because Huxley picked it out."

"Huxley?"

"I am a fool about clothes, Anna—you're right. I go into a kind of coma when I see new things. I went into one this morning and I came out, almost weeping at my stupidity—and Huxley Reals was coming along and I guess he saw I was in despair and asked me what the matter was. I told him—he jerked me into the shop and I had a new suit in ten minutes. It's brown check—and you've got to like it."

Anna laughed. "I'll wait till I see it. Huxley chooses Juliet's clothes—but you're not Juliet. Did you tell him I was missing him?"

"No. No, I didn't. I was engrossed in this suit business."

She was invited to Meg's to supper and she went about four. Meg seemed more quiet than usual. When Elizabeth sat down in the brown chair, she saw Meg's eyes turned on the chair, not herself, and she had an odd sensation as of seeing Adrian sitting here resting, resting. But Meg did not mention Adrian. They talked spasmodically about odd things, but they did not touch much on people. At the table the doctor was full of talk. He laid himself out to be entertaining and he was entertaining, but Elizabeth saw Meg look at him once with something almost scornful in the glance. When Elizabeth left, the doctor said he'd walk home with her. "Good heavens, with that fortune, can I let you out of my sight?" he demanded.

Elizabeth made no protest and the doctor walked along the street with her.

"Almost spring," the doctor said. "Though March can be very wintry in Lakeville."

"Yes, it has seemed like spring today," Elizabeth said without brilliance.

The doctor gave his slow laugh and said, "Let's not talk about the weather, Liz. I told Meg I was going to ask you to marry me, so I'm asking you. I mean it, Liz. I know I'm older than you, old enough to be your father, as Meg is always pointing out. But I don't feel old and I think I have considerable usefulness in me yet. I don't think you're the sort who demands a grand romance—though I might even find I had some romance in me too. But I do think we might make a go of it. Do you?"

"No, I'm afraid I don't," Elizabeth said.

"Why not? I'm not being funny, Liz. I mean it."

"You'd never have seen me if Anna hadn't made you," she said.

"Maybe not. But I do see you now. And I like you a great deal. I'd say I loved you only I know it sounds silly from an old codger like me. Think I do, though. What does it matter how it came about?"

"It might not matter if I wanted to do it," Elizabeth admitted. "But I don't, Dr. McIntry. I just don't."

"Too old?"

"No, you're not too old. I'm not so awfully young myself.

And it isn't even that I want a grand romance. It's just that I don't care about you that way."

"You might get to," the doctor said. They had come to Number Seven and paused at the steps. "You might, Liz. Maybe you think I'm being too light about this, and in the beginning it was more or less of a joke. It isn't a joke any longer, Liz. I want you, like any man wants his woman. I think you're the woman for me, Liz. I've been cynical about marriage because my own was no good, but I want another chance. And I'd try to make it good."

Something about his serious voice touched her. His long figure standing there in the street light's rays was impressive and she felt his loneliness as something very real, very honest, reaching out to touch her loneliness. For an instant she thought, And why not? Why not? We would be good for each other. But she put a hand on his arm and said, "I'm sorry. I'm really sorry. I like you better than I thought I ever would. I wish I could, but I can't. You see, I happen to love someone else. Someone I can't marry—but I never could take second best."

"Adrian?" he said.

"Oh, no. No, of course not. . . . I'm sorry," she said again helplessly.

He was silent a moment. "Oh, well, I tried," he said then, and tried to laugh.

"I'm so sorry," she said again, like a record she could not turn off.

"Believe you really are," he said. "That's something. Well, good night, Liz."

"Good night."

xv

Eʟɪᴢᴀʙᴇᴛʜ ᴛᴏʟᴅ Anna about the doctor. She told it quite calmly. "Anna, the doctor asked me to marry him," she said the next morning. "I said 'No,' in case you're already planning my wedding dress."

"That's stupid," Anna said. "That's really stupid, Liz. And you're not stupid. He's a real person and he'd be good for you."

"I presume he would. I just can't be that practical about it. Now let's not talk about it any more. He's done what you wanted him to do—it's over."

"I don't give up—he'll ask you again."

"No, he won't. He won't, Anna."

"There's the mail!"

Elizabeth went down the stairs and took the mail from Bunce's hands. She saw the letter right on top: "Miss Elizabeth Burke, 7 N.Lake St." and Sarah Horne's address in the corner. She slid the letter into her pocket and went on up the stairs. It was an hour later before she had a chance to read it. She read Mrs. Horne's first.

"My dear Miss Burke: It was with deep sorrow I learned of my friend's death. I have lived a long time myself, and most of my contemporaries are gone, so I am used to death. Still, I was

256

not prepared for this as I should have been. People get set so early and find so little new to learn. But Amanda Daggett began to grow late in life and this always astonished and delighted me more than I can say. It seemed sad that she could not keep on, when there are so few that are willing to grow. I have forwarded your letter and enclose a reply. As my own hold on life is tenuous, I am relieved by the arrangements Amanda made. Sincerely, Sarah Horne."

Then the other letter, with that ugly number on the face of it.

"Dear Miss Burke: Thank you for writing to me about my grandmother. I never saw her but she has been real to me all my life. She has been kind to me these last few years. It would be hard to tell you what her letters have meant to me, putting what she calls 'gimp' into me. I don't have it hard here, because I work in the office, but it's kind of rugged when you're young all the same. There won't be much more of it. I don't know what I am going to do when I get out, but I guess I can get a job somewhere. My grandmother wanted me to come to her house and I was thinking I would, but I don't know now as that would be the thing to do. One thing I didn't agree with her on. She didn't want anybody to know where I'd been. I guess older people get proud that way. But the thing is, I don't think you can keep something like being in stir secret. Somebody always finds out. It isn't that I'm crazy to shout it out to folks, but it doesn't seem practical not to admit it if you have to. You just have to grow a tough skin, I guess. But maybe it would be better for me to start out somewhere where my grandmother wasn't so well known. About the money, I don't know what to say. I wouldn't say it wouldn't come in handy, but, looking at it practically, I can't see any reason why you'd feel you had to turn it over to me. Not legally, or anything like that. It makes me feel good that she wanted me to have it but whatever you feel like doing, it will be all right with me. I'm not going to fight about it. I don't know what I'd do with a house. It isn't likely I'll get married right off—I had a girl but she couldn't take it and maybe no girl could. My grandmother thought she could get me a job with a boat company there, but I don't know whether she had done anything about it or not. A job's what I'm most interested in. What I wish you could tell me is whether it would be foolish to come clear across the country for a job that maybe isn't there now my grandmother isn't there. I am enclosing a five-dollar bill (we earn a little here, you know) and I wish you'd put some flowers on my grandmother's grave for me. Maybe that's silly, but I wish you could do that. In some ways I wish I could come to Lakeville and get a long way off from connections out here. Only I'm not foolish enough that I don't know one place is much like another. If you'd write to me now and then I'd be pleased. I miss my grandmother's letters. Only I don't want to hide anything any more and go through Mrs. Horne. I know my grandmother meant it for the best, but I just don't see it that way. I had things I meant to say, but I'm not very good at letters. I just hope I won't lose my 'gimp.' Very truly yours, Anthony Daggett."

Elizabeth held the limp bill in her hands and the tears ran down her face.

Poor boy! Poor boy! her heart kept saying over and over. There was something about the letter, so half boyish, half mature, that was unbearably pathetic. He was too young to know how very tough a skin he would have to grow. And yet not so young he didn't know a tough skin would be necessary. His grandmother had been right—and yet maybe Anthony Daggett knew the world better than Mrs. Daggett knew it, knew that such secrets cannot be kept, even with the best will in the world. That old-fashioned word "gimp."

She put the letter away, shoved the bill into her pocket, and went in to Anna. "Anna, I have to do an errand. Do you mind if I go out for a little while? I'll tell Cornelia I'm going."

"An errand? What for? Couldn't you wait till I take my nap?"

"Yes, I suppose I could."

But she wanted to go now, this moment. She didn't want to wait.

At two o'clock she stood in the old Lakeville burying ground on the bluff above the lake just out of town. It was one of those soft days that deceive you into thinking spring is at hand. The sun shone and the snow was melting here and there. In her arms Elizabeth carried freesia. She stood there by the new grave that she had wandered a long time to find. She felt strangely peaceful as if it didn't matter whether Mrs. Daggett had forgiven her or not. She put the freesia down on the forlorn grave. It would die soon. After the sun went down, it would freeze. But perhaps till then it would lie there, golden and fresh, a message from a boy in stir.

Maybe it was silly. Silly to spend money for flowers Mrs. Daggett would never see. And yet Elizabeth did not feel it was a waste.

That night she wrote to Anthony Daggett, one of many letters. She thought of Mrs. Daggett's humped figure sitting at that cluttered desk in the corner, with the cats stalking about her or climbing on her as she wrote, and she thought that this could not all be wasted, that some spark of Mrs. Daggett's love had to stay on in the world, go on giving her boy "gimp." It was part of her legacy that she had to do this. But she sent the letter by way of Sarah Horne, in spite of the boy's protests. She wrote sensibly, without much sympathy. She remembered how he used the word "practical" and so she was as practical as she knew how to be. "I do not think you could afford to keep up the house on any salary you could earn at the present in Lakeville," she said. "I did think you might rent it and reserve a room or perhaps two or three for yourself. You would not have any trouble renting it. It is a big house, and full of the possessions of several generations of Daggetts. As to a job with the boat company, I will make inquiries." At the end she said, "I am sending this to Mrs. Horne as usual. I believe you are quite right about secrecy. In the long run you will have to prove yourself, and perhaps a little more thoroughly than most, but for the present I have personal reasons for not wanting to discuss you or your affairs in this household."

She smiled as she read over what she had written. She sounded exactly like The Spinster Aunt in the House. Exactly. She put a postscript on finally: "I took the flowers. Freesia. The yellow was springlike and friendly."

She wrote to him every day after that, often very short brisk letters, and sometimes mailing several together, but she wrote every day. It was an important task and she recognized it as such. Important for several reasons: it gave her a sense of paying a debt to Mrs. Daggett; it gave her a feeling of usefulness; it was something outside of her life in this house. And yet its chief importance lay in none of these but rather in a strange consciousness that it was not important whether her act became known or not, a consciousness that if her letters were seen she would not be ashamed to discuss them openly, that she was no longer afraid of what Anna could do to her in regard to them. She wondered about this, for there seemed no reason for it. She knew very well the story Anna could make of the whole thing, but she felt outside the knowledge, above it. She wondered sometimes whether possession, no matter how ephemeral, did not give power. Whether the fact that the town and Anna believed the old Daggett house and the Daggett money in the bank were hers was armor about her. The thought shamed her, but still, it might be so. She had never had much in the way of possessions. She thought of her box of books in Lollie's apartment. They were all she had owned but they too had been some kind of defense. She sat down one day and wrote asking Lollie to send them wondering why Lollie had not already done so. Did Lollie still expect her to come back? Was she keeping the books as a sort of hostage? Love was a strange thing. She loved Lollie Parsons and yet how little really, they had ever seen each other. Why did she love her and why was she so sure Lollie loved her in return? It could not be because Lollie was so perceptive and saw to her deepest motivation. That was true of Anna also but it did not bring the same response in her. Perhaps it was only that Lollie, though she saw and understood, let her be herself, let her make her own decisions, admitted a maturity as great as her own.

But when the books came and she had set them up on top of the small desk, along the little table by her bed she scarcely looked inside them. She was glad to see them but she did not read them.

One day when she had come home from fetching Johnny the Reverend Mr. Prather was sitting with Anna. He was an interesting-looking man, with Lincolnlike lines deep graven in his long face, deep-set eyes and a stern mouth.

"This is my sister, Liz," Anna said. "We were talking about sin, Liz."

"Let's not. Let's talk about spring," Elizabeth said. "I saw a boy with some pussywillows."

"We've got March to go through yet," Anna said. "Spring may not come this year—but sin we have always with us."

Elizabeth gave the rector of St. Paul's a quick grin and said, "What she is trying to get at is: why wouldn't you take Bill Vine's money for the chapel?"

To her surprise, for he did have a solemn, unsmiling face, he grinned back at her with a quick humor and said, "I wrestled with my angel and got thrown."

Anna laughed and said, "Liz, you're spoiling my subtle approach. But now we're this far, what arguments did your angel use?"

"None. He just scorned the whole thing. I used the arguments. But there aren't any, are there? I just don't happen to believe that money turns holy because used for holy ends."

"And why not? How do you know that Bill Vine might not become saved through pride in his own contribution? How do you know he might not be lured into his chapel? How do you know the Lord differentiates between money from Bill Vine and, say, Mrs. Bunce? How do you know the Lord wouldn't give Bill Vine a good mark for his gift and that you wouldn't be depriving him of it?"

"I don't know, Mrs. Suydam. Indeed, I know very little. But I don't believe it matters to the Lord at all whether we have a new chapel or not. And I do know that to me it was wrong, that's all."

"And that's as far as any of us can go," Elizabeth said.

"I would think," Anna said, "though I'm not a very religious person, Dr. Prather, that it would be like a composition in music, a hymn sung to the Lord, let us say, or a heavenly orchestra—that it wouldn't matter who sang the notes or played the harps, so long as the music went up to God."

"Ah, she's baiting you with music because she heard you used to be a musician!" Elizabeth said.

His deep-set eyes turned to Elizabeth with sudden interest. "So?" he said. "But I don't happen to believe that, either, you see. That it doesn't matter who sings the notes. I believe it matters very much. That is why, you see, I am not a musician. I had a good deal of facility but I did not love music enough to give my life for it and I could not see myself as acceptable in the musical world unless I did love it that much. So I came to a point where I had to ask myself what I did love that much and I found I loved man himself, or perhaps I should say the God-in-man. I happen not to be able to believe that it was the God-in-Bill Vine that made him offer that money, but something malicious and venal. You may well say that I do not know the deepest motivation in any man—that would be true. I had to decide what I thought was his motivation and I found it not good enough."

"That's an awfully hard way to live," Anna said ruefully.

"Yes. Or, no, no harder than any life. We don't want life to be too easy, do we? If I may say so, Mrs. Suydam, your own life is not too easy a one. Yet your courage is a kind of legend already in Lakeville. You say you are not religious, and yet I feel quite sure that your courage makes a true note in that orchestra you speak of, that it goes up to God."

"What a lovely thing to say to me," Anna said softly. "I'm not very courageous, Dr. Prather, but I do love life. I have to pay some kind of debt to life, that's all."

"That's a great deal," Prather said gently. "Well, I must go."

"Oh, but let's have tea!" Anna said. "We always have it now. We were so interested, we forgot."

"Thank you—another time. I must go now. May I come again?"

"Of course."

He shook hands with her, then turned to Elizabeth, held out his hand. "Don't trouble to come down. I'll find my way out."

When the door closed below, Anna laughed and said, "Well! He's really quite nice, isn't he? You were awfully blunt, though, darling."

"It got results," Elizabeth said.

"I think he liked you. I saw the look in his ministerial eye— but having been a musician takes some of the curse off the clericalism, wouldn't you say?"

"What are you doing—spinning webs again?"

"Why not? Oh, Liz, I do so want you to be happy! I suppose I want you to be happy my way, but when he was sitting here, I thought of how selfish that was—that the way you'd really be happy would be with a serious man like that. Always worrying away at the conscience. I think you could have him with half a try. And he does have a little humor."

"Yes, he has humor, but I don't want him, Anna. I just don't want him. I liked him too. I like him better than the doctor. But I'm not going to try for him."

Anna was silent for some time, then she said, "Liz . . ."

"H'm?"

"I think you ought to try. It's so awfully futile to waste your life wishing for something you can't have. Half loaves are better than none. I think you ought to stop dreaming romantic dreams and face reality. Don't be angry, darling—but that's the way it looks to me."

Elizabeth turned from the window, where she had been standing, looked at Anna, and said, "And what romantic dreams do you think I'm dreaming, Anna?"

"I said, don't be angry. I can't bear having you angry at me. I mean Huxley. Oh, I know you deny it, but—well, one gets perceptive, just sitting and thinking. You do have romantic dreams. If you had seen your face when he helped you pick out a suit! I wish it hadn't been that way . . . but the only way to forget it is to make the try at loving someone else. Truly, it is."

"Why?"

"Why? Oh, Liz, don't be that way. You know why."

"Speaking of a hypothetical case—since the one you're dreaming up isn't real—why shouldn't I try for Huxley if I want to? He's free, isn't he?"

Anna gave that breath of laughter which was so familiar. "In a way," she said.

"Well, then? I don't dream about him but if I want to I don't see where any harm lies. How do you know, if I tried hard enough, I couldn't have him?"

"I know Huxley," Anna said. "It's a silly situation, if you like, but it won't change just because it's foolish. Huxley isn't changeable."

"Still," Elizabeth's stubborn voice went on, "if I wanted to try, there wouldn't be any real reason I shouldn't. There wouldn't be anything wrong or even impossible about it. You're willing enough to have me try for the doctor, or even the Reverend Mr. Prather—but why not be willing to have me try for Huxley if I want to?"

Anna's voice became a little sharper. "I don't want you hurt, that's all," she said.

"Well, I have always managed my own hurts. I could manage that one too. But suppose I didn't get hurt? Suppose he came to like me? What then?" •

"My prickly Liz!" Anna said softly.

"I just want it clear, that's all. I'm free too, Anna. And I'm an adult. I'm not going to try for Huxley—but I don't see any reason I shouldn't if I want to. Do you?"

"Only what I said—that you'd get hurt and that is futile. And you'd just make a fool of yourself—you'd hate that, and I'd hate it for you, darling."

"You needn't worry. It's just that I want it understood that I am grown up and that I have a right to try for what I will, so long as it doesn't hurt others."

She was trembling when she went to her own room, as if she had been through a great dramatic scene.

That night at the dinner table Mrs. Suydam said, "I saw Mrs. Reals today and she tells me Huxley is thinking of going to St. Paul to work. He's had an offer it seems."

Adrian looked up quickly. "Huxley? He didn't tell me."

"I didn't remember hearing you mention it," his mother said.

"I hope he doesn't spring it on me right in the middle of this job," he said. "That's not like Hux."

Elizabeth saw he was upset but he said no more then. He took his coffee upstairs to Anna's room. Elizabeth read to Johnny, got him to bed, then sat down in the living room with a book. At last Adrian came down and she rose to leave but he said, "Did Hux say anything to you about leaving?"

"Not lately. Some time ago he mentioned it here one day."

"I should have thought he'd mention it to me if to anyone."

"I don't think he'd made up his mind."

"What time is it?"

"Nearly ten."

"I think I'll drop around and see him."

Without another word he got his coat and went out. Elizabeth went up to Anna. "Where's Adrian gone to?" Anna asked at once. Adrian had put her to bed and Elizabeth at once began to smooth the sheets, arrange the pillows, as she always had to do after Adrian's tender but inexpert ministrations.

"He went to see Huxley Reals."

"At this time of night? With all his fussing about Hux, I should think he'd be glad if he went away. Though Huxley won't go."

"He might."

"No, he won't go. For your sake, darling, I hope he does—but he won't."

Elizabeth gave a quick sigh, then said, "I'll turn in now, I think—is there anything else you want?"

"Just that you don't be cross with me."

"I'm not cross with you."

"You sound uncommonly like it. . . . Sit down and talk awhile. I won't be able to sleep till Adrian gets in."

Ordinarily Elizabeth would have submitted, but now she said, "I'm sorry, but I'm really awfully tired. I'll come in at eleven."

"Well, run along then. You are cross—but don't let it last overnight, darling!"

At eleven Adrian had not yet come in and Anna was restless.

"I do hope Adrian isn't being silly and quarreling with Hux," she said.

"I don't think so. He needs him too much right now."

"It would be strange without Hux in Lakeville. He fills in the chinks. Does it bother you to have me talk about him?"

"Why should it?"

It was nearly one when Elizabeth heard Adrian come up the stairs and go down the hall to his room. He walked quietly, but slowly. He did not go in to Anna, though always he walked at least to the doorway of her room before he turned in. She wondered if Anna was lying awake, listening for him. At breakfast she asked directly, "Is Huxley Reals going?"

He looked at her blankly, or perhaps there was an instant

when his eyes were not blank but almost at once a shutter had
come down across any meaning there.

"I don't know," he said.

"You didn't see him?" she persisted.

"No, I didn't see him," he said.

He refused more coffee, though he always had two cups at
breakfast, went up to say good-by to Anna. He hadn't been
gone more than an hour when a great box of spring flowers
was delivered. "Oh—they're from Adrian," Anna said. "Because
he was a little cranky this morning, I suppose. Do you want
to put them in water before you take off on your great Friday
adventures?"

Elizabeth arranged the daffodils and tulips in a great bowl,
carried them slowly upstairs. They seemed to be telling her
something she did not want to hear.

"They're beautiful," she said. "Nothing so springlike as daffodils."

"Do you mind giving these to the mailman?" Anna said.

Elizabeth took the two letters, turned to go. Mrs. Suydam
was coming down the hall. She was so unobtrusive, Cornelia
Suydam, and yet on Elizabeth's days off she was always there
waiting. "Have a nice day!" she said, and went in to Anna.
Elizabeth walked down the stairs, put the letters on the hall
table, then saw the address clearly: "Mr. Huxley Reals, Lakeville . . ." She hesitated, then put that letter under the other,
for Bunce would be the one to hand the mail to the mailman.

She had no plans for the day, though usually she spent part
of it with Margaret McIntry. But till then? Perhaps Margaret
would go somewhere for lunch with her. She went to her room
and put on her new suit. It was the first time she had worn it.
She put a yellow kerchief in the pocket. She seemed to be dressing up for something, but for what? The brown-and-cream
check suited her—it truly suited her. She ought, she knew, to
go in and show herself to Anna, but she remembered what
Anna had said about her face when she had come home from

the suit's purchase and she could not. She went down the stairs and out into the balmy day. She walked to the McIntry house, walked in, as was her habit now. There was no one about and for an instant, standing there, hearing no reply to her call, she felt an intruder, felt she should not have stepped in without ringing. "Oh, Margaret!" she called again.

Then the doctor stepped in from the office, smiled at her, though with some ruefulness, and said, "Margaret didn't get up for breakfast—but she says she isn't sick. Just go on up."

She began to walk up the stairs, but felt wrong in doing so. Yet perhaps Margaret was sick. She went to Margaret's room and found the door shut. She tapped gently and Margaret said at once "Yes?" but her voice was not welcoming.

"It's Liz. May I come in?"

Did Margaret hesitate? It seemed so. Still, she said, "Yes, come in," and Elizabeth walked into the room. Margaret's room was not so cluttered as the rest of the house. It was almost austere. On the wall were some Audubon prints, but there were none of the fripperies of femininity to be seen anywhere. Margaret McIntry was in bed. Her hair hung in braids and made her look younger, but her eyes were bleak as she said, "Hello, Elizabeth. I'm being lazy today."

"Are you sick?"

"I?" Margaret made mockery of her own good health.

Elizabeth felt again that she was intruding but she went on. "It's too nice a day to lie abed. I thought we might go to the inn or somewhere for lunch. I even put on my new suit for it. Do you like it?"

"Very much. I'm sorry but I just want to be lazy today."

"You are sick, then!"

"Not at all. Didn't you ever want to—to withdraw from the world for a bit?"

"Oh, often. Well, then, I'll go and let you withdraw. But I'm disappointed—my new suit seems so pointless now."

Margaret laughed suddenly and said, "Oh, wait a minute—

I'll come. It doesn't suit me to be brooding—I'm not the type. And what would it get me, anyway? Just a jiffy—I'll get some clothes on."

She slid out of bed and Elizabeth saw with some wonder that Margaret had a graceful, almost beautiful body that didn't show under the somewhat graceless clothes she was wont to wear. With the braids hanging she was like an overgrown schoolgirl and had the appeal of one. But almost at once she was clothed in her usual plain garb and had braided her hair afresh, twisted it up stiffly, adding ten years or more to her age.

"Don't know what got into me," she confessed easily. "I just said to myself I wasn't going to get breakfast, and I didn't."

"It's always fun to break the routine," Elizabeth said. "Exciting."

But she felt confused, felt the right things weren't being said, that there was something between them where heretofore there had been nothing at all.

"I'll tell you what let's do," Margaret said. "I can borrow Mr. Berg's car—he always urges me to take it. Let's go out into the country somewhere, shall we? It is such a good day."

"All right," Elizabeth said.

But once they were in the car, Margaret was silent. There was no flow of easy talk between them. They stopped once in a bare little wood and saw two birds and Margaret fished in her pocket for a pad and pencil. "Here, put 'em down, and the date," she said. "I don't know what good records are, but put them down anyway."

They found a country inn and were all alone in its dining room.

They ate almost in silence, but over coffee Margaret said, "Well, we got out of Lakeville anyway."

"Yes, we got out of Lakeville. Do you dislike Lakeville?"

"Sometimes I hate it. Never for long at a stretch, though. I was born there and I expect I'll die there."

"And this morning you hated it?"

"Yes," Margaret said, no more.

"I'm used to it now. Now I've accepted the fact that I probably won't ever escape it. In the beginning I was always thinking about getting away."

"I realized that," Margaret said. "Don't we get caught in the strangest traps?"

"You make me think of Lollie," Elizabeth said. "She's my teacher friend. She's little and fat—but she thinks like you."

"Poor Lollie. I think I'm getting more like father."

"Why do you think that? You look like him but you're not at all like him."

"Getting like him, I said. Seeing the world with a jaundiced eye. What's it all about? I wonder. Everybody I know is caught in some kind of trap. The devil of it is we help build the traps. Doesn't that sound like father? Very much, I'd say. . . . That's a darned good-looking suit. You must have spent all your inheritance on it."

"Not quite all. Huxley Reals picked it out."

"Huh?"

"He did. I went into that shop where Grace works—she showed me something slinky and I was lost. I walked out, feeling her eying me from the rear as if I were some lowly worm—I cannot decide on clothes. Something horrible happens to my will and my judgment. And Huxley came along and rescued me, walked me right back in and in ten minutes I had bought this."

Margaret poured another cup of coffee and said fiercely, "Traps! Traps, traps! Love or duty or ambition—we call 'em all sorts of fancy names but all they are is traps." Then she gave a grin that was more familiar. "I'm not losing my mind, if that's what you're thinking."

"I wasn't thinking that. I suppose I was agreeing with you—only I gnaw away at mine still. I do gnaw a little."

"You can gnaw till you chew a leg off, but you won't get

out," Margaret said. "Or, if you do, you'll be minus the leg and will have to fight twice as hard to exist—you'll turn wild."

"I should have left you in bed," Elizabeth said.

"Of course you should, I'm no fit company today. Let's go, shall we?"

They went out again into the sunlight, got into Mr. Berg's car, and headed for town. They were silent as they threaded the country roads. Almost at the end of town Elizabeth said, "Adrian sent Anna some of the loveliest spring flowers this morning. Do you think men always apologize for something when they send flowers?"

There was still silence. Then Margaret said, "I wouldn't know. Men don't send me flowers."

"I don't know what he was apologizing for—she said he was cranky, but he never is cranky, not with Anna."

They had come to the house and Margaret made no answer. Then she said, "Wait, I'll just run Mr. Berg's car in."

"I ought to go on home," Elizabeth said. She knew that was true, that she ought to leave Margaret, leave her to her bitter thoughts, whatever they were. Still, she stood there on the steps and waited. Waited for what? They had nothing to say to each other today and there seemed some danger in their even being together, some very real but unexpressed danger.

Margaret returned very soon and opened the door. They stepped into the hall. There, on a small table, lay a florist's box. It hit the vision immediately, perched as it was on top of a pile of books. Margaret walked to it at once, opened it without a word, as if she had forgotten Elizabeth's presence. It was full of the softest yellow roses.

"I thought men never sent you flowers," Elizabeth said helplessly, feeling the danger near now, perilously near.

Margaret sat down on the stair steps, put her head down on her knees, like someone sick. "Go away. Go away," she said.

Elizabeth turned and walked out of the old brown house.

XVI

ELIZABETH, still in her new suit, sat at the dinner table. Adrian was upstairs eating with Anna. Elizabeth tried making conversation with Johnny, succeeded a little, but still the meal seemed a long one. After Johnny had finished, she sat alone with Cornelia over coffee.

"Anna seemed very tired today," Cornelia said.

"Were many in?"

"Jen was here an hour and Peggy Jones dropped in. That's all. When she asks for Adrian, I know she has had to take too much, that she is giving in to being lonely and frightened. She went to bed right after Peggy went."

"I don't see how it can be otherwise—that some days are hard to take, I mean," Elizabeth said.

"No. It can't. I wonder that there are so few of them. . . . I like your suit very much. It becomes you."

"Thank you. I like it too. I like it better than anything I've ever had."

Then a small silence fell. Bunce came in with more coffee, departed.

"I wish Adrian could get away by himself for a few days," Mrs. Suydam said suddenly. Elizabeth flushed, did not answer.

"He hasn't had a letup for almost a year—but of course he won't leave Anna. He'd say he didn't want to, and he doesn't want to, but he is getting nervous and touchy. He's always been so calm and gentle."

"He wouldn't go," Elizabeth agreed.

"I know. But, as Anna says, this is a long-term proposition."

"Anna is the only one who could see that he went," Elizabeth said. "But he has this big job at the plant—he couldn't leave that. And if Huxley Reals goes away, he will be more tied than ever till he finds someone to take his place."

"Adrian has always been so strong," Mrs. Suydam said, with a faint frown in her usually unlined forehead.

"Don't worry, Mrs. Suydam. He is still strong," Elizabeth said.

But through her head went the sound of his slow, quiet footsteps going down the hall, not turning toward Anna's room.

She carried the coffee cups out to Bunce.

"No need to do that," Bunce said. Bunce looked quite herself these days, no sign in her face of inner trouble. She sang about her work and went out of her way to think up tasty dishes to surprise Anna with, went to Pottsy's Thursday nights, and was tolerant of Johnny's muddy overshoes and questions.

"I don't overstrain myself helping you out," Elizabeth said dryly. "I can carry out a couple of cups, can't I, without hurting anyone?"

Bunce gave a deep chuckle. "I'm house-proud," she admitted. "Gets under my skin when somebody touches anything about the house—it ain't my house but I act like it was."

"It wouldn't be much of a house if you weren't in it," Elizabeth said.

"You want to get Mrs. Suydam's tray?" Bunce asked.

"No. No, I don't want to, not really. Adrian'll bring it down." Bunce looked at her in surprise.

"I mean—I don't want to interrupt them. They don't have so much time together, Bunce. I'll wash Anna's things later. . . ."

There's something I want to ask you, only it embarrasses me. I don't quite know how."

"Well, spit it out," Mrs. Bunce said, though she was ordinarily more polite than that.

"You act happy, Bunce. Are you?"

"By and large, I guess I'm happy as needs be. When I heard this morning that the Bentley boy was missing in Korea, seemed like I was happier'n I had any right to be."

"Maybe happy isn't the word. It isn't a happy world. Maybe I mean sure—sure of your way, not regretting anything."

Bunce wiped off the shelf, cleaned the sink thoroughly, hung up her dishcloth. She was not used to such conversations, but she was no fool.

"Well, now, Miss Burke," she said at last, "I don't say I'm too sure about everything. But I've found out this, it's only making up your mind that hurts. Once you've made it up, things gets easier."

"Yes, I suppose that's the way it is," Elizabeth said and went away from Bunce.

She went to her room and wrote to Anthony Daggett. At eleven, in her flannel robe, she went with Anna's milk to Anna's room. To her surprise Adrian was sitting there by the bed. The room was in darkness except for the bed light and Adrian's face was in shadow but for the lower part. His mouth looked inexpressibly tired. Anna's eyes were closed. Adrian reached out his hand for the milk, set the plate down on the small table by the bed, shook his head at Elizabeth as if dismissing her. She hesitated, then went out and left him there. She could not sleep. Daffodils and yellow roses danced before her eyes in the darkness. *Traps—traps—traps!* Margaret's voice dinned in her ears. *Once you've made it up, things gets easier.* But how could you make it up, when everything was so complicated? How could you ever simplify decisions, get them made? How could you really ever know whether you were coming or going? Then she thought of Anthony Daggett and grew a little calmer. That was one thing she was going to see through, make right. One thing.

In the morning Adrian came down to breakfast at his usual time, sat down with the rest. "I won't be home till dinnertime. We're working all day today," he said, and that was about all he contributed to the conversation. But at the door he turned back and said to Elizabeth, "Liz, don't let Anna overdo today. She is overtired."

But Anna seemed quite herself when Elizabeth got her up, did her hair. Indeed, more herself than ever. There was a kind of radiance about her, a kind of secret joy that made her irresistible and extraordinarily beautiful.

"You know," she said, "I've got so I can't take your days off, darling. I think, though I hate to put Adrian to any more expense, that I'll see if Jennie Leavitt will come for those days."

"I don't really need any days off," Elizabeth said. "Don't go to the expense of Jennie—if I need some time, I'll say so. But days I really don't need."

"Of course you do. I like Jennie and she is strong and willing. Besides that, she is a fountain of gossip!"

Elizabeth hesitated, then plunged. "Perhaps you'd rather have her all the time, Anna. You don't *have* to have me here, just because I'm here now."

"Does that mean you don't want to be here?"

"No. But you know what you said about habits once—if you get tired of the habit of me, just say so, that's all."

"And you the same?" Anna asked gently.

"Of course."

"Don't think I wouldn't understand, Liz, if you suddenly wanted to go. Sometimes we simply have to run away—I know that."

"But I don't want to run away," Elizabeth said helplessly. "Why should I?"

When the mail came there was a note from Huxley. Anna laughed softly as she read it but she did not share it with Elizabeth.

That afternoon when Juliet was there, Anna said, "Liz is getting tired of us. She'll be off to new pastures soon—I know the signs."

"Oh, you mustn't leave us, Liz!" Juliet said, with more warmth than usual. "We're so used to you—you're one of us now."

"I hadn't intended to," Elizabeth said. "Anna doesn't read signs as well as she thinks she does."

"Besides, you've got *property* in Lakeville," Juliet said. "You couldn't leave your property!"

"No, how could I?" Elizabeth agreed.

She left them then, went in to Johnny. Johnny was flat on his bed reading. He read everything now, suitable or not. Just words on a page delighted him, whether he knew their meaning or not. The book he had now was one of the loved volumes of his encyclopedia. He was so engrossed she did not even speak to him but wandered downstairs. After half an hour Juliet came down, saw her from the hallway, and came in to her. Juliet, always so self-possessed, looked embarrassed. She came near Elizabeth though and pulled on her gloves slowly. "I wish it might have been so," she said quietly.

Elizabeth was curled up in the yellow chair. Her red dress was very bright against the yellow. She looked up slowly, feeling a cold chill taking her whole body over.

"Wish what might have been so?" she said almost harshly.

"Don't worry—I do not gossip," Juliet said. "Truly, Liz, I do not. I just wanted to say I was sorry. I don't see why it might not have happened that way. I do like you so very much. I'll take back what I said about your going away."

I am going to cry, Elizabeth thought. But she did not cry. She said, "But I haven't any idea of going away. Not unless Anna doesn't need me here any more. That's her idea, not

mine. Well, perhaps I will go, but not for any reason you may
be imagining."

Juliet sat down on the fireside stool. "I wish you could trust
me," she said.

"I do. And of course I know what Anna has been saying to
you. She's been telling you I have a hopeless passion for your
brother and that I want to escape from it. She made that up.
Oh, she thinks it is so, but she made it up—I never told her
so."

"Oh. It isn't true, then?"

It was hard for Juliet Olde to be warm and friendly. This
was, Elizabeth saw, a hard moment for her. She smiled at
Juliet suddenly and said, "It's true enough but I've never admitted it to anyone. You see, I believe you when you say you
don't gossip. But I haven't had any notion of escaping. It's just
one of those things you live through. I'm not going to die of
a broken heart or anything."

Juliet sat there, very still, for a moment.

"I still wish it might be so. You would be the best thing that
ever happened to him. I'm sorry. I'm sorry I spoke."

"Never mind. Forget it. I'm glad you did, rather."

Juliet got up. "Well, good-by, Liz," she said in a confused
way.

That was a stupid thing to do, Elizabeth said to herself, and
yet she could not regret it. And she knew, somehow, that Juliet
would never betray her, even to Huxley. How did she know
that? She didn't know how, but the fact of her trust remained.
She thought of Mrs. Daggett, taking her on faith in the same
way. There was something here to be learned—something about
faith. Something she needed to know. The moment with Juliet
was tied somehow to the experience with Daggett. Perhaps she
felt bound to trust someone because she had been so trusted.
Perhaps it was part of her debt to Daggett. Or was it an admis-
sion to Anna that confession was good for the soul? Was that
it?

I will go away from here, she said to herself. I will go away and all this will be like a dream. It is almost as if I were already gone. My departure has been started—I am on my way out. Should I just go, not wait to be pushed out? Would that be the brave and the sensible thing to do?

But she did not mention Juliet to Anna.

She went down to see Jennie Leavitt and asked her about coming. Jennie, though she often did practical nursing, indeed, earned whatever meager income she had by that method, was hesitant. "Well, I don't know, Miss Burke," she said. "It keeps me awful busy looking after this place. I don't know as I'd want to say I'd do it regular."

"Try it for a few times then," Elizabeth urged. "Could you do that, Mrs. Leavitt? The work isn't so hard. The stairs are a little steep and you will have to go up and down them a few times, for lunch, tea, and so on—but for the most part Anna entertains herself, has friends in."

"Oh, the work wouldn't be anything," Jennie Leavitt said. "Tell you the truth, Miss Burke, Leora Bunce and I don't see eye to eye on some things and I don't know how it would work out."

Elizabeth looked at Jennie Leavitt in some astonishment. Bunce seemed to be liked by everybody. Then she laughed and said, "The only thing is—Bunce likes my days off because she *likes* to wait on Anna. She adores her. She may think it's all stuff and nonsense having anyone in. But Bunce isn't built for climbing stairs. Try it one day, will you? If it doesn't work out, we'll forget it."

"You mean tomorrow?"

"Yes, tomorrow."

It was agreed and Elizabeth went home. She didn't like Sundays off. Fridays she could just manage, but Sundays were queer, formless, unfilled. Johnny almost always went to Margaret's for Sunday afternoon and she did not want to accompany him. He needed to get really away from them all. Besides, the doc-

tor was likely to be at home on a Sunday. There was church,
but she had never gone to church much. She had almost gone
to St. Paul's in order to hear this Reverend Mr. Prather preach,
but that seemed the wrong motive for going, so she had never
done so. Now if she should go, Anna would think her seed of
interest had really been planted. She could walk, but there was
a limit to winter walking in Lakeville. You couldn't fill too
many hours that way. You could write letters, but there were so
few letters Elizabeth had to write. To read was almost all there
was. She had always had a passionate love for books. It was
strange, but since she had come to Number Seven, she could
not lose herself in reading, not in the old way. She ought, she
knew, to have something to do, something creative into which
she could sink herself, lose herself. She had no gift for writing,
nor for painting or drawing. The conquering of the knitting of
gloves had seemed interesting, and still she did not want to
spend her life knitting or doing any handiwork. She might make
a hooked rug—only that took up space and she had so little
space in her tiny room. Oh, what was her gift, that she could
take out into the freedom of her every-other-Sunday-off and
develop? What was it? She had a way with children and she
could spend the time with Johnny happily, but there was that
day gone to Margaret.

Anna asked, "Will she come?"

"She'll try it. She didn't promise for good."

"I'll have to break it to Mrs. Bunce and Cornelia. They
aren't going to like it."

"No, they won't like it. Still, perhaps it will be better."

The doctor stopped in that afternoon. For some reason Elizabeth had no desire to escape him. She felt friendly toward him,
almost anxious for his happiness. Nor did he embarrass her. She
sat down with him and Anna and talked easily enough along
with them. His long, loosely jointed figure looked at home in
Adrian's chair and his sardonic speech was familiar and almost
pleasant. Only when he was leaving he said, "Oh, by the way—

Meg said to tell you she couldn't have Johnny tomorrow. She isn't feeling quite up to par. She's sorry."

Elizabeth was relieved and alarmed at the same time. She would have Johnny but she would also worry about Margaret.

On Sunday morning, when she was almost through with breakfast, she said to Adrian, "Adrian, could I have a talk with you?"

For an instant something old and sick came into his young, hard-fleshed face. "Well, talk," he said.

"In the living room," she said.

He rose without a word, walked into the living room, and she followed. "Well, what's on your mind, Liz?" he demanded then.

"Calm down, Adrian. And sit down. I want to ask a favor of you and I can't do it while you're stalking around."

He sat down, lit a cigarette. He rarely smoked. "I'm sitting," he said impatiently.

"You don't seem in the mood to listen, but now I've started I'd better go through with it. I want you to give a young man a job—not now, but next fall perhaps."

He had expected something else. He hadn't expected this. She saw the relief come to his eyes, saw his hand steady.

"A job? How do I know I'll have one to give next fall? I don't know how I could promise that, Liz. Who is it? . . . I haven't got a big business, Liz. I don't employ an army, you know. What is your young man good for?"

"I don't know. Office work, I expect, though maybe he's good at machinery too. I don't really know. He's been in prison for the past four years."

He stared at her, interested at last, caught out of his own inner distress.

"In prison?" he repeated.

"Yes. His name is Anthony Daggett. He's Mrs. Daggett's grandson. He was driving a car for which he had no license and he killed a man. He was a little wild, but I think not bad. He's getting time off for good behavior and he's been working in the office in prison. He may be caught up into the war—there's no way to know yet. But what he wants is a job. Mrs. Daggett told him she hoped to get him one with you. You see, Adrian, the property she left—that you thought she left for me—is really for this Anthony Daggett. I hold it in trust, so to speak. She didn't want anyone to know he had been in prison, but he doesn't feel that way. He feels you cannot keep it a secret, and I suppose he is right. So I'm asking you. Do you think it would be possible?"

He didn't beat about the bush. "I'll try, Liz. I can't create a job but if it is possible, I'll fit him in."

"That's fair enough. He doesn't want to come clear East unless there is a chance. Mrs. Daggett had expected he would live with her, but now of course he can't."

"I suppose he's the one she wrote to."

"Yes."

"Why didn't you tell us all this before?"

"I couldn't. I feel free to now, but at first I couldn't."

"The place was left outright to you, though, wasn't it? There weren't any strings to it?"

"Yes, there were strings. Not legal, but ethical ones. I never thought the property was mine, Adrian. But let's skip all that. Just so the boy has a chance, that's all I want out of it."

"Do what I can. You're a queer egg, Liz."

"Sometimes I quite agree with you."

"You want me to keep this to myself?"

"Do as you like, Adrian. Of course it would be better if you would—but do as you like."

He went out and up the stairs but she sat quiet, feeling strange, and yet in some odd way at peace. There was nothing to prevent him from going straight to Anna with this bit of news. Nothing at all. And yet she did not think he would. "Twice—twice in a row," she murmured. Yes, twice in a few hours she had trusted people completely, feeling they could not possibly betray her. Juliet, now Adrian. It was strange how certain she felt that they would not betray her.

The bell rang and there was Jennie Leavitt. "Who on earth's that?" Bunce asked.

"It'll be Mrs. Leavitt," Elizabeth said hastily. "Didn't Anna tell you she was coming? Anna wants to spare you and Mrs. Suydam running up and down stairs on my days off. Mrs. Leavitt said she'd help us out."

"Of all the nonsense!" Bunce said, but Elizabeth was already opening the door. There was a brief interchange of greetings between Mrs. Bunce and Jennie Leavitt, then Elizabeth took Jennie upstairs to Anna.

"Hello, Jennie!" Anna said. "What an angel you are to give us a hand. You get to feeling your family is wearing itself out waiting on you—I just had to see they had a breathing space. You are kind!"

Mrs. Leavitt smiled and said, "It's how I earn my living, Anna. Now if you'll just tell me what wants doing . . ."

The telephone rang and it was Peggy Jones. "That you, Liz? This is Peggy. Susie's been begging for Johnny to come spend the day with her. I said that never again could she have anyone 'for the day,' but Johnny's such a little ghost I might just bear it. Could he come?"

"I don't know why not. I'll ask Anna—but I think so. What time?"

"Any time, from now on."

"All right. If I don't call you back in ten minutes, he'll be along."

"Susie's impressed because he can read books. I'll look for him."

She went up and asked Anna. Adrian was in the room and Jennie Leavitt was fussing around the already tidy room as if she didn't quite know what to do with herself.

"Tell her it's a godsend," Anna said. "I didn't know what he could do with the day, now that Meg's laid up. Do you want to take him over, get him ready and so on?"

Adrian was sitting in his chair, facing Anna. In spite of herself Elizabeth's glance turned to him. The natural thing for him to say was "Oh, is Meg sick?" but he did not. He looked toward the window with an extra stillness on his face and said nothing at all.

It was a blustery day. "Like a lion—lion March is acumin' in," Elizabeth said as she and Johnny walked up the street together. "That means flowers are just around the corner."

"I've got to stop at Meg's," Johnny said as they came near the doctor's house.

"What for?"

"I've got to give Meg something. I made it for her."

"Well, all right. We could leave it at the door, if you like. But Meg isn't feeling very well and we can't stop to visit with her."

"That's why I made it for her. She'll like it," he said.

It was a little five-cent notebook, with pictures of birds cut from magazines pasted in it. "That's very nice," Elizabeth said. To her surprise Meg herself opened the door.

"We aren't staying," Elizabeth said. "Johnny has a present for you."

Margaret McIntry, tall and gaunt-looking in the morning light, opened the little book, then gave a warm smile at Johnny. "Now this is a present!" she said. "I do like this a lot. Makes me feel like a new woman." She bent and kissed Johnny.

"I knew you'd like it," Johnny said.

"We're spending the day with Susie, or Johnny is. Be seeing you," Elizabeth finished abruptly and drew Johnny away.

As she walked away from Peggy's house she thought, Poor Johnny! and yet Johnny was happy enough now. His fellow creatures liked him or admired him and he was far less introspective than he had been. So why pity him now? It was just that it seemed wrong that it was such a relief to have Susie want him, such a relief to have him out of the house for a Sunday. Bunce had been loving to him in a new way lately and that was good. But there was no change in his relationship with Anna or Adrian. And Anna was the heart of the house. No little boy had the power to cling so tenaciously to fear or enmity, whichever it was that kept him aloof from his mother.

"It will soon be nothing to me," Elizabeth Burke murmured. For she was going. She knew she was going. How soon? She did not know, but quite soon.

Still, it would be something to her, even away from here. She had touched their lives for some months, and they had touched hers. You did not get lives out of your mind just by going away, and the change in you because of them would not be wiped out in a moment, if ever.

"Oh, Elizabeth! Aunt Liz!" came the voice behind her. She half turned and the wind blew snow against her face. She waited and he was beside her. "We are always meeting in snowstorms," he said. But had they been together in more than one? "Hasn't your new suit come home from Grace's yet? I thought we were going to have a date?"

"It will keep," she said.

"This is a good time for it, wouldn't you say? Suppose I get the car out and we'll go on a binge. You go get your suit on."

"It's a cold day for it," she said foolishly.

"Well, haven't you got some sort of topcoat you can wear over it? That one you've got on—though I can't say I like it much."

"All right," Elizabeth said suddenly. "I'll come."

"Good! I'll wait out in front."

He turned and went back the way he had come and Elizabeth went in, up to her room, put on the new suit. She took the old topcoat over her arm, left her head bare. Then she paused, went back and put on the enamel bracelet, picked up the coat again, walked into Anna's room.

Adrian and Anna were playing cribbage. Anna's hand lifting

a peg looked extraordinarily graceful and delicate. Elizabeth looked straight at Anna and said, "I'm going out to lunch with Huxley Reals. Is there anything you want before I go?"

Anna put the peg in, her eyes lowered to the task.

"Not a thing," she answered casually, not looking up.

It was Adrian who looked up at her, looked away again.

"Good-by, then," Elizabeth said.

" 'By," Anna said, beginning to deal.

The car stood there at the curb and she walked straight to it, climbed in beside Huxley.

He moved away, not asking her where she'd like to go, just starting out as if he had a destination. After they came to the edge of town he said, "You don't look very happy about the whole thing. Why don't we just be happy for a change? Not hunt around for psychological problems or anything?"

She couldn't tell him that she was still shaken from her announcement to Anna, that all her courage had been used up, that she was weak and frightened and half ashamed.

"I'm willing," she said. "But I don't know whether you can just turn happiness on and off at will."

"I got fifty bucks for my article. We can have an elegant luncheon on that."

"Did you really? I'm glad."

"I am too. This is a celebration of my success. All I need now, I said, is a girl in a new suit to take out. And there she was. But do you know, I was surprised when you came."

"I'm surprised too," Elizabeth said. They both laughed and happiness was there all around and in them, in spite of themselves.

"Did you know that Ed Botsworth has asked Pottsy?"

"Already?" Elizabeth said, then flushed and went on, stammering a little, "I mean, it seems only yesterday that Bunce turned him down. She knew he'd turn to Pottsy, I'm sure, but maybe it will hurt her to have him do it so soon."

"They aren't children. They don't have too much time."

"I know."

"Or do they feel just as young inside as we do? We aren't children either, when it comes right down to facts."

"I expect they feel as young as we do," she said. "Or, no, I don't believe the young Bunce would have had the courage to deny herself Ed Botsworth had she wanted him. No, that wasn't young."

"Bless her, anyway. Pottsy is blooming like a rose."

"That's some salvage," she said.

Then they did not talk but drove swiftly through the storm. There was not so much snow, but what there was eddied and billowed, slapped at the windshield in unexpected gusts, blurred the side windows, swept in long wheels across fields.

It was nearly an hour and a half later that they came to the old inn on the back road. It was a famous inn in those parts but Elizabeth had never been there. "If you don't look out, you *will* spend your fifty dollars," she said.

"That's all right. I wouldn't mind."

There was a fire burning on the hearth of a low beamed room and they were taken to a table near the fire. Elizabeth let Huxley help her take off her topcoat, which he did with a little grimace, "Now you look like a girl out on a date." Then he leaned forward and said, "What a nice bracelet! I never saw you wear jewelry before."

"Mrs. Daggett left it to me."

"Has an old-fashioned charm. I like it. Well, what shall we have to eat?"

He made her laugh as they ordered and ate. The fire at her back warmed her and she had an illusion of great happiness, knew it was an illusion, but clung to it, shutting everything out, even Anna's lowered eyes on the cribbage board.

"Speaking of salvage," he said suddenly over the coffee, then stopped.

She waited but he remained silent. At last she said, "Yes—speaking of salvage?"

"My article, that's a small bit," he said seriously. "I know well enough not many people will ever read it, only a few engineers who go right through the *Engineering Journal*. Still, I did write it. I'm going to count it. . . . Would you mind if I told you the story of my life?"

"I know most of it," she said. "Lives are pretty much open in Lakeville, aren't they? I wouldn't mind, but you don't need to."

He laughed aloud and the waiter moved toward him, retreated.

"Oh, Liz, you are good for me!" he said. "You simply won't let a fellow get dramatic. I don't doubt at all that you do know everything there is to know. And that I'm a fool for wanting to repeat an old story. And telling things doesn't change anything—I know that. This purging of the emotions is a lot of tommyrot. Or at any rate, it ought to be done inside, not to others. I'm being defensive, I expect. I know I've been a fool, but I don't want it to show on the outside."

"It doesn't show much," Elizabeth conceded. "Are you going away?"

"No. No, I don't think so. Adrian needs me. He's got this big job ahead and will probably have bigger ones if the country goes on in its present state. No, I won't go. I said I would, then I changed my mind. It didn't seem so important as I'd been thinking it would."

"Or at the last minute you couldn't go," Elizabeth said.

"That happens not to be true. I could have gone very easily. But it would only have been an escape from admitting there was nothing to escape from."

His voice was steady and serious and she looked up at him, looked away again. She did not feel warm now, only still and frightened.

"I've gone through it and come out again," he went on at last. "I thought it was a lifetime affair, and it makes you a little sick to know that you aren't capable of a lifetime affair. It isn't that I don't still see her as beautiful and even desirable. But I

do not any more desire her. That's bitter, if you like, but there
it is. It makes you doubt your own stability, that's all."

Elizabeth, to her own astonishment, felt only a swift sorrow
for Anna.

"Have you told her so?" she heard herself say sternly.

"No. But she knows. Anna knows everything. If you must
know, this was the day I'd set for telling her—but I saw you
and evaded it."

"Let's go home," she said.

"Let's not. I like it here by the fire, with the snow out there
and us here. I can see you are not liking me much right now,
but still I like it here. Aren't you the one who called me a
fool?"

"Yes. Yes, I did."

"Then why are you so hurt because I'm no longer faithful?"

"I don't know."

"You ought to be glad I've come to my senses. But you
aren't."

"I don't know—it's like realizing a fairy story isn't true. But
I can't have it both ways, can I?"

"No, you can't have it both ways. And I'm too old for fairy
stories now. I've been too old for some time. And I don't know
how much I've salvaged, either. Five years of thinking of nothing else does something to you. And even now, if she should
smile at me in a certain wondering way—I don't know whether
I wouldn't recant."

"Please—will you take me home?"

"All right." He stood up rather abruptly, beckoned to the
waiter, paid the bill, got her coat, and stood holding it while
she shoved into it.

They went out again to the car. He wiped the windows off
and they started homeward.

They had driven some distance before he said, "Look, Liz—
Elizabeth I mean—I'm sorry I told you. I shouldn't have, not
first. I'm sorry—ashamed too."

"That's all right. I don't want to talk about it."

"It was Johnny. Johnny doesn't love her. I never thought about it much. I don't know why, but I never did. But he doesn't love her, nor she him. But you have to love your own son, if no one else—don't you? It got to haunting me."

"She loves him," Elizabeth said stiffly. "I don't know why they aren't friends."

"Why aren't they, though? Why? Wasn't it Steele who wrote a story about a man who was going to marry a woman and saw her suddenly through her little girl, who discarded old loved dolls for new and fancy ones? Something like that. Not quite analogous, but almost. Well, I'll stop. I just wanted you to know how it was."

She did not answer. She sat huddled there within the storm, feeling the wind almost physically, though she was safe here inside the car. But she felt buffeted, bruised. Yet had she not wished for this? Why was it hurting so now? Did it make him less desirable, less worthy of love? Was that it? Did she no longer trust him because he had proved faithless to his long love? Did she really want it both ways? And Anna. Anna— Anna—Anna—what would she do? She would do something, that was sure. She would give him that wondering smile that so enchanted and he would recant. Or she would hurt Adrian in some unknown way—or she would send her, Elizabeth, away. That she would do in any event. She would do it for Elizabeth's own good, but she would do it. She would do it no matter what happened about Huxley, if for no other reason, because she, Elizabeth, had made good her remark about the hypothetical case. She knew quite well that she had gone today with Huxley because she had suddenly had to prove to Anna that she had the right to do so—it had almost nothing to do with Huxley that she had gone.

Yet here she was, with his sleeve touching hers. They had eaten together and he had told her the state of his heart. She had, for a little space, been happy, but she had known, even inside her happiness, that this was going to be paid for. That it was going to be paid for too dearly.

Then Lakeville was looming up before them.

He stopped before Number Seven but for an instant did not get out. Then he smiled at her ruefully. "It wasn't much good, was it? We'll have another date, and make it really gay."

"The suit's unlucky," she said. "I've worn it twice now—it's unlucky."

"No, we didn't make any mistake on the suit." He got out, came around and opened the door. "I liked sitting by the fire with you, though. I could as easily have told you the story of my life as not."

"I don't doubt you," Elizabeth said dryly. She murmured some sort of good-by, then, as he stood there, not going back to his place behind the wheel, she turned and said, "I almost told you mine!" Now she really did go, up the steps, inside the green door.

She had such a feeling of doing everything for the last time, as if her hours here were numbered. Leavitt was climbing the stairs with the tea tray and there was the sound of voices upstairs. But Elizabeth Burke did not join the party. She had no more courage left. She went very quietly to her own room and closed the door. Somehow the hours must be got through till eleven. Well, there would be Johnny to get. She looked at her watch. In an hour she could go get Johnny. She kept her mind on that, began to tidy her little desk. She looked at her books, not reading in them, looked at them apologetically, thinking she would soon have to pack them all over again, send them somewhere else. Where? Her room would be gone long before this. But somewhere she would have to send her books.

Presently she was walking through the snow, Johnny's hand in hers. He was talkative, excited. Susie had a trapeze in the basement and wonderful had been his prowess on the trapeze. As soon as he was in the house he went scrambling up the stairs to his grandmother's rooms, and began telling her about his adventures in the air. Elizabeth went to the kitchen and said to Bunce that she would just make herself a sandwich for supper and take it up to her room. She did that. She thought of Bunce holding Johnny in her arms, singing "Jesus Loves Me" to him, felt a longing for someone to hold her. It's too much, she thought once as she ate her sandwich. It's just too much.

She knew when the visitors left. She knew that Adrian had had supper with Anna. She knew when Leavitt shut the front door and departed. She knew that Adrian was reading to Anna. She knew that Mrs. Suydam was putting Johnny to bed. All these small happenings in the house came clear to her through sound, but she sat there in her small room, unable to move out of it. She heard Adrian at last go down the stairs, then come up and go to his own room. It was now bedtime. But she did not undress. She sat and waited in a kind of paralysis for eleven.

She carried in hot milk and toast, set the tray down on the table, fixed Anna's pillows.

"Why, you haven't been to bed!" Anna said.

"No, not yet. I've been reading." Why lie like that? She had held a book but she had not been reading, only waiting. "How did you like Jennie Leavitt?"

"All right. She's very entertaining, a fountain of news. But Bunce is furious. Poor Bunce—but she *is* too fat to climb stairs. Did you have fun on your date?"

"Fun enough," Elizabeth said.

"The lamb—he can't take even a small snubbing!"

Elizabeth did not answer.

"Nor you either, baby!" Anna went on with a small chuckle. "I never knew anybody so hipped on making her points. Liz, I *have* been selfish. You know, I honestly did think that you'd be happier with me than anywhere else. That's how silly I am. I took it for granted—isn't that vain? And now Adrian tells me that you resisted like anything coming. That *was* a slap!"

"Yes, I resisted," Elizabeth said. "Of course I did. Because—

because—well, Anna, you do get tired of people. I didn't want you to get tired of me."

"Nonsense! That's slander, darling. Not remotely true. You know very well I depend on you terribly and love having you with me. But one thing I couldn't bear—and that would be having you here from duty's sake—I couldn't take that."

So this was the way it was going to be. It wasn't going to touch Huxley at all—only her own thorny character, her love-lessness.

"I don't suppose there's any use protesting if you've made up your mind how it is," she said.

"I've had it made up for me," Anna said. "And all your talk about worshiping me from afar—that was fiction, wasn't it? All you've ever wanted was to get away. That hurts, Liz—it really hurts."

"It wasn't fiction," Elizabeth said with difficulty. "Oh, Anna, please don't! Don't pretend you think any such thing. It's no good. You know I'd do anything on earth for you. I try to protect my independence, yes—you knew I was that way. I can't help that. Even that's defense, I dare say. But don't put this on me, because you know it isn't true. I don't want to leave you and I won't unless you make me. But don't say such things to me because I can get hurt too."

"Why, darling!" Anna said.

"I'll go away if you'd rather have someone else. But just say you think Jennie would work out better, if that's what you think. Don't say I want to go or that I don't love you. It isn't true."

"With all your self-probings, you don't see yourself very well, do you?" Anna said, but oh, how gentle her voice was, how tender!

"Probably not. But I try. I try not to fool myself."

"You must try harder, baby. I've got so I can really turn my busybody on lives—I can see all around and into lives, spread them out so clearly. I can see yours too. You've always been special to me, Liz—but really no one is special to you but your-self. You're always being so busy protecting yourself that no one else means anything to you—not deeply. That's cruel, maybe, but that's the way it is. You felt you ought to come be-cause it spoiled the picture of yourself to yourself if you re-fused. You like to see yourself as generous and dutiful—but you didn't really want to come at all."

That rang some bell of truth and Elizabeth's face whitened.

"Perhaps you're right," she said dully. "Perhaps that is the way it is. When shall I go?"

"Whenever you want to," Anna said. "You're not bound here, Liz."

So there it was, said. Clear as crystal. She was to go, and at once. When she wanted to—but she was to want to *now*.

Suddenly she laughed. The sound surprised her, surprised Anna too.

"Oh, but I am bound here!" she said. "And I don't want to go. Because, you see, it isn't any of it true. Not a word of it."

She got up, took the glass and plate, walked out of the room. After she was in bed, she laughed again, but silently. Then as suddenly as the laughter had come, tears came. I've got to be here when she knows he's gone from her, she said to herself. Or should I be? Is that really a reason I shouldn't be here? And maybe he won't go—maybe he's just fooling himself. And—and Adrian. What if . . . ? Does Adrian want me gone too? Is that it?

After a long time she was still awake. The last thing she thought before sleep was: And is it almost true? *Do I hold my-self away from everyone? Do I? Don't I know what love is?*

XVII

*H*OW COULD LIFE be the same after that? How could the
drama be put away, forgotten? And yet for a space it seemed
to be so. Anna said no more about Elizabeth's going. The routine went on. Huxley Reals did not come. Friends thronged the
gay room, played cards there, talked, read poetry, and nothing
seemed changed. The lion March went on roaring and it seemed
like the beginning of winter, not the end. On Friday Jennie
came again, but Elizabeth did not go to Margaret McIntry's.
She wrote a long letter to Anthony Daggett, another to Lollie.
She knitted. She stayed put. She did not know what this re-
prieve signified, but that it signified something she did not
doubt. Once Anna said to Jen, "Liz is so cocky since she came
into money!" And once she said, "Liz, I'm not sure I like that
suit after all—it makes me think of mom's suits that she *thought*
were just the thing for the office." And once she said, "Oh, run
along, Liz—don't *hover* over Adrian and me so!" Still, life went
on after a fashion and Elizabeth was still there. Then on a
Monday night Adrian went out. He sat with Anna till nearly
ten, then without a word went out. It was very late when he
came home.

When it came to the second Friday, Elizabeth went to Margaret after lunch. It had seemed a very long silence between them. She did not walk in but rang the bell. There was no answer. She stood there in the wind, waiting. Rang again. No answer. She turned away, feeling she should have come before. As she started down the walk to the street, the office door opened and the doctor came out. He looked distracted. "Oh, Liz!" he called. "Come in, will you? I'm busy right now, but I want to see you. Just wait in the living room. Be with you soon."

She went back, sat in the room that was so familiar to her now, had been the friendliest room she knew in Lakeville. Then she saw that the picture by Alex Suydam was gone from its place. That gave her a cold, frightened feeling. There was not a sound anywhere and the house seemed curiously deserted. But she sat there, very still, for half an hour, before the doctor suddenly strode in from the office.

"What a mess!" he said. He dropped into the brown chair as if exhausted.

"What's the matter? Where's Meg?" she demanded.

"Yes, where's Meg? That's the question."

"But what's happened?"

"You tell me. I'm going around in circles, and that's the truth, Liz. Meg's gone, bag and baggage."

"Gone?"

"Yes, gone. That's what I said. She's got herself a job in a library, in Rochester. In the office. She's no librarian. Don't you know anything about it?"

"No, nothing." But she did know. She knew it all.

"I can't get anybody to cook for me for love or money. Not that Meg was such a crackerjack cook, but she made out. She was all set to go when she told me, packed and everything. Just said she had decided to take a job and that I would have to make some other arrangements. She thought Jennie Leavitt might come. The truth is that Meg was the heart of the house and I depended on her and I'm lost. I don't know what got into her. She's always seemed contented. But I couldn't budge her. Now I'll *have* to get married!"

Elizabeth laughed. "Yes, I expect you will," she said, then sobered. "I wish she'd told me," she said.

"Thought she would have—she just went this morning. I was coming over as soon as I was through in the office. But what got into her? She's been edgy for weeks now, but she'll be lost in a city. She's a small-town girl if ever there was one. It isn't as if she'd have a fling in town. She's not the kind that goes in for riotous living. I don't understand it."

"It's a good thing. There wasn't much for her in Lakeville," Elizabeth said.

"Just as much as there'll be working in a library in Rochester. Meg made herself a good enough life here. Of course she's never married, but I don't think that's upset her. Thought I knew Meg through and through—apparently I didn't know her at all. Knocked me for a loop and I still feel groggy. Do you think Jennie Leavitt would come?"

"I don't know. She comes to us on Fridays and every other Sunday. But she might. Ask her."

At last she was out in the wind again, but now the wind went into her marrow. She had gone, Meg had gone, without telling her. She had bitten off a leg and got out of the trap. How would she manage, with only one leg? Meg. Meg. Why hadn't she told her? Was their friendship nothing, after all? Or hadn't she been able to trust herself to tell her? Did she believe that all would be known without telling? That that day when she'd sat on the stairs and put her head down on her knees had told all? And what agony had she gone through, alone in that austere room up there, before she packed her things and made her firm announcement?

She sat at supper with the rest, very quiet. She didn't even talk with Johnny much. She saw Adrian glance at her once or twice as if questioning her silence, but she could not talk. She looked at her lemon pie, could not eat it. Then Mrs. Suydam said, "Meg McIntry isn't sick, is she? She didn't ask Johnny for Sunday."

Elizabeth looked up quite calmly and said, "No, she isn't sick. She's taken a job in Rochester. In a library."

"Meg?" Mrs. Suydam said, in astonishment.

"Yes. So the doctor told me."

She couldn't look at Adrian, but was aware that he had risen. He walked out of the dining room without a word.

"Well, that surprises me, Meg's never seemed to have any ambitions like that," Mrs. Suydam said.

"You never know what people's ambitions are," Elizabeth said.

Then she saw that those words had hurt Mrs. Suydam and she added, "Nor what strength they have, either." But that was no better, though she had meant it for better in her thought of Alex Suydam. "I thought I knew her quite well," she stumbled on, "but she never told me—never told me a word about it. Johnny will miss her awfully."

"Perhaps not," Mrs. Suydam said surprisingly. "People have a great deal of influence on the young, then that influence fades when the need for it fades. Johnny has other friends now."

"I know. Perhaps you're right."

Later she was reading with Johnny and she felt sad all through the reading, realizing the truth of what Mrs. Suydam had said, realizing the transitoriness of relations and their importance. That was a strange thing for Adrian's mother to have said to her. What, then, was to be said for faithfulness? What for lifelong friendships? What for marriage, even? If you just took from life what you needed at the moment, passed on, what did that make of you? Or couldn't you help doing just that? Was there something about life that demanded you do so? Had she been demanding something permanent, everlasting, where permanence was impossible?

She put Johnny to bed quietly, bent and kissed him, wondering as she did so whether he would miss her at all should she go away. Her services might be missed for a day or two, but Jennie Leavitt or someone would perform those services and the space she had occupied would fill up. Then she felt a swift blaze of anger going all through her.

No! her heart cried. No, it is not that way! And I am not gone from Meg's heart either, even if she didn't tell me. I am so much there that she knew I would understand. And I am not gone from Lollie's life either.

But that was a selfish cry of the heart, she knew that. A protest against being forgotten. She remembered suddenly old Miss Wilder. Old? Probably she hadn't been more than thirty-five. Old Miss Wilder ran a millinery shop in Katawa where Liz's father had had the newspaper. One day she called Elizabeth in and said, "I made this hat for you, child." It was a simple enough hat of leghorn with velvet streamers, but it was the kind of hat that a child loves beyond measure. She had thought, seeing herself in the long glass in the back of the little shop, that she would love Miss Wilder forever. But beyond a few shy smiles at her when she passed the shop, what had she ever done about it? They moved away and she had never heard of Miss Wilder again. Yet, for a little season, Miss Wilder had had a tremendous influence, making her feel noticed, beautiful, worthy of a hat like that. . . . And there was that Professor Nixon in college—he had deepened her love for and understanding of great poetry beyond measure. "Let me know what you do with your life," he had said to her gently one day. Had she let him know? Was the fact that there was nothing to know important? No, she had forgotten—not forgotten, but she had put Professor Nixon in the past, as if she had no obligation to the past. Was that right? Was it normal? Or was it normal in the young but not in the adult? Was it part of adulthood that you recognized the important and clung to it and paid your debt to it?

Oh, Mrs. Suydam, I wish you hadn't said that! she said to herself.

Anna was right. She did too much self-probing. But if you didn't know the self did you ever know anything?

When, at eleven, tired from too much thought, she came out of her room that night she met Adrian in the hall.

"I've given Anna her milk," he said.

"Am I late?" she asked stupidly.

"No. Good night, Liz."

"Good night," she said.

She didn't tell Anna about Meg. But the doctor did. He came about eleven the next morning. He dropped into the deep chair, said, "You see before you a completely confused man, Anna. Look, you know all, see all—what in the devil got into Meg anyway?"

"Into Meg? What's she done?"

The doctor looked at Elizabeth with a slight surprised frown.

"Didn't Liz tell you? She's left me—gone out into the world and got herself a job. I can't make head or tail of it."

"For heaven's sake! Liz, why didn't you tell me?"

"I don't know," Elizabeth said.

"But what made her? That's what I don't get. She seemed contented enough. I called her a spinster one day and it made her mad, but aside from that everything's been just as usual."

"Well, I don't blame her for being mad at that," Anna said. "What kind of word is that to use to a woman?"

"But she is a spinster. Just a fact."

"Maybe you never feel like one, though."

"Oh, that was weeks ago. And you're the one who made me say it, egging me on to matrimony. You ought to have known better, Anna."

Anna gave him a quick smile and said, "I meant well. My pony balked. . . . What kind of job?"

"In a library. Just walked out on me, as if she'd been planning it a long time. I don't understand it. Jennie Leavitt's going to give me a few hours a day, when she isn't here, but nursing's her line—not housekeeping, and I don't think she's thrilled at the idea. I'm so unpredictable on meals. Meg took that for granted, I will say. But I thought you might know what it was all about."

"I don't. Meg never tells me much. Now I come to think of it, she's the only one in town who doesn't tell me much. But I presume it's a man. It generally is."

"But I'm the only man in Meg's life," the doctor said, with a sorry laugh. "Meg *is* a spinster. If she's yearning over someone she's certainly concealed it. And I don't see how there could be anyone in Rochester, where, so far as I know, she's never been in her life. I must say I miss her."

"Maybe it's just a yearning for independence," Elizabeth said.

"In a library? She's more independent here than she will be in a library."

"Skip that. It's Liz's chief hobby, worrying away at being independent," Anna said. "I don't think Meg worries about that. No, you'll find it's some man."

"I don't know what man. She just seems allergic to men. No, I don't know as that's so, but she seems to consider them as the lesser species, tolerates them, that's all. Huxley Reals drops in, but I'm sure it's not Huxley. She treats him like a small brother. No, I'm smart enough to know there's nothing there. Prather's called a couple of times but she argued with him on some obscure theological point and after he went she said, 'I could preach better sermons than Prather, without half trying.' She was scornful of him, though he seems like a decent man to me. But I'm sure she had no sentimental thoughts about him. Then Adrian has been in now and then, to pick up Johnny or something—and that's all the men she knows much."

Anna gave her warm smile and said, "Well, I hope she hasn't a yearning for my Adrian!"

"Don't be silly. You know, though, once I thought when she was really grown she might marry Alex Suydam. He always liked her and he used to come very often—but of course she was only a child then. A very mature child, however, and Alex

did like her. Yes, I thought that might happen, but of course
he died—she's never paid any attention to boys or men since."

"You never know the repressions in spinsters' souls," Anna
said. "But now you will really have to marry."

"I suppose so. But don't pick me out anyone else, Anna. I
don't have any luck with your pickings."

After he went, Anna said, "Why didn't you tell me? Isn't it
strange? What ever did get into her? I wonder. I can't imagine.
But I'll find out!"

"But maybe she really did just get tired of being the doctor's
housekeeper. It isn't a very thrilling life, would you say?"

"I thought you were such pals. Didn't she ever mention it?"
"No, never."

Traps—traps—traps! The harsh words went in a chain across
the room, circled Elizabeth, wove in and out till the room was
full of them.

Adrian didn't come home for lunch but did come about four.
He came in with his coat still on, as if he had forgotten where
he was, almost, kissed Anna and smiled at Jen, who was sitting
on the stool beside Anna's chair. He took a package out of his
pocket, then flushed a little, shoved it back in again.

"What's that?" Anna asked.

"Wait," Adrian said. "It's a reward for you if you eat your
supper."

But Anna coaxed it out of his pocket again, opened it. It was
a slim bracelet of topazes. "Oh, darling!" she said softly. "How
beautiful!" She put it on her arm. "But why didn't you keep it
till my birthday?"

"Don't know. Just felt like getting it now," Adrian said.

"Gosh," Jen said, "what a husband! At his peak John got me
a dishwashing machine!" Then Jen sobered. "Not that I want
to trade John in—or the dishwashing machine either!"

They all laughed. But Elizabeth thought, Daffodils and topaz
bracelets—daffodils and topaz bracelets.

Jen went away soon and Adrian slid out of his coat, dropped

it across the unused bed, came over and sat where Jen had, on the stool. "Maybe you have all the trinkets you want," he said, "but I saw it—it seemed just the color of your eyes, so I got it."

"It's lovely. And I like trinkets. Did you know Meg McIntry had gone to Rochester, taken a job there?"

"Somebody said something, I think. Yes, I'd heard that."

"The doctor was in. He's going around in circles. I'd give a lot to know exactly why she did go. It just didn't seem in character."

Elizabeth said, "But it did. If she decided she wanted to go away and live her own life, she's the very one who would go. She wouldn't dawdle over making up her mind either. The doctor'll make out."

"The doctor swears she had no love life. And it really is hard to imagine her having one. Hux dropped in there often, but I can't imagine Hux giving her a whirl—though she might have wanted him to, I suppose. The oddest people do seem to go for Hux. But the doctor says no. He might not know, though. He sees a lot, but fathers don't see their own daughters very well."

"That's nonsense," Adrian said too evenly. "She treats Hux as if he weren't quite bright."

Anna's smile had a faint edge of anger, but she said, "You never know what spinsters are thinking. They work up the most extraordinary fantasies."

There was a small silence, then Adrian said, "I don't think Meg has ever been given to fantasies. And spinster isn't a word I'd have thought of for her."

"It's just a word," Anna said. "She's not so old—thirty-two or -three, I imagine, but she seems to have been born exactly as she is now and will always be the same."

"Oh, let her go, Anna. Leave her alone. She's gone," Adrian said, and Elizabeth's heart began to pound in fright. It seemed as if anyone, someone much less perceptive than Anna, could read the desolation in Adrian's voice. But Anna gave her small, loving laugh and said, "Liz, couldn't we have a fresh pot of tea?" But she couldn't let Meg go. She went on, "It's the why she's gone that's so intriguing, darling."

Adrian got up, walked past Liz starting for the door, said, "I'll get some tea, Liz."

"Adrian's working too hard. He's edgy," Anna said.

"Yes, I think he is. If he could only go off somewhere for a week and just rest—he needs it."

"Maybe I could get him to stay home for a week. He wouldn't go away."

"No. No, I don't suppose he would," Elizabeth said dully.

If only Anna would let it go. If she'd forget Meg and the why of her going. If she'd just comfort Adrian, try to let him rest, all might yet be well. But Elizabeth did not think Anna would let it go. And when Adrian came back with the tea, Anna began almost at once. "I wonder about women like Meg. So down-to-earth, so practical, and so smart. She's smart enough, Meg, but what does life mean to her? Birds? Making life smooth for the doctor? I'd have said she had some father complex—only she's gone. But maybe gone to escape it."

"I don't think Meg has any father complex," Adrian said. "I dare say she'd have lived a completely normal life if . . ."

"If what?" Anna asked gently.

Don't! Don't say it! Elizabeth's heart cried out.

"If I hadn't ditched her," Adrian said calmly enough. "I was engaged to her when I met you."

"Why, *Adrian!*" Anna's voice was an amazed whisper. "To Meg?"

"Yes, to Meg. If her mother hadn't happened to die that year and the doctor hadn't happened to need her, I'd have been married to her. But I met you and that was that. So I don't much care to hear you discuss her spinsterhood, Anna. Being, as you might say, the cause of it."

"Darling, I'm sorry," Anna said. "I'm so sorry. But why did you never tell me?"

"It was nothing to be proud of," Adrian said. He was speaking in a grim, hard voice. "And now, if you don't mind, let's drop it."

Elizabeth managed to escape then. She did not know whether Anna dropped it or not. She wished frantically that Adrian had not told Anna that. Suppose Anna made it a story for "the girls"? Suppose she couldn't let it go, but went deeper, came to the real reason for Meg's going? Suppose that?

Conversation at supper was strained, unimportant. Then somehow hours had gone by and Elizabeth sat beside Anna's bed.

"You know, I can't get over my surprise—Adrian and Meg!" Anna said.

Elizabeth did not answer, ate a piece of toast mechanically.

"Think of Meg here—what a cluttered dark hole she would have made of it!"

"Oh, I don't know. Her house isn't beautiful and yet it seems very full of life," Elizabeth said.

"But what did he see in her?"

"Nothing, after he saw you," Elizabeth said. "I think there was enough to see, but after he saw you . . ."

"And that's why she almost never comes here, of course. Why she's had such a passion for Johnny. I wish I'd known— I'd have been kinder."

"It was a long time ago," Elizabeth said. "Let's forget it."

Johnny didn't act very disappointed the next morning when he was told he was not going to Meg's. He said, "I could go and play with Susie." Elizabeth remembered what Mrs. Suydam had said and thought it was true. Johnny had had Meg when he needed her, but now he needed her no longer and would forget her. Perhaps it was right and normal and yet it was sad. She would have liked Johnny to be faithful.

Anna was very tender with Adrian that morning, gay and charming as only Anna knew how to be. When in her busybody she saw Huxley Reals coming down the street, she said, "If only I could say I'm not at home! There comes Huxley. Don't go away, darling—maybe he won't stay long."

But Adrian did go away. He said, "Hi, Hux," briefly, sent him upstairs and went into the living room. Elizabeth heard Huxley coming, turned to go.

"Oh, stay, Liz," Anna said.

"I'd rather not," Elizabeth said.

"I won't let him stay long."

Huxley was in the room. He looked grave and there were long lines down his face that Elizabeth did not remember. How could they have come overnight, as it were? He did not sit in Adrian's chair, but drew the rosewood chair up and sat in that. "That's a very delicate chair," Anna said. "If you break it, I won't forgive you."

"I won't break it," Huxley said. "How are you, Liz?"

"Fine."

"And Anna's fine and I'm fine. We're all fine. So that's disposed of. How would you like to run along and knit or something, Liz?"

"I'd like it," Elizabeth said, but Anna stopped her second attempt with "Oh, don't let him drive you away, Liz. Sit down. Hux and I don't hold private conversations."

"This one I mean to be private," Huxley said quietly.

Anna had on the amber jacket and she had slipped the new bracelet on her arm. She looked down at the bracelet with a small, tender smile, saying she had a new special happiness and was determined to be on her good behavior for Adrian's sake. It had, Elizabeth knew, given her a kind of satisfaction to think that Adrian had ditched a woman for her sake, made him more important.

"But my little sister—she knows everything about me," Anna said. "You can be as private as you like before Liz."

He gave Elizabeth a sudden clear look which she could not

read. "All right, Liz. You can stay," he said. "I just wanted to tell Anna I'd taken her advice at long last. I'm going to be married, Anna, and I wanted to tell you."

"Married? Not really?" Anna said. "Oh, dear—I do hope I'll like her. Is it Charlotte?"

She did it very well, with friendliness, concern for his happiness, pleasure.

"Charlotte? No, I don't think so."

"Don't *think* so?"

"I'll just say 'No' then. Not Charlotte."

"It couldn't be Meg, after all?"

"Meg? No, it couldn't be Meg. But why 'after all'? The truth is that it's only a decision, Anna. There isn't anybody. But I've been bothering you and Adrian long enough."

"Why, Hux! You haven't bothered us. To tell the truth you bolster up my self-confidence no end. And probably Adrian's too! But of course you ought to marry—I've always told you so. If you haven't decided, I can put my mind to it!"

Then Huxley looked again at Elizabeth, smiled suddenly, and said, "I think it'll be Liz. Would that suit you?"

Anna looked at Liz as at a stranger, speculatively, with a little frown. "Liz?" she said. "Oh, I don't know, Hux. She's a darling, my little pony, but she's awfully serious. Besides, she's so awfully independent and prickly—she'd walk out on you, like Meg walked out on the doctor, one of these days."

"Oh, I don't think so. Not if I put my mind to keeping her," Huxley said. "I could always lock her in."

"Do I have anything to say about this?" Elizabeth demanded. "Sorry, but I'm not at your disposal. I'm not at anybody's disposal."

"Well, it just came to me," Huxley said. "I'll have to give it more thought."

Elizabeth walked out of the room then, walked straight out and downstairs. She went to the kitchen where Bunce was getting everything ready before she started for church.

"What's the matter?" Bunce asked. "You're white as a sheet."

"Nothing's the matter. Nothing that can be fixed. I'll watch everything, Bunce."

Bunce went but Elizabeth sat there by the kitchen table, very still, her hands tightly clasped on the table's edge. The house, her life, everything seemed tumbling down about her and she could do nothing but let it crash, bury her in the rubble. She didn't even hear Huxley come down the stairs, but he was there in the doorway. He pulled out a handkerchief and wiped his forehead.

"Well," he said. "That's that."

"I suppose you feel free as the air," she said coldly.

"No. I feel sick. I feel as if I'd taken a beating. But it's done."

"Is it?"

"All right. Perhaps it isn't. Perhaps it never will be," he said, and his voice too was cold. "All the same, Liz, I have wasted enough of life. I am not going to waste any more. On futility. I'm sorry I dragged you in. But, for an instant there, it did seem possible. I mean it seemed like the only real answer. I wasn't being flip. I meant it."

"That's big of you."

"Do you have to be this way? I thought we were friends."

"Did you? Well, we're not. We never will be. I know I'm contradicting myself, but I just don't like faithless people."

"Yes," he said slowly, "you are contradicting yourself. I thought you didn't like slaves."

"I don't. But I don't like faithless people either."

"Well, I do have faith . . . but we'll skip it for now, shall we?" He turned to go, then came back and said, "I wouldn't lock you in, Liz."

She did not answer and he went away. She sat still there by the table, doing nothing, for a long time. She did nothing about the dinner, the table. She just sat there, staring ahead of her or down at her clasped hands, knowing life was cruel, a trap indeed.

XVIII

ELIZABETH WENT DOWN to Mrs. Daggett's house, sat with Jennie Leavitt in the kitchen.

"Mrs. Leavitt," she said, "I'm afraid I am going to have to change my plans. I will have to rent this house, after all. Or most of it. What I was thinking was that you and your brother might perhaps keep those three rooms at the back with the bathroom and all. And then you could keep an eye on the house, collect the rent, and all. How many bedrooms are there?"

"Six," Jennie Leavitt said. "Six, and that little sewing room."

"We'll lock one of them up, one of the big ones. The rest we'll rent, if we can find a tenant. Perhaps the furniture will have to be stored, but I'd rather rent it furnished. Do you happen to know of anyone who would like it?"

"There's Professor Peyton," Jennie said. "He's got three children though."

"Well, children couldn't hurt this house. Does he have furniture?"

"Not much. They've been staying with her folks. They used to be in China and when they come home they didn't bring nothing."

"I think they'd be wonderful. Do you want to see them—or shall I? And what rent could we get, do you think?"

"Well, rent don't go so high in Lakeville, Miss Burke. Not like it is in the city. I guess you could get maybe fifty for it. Maybe more, furnished. Yes, I guess sixty or sixty-five, furnished."

"You sound the Peytons out, will you? I won't be here much longer and I want to leave everything settled. I'll give you full charge and you can send me the rent. Do you think the three rooms would be fair exchange for the work? Of course we'd have to do something about a stove back there, something to cook your meals on. There is a sink, isn't there?"

"Yes, I guess we could make out all right with a stove," Jennie said. "I didn't know you were going away, Miss Burke."

"I am. Quite soon."

She walked away from the old house, having settled that as best she could for the moment. She ought perhaps to have done it before, made the house pay. She didn't know what had restrained her, what she had had in mind. The boy certainly had no need for a big house like that, even should he come to Lakeville. She hadn't, she admitted, been very practical.

Adrian said to her, "So you are really leaving us, Liz?"

"Yes. I thought right after Anna's birthday, if you could find someone else by then."

She sounded, she thought, as if she had decided this.

"We'll try to," Adrian said.

He wasn't angry, just tired.

"I'm sorry, Adrian. I'm very sorry."

"But what are you going to do? Have you a job to go to?"

"I'll get a job. I don't worry about that. Adrian, what I'm most sorry about is that when I came you thought I was reluctant. I was reluctant but not because I didn't love Anna and want to help her. You've always held that against me."

He frowned, then said, "Yes, I believe I did, Liz. I wish you had a job."

"I'll get one. It's the least of my worries."

"Well, you must do as you think best," Adrian said. "You've been a great help to us, Liz."

He too was tired. He could not ask her to stay because he knew that Anna no longer wanted her.

She told Anna. "Anna, if you can arrange things, I believe I'll leave right after your birthday."

Anna did not protest. "I see you've made up your mind," she said, but sadly, as if Elizabeth were deserting her. Elizabeth did not say anything more, did not defend herself. Later she said, "What about that little Mrs. Wilde, Anna? She used to be a nurse and now Jennie has tied up her time by going to the doctor's, you'll have to look for someone. I like Mrs. Wilde but maybe you wouldn't."

Bunce protested. "Why, Miss Burke, you've just got nicely settled in! Whatever do you want to leave us for?"

"It just seems better so, Bunce," Elizabeth said. "But, Bunce, you go on praying for me whether I'm here or not, won't you?"

Mrs. Suydam made no protest at all. She said, "We will miss you, Liz," and that was all.

She put off telling Johnny. Perhaps, she thought, because she could not bear it to have Johnny not care. But now, except for telling Johnny, it was all done.

Anna was very sweet these days. She said to the girls, "I've been as selfish as all get out—keeping my little sister tied to me so long! She just came to 'help out' a few days and here I've kept her months! But you know how you impose on sisters!" The girls made a little flurry of regret, asked her for lunch, for dinner, tried to crowd into a little space more hospitality than they had managed in all the weeks before.

"We are so *used* to you, Liz," Jen said. "It won't seem the same without you here!"

Peggy said, "Oh, Liz don't leave us! You *belong* here!"

Elizabeth was touched and warmed, but she did not change her plans.

Anna even laughed about Huxley's "stand," as she called it. "I do hope he sticks to it—at least for a little while," she said. "He's sweet, but it does get to be a nuisance having him around. I like to have some time with Adrian!" And another time: "Wasn't Hux funny—saying he was going to be married? When he didn't have a notion about the bride? I get to laughing at night sometimes, remembering his 'I don't think so'! I'm sorry his eye fell on you, though, darling—that must have hurt."

"Hurt?" Elizabeth said. "Why should it?"

"Why, it was so plain it had only that moment come into his head. That he had to find someone to make the unreal seem real—but of course, if you tried hard . . ."

"I'm not going to try hard," Elizabeth said.

Anna laughed gently.

Then Bunce said to her one day, "Miss Burke, I was wondering—would you want to come to Miss Potts' wedding with me? It's going to be on next Wednesday morning at ten. At her place. You don't know her well but I thought maybe you'd come with me. It don't seem like it's a wedding without anyway a few there. Maisie says she won't have anybody but just me but I don't feel that would be enough. Likely Mrs. Reals'll come, though you can't tell about her. But Maisie's done for her a long time."

"Why, I'd like to go," Elizabeth said. Of course Bunce couldn't be the only one at Pottsy's wedding. That would be too much to ask of Bunce or anyone. "What could I get her for a present?"

"Well, she's had her heart on a silver butter dish—but maybe that would be more'n you'd want to spend," Bunce said.

"No, I'd go that far."

"There's one at Bafford's," Bunce said.

On Wednesday morning at ten Elizabeth sat with Bunce on the horsehair sofa in Miss Potts' little house. The Reverend Mr. Smith was there, a big, earnest man, and Mrs. Reals, very stiff and dignified, and Huxley Reals. That was the entire wedding party, except for the bride and groom. Huxley smiled at Elizabeth once but except for that one instant he kept his eyes on Miss Potts. Then Miss Potts, in a lavender silk dress, with violets pinned awkwardly, a little rouge on her thin faded cheeks, her gray hair curled unsuitably, stood beside an embarrassed Ed Botsworth in front of The Fern, which had certainly burgeoned amazingly over the winter. Mr. Smith rose, stood facing the pair, began the ceremony. The room was excessively hot. Just as Mr. Smith said, "Dearly Beloved, we are gathered together . . ." Mrs. Bunce rose quietly, moved toward the stove and turned the damper down. Elizabeth saw Ed Botsworth's grateful glance toward her and she would remember it always as one of the funniest and saddest of sights. Then she saw Huxley's eyes on Pottsy and she saw that he looked younger, that he was the boy Potts had got out of scrapes, the boy for whom she had kept the cooky jar full. Why, he really loves Pottsy! she thought.

What a very little time a marriage ceremony took! All these heartaches, all these misunderstandings, all these sacrifices—and in a space of a moment the thing was done, the past discounted.

Done. Done. There was a wedding breakfast laid out in the little dining room and abruptly Huxley Reals took over, with toasts, with laughter, with joking, and Bunce's hearty laugh boomed out and even Mrs. Reals was surprisingly gracious. "Dear Potts!" she said, with real affection, as she kissed Pottsy. And Potts blossomed and didn't need the rouge. "It was so nice you could come," she said to Elizabeth. "The butter dish is just beautiful!"

Then it was really done. Pottsy and Ed were going to drive upstate to his cousin's for dinner and that was to be the extent of their honeymoon. They were too old for Niagara Falls, Ed said. They saw them off with laughter, and then the party was over.

"I told Maisie I'd tidy up here," Bunce said. She wasn't laughing now.

"I'll help," Elizabeth said.

"No, you'd better get back. I left everything ready for lunch. I'd rather take care of things here, I know where everything belongs. You run along."

"Come on, Liz," Huxley said abruptly. Then he went to Bunce, who stood by the table with all the breakfast debris on it, put his hands on her shoulders, bent and kissed her on either cheek. "Bless you, Bunce!" he said. "You made it a real, honest-to-God wedding!"

Bunce's face broke up a little. "Well, a wedding ought to be special," she managed to say. "Now you all run along."

Huxley said, "Where'd Mother go?"

"She told you—she wanted to do some shopping. She walked home. I guess you weren't listening."

Elizabeth was in the street with Huxley. "Come, get in," he said. "I'll run you home."

She got in.

"That was tough going," he said. "But it turned out well. Well for Pottsy, that is."

"I hope so."

"It will be so. I didn't expect you there."

"Bunce asked me. She was afraid of having too few there. Pottsy didn't want people—but Bunce knew there had to be some to make it seem real."

"Adrian says you are going away."

"Yes. Yes, I am. Soon."

They were already at Number Seven.

"The town will seem empty," he said. She got out of the car, moved toward the steps. "Liz!" he said, and she turned.

"The butter dish was beautiful!" he said.

She laughed and went in.

She tried to tell Anna about the wedding but she found

there was little to tell. "It was very plain, very simple—but nice," she said. "Pottsy looked lovely, in lavender silk, with violets."

"Well, I suppose it's our gain—Bunce won't be leaving us. But it does seem hard on Bunce," Anna said.

"Bunce can take it," Elizabeth said.

"To think what women have come to—that Ed Botsworth should seem a prize!"

"He's a decent, kindly man," Elizabeth said. "No beauty, but nice."

"I suppose so. Still, it's hard to see his appeal. I think I'll give myself a birthday party."

"That would be fun."

"A big one. I don't mean with presents and all that—I won't tell anyone it's my birthday, but just ask everybody."

"Yes, let's—I'd like to see all Lakeville together before I go."

"We'll call it a farewell party for you, darling. That's what we'll do. We won't say anything about birthdays at all."

They began to plan the party and Anna was gay and even loving, as if now that Elizabeth was nearly gone she could afford to be. But nothing turned out quite as expected.

March was going now. The lion had ceased to roar, the sky was taking on that soft pale blue of spring, the snow was nearly gone, and Johnny saw a robin in the back yard. Crocuses blossomed here and there about the town.

Then one afternoon Cornelia Suydam was sitting in Anna's room and suddenly said, "I *am* getting old! I must write to Alberta at once."

"Alberta?" Anna said.

"Cousin Alberta—stepcousin, really, no kin. I wondered when I heard that Meg had gone to the Rochester library why that seemed so familiar. Cousin Alberta has been there for years. I think she's head librarian. Now, how could that have slipped my mind? I haven't kept in touch with her, but I'll write and ask her to show some kindness to Meg. I'll do it this minute."

She got up, murmuring something further about her failing memory, went out of the room.

But that was nothing. That passed without comment. It was four days later when Mrs. Suydam received a letter from Cousin Alberta, a note, rather. She was in Anna's room when the mail came, and took her note, read it, looked puzzled. "That's odd," she said. "That's very odd."

Anna looked up from a letter, said absently, "What's odd?"

"She went there *because* Cousin Alberta was there. Adrian sent her to Alberta. How very odd—that Adrian never mentioned it."

"Oh, Adrian's always helping people get jobs," Elizabeth said, casually, she hoped.

"But he never mentioned it when we were talking about Meg. I don't understand it. She says she's grateful to Adrian—that Miss McIntry is proving very satisfactory and that she thoroughly likes her. Adrian spent a summer with them once when he was a little boy—but I didn't know he kept in touch with her. It's strange."

Stop talking! Let it go! Elizabeth wanted to cry out.

"Yes, it's strange," Anna said. "We certainly discussed Meg's departure very thoroughly with Adrian."

Then she turned to her own letter. But Elizabeth had seen her eyes come to Mrs. Suydam's face with a sudden question or the beginning of comprehension in them.

That night she said, "Wouldn't it be funny—wouldn't it be really funny if Meg had all these years had a passion for Adrian?"

"Funny?"

"I mean strange. I'd never have believed it, but it must be so. I think he wanted her out of town."

"I don't know why he would. She's certainly never bothered him."

"How do we know? I think she has—but Adrian wouldn't have it, and he saw that she got away."

"I don't know, Anna. I don't know anything about it."

"I *thought* something was bothering Adrian. He hasn't been himself lately. And that's it—she's been using her spinsterish wiles on him and he couldn't take it. Poor Meg!"

Elizabeth did not answer and very soon said good night and left Anna.

The paper boy brought Anna a little bunch of hepaticas and Anna kissed him. He grinned at her, his face red. He would be her slave forever, Elizabeth thought with pain. Mrs. Campanini came up the stairs to tell Anna about her first grandchild. Jen came with an armful of forsythia. There were signs of spring everywhere. The days went past, the plans for the party grew, and nothing happened to delay the time for Elizabeth's departure. To Elizabeth's surprise and somewhat to her alarm, Mrs. Suydam said nothing to Adrian, at least not in Elizabeth's presence, about Cousin Alberta. Nor did Anna say anything to him, so far as Elizabeth knew. It was only natural that Anna should speak of it, and perhaps alone with Adrian she had, but never before others. That was more frightening than speech.

One day Elizabeth went up the stairs to ask Mrs. Suydam a question and Mrs. Suydam was sitting at her desk writing. She looked up vaguely, then turned. "Oh, come in, Liz. Did you want me for anything?"

"Yes," Elizabeth said, "but I'm almost afraid to ask it."

"Go ahead—ask," Mrs. Suydam said, with some surprise.

"If you could part with one, I'd like to buy one of Alex's pictures. I don't know what they'd be worth or whether I could afford one. Maybe I could afford one of the drawings if I couldn't a painting. I'm afraid you'll think I'm begging, that I want one given to me, but I don't want that at all, Mrs. Suydam. I want to buy one."

Mrs. Suydam looked around the room slowly, then said, "Alex would be pleased. Which one do you want?"

"You'd do it?"

"Yes, of course. Which one?"

"The little one of the docks. I'd like that one."

"Very well, Liz." She rose at once, walked to the wall where the picture hung, took it down. Elizabeth looked down at it and tears came to her eyes. It might have been the very spot where she and Johnny had stood and seen Huxley Reals coming toward them. But it was all dimmed out in mist. "I do love this," she said with difficulty. "How much do you think it should be?"

Mrs. Suydam hesitated, then said, "Do you think fifty dollars is too much?"

"No. No, of course not. And I could pay that—I wouldn't have to get it 'on time.' It—it will make everything different, Mrs. Suydam—to own it, I mean. I can't be grateful enough to you."

"Be grateful to Alex," Mrs. Suydam said.

"I feel wrong, taking it away from you."

"I'm glad you want it," Mrs. Suydam said. "I am an old woman. I cannot take Alex's pictures where I will be going before too long. Not that I am dwelling on the grave, my dear. I shall live as long as I can."

"I was supposed to ask you—should we use that Italian cloth and have the food downstairs—or could we manage eating up in Anna's room? For the party? I think Anna would like it all in her room."

"Then we will have it there. We will keep it very simple and have it there."

Now there was nothing more to say. Elizabeth looked down again at the picture in her hands, then hugged it against her. She was wishing she had come up here more often, had somehow been closer to this reserved, stiff little woman. But Mrs. Suydam kept a great distance away from people. She refused closeness, refused affection. Or did she? Was she as lonely as anyone else, shut away in grief and regret?

As if the longing had been spoken, Mrs. Suydam said, "Sit

down, Liz. You don't come to see me often. And soon you will be leaving us."

"I don't know why I haven't come," Elizabeth said, still standing. "You—you always seem so self-sufficient, Mrs. Suydam. As if you didn't need anybody. And I'm always busy trying to be self-sufficient too."

The older woman smiled briefly. "Yes. So life goes by. But I have, I think, made friends with Johnny."

That was an odd and touching thing for her to say.

"Yes, I feel happy about that," Elizabeth said. "I feel very happy about that."

"It took me too long," Mrs. Suydam said. "Years too long. But Johnny will come through. I feel sure he will."

"He will," Elizabeth agreed.

"As for the rest—I don't know. I'm sorry to be so sober this morning, Liz. I am greatly troubled. I have discovered something that troubles me deeply. It is nothing I can touch or change, but I am grieved. You have found me in a sad mood."

"Oh. Can I help?"

"No. No one can help, my dear. It is done and over. I hope it is over. But I do not mean to be cryptic. I am glad you wanted the picture."

She was dismissing her, but she had said too much. Her face looked old and tired.

"Mrs. Suydam . . ."

Mrs. Suydam had turned toward her desk, but she paused. Her small figure was very erect, as if bracing itself against danger.

"Mrs. Suydam, I think it is all over and done," Elizabeth said gently. "If it isn't spoken of any more, it will be over and done."

Mrs. Suydam gave a sigh, said, "Yes, if it isn't spoken of. So let us not."

So she had talked with Adrian. She knew. She knew, too, that words, that prying, could make it real, make it more than a few hours of peace in a long weariness. Why, Mrs. Suydam knew everything! She was not remote at all. She saw the whole of the lives in this house. Elizabeth walked out and down the stairs without another word.

When she reached the ground floor the telephone was ringing. Bunce was moving to answer, but Elizabeth was there first, took down the receiver, said, "Hello."

"Hello—Liz?"

"Yes."

"Would you help me pick out a birthday present for Anna?"

"No, I'm not much good at that sort of thing."

"All the same, will you? Come down the lake road at four-thirty, will you?"

"No."

"I'll expect you—Elizabeth." He hung up.

She sat with Anna and Anna said, "You are so lucky, Liz. You've got money—you could travel around and see the world for a year if you wanted to."

"I suppose I could."

"Why don't you? Sometimes when I think that I'll be here forever, till I'm old . . . but what's the good of thinking like that?"

"What good indeed? Sometimes I think it would be lovely to be here like this forever, with all the world coming to me instead of having to go out after it."

"The world might get tired of coming."

"I don't think so. People find happiness here, Anna. They love to come."

"They do seem to, don't they? It moves me that they do seem to want to come."

When it was four-thirty, she was still there. She was conscious of the minutes passing but she was still there. She carried the tea things down to the kitchen, lingered a moment in Bunce's shining kitchen.

"Anything you want?" Bunce asked her.

"No. Just dawdling. I've been dawdling all day," Elizabeth said.

Bunce gave a little grunt and went on about her work. Then the doorbell rang and Bunce went at once. Elizabeth stood still there in the kitchen and heard Bunce say, "Yes, she's here— she's right out here in the kitchen, Mr. Reals."

Huxley Reals stood in the kitchen doorway and said briefly, "Where's your coat?"

"It's spring," he said, as they walked in the street together. "Why did you stand me up?"

"I told you I wouldn't come."

"But I did think you would. I don't want to buy a present. I shall send flowers, as usual. Shall we walk down by the lake?"

"Why?"

"Because I want to. Because I've got something to say to you and I don't want to say it in front of Campanini's, or the five-and-ten. And don't say not to talk because I am going to talk." He had his hand firmly on her arm and they were walking down the steep walk to the lake road. They came to the lake, walked along its edge for a moment in silence.

"You're not very approachable, Liz," he said at last.

"I suppose I'm not," she said dully.

"No, you're not. You make it very hard for me. You make me seem a fool, which I am not. You make me a man of little faith—which I don't think I am. But, Elizabeth, why shouldn't it be so—about you and me, I mean? Why shouldn't it?"

Spring was all around them. The air was soft, the light was a spring light. The water itself looked softer, warmer, more friendly.

"Why should it? I just don't like second bests. Even if otherwise it were all right, which of course you know it isn't."

"No, I know it's difficult. Nevertheless, that's the way it's going to be. I've made up my mind, Liz."

"Oh?"

"All I have to do now is make up yours. You mean I'm not

your first choice—or you're not mine? There wouldn't be many marriages in the world if the first choice was the one that led to marriage. I'm sure that in your girlhood you managed to go through a lot of loving that led to nothing. Didn't you?"

"Yes, I suppose I did. But I am not a child now. What I suppose you're trying to say is that now you've had your cake, you feel as if you'd like a little plain bread for a change."

"No. Or perhaps I do feel like that. Do you mind being plain bread?"

"Probably. Most women do."

"I don't know why. The staff of life. Look, Liz—Elizabeth— but I might call you 'Liz' in time—I know all you can say, and something of what you feel. And I don't have any defense. That's the way it's been and you know it. I loved your sister a very great deal. I thought I would love her till I died. I am very much alive and I no longer love her. I don't even know whether it is because you came or because the thing had run its course or what. Let's say I've been sick and now am well. Only, of course, you could say: This too will run its course. And perhaps it will. I do not think so now, but perhaps it will. It seems firm and everlasting, and as if I had never loved before. But I can realize how hollow those words would be to you. You see—well, my love for Anna had nothing to feed on, nothing to grow by. Love's got to be in a state of growth or it's nothing. It does seem as if we could grow together—but you look as stubborn as a rock."

Elizabeth Burke stood still. They had passed the line of somewhat rickety dwellings along the shore and come to the narrow road leading to the plant. She said, "You see, I happen to love you."

He put out a hand to her shoulder, stared at her, took his hand away, for there was no softening in her face.

"Then—" he began.

"No. I happen to love you. But I don't want to marry you— I wouldn't think of marrying you. I would always remember that you had loved Anna for six or seven years and had stopped. In the beginning of—of my love—I prayed that you would stop being a fool, would stop loving her—and then, then it began to frighten me, thinking you might stop. Anna needs love, she needs it very much. She has Adrian, I know, but she needs love and she depended on your love, whether she encouraged it or not. Then you stopped. Well, you could stop again."

He was very quiet, looking straight at her through the soft light.

"Yes. I said I could. I might," he said at last. "But I do not think so. How can one know? I don't see any point in lying or being more prophetic than is possible."

"Let's go home."

He turned and they began to walk back. They said never a word till they reached Number Seven. Then he put a hand on her arm and said, "You love Anna more than me—is that it?"

She put out a hand to the railing, said, "I don't know. It could be. I don't know."

"Shouldn't you make up your mind about that? . . . I'm talking nonsense—I'm feeling about eighteen because you said you loved me. I can't seem to think of anything else. . . . Say it again."

"No. Never again."

It was still light and everything about the street swam in the light, in the soft light of a spring night.

"If you stop—will you tell me that?"

"Yes."

"I think I'll come up and say hello to Anna."

"No, don't."

"But I am going to. I have some things I must say to her. I must tell her I know whom I want to marry. She has put a spell on you too. I will break it, Liz. Because I am going to marry you, you know. I am going to."

Now she could have him. She could have him if she liked. Why, then, did it seem as if life was ended? Why did her heart ache so—why did Huxley himself seem so far away, yet so dear? Why did it seem so horrible that he should go up there to Anna and declare his love? Was it only because of what Anna might do to that declaration? Or was it truly that she loved Anna more than she loved Huxley? Then her heart began to crack, to seem to melt. No, she loved him terribly much. Better than Anna, better than anyone. And yet—and yet . . . But he was going up the stairs, he was going into Anna's room. She went to her own room, huddled on the bed. She heard Anna laugh. The tears began to run down her face. It seemed a long time afterward that Huxley came out and went down the stairs, slowly, quietly, when the front door closed and all was still.

Johnny came in.

"What's the matter? What are you crying for?" he demanded.

"For my sins," she said.

He came and climbed on the bed beside her, cuddled against her. He was a stiff little boy for cuddling, he did not do it naturally or gracefully. He was like a little animal that doesn't know the human ways of showing affection.

"Don't cry," he said.

"All right, I won't. Did you know it was spring?"

"I saw a caterpillar today."

"No joking? Then we'll see butterflies too, soon. What are you going to give mummy for her birthday?"

"I don't know. I don't know anything she'd like."

"Suppose you made her a drawing. Or I could get some clay and you could make something out of that."

"No, she wouldn't like that. I'll get her a handkerchief."

"It ought to be more special than that. Something you did yourself."

"What are sins?"

"Oh, the things you do that you ought not to do, that you know you ought not to do. Are you ready for supper?"

"I guess so."

At supper she found herself looking at Adrian. He did seem

older than when she had come. But he still looked strong. Strong enough to bear his own burdens. He was not going to confess anything to anyone. He had not, she suddenly knew, confessed to his mother. It had been intuition on her part, wisdom. I like Adrian, she thought suddenly.

Adrian had taken Anna's dinner up and Elizabeth had not even seen Anna since Huxley had been there. But when supper was done, she must go into that room. But after dinner Adrian took his coffee upstairs and when Elizabeth went for the tray he met her at the door with it, handed it to her.

"I'll get Anna to bed tonight," he said.

She knew she was banished from Anna's room. She ought, she knew, to have the courage to go now, this minute, not wait for the party, not wait for anything. But she did not have that kind of courage. After the dishes were done and Bunce had gone to her room, she went to the telephone and called Lollie. She could see Lollie bounding across her little room to the telephone.

"Lollie—it's Liz Burke," she said.

"What's the matter?"

"I'm coming up to town next week. Do you think I could get a room there for a few days or is it all filled up?"

"It is. You could bunk in my place."

"Thanks. I'll do that and look around for something."

"Come to your senses?" Lollie asked.

"Something like that. I'll see you, probably Monday. Bless you, Lollie."

Then she went to her room, wrote a letter to Anthony Daggett, giving him Lollie's address. She wanted to write to Meg, but she did not. No, Meg would write her if there was anything to write that should be written. How little preparation it took to change your life!

She sat still, trying to see the shape of her life ahead, failing. She was too bound here now. She had known it would be so and it was so. She had given herself to Anna again, been again rejected. But she had given more of herself than that. She was partly given to Meg, to Jen and Peggy and Juliet and all that bright band who haunted Anna's room, to the doctor, to Mrs. Campanini, to old Mr. Cripps, to Bunce and Pottsy. To the lake itself and that stiff old woman up there on the third floor which looked out toward the lake a boy long since dead had loved and painted and died in. And she had given her heart away, foolishly, uselessly. She was changed, changed all through. What she wanted was some dark hole to crawl into and sleep her sickness away. Not that Lollie would intrude. She would be safe with Lollie. But the sickness of a new beginning had to be lived through nevertheless. *Because I am going to marry you, you know. I am going to.* But of course he wasn't going to. It would never happen, because Anna was not going to let it happen. And even if she were, it could not be. Because of this wall, this something she couldn't help building up against his offer. This lack of faith—it might be wicked, but it was real. Then she thought of how she had trusted Juliet, Adrian. Past reason. *This is not the same,* her heart cried to itself. *This is not the same!*

At that moment the telephone rang. It sounded loud and shrill in the still night. She went out and down the stairs, lifted the receiver.

"Elizabeth?"

"Yes."

"I know it's late . . . just wanted to give you something to go to sleep on."

"What?"

"Wanted to ask you this: is it fair for you to devote so much of yourself to keeping free and not allow me to do the same? Think about that, Liz."

She could not answer, stood there holding the receiver foolishly, not speaking.

"Are you there, Liz?"

"Yes."

"Are you thinking?"

"Yes."

"About me?"

"About Bunce. No, it isn't fair."

Now there was a silence at his end of the line. At last he said more gently, "That's all for tonight. But don't forget, Liz. It'll be all right if you don't forget. Good night."

"Good night," she said.

She stood there in the dim night light in the hallway, feeling light, strange, free in a new exciting way. When she moved up the stairs she still felt light, no substance in her, and yet very much alive. It was like Anna, taking half a life—no, it was like taking the possibility of death for a chance of a whole life. And she had not been fair: she had tried so terribly hard to be strong and she had resented strength in Huxley. She had not been fair to Anna, not giving her credit for being able to live through her losses. She hadn't been fair to human beings anywhere—not allowing them adulthood, the courage to bear their own burdens. Nor to herself, rejecting life no matter how difficult it might be. *She has put a spell on you too.* She had. Even now, with life itself at stake, she had succumbed to the spell. She had felt guilty at taking life when Anna had so little. But Anna *might* have had more, mightn't she? She might, but she had rejected the possibility. She had chosen.

And so do I choose, Elizabeth said to herself, standing in her little room. So do I choose.

XIX

*I*N THE MORNING when Elizabeth woke she thought at once, I must tell Anna. I must tell her now. I have made up my mind. The thought made her feel weak, lonely, and yet she knew she must do it. Do it before the party, before Anna told everyone she was going away. But this was the day of the party. There were so many things to do. There wasn't time for drama. And when she went downstairs Bunce said Mr. Suydam had taken Anna's tray up. So—she wasn't going to be given an opportunity. But sometime in this day she must make the opportunity. She went up finally to fetch the tray.

"Was I late this morning?" she asked.

"No, not much. Adrian likes to have breakfast with me."

"Do you want to get up now?"

"I'll wait till after the mail comes. If you want to give me my writing things I'll try to do a letter or two before then."

Her voice was cool. Elizabeth propped her up, brought the writing pad, pen. Now. Now was the moment.

"Anna . . ."

But just then Mrs. Suydam came into the room with some question about food. Elizabeth went out and down to Bunce, began to help her. She had to go to the store. She arranged flowers. The morning was gone. She went up with luncheon and Anna was still in bed.

"Bunce said she'd get you up," Elizabeth said.

"So she would have. I thought I'd rest this morning," Anna said. "You're all getting in such a dither about this party. I do like parties to be done easily."

"Well, food has to be got ready," Elizabeth said. "And Bunce has to give everything an extra polish. Anna, I wanted to talk with you about—"

"About what? Huxley? If so, don't. I'm not in the mood."

"But I must. You see—"

"Liz, not now. Don't get so emotional over everything. Run along and help polish—but let's not talk about Life and all those things just now. I really do need a little peace before a party."

Elizabeth went away again, defeated. No, not defeated, just balked at the moment. It was going to be said before the party. It had to be.

It was midafternoon when Bunce said, "I hear Meg McIntry's home for over Sunday. Mrs. Suydam'll likely want to ask her for the party."

"Oh, is she? I don't think Anna knew," Elizabeth said.

"Well, you'd better give her a ring," Bunce said.

Elizabeth couldn't do that, though she had a longing to see Meg, to hear her voice, to ask her whether she had escaped the trap or would be forever crippled. Nor did she think Meg would come to the party, nor that Anna would want her to, except perhaps from curiosity.

Then the afternoon too was gone, like a dream, except that she still felt light and curiously free. Then why did she not say so to Anna? Was she still afraid? She dressed for the party at five, though people had been asked for supper at six. She put on the chrysanthemum velvet dress. She should have had something more springlike, but this was her best and she put it on.

She walked into Anna's room. Anna was sitting quiet in her chair by the window, not yet ready.

"Ready so soon?" Anna asked.

"I should have fixed you up first. I don't know why I got dressed so early," Elizabeth said confusedly. "Anna—"

"Why, there's Meg McIntry! I thought she was in Rochester."

"She's home for the weekend. Anna—"

"Go, call her in. I must ask her to the party!"

"She doesn't like parties—you know that."

"But this is a special one, all for you. She'll want to come to that! Quick—call her!"

"No. I don't think she will want to come."

"Why ever not? Anyway, I want to see her whether she comes or not. I want very specially to see her. There's something I must ask her."

"Couldn't it wait?"

It was like the moment when Mrs. Daggett had come hobbling up the stairs, with the same premonition of disaster, the same helplessness at staving off disaster.

"No," Anna said, "it couldn't wait. Hurry, Liz."

Elizabeth walked out and down the stairs. I should take a stand on this, she thought. This is more important than taking a stand on Huxley. I mustn't let Meg go up there.

But she opened the door and called, "Margaret!"

Margaret McIntry was almost at the corner, but she heard. She turned, put up her hand in greeting, and began to walk back toward Number Seven. "Hi, Elizabeth!" she said as she came nearer.

"How good to see you!" Elizabeth said. "How awfully good to see you! Are you all right?"

Margaret looked just the same as ever. She laughed and said, "I'm fine. And you?"

"Fine," Elizabeth said. Such a silly conversation. "Anna wants you to come up. She saw you in her busybody."

"I dare say," Margaret said.

"Don't come, Margaret."

Margaret gave her a suddenly grave glance. "Why not?"

"Just—don't come. Have an errand anywhere, but don't come."

"I see," Margaret said. "Well, thank you for the warning, but I think I will come. You're awfully dressed up."

"We're going to have a party. Anna wants to ask you to come. Margaret—Meg—I do wish you wouldn't come in. I mean it."

"I can see that. I'm not blind. But you see, Liz, Anna can't do anything to me any more. I'm not afraid of Anna."

She was moving up the steps with Elizabeth, she was inside the hallway with her, moving up the stairs behind her.

"Hello, Meg!" Anna said with gaiety and warmth, as if she loved Meg. "And how's the job?"

"How are you, Anna? No need to ask. You look blooming. The job's fine."

"Sit down—I shouldn't ask you to because you must run home and put on your best bib and tucker and come to our party tonight. But sit down a minute."

"This is my best bib and tucker," Meg said dryly, "but I'm not one for parties, Anna. Never have been."

"You ought to be. First thing you know you'll turn into one of these dry-as-dust spinsters! You're much too nice for that."

"Yes, I think I am," Meg said calmly. "Still, I'll skip the party."

"Well, tell me all about your job. What do you *do*?"

"I keep books," Meg said briefly.

"I'm so pleased with myself for suggesting Cousin Alberta to Adrian! If you do want to get off on your own, it's so comforting to have a friend at court!"

Elizabeth shivered. Meg said only, "Yes, very comforting." She did not contradict Anna or anything.

"Meg . . ."

"Yes?" Meg said, but not dramatically.

"There's something I want to say—have wanted to say for a long, long time, almost ever since I've been married—but you're hard to talk to, Meg. You're so awfully self-sufficient and stand-offish—but still, I do want to say it."

"Well, say it," Meg said.

"It's just—I didn't know at the time I was taking Adrian away from anybody. I didn't know that. It wasn't a thing I could have done had I known."

Meg gave a quick smile. "Of course not," she said evenly. "It's a long time ago, Anna. There's no need to speak of it now."

"I suppose not. But I've never felt you liked me awfully much and I wanted you to know that. I—I've almost felt I ought to share Johnny with you. And I have, what I could. But of course I can't share Adrian." Her voice was sweet, kind, regretful.

"Did anyone ask you to?"

"Of course not! I knew you'd get prickly! But I know how it must feel living in the same town with Adrian—how you felt about getting away. Adrian's pretty special, I think—and you must have thought so too, once. So I'm awfully glad that you've got a job and are happy in it. And of course Adrian's glad too. He was really pathetically glad to have Cousin Alberta suggested—I suppose you prick his conscience!"

"I don't think so, Anna."

"But you see, Meg—it *shows* so when you're fond of some-one— still, everything's all right now. Everybody's happy, and that's the way it should be."

Meg looked at Liz, but as if she didn't see her, and said, "It shows, does it? I've never thought I had a face that registers emotions. An old horse face, didn't you say once?"

"Oh, Meg, do you remember *that* and hold it against me? And it was such a nice horse I was reminded of!"

"Oh, no, I don't hold it against you. My face is like a horse's. I admit that."

"Aren't we being silly? Go home and make yourself gay and

come back at six, Meg. I'd really love to have you come—your father's coming."

"But I'm not coming. I'm never coming to this house again, Anna." Her voice was calm enough, but firm too.

"Why, *Meg!* Oh, I've hurt you and I meant something so different! I wanted us to be *friends!*"

"There has to be honesty between friends," Meg said.

"But I've been honest! You mean you don't want me to be too honest—is that it?"

"No, I didn't mean that. I'm speaking of just plain, everyday honesty. You can pretend to yourself, Anna, that you've been speaking the truth, but of course you know very well you haven't."

"Are you sure you aren't pretending to yourself?" Anna asked gently.

"Quite sure. If you'd like me to list the lies, I can, but I'm sure you know them. I was away. Couldn't you let it go at that, Anna?"

"Why, *Meg!* You shock me—you really do. I've never lied in my life and I wouldn't begin to you."

"First, you don't want me at your party. We'll put that down as a social lie and forget it. Next, you didn't think of Cousin Alberta at all. Next, you wouldn't have dreamed of sharing Johnny with me had you known. You didn't know, that's another lie. Another: you'd have taken Adrian if you'd wanted him no matter who stood in the way. You'd even take Huxley when he wants to marry your sister, if you could. But that, thank God, you cannot do. And my face shows nothing. No one in this town has ever dreamed I was hurt about Adrian, no one. I have never talked of it except to one person I trust implicitly, and I am sure that Adrian never has. He saw you, he loved you, and that was the end of it. But you cannot bear it that anyone has ever touched your possessions. That you cannot bear. I am not taking any of your possessions, but I think it might be very good for you to know that I could have had I so desired."

"Could you, indeed?"

"Yes. And not because Adrian does not love you. But because he was so dead tired that he would have turned to anyone who could let him rest. I know how, you see. You have a kind of courage, I grant you that, but you haven't got the kind of courage to go through another operation so that Adrian might possibly have a whole wife instead of half a wife. I know it was dangerous—I know that. I do not know what was right for you to do—but I do know that you have to give a man great tenderness to compensate for not having a whole body to give him. I think you could have given it to him, but no, you thought only of yourself, of what people thought of you, not what you could do for them."

"So. So that's what you think of me," Anna said slowly. "But, then, I suppose that's what I might have expected. If you've been hurt you can't bear kindness."

"Oh, I could bear kindness if I received any. But that wasn't kindness, Anna. Why don't you look in your busybody and see yourself? . . . And sharing Johnny! You mean you were glad to have him out of the house, because he *did* see you. You can't bear it to have him see you. But he remembers the kittens, you see. He may forget someday, but he remembers the kittens. And you know that. You know it too well but you pretend not to. You pretend he's afraid you're going to die. It's not that— he's afraid of you. . . . And now I think I've said all and more than needs saying. But never ask me here again, Anna."

She rose and walked toward the door. Elizabeth saw that Anna's hand was moving in a curious circle, round and round, on her table, but she went after Margaret, walked down the stairs with her, opened the door.

Margaret turned and looked at her steadily. "A fool's effort," she said, "but I had to do it." She walked steadily down the steps, away in the gathering dusk.

Elizabeth went up the stairs. Her body was not light now. It was heavy and tired and cold. The hall door opened and Adrian came in. She wanted to say, Not now, Adrian—you must not go in to Anna now. You must not! She paused on the stairs hunting a barrier to his coming upward. She said, "Oh, Adrian, Bunce was waiting for you to crack some ice. Would you have time?" Bunce would be surprised. Would she deny it? Would she have cracked the ice already? But Adrian was walking along the hall toward the kitchen and Elizabeth was going along the upper hall toward Anna.

Anna sat just where she had left her, her hand still making that circle on the table. She did not look up, and that fact was frightening. Elizabeth found no word, no word at all to break the silence. She stood there in the velvet dress. The lights were not on and shadows were gathering in the room. What light there was fell on Anna by her table, Anna with her glance down on her slowly moving hand.

It was Anna who spoke first. She spoke not to Elizabeth, it seemed, but to her own moving hand.

"I told him not to let her in," she said. "I told him a hundred times. She was mangy and she had a bunch on her neck. She couldn't have taken care of them. . . . It wasn't my bedspread—she was mangy and she had a bunch on her neck. . . . Someone had to do it."

The cold was in Elizabeth's spine now, in her marrow. The voice was not Anna's voice, but one tired and flat and defeated. These were the kittens Meg meant. These must be the kittens, born on Anna's bedspread and probably drowned—and Johnny had seen. Little ghost Johnny had materialized out of mist and seen. . . . The little clay cat fell on the floor, its tail off, its ears flattened. "I'll make her another cat!" Johnny cried.

"He looks at me as if I were a murderer. You all do. Adrian does."

"No, Anna. That's not so." Her voice came like a whisper.

" 'They look like a married pair,' I said. And you laughed inside."

"I didn't, Anna. No, I didn't."

"Of course you did. Or did you cry? You promised not to pity me but you probably felt sorry for me."

"Anna, stop making that circle."

Anna's delicate fingers stopped suddenly their monotonous tracing.

"And I suppose Adrian thinks I should have had the operation. He thinks so too. He'd rather have me dead than half alive."

"Adrian's never mentioned it."

"But he did. They walked along so still, like a married pair, just like a married pair."

"But she did go away. She did go away," Elizabeth said. She felt that her words were spoken to herself, that Anna didn't even hear her. Yet Anna answered.

"Does that change anything?" Anna said. "And suppose I had the operation? Suppose I did? What would there be to hope for? Would it be better to walk around dead inside than to sit here dead inside?"

If only she would lift her amber eyes, laugh, even if it was a false laugh! If only she had never looked into the busybody and seen herself!

"Damn the busybody!" Elizabeth said aloud.

"You can't take it down now. It wouldn't matter—I've looked," Anna said.

"Oh, Anna!"

"You sounded just like mom," Anna said oddly.

Elizabeth was the ghost of Fanny Burke walking across the floor, putting her hand on Anna's hair, smoothing it back from the forehead, saying, "It's time to dress for the party. Will you wear the gold jacket?"

Then there was Adrian in the doorway.

"What's the matter? Aren't you ready yet?" he asked.

Elizabeth moved a space away, giving Anna room to breathe. Anna took her hands from the table, let them lie hidden in her lap.

336 Woman at the Window

"Don't rush me, darling," she said, and her voice was just as always, gay, amused, bright. "Are you feeling awfully strong?"

"Strong?" Adrian said.

"I thought maybe you could carry me down to the living room for the party. It does seem silly to make everybody climb those stairs."

She sat in the round-backed chair with the angel-head carving. White tulips sat on the octagonal table beside her in a circle of light. The room was full of laughter and there were gifts strewn across the afghan on her knees, on the floor at her feet. "Happy birthday, darling!" . . . "Happy birthday, Anna!" Over and over the words sounded, like a chorus. . . . "How wonderful to have you down here, Anna!" . . . "Oh, you angel!" said Anna. "How lovely! . . . But it was supposed to be a secret!" . . . "Oh, Jen, that's *beautiful!*" And the light was on Anna, on her gold jacket, on her eyes, in her warm, loving voice. And people said as they had said before, "Anna's wonderful!" or "Isn't she magnificent?"

They brought plates of food and sat on the floor and the laughter was high and the talk exciting. And through it all Anna's voice came, tying them together in friendship, in warmth, making it another of "Anna's parties." And Adrian sat near Anna, quiet and strong, watching her. Some of the tiredness seemed to have gone out of him.

Elizabeth went to the kitchen for another bowl of salad and Huxley was there with Bunce. He smiled at her and then he said, "Did you know I was going to marry Liz here, Bunce?"

Mrs. Bunce almost dropped a pan of rolls. "Good Lord, you startled me, Mr. Reals!" she said. "I guess Miss Burke's got more sense'n that."

"No," she said slowly, "I haven't, Bunce."

"Well, for goodness' sake!" Bunce said. "Take these rolls in, will you, Mr. Reals? I don't suppose you're going to get married tonight."

"Not tonight, but soon, Bunce. Soon," he said.

"*Them* two!" Mrs. Bunce mumbled after them. "I'd never have thought of it. *Them* two!"

Then it was over. "This was the best ever!" . . . "Wonderful party, Anna. You always do have wonderful parties! And to have you down here—that's the best part of it, darling!" They were reluctant to go, but at last it was over. Adrian carried Anna up the stairs and Elizabeth watched the gold of her jacket making a path of light. "Do you need me?" she called after them.

"No," Adrian said.

But presently she followed them slowly up the stairs, went first to Johnny's room. He was sound asleep, looking childish and good. She bent and kissed him. "It'll be all right. It'll be all right, Johnny," she whispered. He did not stir. She stood there a moment, looking down at him, seeing him, a small ghost, standing in the kitchen door, watching his mother, filling up with horror and hate. "It'll be all right," she murmured again.

Then, though Adrian had said he didn't need her, she walked toward Anna's room. I never told her I was going to marry Hux, she said to herself. But that didn't seem important any more. It was a private matter that had nothing to do with Anna at all. The telling would have been defense, bravado. No, it didn't have to be told. Still, she felt compelled to go to Anna, whether Adrian wanted her there or not.

Adrian had got Anna into bed. Clumsy, though tender, Adrian was. Elizabeth wanted to smooth the sheets, fix the pillows. But she stood there in the doorway and did not come into the room. "Is everything all right?" she asked.

Adrian was standing by the bed. He turned and looked at her, angrily.

"Is this some of your doing?" he demanded.

"What? I don't know what you mean?" she said.

"Darling, don't jump at Liz like that. It's nothing to do with Liz," Anna said.

"Well, I'm not going to let you," Adrian said.

"Oh? You like me like this?"

"Rather like this than not at all," Adrian said.

"But it might not be 'not at all,' " Anna said. "Adrian, don't get all worked up. I'm going to do it."

"No," Adrian said.

"It's my life," Anna said. "Isn't it? Haven't I the right to decide what to do with it?"

"It's mine too," Adrian said.

"No, it's mine," Anna said, and her voice was almost cold. "It belongs to no one but me. I've been too weak to decide before, but now I have decided. Half a wife is no wife—I'll either be whole or nothing. Half a life is no good, Adrian. Liz knows that."

"I don't know," Elizabeth said. "I don't know, Anna."

"Liz!" Her voice was sharp.

"But I don't know."

"I thought you promised me not to pity me."

"I'm not pitying you."

Strange, but she wasn't. She wasn't pitying Anna at all. She wasn't even pitying Adrian, with his lined, hurt face, desiring a whole wife, ashamed of his desire.

"I told Doctor McIntry that I'd go Monday," Anna said. "He'll call Graner in the morning."

"I won't have it," Adrian said.

"But I said it was my life. It's settled, darling. If it were you, you'd do the same—wouldn't you?"

Adrian turned away from the bed. He walked over to the hearth, but did not look at them even then.

"I suppose I would." His voice was close to harsh.

"Well, then!"

"I can't go through it all again," he said. "I can't let you go through it. I thought you were happy."

"Happy?" Anna said. "Did you?"

Elizabeth had a moment's fear that Anna would say: But

you weren't happy. You went to Meg. But she did not. She did not mention Meg.

"You've seemed so," Adrian said.

"Seemed so," Anna echoed. "I'm very tired. I must sleep now. . . . Do you want to bring me some milk now, Liz?"

Elizabeth went out and down the stairs, heated the milk, made some toast. When she came back Adrian was gone. She put the tray down, then turned to put the pillows behind Anna.

"You drink it," Anna said. "I'm not hungry."

Elizabeth sat down by the bed, drank the milk obediently, even ate a piece of toast. "Shall I sleep in here?" she asked then.

"No. Adrian is coming back," Anna said. "You *do* look like mom, Liz."

"Do I?"

"You'll stay till I get home, won't you?"

"Yes, I'll stay."

"Want to pound these pillows up a little?"

Elizabeth smoothed the bed, patted the pillows, then she lifted the tray.

"Good night, Anna," she said. Surely there must be more to say, but Anna said, "Good night," and that was all.

She was back in her own room. She sat down, still in her velvet dress.

How peaceful this room is! she thought. But of course it wasn't the room. Often she had hated the room.

I suppose I never loved her before, she admitted. Never before, even if I've said I did so many times. I worshiped her and I envied her and I pitied her—and that was all. And why now? Because she's walking into danger with her head still high? Did I want her to walk into danger? Was I glad when Meg said what she said to her? No—oh, *no!* Oh, Anna, I wish I were like mom! She knew all about loving! . . . It's because you did it for *love's* sake—it sounded like for your sake—but it wasn't. It was for *love's* sake. . . . Those were the only words you knew—you didn't know how to talk any other way—but words don't mean any-thing if you *know* somebody. . . . It sounded as if you were just going to make another picture of yourself to hang up—but it wasn't that way. You're *afraid*—but you're going to do it, be-cause that's the only way you know how to say "I love you." Oh, *Anna!*

The house grew very still, but still she sat there in the little room. Nothing was finished, but the peace remained with her, wrapped her round. And out of the peace came Huxley's face, across a table, through snow. A face with sober eyes and a firm mouth, a face to love and trust forever. And Johnny's small face, and Mrs. Suydam's proud face. Bunce's dark little eyes. Her people. She would walk these streets for the rest of her life. She would see Johnny grow up and Mrs. Suydam die—she would grow old here and die herself. And Anthony Daggett might fall on some foreign soil or he might come to this town and be her friend. And Mrs. Daggett—she would never, never know whether Mrs. Daggett had trusted her to the end or not. It was all unknown, the future, and there was pain ahead, and anxiety. But the peace persisted. If you just loved enough, just trusted enough . . .

"Why, I know—I know whether I'm coming or going!" she said aloud. "I must call Lollie . . . it's not too late. I must call Lollie now."

JUN 19

MAY 21

JUL 30

MAR 9   1976

DEC 2 - 1976   Cnt. R.

7

APR 9   1977   58

26   968

APR 26   16